Rachel Knowles is the a
History blog. She lives in
husband, Andrew, and has four grown-up daughters.

Please visit Rachel Knowles online:
Website: www.regencyhistory.net
Twitter: @regencyhistory

A Perfect Match

Rachel Knowles

Rachel A. Knowles.

Sandsfoot Publishing

Published by Sandsfoot Publishing 2015

Copyright © Rachel Knowles 2015
Cover design © Mirabelle Knowles 2014

Rachel Knowles asserts the moral right to be identified as the author of this work

A catalogue record for this book is available from the British Library

ISBN 978-1-910883-00-6

Sandsfoot Publishing is an imprint of Writecombination Ltd
28, Sunnyside Road,
Weymouth, Dorset. DT4 9BL

For Andrew
My perfect match

Chapter 1

November 1788

Mrs Westlake could barely conceal her excitement. It was almost thirty years since she had been to London, but the memory of her last visit was as fresh in her mind as if it had been yesterday. For one glorious season, she had been the toast of the town and now, at last, she was on her way back to the scene of her triumph. The prospect of reentering the ton – the highest order of fashionable society – made her feel positively young again.

Even though she was past the bloom of youth, Mrs Westlake was still a very fine-looking woman. She had maintained her figure into middle age and her face was remarkably free of wrinkles, thanks, she believed, to the Olympian Dew which she religiously applied every day. Her hair was as thick and golden as it had been in her heyday without the slightest hint of grey. She wore it fashionably powdered and carefully arranged into a style 'au naturel' that her fashion arbiter, the Duchess of Devonshire, had lately adopted.

It did not take long for the novelty of the journey to wear off. Mrs Westlake began to bemoan how many hours it would be before they stopped to change horses. The time would pass much more quickly if she had someone to talk to. She glared resentfully at her companion and was on the verge of waking her when she stirred of her own accord.

"I was beginning to think that you were going to sleep all the way to London, Alicia," Mrs Westlake grumbled. "It is very tedious not to have anyone to talk to."

"I am so sorry, Mother," her companion replied, in a tone designed to soothe her mother's ruffled feathers. "This carriage is so comfortable that I just could not keep my eyes open."

Mrs Westlake was somewhat appeased. She was very proud of her brand new travelling chariot which had been built to the latest design and offered the most comfortable ride that money could buy. Its well-sprung body absorbed much of the jolting from the uneven carriageway, despite the speed at which they were bowling along the turnpike road, drawn by two pairs of matched bays from the late Mr Westlake's stable. The carriage was painted a lovely dark emerald green. She had chosen the colour herself and was very pleased with the result. Her only regret was the lack of a coat of arms on the door. But there was nothing she could do about that. She had made her choice a long time ago.

"It is a very comfortable ride, is it not? I do not suppose that my cousin has a vehicle this smart."

Considering the exorbitant amount of money that her mother had spent on the chaise, Alicia thought it very unlikely indeed.

"Nevertheless, she does live at a good address," Mrs Westlake continued. "I would never have agreed to stay with her otherwise."

Alicia did not doubt it for a moment. She had been surprised when her mother had accepted Lady Granger's invitation to spend the season with her rather than buying, or at least leasing, her own fashionable address. But for some reason, it suited her mother to live as the guest of a cousin whom Alicia had only met once, when she was still in the schoolroom.

"Elizabeth did rather well for herself catching Sir Charles Granger," her mother continued. "She was never handsome and her dowry was moderate to say the least, but somehow she managed to attract his eye. It was as well for her that she had little competition. There was more money and grander titles to be won elsewhere. The Earl of Harting was the biggest prize on the matrimonial market that year, but he never paid the least heed to Elizabeth."

She paused dramatically. "The Earl wanted to marry me, you know."

Yes, Alicia knew. Her mother had often boasted of her youthful conquest. She seemed inordinately proud of the fact that an earl had wanted to marry her and had often regaled her with the tale of her triumph. Alicia made an innocuous comment, knowing that her mother would need little encouragement to continue her monologue. All that was required was the occasional "indeed" or "really" and her mother could keep talking for hours.

"I remember the dress I wore when I met the Earl for the very first time. It was white and richly embroidered with silver thread and edged with the finest lace, and worn over such a wide hoop that I had to glide through the door sideways. My hair was arranged in a very French mode – la tête de mouton – with row upon row of curls across the front of my head and powdered thickly like they did in Paris."

Mrs Westlake sighed. "I was sorely tempted to accept the Earl, but there was so little money with the title. And your father had already made it quite clear that he was prepared to lay all his worldly wealth at my feet. The Earl was heartbroken when I refused him, but if I had accepted, his mother would probably have made my life very uncomfortable. She wanted him to marry Lady Margaret Randolph of Lincoln who had nothing to recommend her except her father's title and a dowry of £40,000. His mother may even have persuaded him to cry off. The Earl was somewhat lacking in resolve, you see, and I doubt very much that he could have stood up against her for long."

She sighed again. "Lady Harting—how grand that sounds. It would have been very agreeable to have a title."

Alicia sat quietly and listened, biting her bottom lip, and resolutely refusing to respond to her mother's words. She did not like to hear the wistful tone in her voice when she talked of the Earl. It sounded remarkably like regret.

For a moment it seemed that Mrs Westlake would be lost in silent reverie, but no, a moment or two later she started again.

"Then again, I would have had to look at the Earl's face over breakfast every morning and I much preferred looking at your father. Such a handsome man! Well-defined features and a firm chin. He had resolution written all over his face. He was quite determined to have me despite my parents' opposition to the match. They could not accept that your grandfather had been in trade, but I never saw that it made much difference where the money came from. Your father was brought up a gentleman and that was good enough for me." She sniffed, more for effect than from any real need to do so. "Your father was a good man." She then rather spoiled the result by adding: "Besides, he was far wealthier than the Earl and much better looking."

It was Alicia's turn to sigh now. How could her mother have such a selective memory where her father was concerned? She could remember his fine looks and his wealth, but conveniently forgot how she had made his life a misery with her constant complaining. She claimed to admire his resolution, but had fought against it relentlessly when it had conflicted with what she wanted.

"Within a week of proposing to me," Mrs Westlake continued, "the supposedly heartbroken Earl had rushed to do his mother's bidding and was engaged to Lady Margaret with her £40,000! She was quick to circulate the rumour that the Earl had jilted me—that he had not proposed marriage at all. I suppose she could not stand the thought of being his second choice. As if anything but her money could have made the Earl prefer her to me! It was horrible," she said, shuddering. "But your father and I were married and he took me away from it all."

And there, thought Alicia, the line should be inserted: "And they lived happily ever after." But of course, they had not.

What her mother had not counted on was that her father would not take her back to London when the gossip had died down. He had allowed her to rebuild his house in the Neo-classical style and fit it out with the latest Chippendale furniture. He had permitted her to squander enormous amounts of money on the latest fashions so that she had soon gained the reputation of being the best-dressed lady in Oxfordshire. He had even taken her on a Grand Tour of Europe, but he had stubbornly refused to take a house in London for the season, determined to separate his wife from what he considered to be the destructive influence of the ton.

Alicia had come to the conclusion that her parents had nothing in common except her. Her father had been a classical scholar with a deep religious conviction and he had mistakenly thought that he could mould the character of his giddy young bride. But her mother had not wished to give up balls and card parties for sermons and good works. She had not been clever enough to partake in his studies and saw attending church more as a chance to show off a new hat than as an opportunity for spiritual development.

For as long as Alicia could remember, her mother had complained about her lot in life. She had moaned about not going to London. She had moaned that Alicia preferred her father's company to her own. She had moaned that with all that learning, her husband was turning Alicia into a veritable bluestocking, ruining her chances of making a good match. Mr Westlake had taken refuge in his library and in frequent trips abroad, visiting his beloved Roman ruins; Mrs Westlake had moaned that she was neglected.

It was now more than a year since the premature demise of Mr Westlake. Alicia reflected that her mother had long since recovered from the shock of becoming a widow, but she still missed her father dearly. It was perhaps as well that Mrs Westlake chose that moment to draw out a folded piece of paper from her pocket. Alicia groaned inwardly. A letter! She had little expectation of escaping its contents, but at least it prevented her thoughts from becoming too melancholy.

"I received this note from Lady Granger yesterday, but I did not have the chance to tell you about it. I swear I did not stop for a moment, making sure that Marie was packing my things the way I like. That is the trouble with servants—you always have to keep an eye on them."

Alicia thought it more likely that her mother had got in the way of her highly superior lady's maid, but she did not think it would be helpful to point it out.

"Indeed, I can hardly remember what it says, I was so distracted yesterday," Mrs Westlake continued. She unfolded the letter and began to read, stopping every moment or two to share the contents with her daughter.

"Elizabeth writes that everything is ready in anticipation of our arrival. She promises us rooms overlooking the Square with a very fine prospect of the gardens." She paused as she read a few more lines of her letter.

"Apparently the King is still far from well. There are rumours that he will not get better and that the Prince of Wales will form his own government. Elizabeth says that would be beneficial for them, as Sir Charles is hopeful of a good position."

Another pause and then Mrs Westlake began again. "Oh! The Duchess of Devonshire has not yet arrived in town. What a shame! I hope she does not stay away too long. I am so looking forward to meeting her. Perhaps she cannot bear to leave her little girls. I have heard that she is a devoted mother and London is certainly not the place to bring up your children."

Mrs Westlake read on. "Ha! The Earl of Harting has grown very stout and goes around with a sour look on his face. It must be the effect of being married to the Countess! However, it would appear that we will not have to endure their company for a while at least. Elizabeth says that they have gone abroad for the winter because of the Earl's health. Though if he is suffering from an ill-tempered wife, I do not suppose that the visit will bring much relief!"

She laid the letter down in her lap and sighed. "Ah, what it would be to be young again, surrounded by admirers, vying for a dance." For a while, she sat unseeing, lost in nostalgic thought, but gradually her thoughts drifted back to the present. It would not do to dwell on the past. All her ambitions were centred on Alicia now.

Chapter 2

At length, the open fields were replaced by houses as the carriage reached the outer edge of London town. As it moved on toward its destination, the buildings became more and more densely packed together and the thoroughfare became busy with activity. For what had seemed like hours, all that Alicia had been able to hear was the constant rumble of the wheels on the road. Now, all manner of different sounds disrupted the monotonous noise. Street vendors loudly advertised their wares to potential customers; dogs barked and children cried. Despite her mother's protests, Alicia could not resist leaning forward in her seat and peering through the window. It was all so new and exciting.

Mrs Westlake's only desire was to be at her journey's end. The smell emanating from the squalidness of so many people living in close proximity to each other was almost overpowering. Holding her vinaigrette to her nose in an attempt to mask the unpleasant odour, she sat back against the cushions and closed her eyes until the hubbub quietened.

As they entered Mayfair, the streets became peaceful again and Alicia noticed that the houses were larger and more widely spaced. This, she correctly surmised, was where the ton lived.

When the carriage stopped, Mrs Westlake opened her eyes. They had arrived in Grosvenor Square. The carriage had drawn up outside a large house with elegant stone pillars flanking an impressive front door, with a huge brass knocker in the centre of it, shaped like the face of a lion.

Almost before the carriage came to a halt, the front door opened and a liveried servant emerged from the house and hurried toward them to offer his assistance. They were ushered into a spacious hall with a black and white marbled floor that Alicia thought looked rather like a chessboard.

An exquisitely gowned lady of immense proportions, whom Alicia correctly assumed was Lady Granger, enthusiastically greeted the weary travellers.

"My dear Susannah. How glad I am to see you at last," she effused, taking her cousin by the arm. "My, my—how your daughter has grown. And what a beauty! There will be hearts broken, you mark my words. Now do you want to see your rooms and lie down for a while to recover? But no, I am sure that you are as eager as I for a comfortable chat. Let us go into the drawing room and I will ring for some refreshments."

They had little choice but to follow Lady Granger up the stairs and into a large room furnished in Neo-classical elegance. "It is the height of fashion," she confided with pride as she lowered her immense bulk into a chair. "The Prince of Wales has a desk just like that," she mentioned casually, pointing to a perfectly symmetrical mahogany desk with gold trimmings. "Sir Charles saw it at Carlton House and when he described it, nothing would do but for me to order one myself."

Mrs Westlake was extremely impressed. She had only to hear that it was fashionable and she must like it. Alicia wondered, not for the first time, whether her mother had any real taste of her own.

Lady Granger looked at Alicia and nodded approvingly. "I have no doubt that you will be able to make an excellent match for your daughter, Susannah." She paused for a moment to consider the options. "It is rumoured that the Marquess of Worcester is looking out for a rich wife," she whispered confidentially, "but then again, he is one of the Prince of Wales' set and a bit wild. Of course, the royal princes are always short of money, but that would be no good at all. The King wants his sons and daughters to marry royalty. Only look at poor Mrs Fitzherbert. They say that the Prince of Wales actually married her, but if the King does not acknowledge the marriage, what good is that? She is little better than a royal mistress!"

"Is she much received?" Mrs Westlake asked, awed.

"O yes, indeed. For who would risk offending the heir to the throne? And besides, she is not without connections, despite being a Catholic. She is related to the Seftons and her first husband was one of the Welds of Lulworth. Talking of Lord Sefton—his son would be a good match. Perhaps a little young to be settling down and it is an Irish title, which would not be our first choice, but a good family."

Alicia sipped her tea in silence whilst the two ladies discussed all the eligible and not so eligible contenders for her hand. She let them talk. Though wishing they would not make her feel as if the sum total of her attractions was in the size of her dowry, she had not the heart to interrupt their conversation. Clearly both ladies were enjoying themselves hugely and she felt it would be cruel to deprive them of their temporary diversion.

It was not as if she had to agree with what they were saying. They could not force her into marriage with the first titled gentleman who offered for her. When she thought about it, Alicia was not sure that she was interested in making a good match at all. She had no objection to the principle of marriage, but she certainly did not want to marry someone who was motivated solely by the wealth in her pockets. She had also witnessed firsthand the disunity that arose from a marriage where the parties had different outlooks on life and was determined not to make the same mistake as her parents.

What Alicia wanted was to marry someone who was her equal on every level—socially, intellectually and spiritually. She was not looking for a good match. What she wanted was a perfect match.

Alicia awoke the next morning refreshed by a good night's sleep and eager to explore what the city had to offer. There was so much she wanted to do. Her mother had talked of Vauxhall Gardens, the Opera House and the Drury Lane Theatre and she was eager to see them for herself. She was even keener to discover the treasures of the places that her father had enthused about—the British Museum and Mr Townley's collection of antiquities. She also wanted to visit his dear friends Mrs Montagu and Mr Reynolds. He had told her about them after his visits and had always meant to take her to meet them, but he had never got the chance. He had become ill travelling back from his last trip to Rome and never recovered.

However, before she could suggest a visit to the British Museum, her mother informed her that their first appointment was with Lady Granger's dressmaker, Madame Dupont. Alicia was disappointed that she could not go out and explore, but she had no choice but to submit.

Mrs Westlake found her daughter's lack of enthusiasm disconcerting and scolded her all the way to Tavistock Street. "Stop looking so down in the mouth, Alicia," she grumbled. "You are going to purchase a new wardrobe, not have a tooth pulled!"

When they arrived at Madame Dupont's smart establishment, a girl greeted them at the door and led them to an elegant sofa before scurrying away to fetch her employer.

Madame Dupont sighed when the girl told her it was Lady Granger with two unknown ladies. Lady Granger always paid her bills, so she could not really complain, but her client was not exactly a good advertisement for her creations. Her figure was deplorable, try what she did to disguise it, and she skirted on the edge of the ton. Madame Dupont dreamed of being exclusive—dressing only the cream of society and those that showed off her designs to perfection.

But it had to be said that members of the ton were notoriously bad at paying their bills and so Madame Dupont accepted the clients who came to her with a good grace and continued to dream of universal recognition for her brilliance. Resigned to dressing two more ladies who did not quite fit the image of her ideal client, Madame Dupont went through to where her customers were waiting, forcing a pleasant smile onto her face.

She brightened considerably when she saw Lady Granger's companions. Although not dressed in quite the latest fashions, she could tell at a glance that their garments were of the highest quality. And when she realised that the young lady was about to make her debut in society, the smiles were no longer forced; she was thinking of the cachet to be gained if such a beautiful girl was presented to the ton in her gowns. Maybe her chance had come at last.

Madame Dupont took control, enthusiastically discussing colours and designs as her assistant brought out swathes of fabrics and held them up to Alicia's face. Alicia was not averse to acquiring new clothes, but she did not find the process as pleasurable as might have been expected; she was prodded and measured and generally ignored whilst her mother and Lady Granger were deep in consultation with the modiste.

"Alas, mademoiselle will not be requiring a court dress," she said sadly. "The Queen will not be holding any drawing rooms until the King is better."

Mrs Westlake agreed that it was sad and joined the modiste in bemoaning the King's debilitating illness. However, she secretly rejoiced that there would not be a drawing room. Although she herself had been presented, she was not at all sure that she would be allowed to present her daughter. The Queen had been known to refuse permission for a lady's presentation because of her father's occupation and although Mr Westlake had been a gentleman, there was no denying that his fortune had come through trade. There were still some things that money could not buy. Mrs Westlake was relieved that she did not have to risk the humiliation of being refused. She dispelled her gloomy thoughts by ordering a great many new gowns for herself and left Madame Dupont's feeling very satisfied with her morning's work.

Chapter 3

Until the first of her new gowns was ready, Alicia was confined to the house. There were to be no public appearances until the Westlakes were fit to be seen. Alicia practised the pianoforte and tried unsuccessfully to sketch the view from her window, but she missed the countryside and longed to go for a walk in the sunshine. She also missed her books. At home, she had access to a library filled with her father's books. Sir Charles was clearly not a great reader and his shelves were filled with volumes that Alicia was quick to see were intended mostly for show.

She tentatively suggested that some new books would help to while away the hours and asked whether she could visit Hookham's circulating library. Her mother's reaction was so severe that she was sorry she had found the temerity to ask. Mrs Westlake delivered a lengthy tirade on the ungratefulness of daughters in general and specifically on the stupidity of her own in suggesting such a thing. Mrs Westlake absolutely forbade her to venture out of the house. First impressions were of the utmost importance. Appearances were everything. She did not want to give anyone the opportunity of stigmatising her daughter as a dowdy girl fresh from the country.

In the meantime, Mrs Westlake deliberated long and hard about how to promote her daughter's introduction into the ton. She had to admit to having been wrong about her cousin's standing in society. Lady Granger's letters had been so full of gossip about members of the aristocracy that she had mistakenly thought that her cousin was on intimate terms with the people she spoke of. It had not taken her long to realise her mistake. Her cousin did not move in the circles to which she aspired. Lady Granger's husband might be a baronet and she might live in the right part of town, but that did not give her an entrée into all the top houses.

Mrs Westlake was not easily daunted when in pursuit of her ambitions. She needed to develop a new strategy. Although Lady Granger might not belong to that coveted higher echelon of society, she was the wife of a Whig Member of Parliament. In Mrs Westlake's mind, most of the leading ladies of the ton belonged to the Opposition rather than to Mr Pitt's Tory party. Surely Lady Granger could secure an introduction for her and Alicia to one of the Whig hostesses?

The Duchess of Devonshire would have been Mrs Westlake's first choice. Lady Granger had proudly admitted visiting Devonshire House several times, and if the Duchess had been in town, Mrs Westlake might have begged her cousin to secure them an introduction. The Duchess might have taken one of her fancies to Alicia and that would have ensured her success. Then again, she was a duchess and Lady Granger might have objected to imposing on someone of such high rank.

She quickly dismissed the Duchess' sister, Lady Duncannon, as a possibility. The rumours were that the Viscountess was flirting with disaster by conducting a less than discreet affair with the brilliant playwright, Mr Sheridan. Wisdom decreed that they keep their distance from any hint of scandal.

Then there was Viscountess Melbourne. Though some ten years her junior, Lady Melbourne's reputation was not calculated to instil Mrs Westlake with confidence. Despite her name being linked with that of the Prince of Wales for a number of years, she had emerged from the affair unscathed, having maintained her position at the forefront of society. Mrs Westlake was somewhat in awe of her reputed cleverness and wit, but, rampantly ambitious herself, she admired rather than feared this trait in another.

She decided that Lady Melbourne was in the best position to help them, if only she could be persuaded to do so.

First she had to coax Lady Granger to effect the introduction.

"Impossible!" Lady Granger declared, when Mrs Westlake first broached the subject. "I cannot force the introduction upon Lady Melbourne, Susannah. She is a viscountess for goodness sake."

"But surely you are political allies, Elizabeth? I was sure that you would be able to arrange it," Mrs Westlake said sulkily.

Lady Granger wriggled uncomfortably. She was not immune to her friend's entreaties, but she had no great liking for Lady Melbourne and wished very much to avoid putting herself on the receiving end of one of the Viscountess' famous set-downs. "What of your old friends, Susannah?" she said desperately. "There must be those who will still receive you?"

Mrs Westlake had no such certainty. Her old rival, the Countess of Harting, had set her peers against her once, labelling her a fortune hunter, and she felt in urgent need of new connections to support her readmission to the ton.

"You are our only hope, Elizabeth," Mrs Westlake pleaded. "If you cannot introduce us to anyone of consequence, we may as well retire from London now!"

Lady Granger sighed. She was naturally indolent and did not like to be bullied into doing things that she would much rather not do. But her aversion to unpleasantness was competing with a stronger emotion: the simple enjoyment of female companionship.

Her life was tedious in the extreme. She had not been blessed with any children and Sir Charles was always at his club. She did not want Mrs Westlake and her daughter to go home. It would, of course, mean that she had to exert herself, but it would be worth it if it meant that her cousin would stay and keep her company for the season.

Reluctantly Lady Granger admitted that she had been invited to an evening party at Lady Melbourne's the following week. It had been her intention to cry off, but she grudgingly consented to go and, if the opportunity arose, promised to mention that she had visitors staying with her.

"And then maybe, though I cannot guarantee anything, she will invite me to take you to call on her. But I cannot think why you wish to take up with Lady Melbourne. She is such a disagreeable woman. If there is the slightest thing wrong with my appearance, she is sure to notice and point it out. She despises any show of weakness or sensibility. If she finds you have a sore spot, she plays on it. The gentlemen all seem to love her though. Sir Charles is often at Melbourne House. He says that all the talented young party members go there. Rather like an exclusive Whig club."

Lady Granger resigned herself to the sacrifice and duly attended the party. Lady Melbourne always made her feel nervous. The Viscountess' propensity to deliver barbed comments kept poor Lady Granger on tenterhooks and made it quite impossible for her to relax and enjoy the evening. She knew she could not go home without attempting to secure an introduction for her cousin, but dreaded the possibility of Lady Melbourne giving her a set-down. With the attitude of a martyr, she managed to secure a few minutes' conversation with her hostess.

Lady Melbourne was amused. Any woman that could persuade another to do something that they so clearly did not want to do was worthy of her attention. But the name was enough in itself. If she was not mistaken, and she rarely was, Mrs Westlake was none other than the beautiful Miss Etherington who had once been courted by the Earl of Harting. Lady Melbourne had still been in the schoolroom when Miss Etherington had taken the town by storm, but she had heard the rumours and was curious to know what she was like.

"By all means bring them to visit," she said graciously.

Lady Granger did not return in triumph, although she had succeeded with the object of her visit. She was not best pleased. It would mean another visit to that woman, laying herself open to the possibility of being snubbed. Not that Lady Melbourne had made any cutting remarks in their last conversation. In fact, she had been remarkably pleasant. Nevertheless, Lady Granger could not help thinking that Lady Melbourne was laughing at her and feared that on the next occasion, she would give her an almighty set-down.

It was with some trepidation that Lady Granger accompanied Mrs Westlake and Alicia to Melbourne House. "I am not responsible, Susannah, if that woman is unpleasant to you. Remember that it was your idea to court her favour, not mine."

Lady Granger performed the introductions and Lady Melbourne greeted the visitors with effusive professions of delight that were belied by her smile—a cold, superficial smile that waited to pass judgement. Curiosity had prompted her to beg Lady Granger to bring her visitors to call. It was a sacrifice. Lady Granger's conversation was desultory and if her other visitors were equally tedious, she would make sure that she never saw them again.

"How lovely to meet you, Mrs Westlake. I understand that this is your first visit to London for many years. How have you kept away from the metropolis for so long? Have the ties of parenthood kept you ensconced deep in the country?" she asked, trying to provoke a response from her visitor.

Mrs Westlake bristled, but determined not to allow Lady Melbourne to get under her skin. "Indeed, no. Sadly Mr Westlake and I were blessed with only one child, my daughter Alicia, but my husband did not care for the town, and so we stayed away."

Lady Melbourne nodded with approval. She had not expected to find Mrs Westlake so well in charge of herself. She had heard that she was somewhat garrulous and was pleasantly surprised to see that she had learnt some diplomacy with age. She turned to Alicia. The girl was as pretty as a picture and well-dowered too, if her sources were correct. Even in the schoolroom, Lady Melbourne had managed to keep abreast of what was happening in society. One never knew when a snippet of information might prove invaluable. If Mr Westlake had been half as rich as she had heard reported, then Mrs Westlake and her daughter were very comfortably off, very comfortably off indeed. If only they were better connected, Lady Melbourne thought, she would not be sorry to see her son Peniston married to the girl.

Lady Melbourne plied Mrs Westlake with questions, asking about her husband and his estate in a manner that would have seemed rude in a less important personage, but somehow seemed perfectly natural coming from the Viscountess. As Mrs Westlake talked, Lady Melbourne drew her own conclusions. Mrs Westlake's understanding might not be strong, but she was exerting herself to entertain, and underneath the trivial conversation, she caught a glimpse of the ambition that ruled her own life.

Lady Melbourne then turned her attention to the daughter. "This is your first visit to London, Miss Westlake?" she asked.

"Yes, Madam," Alicia replied.

"And do you like London?"

"It is hard to say," she replied, "for I am yet to venture much abroad, but the views from my window are interesting enough. Though not, perhaps, comparable to Rome," she added.

"And when were you in Rome?" Lady Melbourne asked, surprised.

"Sadly, never, Madam," Alicia replied, her eyes twinkling. "I should explain that my father painted many different views of that city and the ruins at Pompeii and I cannot help but think they are more majestic than what I have so far seen from my window."

So the girl had a sense of humour. Better and better, Lady Melbourne mused.

"But you must admit that London is the social axis around which the whole of the civilised world rotates," said Lady Melbourne, attempting to throw her young guest off balance.

"Possibly," replied Alicia, "but surely Paris could vie with London for that honour? After all, it is to France that we look for the latest fashions."

Lady Melbourne was amused. A girl with opinions was original, to say the least. A brief conversation was enough to inform her that mother and daughter were not cast in the same mould. Miss Westlake was of a much more serious frame of mind than her mother. Or was she? There was something in her eyes that suggested she was not taking the visit seriously. Mrs Westlake was vociferously courting her interest; Miss Westlake, on the other hand, was enjoying a stimulating conversation and appeared not to be the least bit bothered what impression she was making. How interesting.

"I would be delighted if you would accompany me to the theatre on Saturday," Lady Melbourne said, acting on impulse. "My husband does not care for *Macbeth* and I have it in mind to make up a party. Can I tempt you, Mrs Westlake?"

Mrs Westlake glowed with pleasure, enthusiastically accepting the invitation before her ladyship could change her mind. For her part, Lady Granger declined with equal rapidity. Such an evening's entertainment would yield her no pleasure; she would be worrying all the time that Lady Melbourne would say something cutting.

"And you, Miss Westlake?" Lady Melbourne asked, turning to face Alicia. "Would you like to visit the theatre?"

"Yes, Madam. My father often spoke of having seen Mrs Siddons at the Drury Lane Theatre. He was very taken with her performance as Lady Macbeth and more than once tried to represent on canvas the scene where she walks in her sleep. It has given me a great desire to see her," Alicia said eagerly.

"I cannot promise you Mrs Siddons, Miss Westlake, but I hope you will find the play enjoyable even without the great muse herself."

Mrs Westlake immediately took over, assuring Lady Melbourne that it made no difference at all to her who was performing if they were to enjoy her company. Lady Melbourne smiled her hollow smile again, and murmured, "I shall look forward to it," wondering why she had voluntarily chosen to spend a whole evening in such insipid company.

But then she happened to glance at Miss Westlake, and saw the resigned look on her face, as if her mother's fawning behaviour was to be endured rather than challenged. It would be entertaining to observe how the ton took to Miss Westlake. She would definitely have to secure her entrée; it would be most amusing.

Chapter 4

Mrs Westlake could speak of nothing else except her friend the Viscountess. Even Lady Granger began to tire of her effusions and think that companionship had been bought at too great a price. Alicia thought that it was a great pity that her father had not been a viscount or an earl or at very least a baron. Maybe then her mother would have grown accustomed to moving in exalted circles and not talk in this embarrassing manner as though she lived for nothing else but to consort with people of rank. How vulgar her mother seemed to her, chasing after connections as if her very life depended on it. Alicia wondered whether her mother really believed that being taken up by the nobility would supply what was missing from her life.

Alicia was not at all sure that she liked Lady Melbourne. Her brief encounter with the Viscountess was enough to confirm to her that Lady Granger's scruples were quite justified. For some reason, it pleased that lady to pick them up, but she had no doubt that she would drop them again, equally quickly, if it suited her.

The company Alicia sought was of a different kind. She was eager to call upon her father's old friend, Mrs Montagu, but she knew that her mother was somewhat afraid of the intellectual set that her husband had moved in and would quite likely respond with a negative reaction.

For the third or fourth time, Mrs Westlake was discussing with Alicia what they should wear to the theatre. As often happened in their discussions, Mrs Westlake was doing most of the talking. When her mother paused for breath, Alicia, having failed to find a more suitable time for broaching the subject, casually mentioned that she was planning to call on Mrs Montagu.

"Good heavens!" her mother exclaimed in alarm. "Do you want to ruin your chances before you have set one foot in a London ballroom? If you are labelled a bluestocking, you will stand no chance at all of making a good match."

As Alicia was tired of hearing about the good marriage she was supposed to make, she thought wickedly that this was hardly the way to discourage her from calling. However, she adopted a more diplomatic approach, and appealed to her mother's strongest motivator—what other people thought of her.

"I wrote to Mrs Montagu when Father died and it would be rude not to pay her a visit now that we are in London," Alicia said calmly.

Mrs Westlake shuddered. "I am sure it is not necessary to pursue the connection, Alicia. You have not even met the lady and there is not the least requirement for you to call."

On this occasion, Alicia was determined to win her point. Mrs Montagu had written such a warm letter in reply to the news of her father's death that she was eager to talk with her as someone who appreciated the depths of her father's character.

Knowing that her mother hated any suggestion of meanness, she subtly played on her mother's feelings. "I will not go if you object very much, Mother, but I am afraid that people will say that you have abandoned

father's old friends. Surely it would be considered bad
ton to be backward in any attention to a lady who used
to know him so well?"

Mrs Westlake began to waver. She meant no disre-
spect to Mrs Montagu but she hated the bluestocking set
that she represented. Mr Westlake had belonged to that
set, but she most assuredly did not. She had once
attended one of Mrs Montagu's bluestocking assemblies
with her husband and had felt totally out of her depth.
Mrs Westlake shuddered at the memory. She had made
very sure that Mr Westlake had not repeated the exercise.

On the other hand, she did not want to be accused
of cutting her husband's old friends, though she had no
taste for their company. She reluctantly conceded that
perhaps Alicia should call, just the once, to show that
there was no bad feeling.

Having won her point, Alicia was eager to pay the
visit before her mother had the chance to change her
mind. She placed no reliance on her support; she was
well aware of her mother's talent for procrastination
when it came to doing anything that she did not want to
do. She determined to go by herself, with just her maid
for company. Martha would moan. She would say that it
did not become her position to go gadding about the
town without a proper chaperon. But surely there could
be no objection to calling on an old lady by herself? She
would not put her mother through it; she was just not
cut out for intellectual conversation.

Both her mother and Lady Granger were still above
stairs when Alicia ordered the carriage to be brought
round. As she had predicted, Martha was forthright in
her opinions. Although a year younger than Alicia,
Martha was the daughter of the Westlakes' housekeeper
and seemed to have inherited all the rights of an old

family retainer, taking liberties with her young mistress that other servants would not have dared.

"You'll pardon me speaking my mind, Miss, but I hardly think as how your mother would be pleased to have you going a-visiting all by yourself. You should ought to have your mother or Lady Granger with you."

"Martha, I am going to visit an old lady—a friend of my father's. I hardly think a chaperon is necessary. And besides," she added, with a wicked smile on her face, "I am not alone. I have you to protect me!"

"It is not right for a lady of consequence," Martha muttered as she followed her mistress up the steps and into the carriage. She continued to mutter all the way to Portman Square. Alicia laughed at the degree of importance that Martha liked to give to herself and her young mistress and could not help thinking that she was cut out to be a maid for a duchess, not just a plain 'Miss'.

However, as they approached the impressive portico of Montagu House, some of Alicia's confidence deserted her and she was aware of just a touch of nervousness. She sat fidgeting in her carriage seat while the footman jumped down and advanced toward the house. She held her breath while he knocked on the door and waited for an answer. The door opened almost immediately and Alicia nervously bit her lip as the footman sent in her card. She was relieved when the footman returned to the carriage and informed her that Mrs Montagu would be happy to receive her. Once inside, she was accorded all the welcome she could have wished for from her father's old friend.

"How kind of you to call, Miss Westlake. Your father was a very dear friend." She waved her hand at the wall behind her where an oil painting of Pompeii was hanging. It was a view with which Alicia was very familiar, having seen numerous variations of it over the years. "That picture is one of his," Mrs Montagu said. "He was a very talented man—as gifted with the brush as he was with words. I loved the way that he would always tell you the story behind what he had painted. I could listen to him talk for hours." For a moment she was lost in her reverie, but then she seemed to refocus on her young guest.

"You must miss him very much," she said.

"Yes, Madam."

"And your mother?"

"She is glad to be wearing colours again."

"Ah!" Mrs Montagu nodded wisely. "It is hard for butterflies to dress like moths." The silence hung comfortably between them, both lost in thought.

"And you, Miss Westlake. Are you to make your come-out in society?"

"Such is my mother's intention in coming to London, but ..."

"But?"

Alicia chose her words carefully so as not to cast aspersions on her mother's character. "My mother is anxious to introduce me into the circles in which she once moved, but I fear that those who cut her acquaintance when she married my father will not readily welcome her back now that she is a widow."

"A widow, yes, but a wealthy one, Miss Westlake. Money opens many doors. In the meantime, I can offer you good company if you would care to attend a small gathering here tonight. Not a full assembly, just a few friends, but there are those who will remember your father, Miss Westlake—Mrs More and Mr Reynolds amongst them. Would your mother permit you to come?"

Alicia quickly quashed the suggestion that her mother might forbid her from mixing with her father's old friends, feeling only slightly guilty for giving a false impression. She eagerly accepted the invitation, subduing any misgivings she might have had that her mother would not be quite as thrilled with the invitation as she was. She was not.

"Alicia, how can you be so stupid? If you associate with that bluestocking circle you will be labelled as one of them. What gentleman wants a clever wife? Reflect on what has happened to Miss Burney. Now I have nothing to say against her writing novels, and I did so enjoy *Evelina*, though I think perhaps that *Cecilia* was my favourite, but as soon it was acknowledged that she was the author, she was drawn into that set by her father's intellectual friends. And what good has come from that? Nearly forty and not a hint of a husband. Becoming one of the Queen's ladies was all very well, but Lady Granger says that last time she saw her, she looked positively worn out and it seems highly unlikely that anyone is going to look at her now. She may have the Queen's ear, but I would rather have a daughter to comfort me in my old age."

Alicia raised her eyebrows at that. Her mother did not conduct herself like a lady sinking into old age and did not appear to be in the slightest need of comfort.

"Mrs Montagu is very well respected and I am hardly going to be drawn into her set through a single visit."

Mrs Westlake was not so sure. Alicia was too like her father for her peace of mind. No doubt Alicia would fit in all too well with her husband's old friends. It was an alarming thought. It was no bad thing for a gentleman to be educated, but if a woman showed more than a moderate amount of learning, it could ruin her chances.

"I grant you that Mrs Montagu is respectable enough, but what of her friends? Mrs More might be there, Alicia. I met her once. A supremely intelligent woman and so religious that she made me feel quite uncomfortable. Learning is all very well, but it will not get you a husband. Mrs More herself is not a married lady. Why single women must call themselves 'Mrs' is beyond my comprehension. What is more, she interferes with politics more than is right for a woman. I shudder to think of the same thing happening to you, Alicia."

"But Mother, how can you say that politics is the province of men when the Duchess of Devonshire, whom you so admire, is the truest Whig of them all?"

Mrs Westlake shook her head. "You do not understand, Alicia. A married woman has licence to do many things that a single woman should never attempt. The Duchess has embraced the politics of her husband. And even so, it caused some nasty talk after the election of '84. If the press are to be believed, she won votes for Mr Fox by kissing the common people."

"But I thought you admired her?"

"And so I do," Mrs Westlake assured her, "but I have to admit that she overstepped the mark on that occasion. A man may do many things, but a lady – even a lady of wealth and importance like the Duchess – has to be careful or her reputation will be torn to shreds."

Alicia saw that she was getting nowhere and resorted to her original tactics. "Mother, I have accepted Mrs Montagu's invitation. If I send my apologies now, I fear that they will blame you for keeping me away."

Mrs Westlake pouted. Alicia was right. It would not do for her to appear discourteous. "Well I am not coming with you to be made to feel ridiculous. Just the mention of bluestocking gatherings sets my heart fluttering with nerves. Not that Miss Burney was unpleasant, but she was far too reserved to put me at my ease. My, what a shy creature she was! You go, my dear. Just this once. To be polite. Martha can go with you. There can be no need for a chaperon at such a gathering as that."

Alicia gratefully agreed and escaped to her bedroom before her mother could change her mind.

She was not feeling quite so confident by the time she arrived at Mrs Montagu's house. Martha had muttered her disapproval all the way there and Alicia was obliged to admit that her maid had some justification for her disapprobation. It was one thing to pay a morning visit on your own, but Alicia had to acknowledge that it was not quite comfortable to go to an evening party without a companion. At least she had the assurance that she was dressed in the height of fashion. Her mother had insisted, on the basis that there was always the possibility that she might meet someone of consequence, though she rated the chances very low. Alicia reflected that had she thought it likely, her mother would no doubt have overcome her dislike of bluestocking gatherings and accompanied her to Mrs Montagu's after all.

Mrs Montagu was not surprised that Mrs Westlake had declined to accompany her young friend and immediately began presenting her to the other visitors and setting her at her ease.

"Miss Westlake, allow me to introduce you to Sir Joshua Reynolds, President of the Royal Academy. Sir Joshua, Miss Westlake, the daughter of our old friend, who is visiting London for the first time."

Alicia curtseyed. So this was the famous portrait painter. She was aware of a touch of disappointment.

Perhaps she had expected his person to be as imposing as his portraits. Sir Joshua was neither tall nor handsome. His face was dominated by a pair of round-rimmed glasses and was somewhat disfigured above his mouth. She immediately chided herself for such a superficial reaction. There was something in his bearing that was very gentlemanly and when he smiled, his whole face lit up. He had known her father and they spent a happy half hour exchanging reminiscences. Mr Reynolds adverted to his failing eyesight.

"At least that was something your father did not have to endure, Miss Westlake. It is frustrating beyond measure to see the exercise of your talent threatened because you can no longer see what it is you are painting clearly enough to translate it onto the canvas. Perhaps there will come a time when I will not even be able to see my paintbrush. And then what would I be? A painter who cannot paint. But come, Miss Westlake. These things are not upon us yet. Let us not be melancholy but enjoy the day. Let me introduce you to another friend of your father's."

Mr Reynolds led Alicia across the room to where a lady and gentleman were deep in conversation. Alicia judged the lady to be about the same age as her mother, but thought, perhaps, that she was not taking such troubles to resist the signs of ageing as her parent was or maybe that she had not led such a cossetted life. The gentleman was younger. He had long blond hair, very indifferently tied back at the nape of his neck, and his features were severe, clearly intent upon the subject in hand. The lady looked up as they approached and immediately broke off her discussion in answer to Mr Reynolds' unspoken request and rose to greet them. The gentleman reluctantly stood up as well but made no move to leave his place. Alicia was surprised to notice how tall he was and mused how impossible it was to guess someone's height when they were sitting down.

Mr Reynolds introduced the lady as Mrs More and then withdrew.

"I was sorry to hear of your father's passing, Miss Westlake. He was a good friend of mine and is missed by many in this circle."

"Thank you, Madam. It is comforting to be amongst his friends."

"And do you follow in his footsteps, Miss Westlake? Are you a great artist and student of history?"

Alicia laughed. "I am afraid that my drawing skills are so inferior to my father's that they are really not worth mentioning, but I share his love of antiquities. I have studied all my father's notes on Pompeii and would dearly love to go there to see the site for myself."

"Will you permit me to introduce Mr Merry? He is a great friend of Mr Wilberforce and if you want to talk about antiquities, I know of no one else in this room that is better qualified." Alicia willingly gave permission for the introduction and followed Mrs More over to the gentleman in question who was nonchalantly propping up the wall while waiting for them to join him.

When Alicia had first seen Mr Merry, he had been deep in conversation with Mrs More, but now that he was not concentrating so intently, his features had relaxed and Alicia saw that he was a much more handsome gentleman than she had at first supposed.

"Miss Westlake, I present Mr Merry. Mr Merry, Miss Westlake. Miss Westlake and her mother are staying with Sir Charles and Lady Granger for the season. Miss Westlake's father was an excellent man and one quite after your own heart, Mr Merry. He was a very keen classical scholar. Did you never happen to meet him in Rome?"

"Miss Westlake, I am charmed to make your acquaintance," he said, in the clear musical tones of a natural orator. "I met your father once when I was making the Grand Tour with my elder brother. He was able to satisfy my thirst for knowledge about Pompeii. I do not believe he had his equal on the subject in the whole of Italy."

Alicia was gratified to find her father so admired. "It was his favourite subject. He was writing a book about it when he died. He had already completed the illustrations but sadly he never managed to write more than the opening chapter."

Alicia discovered that Mrs More had moved away to talk to someone else whilst they had been deep in discussion. She decided to settle her curiosity.

"Tell me, Mr Merry," she asked eagerly, "what was it you were talking about so earnestly with Mrs More when I first saw you?"

Mr Merry's carefree expression disappeared. "We were talking about the poor King. Pitt says that there will have to be a Regency if he does not recover soon. A Regency with the Prince of Wales as Regent. Better a mad king than have his good-for-nothing son in power!"

Alicia was shocked. Her mother and Lady Granger had spoken so enthusiastically about the Prince that she had not really considered that he could be anything but the worthy figure they had painted.

"You look quite taken aback, Miss Westlake. Does it offend you that I support the King over his son?"

"No indeed," replied Alicia honestly. "It is our Christian duty to support and pray for the King in sickness and in health. But is the Prince of Wales really so very bad? Sir Charles believes that the country needs the reform that only the Whigs can bring."

"Ah, but of course. You are living in a Whig stronghold and you have been imbued with Whig party politics!"

"I form my own opinions, Mr Merry," Alicia replied haughtily, "but it is hard to make good judgements when one's information is limited. My mother does not believe ladies should be involved in politics."

"A lady after my own mother's heart. She would never demean herself like the Duchess of Devonshire and run after votes for her husband's party. I am no Whig, but you cannot but admire Her Grace's commitment. Alas, I fear that my dear Pitt has not the ability to inspire such female devotion. Then again, the Duchess of Gordon has recently become his ardent supporter and if she continues to entertain the Tories on such a lavish scale, she will be in a fair way to rivalling the Duchess of Devonshire's position."

Alicia was struggling to keep up with the fast flow of his conversation. She knew so little of politics. Her knowledge was restricted to the gossipy bits that her mother sought out eagerly from the papers. However, she latched onto the way Mr Merry had referred to Mr Pitt and asked whether he had met him.

"Met him? Pitt and I were up at Cambridge together. I wanted to go into politics like him and Wilberforce, but my parents did not take to the idea. I think they thought I might desert the Tories and join the reformers. How embarrassing would that have been? You see, I do not see eye to eye with my parents. I have the temerity to have my own opinions rather than adopting theirs without question. To put it simply, they did not trust me to behave as they wished. To ensure that I should not disoblige them, they sent me on the Grand Tour with my elder brother. I suppose that I am grateful to them for that at least. I fell in love with ancient Rome and the rest is, shall we say, history!"

Alicia laughed. "Do you see much of your friends now?"

"Very little. Wilber is a good fellow and his home is always open to me, but since he became religious, he does have a tendency to make me feel somewhat inadequate, so, I confess, I tend to avoid his company. And Pitt? Pitt is rather busy running the country. He has the King's ear. Not that that is going to help him if the King does not recover. I very much doubt whether his government will survive if the Regency goes ahead. It stands to reason that the Prince will bring in his Whig friends. Fox is one of his intimate friends, you know, though not quite so intimate since he upset Mrs Fitzherbert."

Of course, Alicia knew all about the Prince and the lady he was rumoured to have married. Her mother thrived on society gossip, but she was eager to hear Mr Merry's opinion. "Do you believe that the Prince and Mrs Fitzherbert are actually married?" she whispered.

"I do, but the marriage will not stand up in law. The Prince knows that he cannot marry without the King's consent and he certainly never bothered to seek it for a marriage that he knew the King would deplore in every conceivable way. No, in his own inimitable style, the Prince is making out that she is his wife because those were the only terms on which he could get her."

"I think it hard that the Prince of Wales cannot choose his own wife," Alicia said with conviction. "If he truly loves Mrs Fitzherbert, then it is cruel to keep them apart."

"I am afraid that you have been misled, Miss Westlake. The Prince is by no means constant. He will not give up the throne for the sake of his Catholic wife. Mark my words: he will put her aside just as soon as it is convenient to him."

"Is it so terrible that she is a Catholic? Surely they, too, believe in God?"

"The King is vehemently opposed to Catholics. He believes they would take his throne. Much evil has been done in the name of religion, Miss Westlake. I find that life is far simpler without it."

"Without religion, Mr Merry?" asked Alicia in disbelief.

"Yes, indeed."

"I do not think that I have ever met someone who openly discarded religion. Even my mother dutifully attends church and says her prayers. Do you not believe in the bible at all?"

Mr Merry laughed. "To be sure I do. I live by the bible: 'Eat, drink and be merry for tomorrow we die!'"

Alicia digested his response. He was laughing at her, but she was not ready to abandon the subject. Her curiosity was piqued. She wanted to know more. "You must have believed in God once. I cannot accept that you just woke up one morning and decided that religion had caused too many wars and so you were not going to believe any more. No, it must have been more personal than that," she reasoned. "Am I right? Did something happen to make you stop believing?"

Mr Merry stood with a closed-in look on his face and Alicia wondered if she had overstepped an unwritten line and committed a social solecism.

After what seemed like hours, he finally spoke. "Yes, you are right. And now, you will have to excuse me, Miss

Westlake. I need a drink." And with this, he gave a brief bow and walked off without another word.

Mrs More soon drew Alicia back into conversation, but out of the corner of her eye, Alicia noticed Mr Merry taking his leave of their hostess. Alicia enjoyed several other conversations with her father's old friends, but none of them was quite as stimulating as that with Mr Merry and she came away feeling a twinge of disappointment that her new-found friend had deserted her so precipitately.

Chapter 5

Alicia was relieved that her mother showed only a perfunctory interest in her visit to Mrs Montagu's. Her mother was not likely to be impressed that she had spent the majority of the evening in company with an untitled gentleman who by his own profession was a younger son who did not get on with his parents. Mrs Westlake listened half-heartedly to her rhapsodies over Mrs Montagu's kindness and the pleasantness of the evening, evincing a modicum of interest when she mentioned that she had met the great Sir Joshua, but not encouraging her to expand on it.

Having successfully visited her father's old friends, Alicia was determined to achieve another of her goals. Over dinner, she casually dropped into the conversation that she was eager to see the British Museum, as she had heard the antiquities were unequalled.

Sir Charles took the bait beautifully. "But of course, Miss Westlake. Everyone must go to see the collections. Even Lady Granger has been. Is that not so, my dear?"

Lady Granger smiled weakly. Yes, she thought. She had been to that awful museum and nothing was going to convince her to make such a fatiguing visit again. All those stairs. It made her feel exhausted just thinking about it.

"Yes, my dear. A most interesting experience."

"Would you like me to procure tickets for you to go,

Miss Westlake? I fear I am too busy to accompany you,
but I am sure that your mother and Lady Granger would
be happy to take you."

Mrs Westlake hesitated. The last thing she wanted to
do was to visit the British Museum. But if everybody
went, it would be unfashionable not to. They need not
stay long. A quick look round and then she could say
that she had been. Yes, it was a sacrifice, but these things
had to be done for the sake of fashion.

"Thank you, Sir Charles. I would be most grateful if
you could make arrangements. What day shall we go,
Elizabeth?"

Lady Granger was quick to decline. "I do not think
that it would be wise for me to go with you, Susannah.
Delightful though it would be to accompany you, I must
think of my health. No, pray do not try to persuade me. I
would not spoil your visit for the world."

Mrs Westlake was not fooled by her profusions and
wished that she too might cry off. But when Alicia tried
to release her from the engagement, predicting that her
mother would be bored and saying that she could very
well go on her own, Mrs Westlake was outraged and
determined to martyr herself to the cause.

The visit was set for Thursday and Sir Charles kindly
applied for tickets for the afternoon session and
collected them in advance. Alicia looked forward to an
afternoon of delight marred only by her mother's lack of
enthusiasm.

Mrs Westlake was bored after a quarter of an hour.
She groaned inwardly and wondered how soon it would
all be over. She could not understand why her daughter
was so obsessed with history. Why would anyone want
to spend their time walking around rooms crammed with
bits and pieces that belonged to days gone by? Most of

the relics were incomplete as well. No one would think they were worth a second glance if they were not old. She blamed Alicia's father. It was he who had put all this antiquarian nonsense into her head.

Their guide was one of the under librarians, a rather elderly gentleman attired in a full-skirted coat and wig that appeared to be at least twenty years out of date. Although Mr Brown clearly knew his subject, Alicia felt that his delivery would have benefitted from a little more animation.

The other visitors in their group gave the impression of being as bored as her mother. Alicia doubted whether they had the slightest interest in what they were examining. The older gentleman looked elegantly detached, his extremely stout wife seemed to be in danger of expiring before reaching the end of the tour and the younger gentleman, whom she assumed was their son, was as restless as her own mother.

"Alicia, could we go out into the gardens now. It is a beautiful day," she whispered in a low voice so that their guide could not hear.

"Mother, we have only just got here. I told you not to come. I knew you would be bored," Alicia whispered back.

Mrs Westlake sniffed. "That is all very well, but it would have given such an odd appearance if you had come on your own."

"But I would not have been completely on my own—Martha would have come with me."

"If only your father were alive, he would have come with you, most willingly. And the pair of you would have lost yourselves in here for a week or more with no consideration for those not blessed with your predilection for antiquities," Mrs Westlake moaned.

Alicia bit back a harsh response, thinking wistfully how true her mother's words were. She knew that her mother struggled to see anything from any point of view other than her own. Her mother did not mean to hurt her. The truth was, Alicia was very like her father and her mother did not like to be reminded of it. But it was no use regretting the loss of her beloved father and how he would have enjoyed talking to her about all the strange objects collected together in the museum.

Mrs Westlake gazed longingly out of the windows to the well-tended gardens outside. Twice the guide called out "Madam" in an effort not to leave her behind as they moved on to the next exhibit.

"I think you will find the gallery more interesting."

Alicia turned round to see who had spoken. A pair of blue eyes sparkled down at her from the handsome face of Mr Merry. The cloud over their last parting seemed forgotten and she for one did not want to bring up that melancholy moment. "Good afternoon, Mr Merry," she said warmly, smiling with pleasure. "Are you visiting the museum too?"

"Not exactly. I have permission to use the reading room to study the manuscripts and so come and go quite freely." He glanced toward their guide and grimaced. "Oh dear! I am sorry that old Brown is taking your party round. A marvellous antiquarian but not the most stimulating of guides."

"No, I am afraid not. If he becomes any less lively, he is in danger of turning into one of the exhibits. I fear he will send my mother to sleep."

Mr Merry laughed out loud and the whole party stopped and stared at him. Mr Brown looked irritated at having his tour interrupted, but Mr Merry, oblivious to his discomfort, gaily asked whether he minded him joining the party and continued talking to Miss Westlake without waiting for an answer. Mr Brown sniffed loudly to show his disapproval and continued the tour. The other visitors followed meekly in his wake, anxious to get the tour over with as quickly as possible, but Mrs Westlake held back, waiting for her daughter and the strange young gentleman to draw level.

"Alicia."

Alicia broke off from her conversation immediately. Mrs Westlake studied the gentleman whilst her daughter made the introductions. He was a very attractive young man, to be sure, and most obviously a gentleman. There was something vaguely familiar about him, but surely she would have remembered if she had met him before. She never forgot a handsome face. But where could her daughter have met him?

"... at Mrs Montagu's house," Alicia finished. Ah, Mrs Montagu's. That was no recommendation. What had Alicia said his name was? She had been concentrating so hard on trying to place him that she had quite failed to take it in. Ah, well. She would have to ask Alicia later.

By this time, the assiduous Mr Brown was already halfway up the grand staircase, with the other members of their party trailing dolefully behind. Mr Merry suggested that they should catch up with the group before Mr Brown scolded them and led the way up the stairs with Mrs Westlake. Determined to make a good impression, he began to engage her in conversation. It did not take him long to realise that she was not at all interested in antiquities and he immediately launched into a discussion of the King's health which Mrs Westlake entered into enthusiastically.

Alicia smiled. Nothing could have delighted her mother more than to be entertained by a handsome young gentleman in a public place. Alicia was very grateful to Mr Merry for sparing her from her mother's moaning. Mrs Westlake rejoined the rest of the party in a much improved state of mind. Being attended by a personable young man lent a certain distinction to the outing.

Mr Merry turned back to wait for Alicia to join him; she had lagged behind on purpose to allow herself a little space. When she reached the top of the staircase, she looked up to find that she was staring at a stuffed giraffe which had been carefully preserved.

"Oh! How horrible!" she said, shuddering, turning her eyes away.

Mr Merry raised his eyebrows. "That is not the fashionable response," he mocked. "I believe the correct response is 'how interesting'."

Mrs Westlake was a few paces ahead.

"Look, Alicia, a giraffe. How interesting!"

Alicia swallowed hard to hold back a giggle and she had almost succeeded when she looked at Mr Merry who clearly wanted to share the joke. That was too much for Alicia and she had to cough violently in order to avoid an undignified burst of laughter.

To her surprise, Mrs Westlake found the natural history exhibits quite fascinating and insisted on pointing out particular specimens that caught her eye. Alicia smiled sweetly and murmured "how interesting" once or twice. When her mother drew her attention to a brightly-coloured snake which had been pickled in spirits, she made the mistake of looking up desperately into Mr Merry's face as she uttered the tired phrase for a third time.

Mr Merry shook his head in silence with a grim expression on his face but his eyes were sparkling with mischief and Alicia had to bite her lip in order to prevent herself from laughing.

At last they reached the gallery and Alicia was faced with cabinet after cabinet of treasures—Roman sculptures and Etruscan vases, Egyptian mummies and all sorts of medals and coins. She had never seen so many antiquities in one place. Mr Merry was amused by the glow of expectation on her face as she took in each new discovery. He found that he was experiencing all the antiquities with which he was so familiar in a new light.

Mr Brown was still chattering on in his monotonous voice, but Alicia now listened with interest. She could not hear enough about these objects, but unfortunately, Mr Brown had his eyes firmly fixed on the end of the tour and was inclined to hurry them through the displays. Mr Merry saw her frustration and took Mr Brown aside. A quick word in his ear and Mr Brown uttered a curt response, "Very well," but gave Mr Merry a venomous look which expressed his disapproval of that gentleman's actions.

Mr Merry went back to Alicia very well pleased with himself. "I have procured us a little extra time, Miss Westlake, so that I can better show you Mr Hamilton's collection of Etruscan vases. Mr Brown has agreed that I can take over as your guide as long as we are finished by the time the museum closes." Alicia smiled her appreciation, certain of a pleasant hour to end her afternoon.

Mrs Westlake was quite content. She could endure a little boredom in order to allow her daughter time to further her acquaintance with such a handsome gentleman. Moreover, his presence relieved her of having to pretend an interest in any of the relics on display.

All too soon, the hour was over, and it was time for the party to break up. Mr Merry conducted them to the exit of the museum and took his leave. Alicia resigned herself to enduring her mother's nonsensical chatter for the rest of the day and, of course, the inquisition into Mr Merry's status and wealth, of which, she realised, she knew very little. But in the event, she was spared both. No sooner had the carriage drawn away from the museum, than Mrs Westlake fell fast asleep, worn out by the exertions of the afternoon, leaving Alicia alone with her thoughts.

Chapter 6

The expected interrogation about Mr Merry never came. Saturday was fast approaching and Mrs Westlake was single-mindedly consumed with preparing for an evening in Lady Melbourne's company.

When the day finally arrived, Mrs Westlake fidgeted and fussed over her finery until her ladyship's carriage arrived to carry them to the theatre. Alicia was feeling rather pleased with her own appearance. She knew that her new cream silk suited her very well and that it was trimmed in the latest fashion. The gown was exquisitely embroidered with garlands of flowers and edged with blue satin ribbon whilst the sleeves were trimmed with Brussels lace. She might doubt her mother's intelligence, but she certainly had a good eye for fashion. Martha had spent a long time coaxing her hair into the style that everyone was wearing—full curls on the sides of her head with ringlets falling down beneath.

Lady Melbourne was accompanied by her eldest son, Peniston, who made no attempt to hide his admiration when he was introduced to Alicia. For a moment, Lady Melbourne wondered whether she had made a mistake. She had no wish for her son to make such an alliance. On the other hand, he was at that impressionable age where he could fall for the most unsuitable women. She judged that Miss Westlake was far too intelligent a young lady to keep Peniston's fancy. A light flirtation would do him no harm and might very well push the girl into the public eye and that would be amusing. No, she need not worry about Peniston.

Attending the theatre with the Viscountess certainly had its advantages. The number of people gathering for the play was quite overwhelming, but a footman went before them, carving a path through the throng waiting in the lobby of the Theatre Royal, saving their gowns from being crushed. Her ladyship was repeatedly hailed as they progressed and more than once she stopped and introduced her companions to those who claimed her attention. Eventually they made it through the crowd and into the seclusion of her ladyship's box.

The theatre was ablaze with light from the hundreds of candles that flickered in the elegant chandeliers all around the auditorium. Alicia was glad that they were safely tucked away in a box and not at risk of getting dripped on by wax if the wicks were left too long before they were trimmed. What a large chandler's bill the theatre must have, she thought.

It was very noisy in the theatre with hundreds of people talking to each other all at once and Alicia began to get a headache. She was not used to such crowds of people and longed for the play to start and grant her poor head some relief. Although the pit was already full, many of the boxes stood empty until the last minute when there was a sudden influx of those who had hurriedly finished their suppers so that they could see the great Mrs Siddons perform.

Alicia was annoyed that some people continued to chatter throughout the play but she did her best to block out the sound. During the interval, she expressed her frustration to her mother.

"But no one has come to watch the play, Alicia. They

have come to see and be seen. What is important is to discover who will come knocking on Lady Melbourne's door. That is what this is all about."

Sure enough, a moment or two later, there was a sharp rap on the door of the box which was opened to admit two gentlemen. Mrs Westlake was not impressed to be introduced to Mr Sheridan and Mr Grey. She was hoping to make grander connections than a couple of Whig politicians, even if Mr Sheridan was a famous playwright. However, she did glean one useful piece of information from Mr Grey: the Duchess of Devonshire was back in town.

Whilst Mr Grey vied with her son for Alicia's attention, Lady Melbourne drew Mr Sheridan to one side and dropped a hint in his ear that Miss Westlake was possessed of a very handsome fortune. She knew that her friend would not be able to keep such a juicy morsel of gossip to himself, and felt that she had done all that was required to launch Miss Westlake into society.

Macbeth was as horrible as Alicia had hoped it would be. Mrs Siddons was perhaps past the best of her acting career, but her performance in the sleepwalking scene was every bit as eerie as her father had described it. When the curtain fell, Alicia clapped enthusiastically, only to discover that the occupants of the neighbouring boxes were offering applause in a much more restrained manner.

There was a longer break before the musical entertainment, a piece called *Doctor and Apothecary* of which Alicia had never heard. Once again, there was a knock at the door, announcing the arrival of visitors begging entry to Lady Melbourne's box. Mrs Westlake glowed with pleasure as she was introduced to the Marquess of Worcester and the Duke of Bedford. She had known that Lady Melbourne's patronage would open doors for them and it was gratifying to discover that she was right. Not that she thought either gentleman would be a suitable match for her daughter. Lady Granger had labelled the Marquess as a fortune hunter and she guessed that the Duke was no better, but to be seen to draw their attention would help bring them to the notice of others.

Lady Melbourne smiled to herself. Sheridan had worked fast! Word that she was entertaining an heiress in her box had evidently reached Worcester's ears already. The news had passed round even more quickly than she had imagined. It was just as well. She had noticed the look of chagrin that had descended over her son's face as these latest visitors had ousted him from his place at Miss Westlake's side and decided that it was a timely interruption. Miss Westlake was not quite what she wanted as a wife for her son. A little heartache would do him good, but it would not do for Peniston to become too infatuated.

Alicia was not sure that she liked the fulsome compliments that the gentlemen were paying her. She was not practised in the art of flirtation and had no defences against such behaviour. She was not sure that it meant anything at all; she rather thought that it did not. It was just some fashionable game for which she did not know the rules.

She looked in vain for the reassuring smile of Mr Merry. There was a gentleman with whom she could have a rational conversation without him making absurd references to her eyes that put her to the blush. He might have been willing to discuss the play rather than talk nonsense. She was not ready to admit, even to herself, that she felt a marked preference for his company. It was merely that it would have been a relief to have had five minutes of sensible talk with him.

Alicia had quite given up the expectation that Mr Merry would appear. However, when there was another knock on the door, she realised that she was still hoping he would come. It was not him. The latest visitor was introduced as Mr Hampton, nephew to the Duke of Wessex. A good connection, thought Mrs Westlake, but alas, no title.

Lady Melbourne was intrigued. Mr Hampton had not visited her box before. Had he been drawn by a sight of her young visitor's beautiful face or was he more in need of a fortune that she had supposed? She took pity on him and unceremoniously ejected her other visitors from her box, encouraging him to take a seat at Alicia's side.

"Did you enjoy the play, Miss Westlake?" Mr Hampton asked.

"Very much so," she replied, delighted to have the opportunity of discussing the performance of Macbeth at last. "I thought Mrs Siddons was wonderful."

"Very fine acting indeed," Mr Hampton agreed.

"I believe there are few that can compare to her, though many aspire to follow in her footsteps. I am inclined to think that my father was right and she is the best actress that the London stage has ever seen. Would you agree, Mr Hampton? Is Mrs Siddons incomparable?"

"Absolutely," Mr Hampton replied.

Whilst Mr Hampton made polite conversation with Alicia, Lady Melbourne stirred up Mrs Westlake's interest in him.

"Mr Hampton is practically the Duke's heir," she said nonchalantly. "Only Mr Hampton's father stands between them and alas, poor Lord Richard is not in good health. Mr Hampton is a very well-behaved young gentleman. Only recently come to London at his uncle's request, to get a little polish and take his place in the ton. If you ask me," she added confidentially, "the Duke has sent him to London to find a wife, to secure the succession."

Mrs Westlake started to look at Mr Hampton in a new light. There was little in his appearance to suggest his noble lineage. His clothes were fine but they lacked the magnificence that she associated with the aristocracy. His waistcoat was disappointingly plain and there was no gleaming jewel in the lace at his throat.

However, now that she looked more closely, she saw that his face had good, strong features and there was a slight haughtiness in his voice which suggested that he was well aware of his worth. She chose to overlook the deficiencies in his dress; if Mr Hampton showed an interest in her daughter, she was certainly not going to stand in his way.

Alicia was sorry to see Mr Hampton go. Unhampered by the knowledge that her mother had already approved of his suit, Alicia decided that she was not averse to getting to know Mr Hampton a little better. Although she was disappointed with the brevity of his comments and felt that she had failed to elicit any real discussion about the play, it was a relief not to be subject to the flirtatious remarks of the other gentlemen. She thought perhaps he was shy and looked forward to the challenge of drawing him out if they were to meet again.

The musical that followed was somewhat mediocre after the brilliance of Mrs Siddons and Alicia decided that it was rather a flat way to end the evening.

Chapter 7

Mrs Westlake sat at the breakfast table with a pile of envelopes and a cup of hot chocolate and let out a very satisfied sigh. She was extremely pleased with herself. Securing Lady Melbourne's patronage had been inspired. Within a few days of their visit to the theatre, the invitations had started to arrive. Sometimes they came in the guise of a note to Lady Granger, apologising for the oversight and begging her to bring her guests to an entertainment to which she had already been invited. But more often than not, the invitations were addressed directly to Mrs Westlake, with Lady Granger tagged onto the end of her invitation or even, in one case, forgotten completely.

"We shall not have to spend an evening at home until after Christmas," she boasted.

Lady Granger made a guttural noise that sounded remarkably like "Humph". She had hoped for female companionship, but she had forgotten how tiring a full social calendar could be. After only a few weeks, she was feeling pulled and wishing that her cousin would go away and leave her in peace.

It appeared that the doors of all the leading Whig houses had opened up to Mrs Westlake and her daughter. Lady Granger discovered that she was being invited into the houses of people that under normal circumstances rarely gave her a moment's attention.

For this, Lady Melbourne's tongue was largely to blame. The words she had purposefully dropped into Mr Sheridan's ears had, as she had predicted, spread like wildfire. The rumour that Lady Melbourne's new protégée was in possession of a large fortune had passed around half the ton before they had left the theatre. Such a report was bound to attract fortune hunters, but with the added advantage of Lady Melbourne's patronage, which seemed to confirm the Westlakes' respectability, aristocratic families with a son needing to find a richly dowered wife hastened to make the acquaintance of the Westlakes.

"Now do you see how extremely beneficial it is to have good connections?" she asked her daughter.

"Yes indeed," Alicia replied automatically, but she was not really paying attention. She was studying the handwritten note in her lap. It was an invitation to an evening party at Mrs Montagu's. The company was to be much the same as before, though Mrs Montagu hoped that Miss Burney, the celebrated author, might be able to join them. She chewed her bottom lip as she often did when lost in thought. It was a habit that her mother deplored, but no amount of nagging had succeeded in eradicating it.

Alicia desperately wanted to go to Mrs Montagu's— she had been starved of intelligent conversation since her visit to the museum. She was under no illusion that her mother would be so enthusiastic. She needed a strategy – a way of persuading her mother that letting her visit Mrs Montagu's was completely harmless. What if she could convince her mother that it was the lesser of two evils?

"Mother, I was wondering whether—"

"Argh!" Mrs Westlake let out a little shriek. Alicia stopped mid-sentence. Surely her mother could not have a premonition about what she was going to say? But no, her mother was not reacting to her at all. She was sitting staring at a card in her hands with a rather dazed look on her face.

"Mother? Are you quite well?"

"Well? Of course I am well," she snapped, instantly coming back to life. "This," she said, holding the gilt-edged card up with reverence, "is an invitation from the Duchess of Devonshire! A ball at Devonshire House. Oh, Alicia. This is just what I had hoped for."

Leaning back in her chair, Mrs Westlake silently digested the wonders of the opportunity that had presented itself. Even when she had been living in the backwaters of Oxfordshire, Mrs Westlake had kept up with all the exploits of the Duchess of Devonshire. The press adored the Duchess who kept them busy with her ever-changing hairstyles and extravagant parties. Mrs Westlake had eagerly followed the reports in the Times. The newspapers were not always kind, but they had left her in no doubt of the leading role that the Duchess played in fashionable society.

She had never dared to copy the towering creations that the Duchess had worn on her head. Appearing with a three-foot hairstyle topped with a sailing ship may have been the height of fashion, but it would have been quite out of place in the local assembly rooms, and she shuddered to think what her husband would have said.

On the other hand, the huge wide-brimmed hats that the Duchess had introduced were another matter. Mrs Westlake had been quick to commission several from London and had received many admiring comments from the local gentry. And when the Duchess had adopted a more natural hairstyle, she had been one of the first to copy it.

The Duchess was at the very centre of the world that Mrs Westlake wanted to belong to. She would have given anything to take the Duchess' place in society. She was beautiful and charming and every gentleman in the ton was in love with her, with the exception, so it was rumoured, of her own husband. Mrs Westlake thought this was a pity. It was distinctly preferable to be adored by one's husband, although, she reflected bitterly, this did not always guarantee that you got your own way.

However, the Duchess' ball did present Mrs Westlake with a dilemma. Should they wear the prescribed colours to the ball? As the season had progressed and the King was still showing no signs of recovery, the Whigs had grown increasingly confident that they would soon be taking over the government. The rivalry between the Whigs and the Tories was reaching endemic proportions and they had begun to wear particular colours, like a uniform, at their entertainments to declare their loyalties.

Mrs Westlake wanted to remain neutral. Although she valued her connection with Lady Melbourne and was delighted to be noticed by the Duchess of Devonshire, she did not want to rule out the possibility of Alicia's hand being sought by a rich and titled Tory. She was beginning to harbour hopes that something might come of Mr Hampton's obvious admiration for her daughter. Lady Melbourne had been quite open about the fact that the Duke of Wessex was a King's man. She did not want to scare his nephew away by wearing the colours of the Whigs too openly. On the other hand, she reasoned, it was too great a risk to offend the Duchess, and it was by no means certain that Mr Hampton would attend a ball in the Whig stronghold. No, they would wear the prescribed white and gold and hope for the best.

"Are you not excited, Alicia? Devonshire House!"

Alicia had to admit that she was impressed. She was not averse to meeting the celebrated Duchess and discovering what it was like inside Devonshire House. She was always interested in other people's houses. Their size and style told you a lot about someone's wealth and position; how they were decorated and furnished told you about their taste.

But her mind was still playing with the question of how to get her mother to agree to her visiting Mrs Montagu's again. She thought that perhaps her best chance was now, whilst her mother was distracted by the Duchess' invitation.

"Mother, I was wondering whether you could spare an afternoon to accompany me to visit Mr Townley's collection of antiquities. Father often talked about them and I would very much like to see the collection for myself."

Unsurprisingly, Mrs Westlake did not take kindly to the suggestion. She was astounded. They had been invited to the Duchess of Devonshire's ball and Alicia was talking about antiquities. How like her father!

"Absolutely not, Alicia. I am not going to spend another dreary afternoon dragging myself around another lot of old things. Visiting the British Museum was quite unexceptional. In fact, it may even be considered desirable, for everyone goes there. But it is quite unnecessary and even detrimental for a young lady to have more than a passing interest in antiquities."

"I know that it does not appeal to you, Mother, but you need not come," Alicia said. "I am sure that the Marquess of Worcester would be happy to accompany me to Mr Townley's house if I were to ask him," she added innocently.

Mrs Westlake took a deep breath and struggled to control her rising temper. "Alicia, how many times do I have to tell you that it is not to your advantage to appear bookish? I suppose there are gentlemen who wish for an intelligent wife, but they are few and far between. Under no circumstances are you to ask the Marquess or any other gentleman to accompany you. Have you learnt nothing about the way to behave correctly? I want your word that you will not ask anyone to take you."

"Very well, Mother. You have my word. But what if a gentleman were to ask me to accompany him? Surely if the invitation came from him, he could not object to my interest in antiquities?"

Mrs Westlake thought for a moment. "That would be a different matter," she agreed. "If the invitation came from the gentleman, then I would have no objection. That nice Mr Hampton, for instance," she continued, warming to the idea. "He seems to be of a more serious frame of mind than some of his contemporaries. Perhaps if he knew of your interest, he would take you."

Alicia did not hold out much hope of Mr Hampton inviting her to visit a collection of antiquities. They had met twice since the evening at the theatre, and, much to her mother's delight, on both occasions, Mr Hampton had singled her out. Alicia found Mr Hampton's company restful as he did not embarrass her by flirting, but although he always responded politely when she asked a question, she was beginning to think he must be of a naturally taciturn nature as he rarely continued the conversation. When she had mentioned how much she had enjoyed her visit to the British Museum, Mr Hampton had responded that he believed it was very fashionable to visit and ventured no further observation. No, she did not think that Mr Hampton would want to accompany her to Mr Townley's house in Park Street; she doubted whether he even knew it existed.

"I am afraid that Mr Hampton has given me no reason to believe that he is at all inclined toward history," Alicia replied.

"Then you will have to abandon the visit altogether," Mrs Westlake replied in a matter of fact voice.

Alicia put on a crestfallen face. "How disappointing! I had set my heart on going," she said in her sulkiest voice.

"You have the Duchess of Devonshire's ball to look forward to," Mrs Westlake reminded her. "Surely that is more exciting than a visit to some collection of old pots and broken statues?"

"But I will not find any stimulating conversation there," she moaned, "and no doubt you will forbid me to visit Mrs Montagu again, where I could at least enjoy a little rational talk."

Mrs Westlake hesitated. Alicia had always been an easy-going child, very ready to fit in with her mother's plans, beautiful in person and gracious in her manners. But from time to time, she exhibited her father's stubbornness and she had no wish to come up against her daughter's will just when they had received the most flattering invitation of the season.

"If Mrs Montagu were to invite you again, then I suppose there would be no harm in you accepting," Mrs Westlake said, though she could not keep the reluctance out of her voice as she made the admission. "To be sure," she added in a more cheerful voice, "if you did visit Mrs Montagu again, perhaps it would fulfil your need for intelligent conversation, and you would not feel the need to flaunt your scholarly inclinations every time you open your mouth in company."

"Thank you," Alicia replied, kissing her mother spontaneously on the cheek, overjoyed to have achieved her objective so easily. She refused to feel guilty about the subterfuge. After all, she had not been lying; she ardently wished to visit Mr Townley's collection, though she doubted whether she would have had the gall to ask the Marquess of Worcester to accompany her. "I will write immediately and let Mrs Montagu know that I will be there on Friday."

"But Mrs Bellingham's concert—" Mrs Westlake objected. But Alicia had already left the room; she was not going to give her mother a single chance to change her mind.

Chapter 8

Alicia found to her surprise that she was quite nervous about going to Mrs Montagu's again. She did not really understand her anxiety. She was sure of her welcome and, though excited at the prospect of meeting Miss Burney, it hardly explained why she had changed her choice of gown three times and had ended up wearing a new one that her mother had set aside for an evening party the following week.

She guessed that it had something to do with Mr Merry. After the trip to the British Museum she had found it hard to put him out of her mind. It was not that she had any serious intentions toward him, but she could not deny that she preferred his company to that of anyone else she had met in London.

He was the only gentleman of her acquaintance who talked to her about subjects of real interest. Everyone else made polite conversation on commonplace topics like the weather or the company in London, or paid her such fulsome compliments that she was continually colouring up.

Furthermore, Mr Merry made her laugh and she did so love to laugh. She had been convinced that he liked her, that he was her friend. Surely he would not have devoted an entire afternoon to her entertainment at the British Museum unless he enjoyed her company? But she had looked in vain for him at any of the social events that followed and had reluctantly concluded that she must have been mistaken.

"How lovely to see you, Miss Westlake," greeted her hostess, "but I fear you are in for a disappointment. Miss Burney is not here. The Queen had need of her support and so our poor friend was unable to join us. It grieves me to see such a talented author too worn out by her duties to embark on any new project. I fear that the Queen does not allow her much respite. Since the King became ill, her Majesty has depended upon her female companions more than ever. And now the royal family has removed to Kew and Miss Burney has gone with them. I believe she is as much imprisoned at Kew as the poor King."

Alicia expressed her regret at not meeting the famous author. Even her mother praised Miss Burney's books, though she had not been so flattering about her shyness on the one occasion that they had met. She glanced around the room and was quick to spot Mr Merry talking to Mr Reynolds.

As if he felt her eyes upon him, Mr Merry broke off his conversation and sauntered across the room to greet her.

"How do you do, Miss Westlake? Have you been plaguing your mother to death with requests to visit the British Museum again?"

Alicia raised her eyebrows at the familiarity of the greeting, but was not offended. "My mother believes that one visit is quite unexceptional. A second would show a degree of interest in antiquities that exceeds what is required. I do not waste energy on lost causes, Mr Merry. It really is not worth my while to try and persuade my mother to make another visit. I would rather save my energy for other purposes."

"Such as?"

"Dancing, Mr Merry. I love to dance. But perhaps you do not care for the exercise?"

"I ... I ..." Mr Merry found that he was momentarily lost for words. "To tell you the truth, Miss Westlake, I do not dance very well. I can stand in front of a roomful of strangers and give a lecture on ancient Rome with ease, but when I walk out onto a dance floor, I become unaccountably nervous. My nerves communicate themselves to my feet and I have to work extremely hard to ensure that my clumsiness does not leave my partner's toes covered with bruises."

Alicia laughed at the forlorn look on his face. "It is usually possible to improve your skills if you practice," she said, in a tone of voice that was more suited to encouraging a child to play their instrument than chiding a gentleman on not making the effort to improve his dancing. "Is that why you avoid the round of balls, so that you do not have to dance?"

"People attend the season to dance and flirt and make small talk. I cannot dance, I do not flirt and small talk bores me rigid. I do not shine in the ballroom, Miss Westlake."

"Then I shall not look for you at the Duchess of Devonshire's ball," Alicia replied nonchalantly, for some reason eager to display their new-found connection. "Yes, you may well look shocked, but we have risen to the dizzy heights of the Duchess' notice and my mother is in raptures."

"I am sure that it is no more than you deserve, Miss Westlake."

Alicia acknowledged the compliment and asked him how his studies were progressing. No subject was more calculated to please. Mr Merry launched into the details of a letter he had discovered in the manuscript room of the British Museum. It was about the recent discoveries at the excavations at Herculaneum and Mr Merry explained how it was filling in some gaps in his knowledge of the area. With a little encouragement, he reminisced about the various excavations he had visited in person and the marble statues and other antiquities he had been able to acquire.

"I have heard that Mr Townley has a superior collection of marble statues," Alicia interposed. "Have you seen them?"

For a moment, a shadow passed over Mr Merry's face, as if the thought of those particular marbles had given him a bad taste in his mouth, but in a second, it was gone and Alicia thought she must have imagined it.

"Mr Townley is a great friend of mine," Mr Merry replied. "I am a regular visitor to his house in Park Street. Each room hides some fresh treasure. I find something new every time I visit. He is somewhat addicted to his collections. When he runs out of room to house them, he simply throws something else out to make more space. The last victim was his carriage—he no longer keeps his own chaise, but has filled the space with more antiquities."

Alicia's eyes glazed over trying to imagine a house overflowing with ancient curiosities. "It must be a breathtaking sight," she said wistfully.

"Walking through Park Street is like stepping back into ancient Rome. It even smells of the first century."

Alicia gave a little sniff as she listened. It sounded entrancing.

"It reminds me vividly of Rome. When I suffer from homesickness, I go round to Townley's house and pretend that I am back there."

"I did not know that you considered Rome your home," Alicia said, surprised.

"I do not," Mr Merry replied.

"But you just said you went to visit Mr Townley's house when you felt homesick."

"Yes—when I am sick of my home, I go and visit Townley and remember the freedom and wonders of Rome."

Alicia bit her lip. She knew she should not smile at such a comment, but she could not help it. She never knew what Mr Merry was going to say next. It was most entertaining.

"It is possible to forget that you are just a stone's throw from St James' Park when you are deep in rooms crammed full of antiquities from lost civilisations. Sometimes I wander, sniffing out new treasures, but mostly I just like to sit and look. There are one or two pieces that I am particularly attached to—a very fine statue of a dog and a few others that I helped to acquire for Townley when I was in Rome."

"I wish I could go to Rome," Alicia moaned. "It seems so unfair that gentlemen are sent abroad for months and months, to travel and observe the way of life of different peoples, while young ladies are left at home."

"Now admittedly the Grand Tour is generally the province of men, but there are women who have travelled."

"Such as?"

"Mrs Piozzi."

"Mrs Piozzi does not count," Alicia replied, unimpressed. "She was travelling with her husband."

"But there were others," Mr Merry assured her, "and not all of them were married." He screwed up his face in mock concentration. "I am afraid their names at present elude me, but I met several whilst staying in Rome."

"I think that you are making it up," Alicia replied.

"Well, the next best thing to visiting Rome itself is to immerse yourself in its antiquities. You have already seen what the British Museum has to offer. I would highly recommend a visit to Mr Townley's. He is quite ready to welcome visitors into his home to see his collection. There is nothing he likes better. Lately he has been talking about having a catalogue printed so that people can still enjoy his treasures even when it is not convenient for him to show them round himself. With the numbers of people visiting, he is in danger of becoming a full-time guide!"

"I would like very much to visit Park Street, Mr Merry," Alicia declared. "I need no more convincing."

Mr Merry was amused. Miss Westlake was most definitely angling for an invitation. He was most happy to oblige. In fact, he would be flattered if he thought that she was interested in his company and not just his obsession with antiquities. But he could not resist teasing her a little before giving her what she wanted.

"Then what are you waiting for? Ask your mother to take you at once," Mr Merry quipped.

"Mr Merry," Alicia said with growing frustration. "You must be well aware that my mother and I do not share the same taste in these matters. I do not think – in fact, I am quite sure, because she told me so – that she would wish to accompany me to see Mr Townley's collection."

"Ah, maybe not," Mr Merry said, nodding wisely. "But surely the good Lady Granger would not refuse you?"

The thought of Lady Granger navigating her corpulent figure around a collection of valuable antiquities, even supposing she could be persuaded to go in the first place, was too ghastly to contemplate. If Mr Townley's rooms were as crowded with antiquities as she had been led to believe, she would be in constant fear of Lady Granger knocking something over.

"I do not believe that would be wise," she said sweetly, "and without an amenable companion, I will sadly have to forego what would no doubt have been a fascinating experience," she snapped. She curtseyed abruptly and turned to leave.

Mr Merry took pity on her. He saw that he had gone too far. He had hoped to make her beg him to take her, but he realised that there was a limit to how far she would forget herself. He quickly sought to retrieve the situation.

"Miss Westlake."

Alicia turned back.

"If you would care to accompany me, I would be delighted to show you Mr Townley's collection myself."

"You would?"

He smiled. "It would be a pleasure. Would Thursday afternoon be convenient?"

Alicia hesitated. It was the day after the Duchess' ball, but that might even prove to be an advantage. Perhaps she could avoid telling her mother about the visit at all. Although Mrs Westlake had given her permission for the visit in principle, Alicia had no assurance that she would not change her mind if she realised that she was going with Mr Merry rather than Mr Hampton. Mrs Westlake often slept well into the afternoon the day after a ball and would doubtless keep to her room until dinnertime in order to build up her energy for another evening's entertainment. Yes, it was the ideal day to go.

Alicia nodded, a wide grin spreading across her face. "I thought you would never ask."

Chapter 9

At last the day of the Duchess' ball arrived and, as far as Alicia was concerned, it was not a day too soon. Ever since they had attended the theatre with Lady Melbourne, her mother had delighted in dropping the Viscountess' name into conversation whenever she could.

But the effect of the Duchess' invitation was even more embarrassing. Her mother could not resist talking about her friend the Duchess or her invitation to the forthcoming ball at Devonshire House at every available opportunity. Alicia cringed at each mention. Her mother had never even met the Duchess and she talked as if she had become the Duchess' intimate friend.

Devonshire House was already buzzing with activity when they arrived. Mrs Westlake had determined to arrive at a fashionable time, refusing to go too early, despite the temptation to savour the experience for as long as possible. They had to wait in a queue for over thirty minutes before their carriage could get close enough to the door to deposit its burden.

The Duchess greeted them graciously and smiled warmly at them, but she clearly had no idea who they were. Her attention was soon drawn away from them to greet the latest arrival. Mr Grey had just walked through the door and only a fool would imagine that she was more interesting to the Duchess than this handsome young Whig politician, who was clearly besotted with her.

Alicia sighed. She did not pretend to understand the complicated lives of the people around her. It was so sad to see the Duchess lapping up the attention showered upon her by Mr Grey when her own husband was coldly indifferent to her. Her mother had told her the whole sad story.

The Duke had made an alliance of convenience and had not required or desired any emotional input from his wife. All he required was a son—a son which she had failed to give him. Alicia thought how different her life would have been if her own father had been like the Duke. Mr Westlake had doted on his daughter and she had never once heard him say that he wished she had been a boy.

As Alicia moved away from the door, the Marquess of Worcester appeared at her side and claimed her hand for the next dance. He informed her that the Prince of Wales was expected. Alicia wondered what His Royal Highness was really like. Her mother and Lady Granger had painted a very different picture of him from that drawn by Mr Merry, though she supposed that Mr Merry was unlikely to be influenced by his good looks and had reached all his negative conclusions from what he had seen of his character.

The Marquess flirted outrageously, but Alicia refused to give him any encouragement. The Marquess might be willing to exchange marriage vows for a fortune, but she was not. At the end of the dance, her mother was nowhere to be seen, and so Lord Worcester returned her to Lady Granger who had planted herself on a chair at the forefront of the dowagers and was clearly not going to budge for anything except supper.

Lady Granger tapped Alicia's hand lightly with her fan and gently chided her for encouraging the penniless Marquess to dangle after her.

Alicia vehemently denied the accusation. "I assure you, Madam, it is no such thing, but how am I supposed to depress his attentions without being rude? He is, after all, a peer of the realm, and even I know that it would be unwise to alienate someone with so many connections."

Lady Granger shook her head. She did not sound as if she believed Alicia. "A title is not everything, my dear. Being married to a gambler would cause you nothing but heartache; he would run through your fortune as if it were nothing more than a mere competence. And do not place your confidence in being able to hold his devotion. It is not fashionable for a husband to be forever in his wife's company. Mark my words, he is far more likely to flirt with someone else and leave you to do the same. Just think of your sponsor, Lady Melbourne. Before she was married a year, her husband took up with that Baddeley woman. But do you think that her ladyship stayed at home and sulked? No, indeed. She has had her own affairs and who is to say who has fathered her brood? And I have just heard," she added, "that her ladyship is increasing again. I wonder whether this one is her husband's. They say that William is so like Lord Egremont that there is really no doubt, whereas George—"

"Lady Granger." A silkily soft voice interrupted the flow of Lady Granger's seemingly interminable flow of gossip. She jumped violently, like a small child who has been found with her hand in a jar of sugar plums.

"You must introduce your charming companion," the smooth voice continued.

Alicia instinctively rose from her chair. Although the

voice spoke in little more than a whisper, she felt sure it belonged to someone of importance to have caused such a violent reaction in Lady Granger. The speaker was a rather thin but very beautiful lady—certainly not young, but with the sort of charismatic good looks that tended to attract a great deal of attention from the opposite sex.

Lady Granger hurried to drag her bulk from her chair in order to make the requested introduction. Alicia discovered that her instinct had not erred—the lady was no lesser personage than the Countess of Jersey. It took all Lady Granger's efforts not to shudder in her presence. She feared Lady Jersey even more than Lady Melbourne—her spitefulness was legendary. She had heard it said that the Prince of Wales had been infatuated with her for years, but that she liked to keep him hanging on.

Lady Jersey did not waste any time with the preliminaries, but started bombarding Alicia with questions about her family and connections. Alicia did not care for the interrogation, which Lady Granger just stood helplessly by and watched, and was grateful when she saw the Duchess of Devonshire approaching, accompanied by a gentleman. Alicia's eyes lit up with pleasure as she recognised her friend, Mr Hampton.

Although only of medium height, Alicia thought there was something in his bearing that declared his high connections. His rather heavy aristocratic features sat well on his serious-looking face. Not, perhaps, the most handsome gentleman of her acquaintance, but certainly not unpleasant to look at. And it was most definitely a pleasure to look on anyone who was able to save her from Lady Jersey's intense questioning.

"Pray let me interrupt you," the Duchess said, breaking in on Lady Jersey without waiting for her to finish her sentence. "This young lady needs to dance and as Mr Hampton has dared to brave our stronghold, the least I can do is allow him to dance with the prettiest girl in the room." She smiled kindly at Alicia. "Miss Westlake, I believe you are already acquainted with Mr Hampton?"

"Yes indeed, Your Grace," Alicia replied, smiling warmly in response. It was not difficult to see why the Duchess had such a reputation for charm. She was addressing Alicia with what appeared to be sincere affection, and yet, unless Alicia was very much mistaken, when she had arrived not an hour since, the Duchess had not even known who she was. Clearly Mr Hampton's interest had been enough to change that, and Alicia could not regret being noticed by her charming hostess.

Lady Jersey hurried to support the Duchess, encouraging Alicia to dance, but there was no warmth in her words. Alicia had not missed the flicker of annoyance that had passed over her interrogator's face when the Duchess had interrupted her. Alicia wondered whether the Duchess had noticed. It was gone in an instant, but it was at odds with the gracious words that now oozed from the Countess' mouth.

Alicia was surprised that the two ladies were supposed to be friends, for a more mismatched friendship she could not have imagined. From all she had heard, the Duchess was all graciousness whereas Lady Jersey was renowned for her spite. If what Lady Granger said was true, Lady Jersey had even had an affair with the Duchess' husband. Alicia did not pretend to understand why the Duchess maintained even the appearance of friendship with such a woman.

Alicia was relieved to make her escape.

"Thank you, Mr Hampton. I was never more grateful for an invitation to dance."

"You looked in need of rescuing," Mr Hampton confided, leading her into the set that was forming.

Alicia smiled. "I did. Lady Jersey seemed to want to know everything about me and she is not the sort of person it is easy to refuse."

Mr Hampton nodded solemnly in agreement. "She is a most persuasive lady."

Alicia noticed for the first time that Mr Hampton was not dressed in the prescribed colours for the evening. "No uniform?" she teased, as they took their places in the dance.

Mr Hampton did not seem to notice her playful tone and gave a serious reply. "I am the Duke of Wessex's nephew, Miss Westlake. We are King's men."

"I am surprised they let you through the door then"! Alicia exclaimed with a wicked grin, but it was lost on her partner.

"The Duke is far too influential to be ignored," he replied ponderously. "And thankfully, our guest lists are not yet limited to a single political allegiance."

Alicia thought it a pity that Mr Hampton did not respond well to her playful banter, but decided that, as he did not know her very well, perhaps he genuinely believed she was in need of reassurance.

"I am very glad of the opportunity to dance," she said, changing the subject. "It is one thing to practise the steps at home, but quite another to dance in public. I do not believe that any number of lessons could have prepared me sufficiently for the exhilarating experience of dancing at a real ball. Do you like to dance, Mr Hampton?"

"I do indeed, Miss Westlake, but I have been in company so little of late that I was half afraid that I had forgotten how to dance."

"Then you must get out more, Mr Hampton," Alicia urged.

"Alas, it has not been in my power," he said quietly.

Alicia waited for him to offer some explanation, but, having aroused her curiosity, he did not rush to satisfy it. Mr Hampton lapsed into silence, passing only desultory remarks until the dance was over.

"I declare you have deceived me, Mr Hampton," Alicia chided playfully as they went in search of refreshments. "You led me to believe that your dancing abilities were dubious, but your skill is far superior to my own."

"It was not my intention to deceive, Miss Westlake. I was able to dance well enough when I was an officer in the Horse Guards, but I could not be sure whether my skill would have deteriorated through lack of use."

"You were a soldier?" Alicia asked, surprised.

"Yes," Mr Hampton replied. "If you had danced with me eight years ago, I would have been attired in regimentals."

Alicia stifled a laugh. "If I had danced with you eight years ago, Mr Hampton, it would have caused a scandal."

Mr Hampton looked confused.

"Do not look so shocked, Mr Hampton," she hastened to reassure him, wondering with a touch of impatience, if she would have to explain every rejoinder she made. "Eight years ago, I was only ten years old. Schoolgirls are not generally welcome in the ballroom."

"No indeed!" Mr Hampton responded.

"So where is your uniform now, Mr Hampton?"

"When my cousin died, I felt it was my duty to sell out. So I hung up my red coat and took on estate management instead."

"That must have been hard—giving up a profession you loved."

Mr Hampton smiled non-committedly. He was not going to be churlish and refuse Miss Westlake's sympathy, though in truth, he had been only too glad to switch roles. "It is always hard to give up something you love, but it was the least I could do for the Duke."

"And is the Duke with you in town, Mr Hampton?"

Mr Hampton shook his head. "The Duke rarely leaves Swanmore—his main seat in Hampshire."

So that was why Mr Hampton had been so little in town, Alicia thought. No doubt, he had been keeping the Duke company. "I am sorry. I did not realise that the Duke was an invalid."

"No, no, Miss Westlake. You mistake my meaning. The Duke is well enough for a man of his age. It is an affliction in spirit that he suffers from. He has not been the same since the death of his son, the Marquess of Denmead."

"How sad," Alicia replied. "But forgive me—does the Duke still mourn after all these years? Did you not say that he died eight years ago?"

Mr Hampton nodded. "Yes, you are right. My cousin was killed in the riots of '80."

Alicia was quick to offer her sympathy: "How dreadful." She had heard about the riots. Her father had ranted about the tragic loss of life that had occurred, all because some Protestant fanatics had objected to the Catholics being granted a little more freedom and stirred up a mob to descend on Parliament.

"It was a long time ago," Mr Hampton said quietly.

"But not forgotten."

"No, not forgotten," Mr Hampton agreed. "It will never be forgotten. Denmead was like a brother to me."

Impulsively she laid a hand on Mr Hampton's arm.

"I am so sorry."

Chapter 10

It was at that moment that Mr Merry first caught sight of Miss Westlake. He had arrived at Devonshire House whilst she was dancing with Mr Hampton. It had not been his intention to arrive so late, but he had forgotten how long it took to get ready for a ball. His valet had chided him for his impatience.

"It is hardly surprising that your coat is a mite tight, Sir," John muttered as he helped his master to dress. "It is a few years since you have worn it. If you had given me any warning that you intended to go to a ball, we could have arranged for a new one. But no, you never were one to plan ahead."

Mr Merry looked down at the beautifully tailored garment with something akin to revulsion and fidgeted uncomfortably. Unfortunately what had been well-cut when it was made was now proving to be somewhat inadequate.

"It's as well that your brother is not going to be at the ball tonight," John continued, undaunted by the disgruntled look on Mr Merry's face. "Wearing a coat that was in fashion three years' ago is not his style and no doubt he would tell you that it should not be your style either."

"My brother's opinions are of no consequence, John. They never were."

"Your mother would have something to say if she knew that you were running off to the Duchess of Devonshire's ball. She would fear that the Queen of the Whigs had cast her spell over you and sent you running into the arms of the Opposition."

"Does my own mother really know me so little? Surely she has learned by now that I will not side with the Whigs just to annoy her?"

"I think your mother believes that everything you do is specifically intended to annoy her," John replied. "Of course, there must be a woman involved," he continued, goading his master with the provocative words. "Can't think of anything else that would get you into these clothes."

"Your opinions are, of course, as edifying as ever, John," Mr Merry quipped, refusing to rise to the bait.

"Aha! So there is a woman!" John retorted. "And about time too, Sir. If you don't find yourself a wife soon, no doubt your mother will find one for you."

Mr Merry paused for a moment and looked at his manservant in surprise. "Oh no, do you think so, John? I am sure she has never taken so much trouble over me in the past."

"Now, now, Sir."

"John?"

"Yes, Sir?"

"My hat, if you please."

John handed Mr Merry his hat and cane and grinned. For once, he had managed to persuade his young master to stand still for long enough to powder his hair thoroughly, heightening the blondeness of its colour. John secretly thought that there were few gentlemen who could wear powder to such good effect. But it confirmed his opinion that a woman was involved. Nothing less would make his master take one jot of care over his appearance.

Mr Merry stood awkwardly at the entrance to the ballroom wondering why he was there. He pulled restlessly at the despised coat that had hung, unworn, in his wardrobe for three years and heartily wished that it had remained so.

It was some consolation to know that through the efforts of his valet he made a creditable appearance. His red silk velvet coat was not in the height of fashion and only modestly embroidered with silver thread, but anyone could see at a glance the quality of the workmanship. His hair was neatly tied and powdered; the silver buckles on his shoes glistened in the candlelight. He knew he looked the part, but he never felt at ease in the ballroom. His elegance was challenged the moment he started to dance and he hated that feeling of inadequacy that crept over him if he should happen to make a mistake.

The Duchess of Devonshire had moved away from the door, but caught sight of the newcomer and hurried over to greet him. Mr Merry was not a frequent visitor to Devonshire House, but the Duchess had ever a soft spot for a handsome face and a quick tongue.

"Sounding out the Opposition, Merry?" she teased.

Mr Merry swept a deep bow. "Your Grace could never be in opposition to me," he replied suavely.

She rapped his knuckles with her fan. "I swear you are almost a stranger."

"But if I were a stranger, you would not have invited me," Mr Merry retorted smoothly.

"Ha, very true," she replied, looking up at him with a flirtatious smile on her lips.

At that very moment, Alicia looked up and caught sight of Mr Merry. This was unexpected. How delightful! He had led her to believe that he did not attend balls, and yet here he was. But her initial delight was quickly dampened by the realisation that he was flirting with the Duchess—something else that she did not think he did. He had never attempted to flirt with her. Something akin to jealously flared up inside her. It was not that Mr Merry owed her anything, but he was her friend and as he clearly did not depend on her company, she would make sure that he realised that she was doing very well without him.

"And are your parents in town, Mr Merry?" the Duchess continued.

"Sadly no, Your Grace. They are spending the winter in warmer climes for my father's health," he replied, as he surreptitiously scanned the room until his eyes eventually alighted on Alicia. He was relieved to see that she was there. Otherwise all this effort would have been wasted. She seemed to be having a good time—too good a time. He was not best pleased to see her listening intently to her companion and when he saw her reach out and lay a hand on his arm, in what could only be deemed an intimate gesture, he had difficulty restraining himself from marching across the room and demanding an explanation for her behaviour.

What was she playing at being so familiar with her companion? She was as inexperienced as a new born babe! He looked at Alicia's partner with unmitigated dislike. Who was he? He did not recognise him. Could he be trusted to behave with propriety and not take advantage of her obvious innocence? He watched as the unknown gentleman led her into the dance that was forming.

And then Alicia's partner turned and Mr Merry caught sight of his face. The man's features seemed familiar, but he could not quite place them. Then it came to him and, for a moment, he stood, staring, hardly able to believe his eyes. Surely he must be mistaken?

The Duchess was asking Mr Merry about his brother, but he interrupted her without any preamble. "Who is that gentleman with Miss Westlake?" he asked in a constrained voice.

The Duchess shook her head. "Merry—you really are an ungracious wretch. Could you not at least make the pretence that you came to see me?"

Mr Merry looked penitent. "Your Grace, I …"

The Duchess took pity on him and followed his gaze until she spotted Alicia. She recalled the young lady she had rescued from Lady Jersey's clutches and gave a knowing smile. So this was the magnet that had drawn Merry to her ball. "Miss Westlake's partner is Mr Hampton, Merry. He is the Duke of Wessex's nephew. He is only recently come to town. Sent by the Duke to find a wife, if the gossips are to be believed. Only his uncle and father stand between him and the dukedom. A good match for Miss Westlake if she can get him. Have you never happened to meet him before?"

"I am not sure, Your Grace. I think so, once, but his name eluded me."

"Oh, now. Here is poor Lady Castleford, neglected by her husband again. Take pity and dance with her, Merry. She is a sweet little thing and Castleford bullies her mercilessly. I am surprised that he even brings her to town with him. All for the sake of appearances, I suppose, and yet the whole world knows that his name has been linked with Lady Jersey's for months."

Mr Merry panicked. He was not a great dancer and

had only been drawn to the ball to see Alicia. He tried desperately to make his excuses. "Your Grace, I do not mean to disoblige you, but I do not intend to dance."

"Nonsense, Merry. Why would you come to a ball if you did not mean to dance?" the Duchess scoffed.

Mr Merry took one look at the forlorn Countess and was moved with compassion. When the Duchess renewed her entreaties, he did not resist and was rewarded with such a look of gratitude that he felt it was worth the risk of treading on a few toes. The Countess responded to a gentle enquiry after her family by talking animatedly for the entire length of the dance about her two little boys. It was clear that they alone made her life worth living.

Alicia's temper was rising. Mr Merry did not go to balls and yet here he was. Mr Merry did not flirt and yet he had been flirting with the Duchess of Devonshire and now he was hanging on every word that his elegant partner said. And moreover, he was dancing, and Mr Merry had definitely told her that he did not dance.

By the time the dance had finished, Alicia had gone through the full range of emotions, from jealousy to anger to a horrid feeling that she had read more into Mr Merry's friendliness than he had meant. She had just resigned herself to the possibility that he had not come to the ball to see her after all, when he appeared, directly in front of her. Mr Merry looked Alicia's partner in the eye, but there was no glimmer of recognition.

"Forgive me," Mr Merry said, "but I do not think I am familiar with your partner, Miss Westlake."

Alicia was surprised, but hurried to perform the introductions. The gentlemen bowed in acknowledge-ment of each other, but there was no warmth on either side. It was as if war had been declared between them and she had the awful feeling that she was the cause. Mr Hampton excused himself and Mr Merry led Alicia into the next dance before she had the chance to refuse.

"I do not like the company you keep, Miss Westlake," he said curtly.

Alicia was lost for words. She had not been expecting such a forthright attack.

"I do not trust Mr Hampton. Stay away from him."

"Mr Merry, what right have you to dictate whom I associate with?" Alicia demanded, annoyed by his suddenly peremptory manner. "It is not as if you have been trying to monopolise my attention. You seemed to be happy enough making sheep's eyes at that beautiful lady a moment ago."

Mr Merry laughed. "Do not be a goose, Miss Westlake. That was the Countess of Castleford. She is married with two small boys. Her husband is a bully and the Duchess felt sorry for her and asked me to dance with her. If it looked like I was making sheep's eyes at her, it must have been because I was thinking of you."

"Oh." It was the first compliment that Mr Merry had ever paid her and it threw her quite off balance. Anxious to quell the disturbing feelings that his words stirred up, she resorted to anger and returned to his condemnation of her previous partner. "But what of Mr Hampton? How can you judge a man you have only just met?"

"I did not say that I had only just met him."

"But you asked me to introduce you."

"Now that is another matter."

"I do not understand."

"I have encountered Mr Hampton before under – shall we say – unfortunate circumstances."

Alicia looked enquiringly at Mr Merry. "What circumstances?" she demanded.

"Miss Westlake, you ask far too many questions for a gently bred young lady," he said abruptly. "You should accept the advice of one older and wiser than you who has only your best interests at heart."

Alicia bit her bottom lip. She had not expected such a set-down. A ready blush rushed to her cheeks, but she maintained a dignified silence for the rest of the dance, and then curtseyed formally when Mr Merry returned her to Lady Granger's side.

What could have set Mr Merry against the Duke's nephew, if indeed it was anything more than jealousy? Alicia very much wanted to know—she hated unanswered questions. It was arrogant of Mr Merry to assume the right to dictate her friendships. She failed to see what threat Mr Hampton could be to her. He was always courteous, danced well and made polite if undemanding conversation. His connections were such that he could hardly be deemed a fortune hunter.

On the other hand, Alicia had seen the look of enmity on Mr Merry's face and, if she was honest, it scared her a little. She thought she had learned to read his feelings rather well. His countenance gave away his mood more often than he probably realised. Sometimes his eyes were smiling when he said something serious and Alicia knew that if she met his gaze she would probably burst out laughing. But this time, his eyes were cold whilst he muttered polite words and there was no twinkle in them as he warned her against Mr Hampton. It was all most disturbing.

Too late she realised that her trip to Park Street was in jeopardy. Would Mr Merry still accompany her even though they had parted on such bad terms? It was a melancholy thought with which to end the evening. Worse still, her mother chattered on and on about how glorious the evening had been and of all the middle-aged gallants who had begged her to dance so that she felt quite young again.

Chapter 11

At one o'clock the following afternoon, Alicia sat nervously waiting to see whether Mr Merry would keep his appointment. As she had predicted, the exertions of the previous night's entertainment had exhausted the older ladies and both her mother and Lady Granger had kept to their beds all morning and had still not made their appearance. She felt just a tad guilty that she had managed to avoid telling her mother about the proposed visit, but she reasoned that she was only saving her from unnecessarily worrying that her daughter was turning into a bluestocking.

When Mr Merry's carriage drove up to the front of the house, Alicia let out a sigh of relief. Despite their falling out, he had not let her down. If necessary, she was prepared to apologise in order to restore harmony. She did not care for Mr Merry's disapproval and was eager to put herself in his good books again. Nothing was more calculated to do this than an afternoon spent looking at antiquities, she reasoned. Here their interests met and surely they could converse amicably.

But it appeared that no apology was to be offered or required. Mr Merry talked cheerfully all the way to Park Street. No mention was made of the harsh words that had passed between them the night before; it was as though they had never been spoken. Alicia remembered that it had been just the same after Mr Merry's abrupt departure from Mrs Montagu's house the first time she had met him. When next she had encountered him at the British Museum, all previous animosity had been forgotten. Alicia had to confess that it made her feel rather uneasy. She had been brought up to admit when she was wrong and seek forgiveness and reconciliation. It seemed that she was perfectly reconciled to Mr Merry without having to deal with anything. It was most disconcerting.

Martha had hoped that Mr Merry would not turn up. She had no wish to spend the afternoon in a gloomy house in Park Street. It was a hard life, she grumbled, waiting around while your mistress amused herself. Not that she wanted to accompany Miss looking round some old bits of stone. What she wanted was a comfortable chair and a nice cup of tea in the butler's pantry. That was her idea of a pleasant afternoon. Of course, it was better than wandering around one of those ruined castles that Miss was so fond of. At least it was warm inside Park Street and, if she was lucky, she might get some refreshments. She liked Mr Merry. A handsome, unaffected young gentleman, although he seemed to share her mistress' love of old things. Modern was more comfortable. Martha could not understand the attraction of antiquities at all.

Mr Townley himself met them at the door and Mr Merry performed the introductions.

"Merry, dear boy, what a pleasure to see you, and with such a lovely companion. Come along, come along, Miss Westlake. You must come and meet my wife. She owes her very existence to this man. There was a nasty moment some years ago when I thought I was going to lose her, but this young gentleman," he said, pointing at Mr Merry, "most nobly and unexpectedly came to her rescue. I will always stand in your debt, Merry," he said with the utmost seriousness.

Mr Merry looked uncomfortable. "It was a false alarm, Townley. She would have been perfectly safe here—we just did not know it."

Alicia looked at Mr Merry with new respect. Here was a true hero.

Mr Townley led the way into the drawing room. Every surface was covered with vases and sculptures and the walls were hung with classical scenes. Alicia wrinkled her nose. The musty smell had more to do with dust than ancient Rome. What a horrendous task cleaning a room like this must be! She pitied Mr Townley's poor servants. She gazed around the room in wonder, but could not see Mrs Townley anywhere. She looked at Mr Townley expectantly.

He stood by a fine marble bust of a woman—a beautiful woman from centuries past. "Meet my wife," he quipped, putting his arm around the exquisite marble.

Understanding dawned, making Alicia smile. Looking around the haphazard arrangement of ancient curiosities, she wondered what woman could live with it. How appropriate that Mr Townley should claim a favourite marble as his wife!

"I call her Clytie," he continued. "Clytie and I go back a long way and have had our adventures together."

Alicia smiled. "I am sure she is devoted to you!"

Mr Townley laughed. "As I am to her!"

"But I am intrigued, Mr Townley. What happened to put your wife in danger that Mr Merry need rescue her?"

Mr Townley scowled. "The riots of '80 which that rascal Lord Gordon stirred up against us Catholics. The rioters were gathering in the streets outside. I thought I would never see my lovely collections again. The rioters were not very discerning. They would not have cared if they had destroyed hundreds of years of history along with the buildings. They wrecked poor Lord Mansfield's house and all his precious manuscripts were lost. The protestors' ranks were swollen by people broken out of prison by the mob. I was terrified. Not for my life, but for my life's work—these collections, and most of all, for her. I would have carried her away with me myself, but I am not a strong man, and she was too heavy for me to carry so far. But then Merry turned up to the rescue and urged me to leave quickly while I still could. He picked up my wife and carried her downstairs and out to the hackney carriage that was waiting to transport us to safety."

Alicia smiled admiringly up at Mr Merry. "How gallant of you to come to a lady's rescue! It must have been a night to remember."

But Mr Merry did not respond in kind to her playful sally. He was lost in a silent reverie. "It was certainly a night that it has been impossible to forget," he said abruptly, and then walked out of the room without another word.

Mr Townley and Alicia followed in his wake. By the time they had caught up with him, Mr Merry had lost his solemn mood and was examining a life-size marble of a discus thrower that Mr Townley referred to as Discobolus. Mr Merry shook his head in despair.

"I tell you, Townley, the position of the man's head is all wrong," Mr Merry argued. "Hamilton admitted to me that he had restored it and I am convinced that he has put it back at the wrong angle."

"How can you say that, Merry? To be sure, there is a crack, but many of the sculptures have cracks."

"If a man were throwing the discus, he would have

his head down, like this." Mr Merry mimicked the stance that he believed the discus thrower should have. "Your statue is looking up. It is simply not right. Hamilton should have spent more time researching before fixing the head like that. Would you not agree Miss Westlake?"

"I ... I am afraid I know little of the subject. The statue looks magnificent to me, but then, I am no sportswoman."

"Have it your way, Merry, but I am not breaking off the head of my precious discus thrower and having it reset to please even you. So hands off! It stays as it is."

Alicia moved from one exhibit to the next, overwhelmed with the variety of antiquities. She wished that she could paint with her father's skill. Then she could have recorded them all – well, maybe not all, but the best at least – so that she would not forget them. Mr Townley knew his collections intimately. Every object that caught her fancy, she eagerly sought its history. She wanted to know how old it was and where it had come from. She also wanted to know which objects Mr Merry had acquired for him. Mr Townley had all the answers and was delighted to have such an enthusiastic visitor.

"I do hope you will bring Miss Westlake back one day, Merry. You know how it is with my collections— always something new to see. A pleasure to meet you, Miss Westlake. An absolute pleasure."

Chapter 12

Alicia returned from her visit to Park Street full of all that she had seen, her enjoyment only very slightly tempered by the knowledge that she would now have to answer to her mother for her absence. Moreover, she would have to explain why she had failed to mention that she had agreed to such a visit without her mother's explicit approval.

In the event, Alicia did not have to explain her absence at all. She arrived home from Park Street to be met by the news that her mother was still in bed. She had woken well into the afternoon with a throbbing headache and had stayed in bed to regain her strength.

It soon transpired that Mrs Westlake was suffering from more than the repercussions of dancing all night at a ball. As time progressed, instead of feeling better, she felt worse. Her throat was sore and she was finding it hard to breathe. She had fallen victim to the common cold.

Lady Granger was full of sympathy and immediately sent for the doctor. Unfortunately, there was nothing he could do for his patient except prescribe her a syrup to soothe her inflamed throat and reassure her that she would soon be feeling much more the thing if she stayed in bed for a few days.

Mrs Westlake was distraught. To become ill at this point in the season was too galling. Just when they had been accepted into the height of society through the invitation to the Duchess' ball. It was so upsetting. To Alicia's distress, her mother would not let her near the sickroom.

"If you lose your bloom now, you may never recover it!" she declared dramatically. "I will do very well with Marie to look after me."

By the time Mrs Westlake was sufficiently recovered to leave her bedchamber, Christmas was almost upon them. She had been gratified to receive many enquiries after her health and determined to be well enough to attend church on Christmas morning, before her new connections had a chance to forget her.

The church of St George's in Hanover Square was packed with the ton, impatiently waiting for the service to finish, so that they could greet their acquaintances. Alicia had begun to feel cooped up in the house in Grosvenor Square and if her mother had not been well enough, she thought she would have found the courage to venture forth without her.

Lady Melbourne made a point of noticing Alicia and her mother and introduced them to the Duchess of Gordon. The Duchess immediately promised them an invitation to her ball to be held early in the New Year. It was the first time a leading Tory hostess had extended them an invitation and Mrs Westlake simply glowed with pleasure as she added another duchess to her list of connections.

Alicia looked in vain for Mr Merry. It was most disappointing to be deprived of his enlivening conversation after days of listening to nothing but her mother and Lady Granger talking about their ills, interspersed with juicy scraps of gossip that she would much rather not hear. She thought she would go mad if she did not have a rational conversation with someone soon. Her eyes lighted upon Mr Hampton and she gave him her warmest smile as he walked over to talk to her.

"Christmas greetings to you, Miss Westlake. I trust your mother is fully recovered?"

"Thank you, Mr Hampton. As you can see, my mother is quite herself again," she said drolly, rolling her eyes as the sound of Mrs Westlake's loudly chattering voice reached them.

"I am so glad," Mr Hampton replied with a smile, but Alicia had the feeling that he did not understand the joke. Perhaps he disapproved of her laughing at her mother. Or maybe he just did not think it was funny. She was sure that Mr Merry would have understood. Alicia sighed. She should have known that he would not turn up to church, even on Christmas Day. She realised she had been trying to forget that he did not believe in God. Even so, she could not help wishing that Mr Merry was there to share the joke.

Chapter 13

The Duchess of Gordon's ball was the first event of the New Year and was designed to outshine that of her political rival the Duchess of Devonshire in every respect. The King was still far from well and it looked increasingly likely that the Prince of Wales would shortly be appointed Regent. No one doubted that if this happened, Pitt's government would fall, but the Duchess of Gordon, one of Pitt's most fervent supporters, was not backing down. The Whigs might be on the verge of political breakthrough, but she was determined to give the most successful ball of the season.

Both sides of the political spectrum were bent on descending upon the Duchess of Gordon's Pall Mall home. The Duchess of Devonshire was rebelliously wearing the Regency cap which she had designed, sporting the three feathers of the Prince of Wales and bearing his motto. The Duchess of Gordon ignored this and greeted her rival with the utmost politeness. The atmosphere was so taut that Alicia felt it would take very little to spark a war.

Political tension was the last thing on Mrs Westlake's mind. The season was advancing and none of Alicia's admirers had so far made her an offer. Of course, Mrs Westlake was not to know how little encouragement her daughter had given any of them to do so. Mrs Westlake hated skirting on the edge of the society to which she felt she belonged and was depending on Alicia to make a good match to establish their place in the ton. Despite bragging about her exalted connections, she was all too aware of the precarious line that they were treading. One ill-judged step and they risked being put out of society. She wanted the security of knowing her position in the ton was unassailable and that kind of security would only come through a good marriage.

Mrs Westlake had by no means given up on Mr Hampton who appeared to be the most desirable of her daughter's circle of admirers. If he could just be given a little nudge, she felt sure that she could bring him to the point of proposing. He was a far more serious young man than many of his contemporaries, but Alicia always seemed happy to see him. Mrs Westlake could see no possible objection to the match on her daughter's side.

Eager not to lose any opportunity of forwarding Mr Hampton's suit, Mrs Westlake led the way toward the ballroom with Alicia following closely behind. It was not a very dignified passage. The Duchess had invited hundreds of guests, half of whom seemed to be loitering in the hallway making it almost impossible to move. But step by step they progressed and Alicia was relieved to find that, once in the ballroom, there was a little more breathing space.

Mrs Westlake positioned herself to the right of the door so it would be possible to see every newcomer as they entered the room. She had not been able to discern any sign of Mr Hampton in the ballroom as yet and she did not want any other young lady stealing a march on her daughter. If Mr Hampton was to be present, then Alicia must be poised ready to partner him in the first dance.

As they stood, watching and waiting, Alicia thought

she spotted Mr Merry on the other side of the doorway. He had his back to her, but he was conspicuous because of his height. Of course, she should have expected to see him here. She knew that he supported his friend Pitt and the Tories, but having seen nothing of him since before Christmas, she had supposed that he had sunk back into his studies and forgotten her very existence.

But even as she looked, the gentleman turned and she saw that she had been mistaken. She felt a rush of disappointment; she would have liked to see a friend in this Tory stronghold. At that very moment, her mother grabbed her arm. A rather stout older gentleman whom she had never seen before had stopped right in front of them, holding up the movement of people trying to enter the ballroom.

The gentleman just stood there, staring at Mrs Westlake, then at Alicia, and then back at Mrs Westlake, looking as if he had seen a ghost.

Mrs Westlake curtseyed and murmured, "My Lord," and waited for a response. None came.

The gentleman seemed to have been struck dumb. Thirty years rolled back before his very eyes and Miss Etherington was curtseying to him again. He looked at the young lady to her right. She was so like his Miss Etherington that it made him feel quite faint. But no, this girl must be her daughter. She was not Miss Etherington anymore. She had married that man—what was his name? "Mrs, um, Westlake," he mumbled after what seemed like an eternity.

Mrs Westlake breathed again. For a moment, it had seemed as if he was not going to acknowledge her. He nodded toward Alicia. "Pray introduce me."

"Alicia, the Earl of Harting. My Lord, my daughter, Miss Westlake."

So this was the Earl of Harting. Alicia sunk into a curtsey whilst she assessed the man who had once proposed to her mother. Though he could not be much more than fifty years of age, the Earl's features, which had never been strictly handsome, looked pulled. His eyes were tired and his cheeks ruddy from too much port. Whilst her mother had retained her youthful figure, the Earl had not. If she were being polite, she would describe him as portly.

"Harting." A clipped female voice sounded from behind the Earl, breaking through the grumbles of those that were unable to move into the ballroom, loud and clear. "Can you not progress?" The piercing voice carried across the entire ballroom, until it seemed that every head was turned toward them.

"My dear, I have stumbled across an old friend. You remember Mrs Westlake?"

The venomous look on the lady's face said it all. She stared at Mrs Westlake and then moved on, refusing to acknowledge the acquaintance or wait to be introduced to her daughter.

"Come, Droxford. Your father has been detained. It is too crowded in here. I need air."

The tall gentleman that Alicia had mistaken for Mr Merry responded to the Countess' summons and stepped forward. He followed her across the ballroom toward an exit on the far side. The onlookers held their breath, waiting to see if the Earl would follow his wife's lead. The Earl sighed, smiled apologetically and followed in their wake. "Pray excuse me," he murmured.

The silence was broken. Word quickly spread around the ballroom that the Countess of Harting had cut Mrs Westlake and her daughter.

"Well!" fumed Mrs Westlake to Alicia. "What a rude

woman old Harting has married. I suppose she got what she wanted. But why in God's name did he marry such a harridan? And there is her son, a grown man, running around after her as if he had nothing better to do."

"Calm yourself, Mother," Alicia urged in an undertone, "or someone will hear you." She took her mother forcibly by the arm and guided her to a seat at the side of the ballroom. The Countess' behaviour had been rude, but creating a scene at a ball was tantamount to social disgrace and Alicia knew that it had to be avoided at all costs.

She could tell from the tone of her mother's voice that she was quickly working herself up into a frenzy. Alicia knew all too well what her mother was like if she descended into hysterics. She thrust her hand into her pocket, desperately searching for her vinaigrette whilst all the time encouraging her mother to control herself, speaking in a very calm, very quiet voice. Mercifully, Alicia quickly found what she was looking for. She flicked open the little silver box and thrust it under her mother's nose.

Mrs Westlake took a long sniff at the vinaigrette and continued talking in a loud whisper. "That awful woman—how could she cut me like that? Right here, in front of everybody. You could see the Earl was shocked. It was probably seeing you, Alicia. You look very like I did when I first met the Earl and it must have struck him too. But then that woman saw who he was speaking to and demanded his presence immediately as though I was not even there. She stuck her nose in the air and walked off as if I were some cast-off mistress or complete nobody. I cannot believe that she would hold a grudge after all these years. I feel so humiliated, I could scream with vexation."

Over and over, Alicia begged her mother to control herself. Eventually, her words seemed to have an effect. Mrs Westlake took another long sniff at the vinaigrette and began to grow calmer, though now she looked on the verge of tears.

"Alicia, I cannot bear it," she whimpered. "We must leave. Now."

Alicia did not think that a precipitate flight would aid her mother's cause. Once again, she had to exert all her influence over her mother to prevent her from acting imprudently. "Come now, Mother, surely you are over-reacting? The Countess is only one person in the whole of London."

"But Alicia, everyone saw. The gossips will see to it that everyone knows. Gillray will probably publish some horrid cartoon laughing at me. I will never be able to show my face in public again."

"You must rally, Mother," Alicia said firmly. "If you leave now, everyone will say that the Countess has chased you away. Do not give her the satisfaction of putting you to flight. You must rally."

Mrs Westlake sniffed hard at the vinaigrette again and closed her eyes. Alicia had a good point. The Countess had humiliated her, but she must not let that woman win. Gradually the misery turned to anger. She opened her eyes and Alicia could tell at once that her efforts were paying off. "That man has no strength of character!" she whispered crossly. "No strength of character at all. How could he let his wife bully him like that? Just shrugging his shoulders at me and looking embarrassed and running off to do her bidding? I will show more strength of character than him. You just watch me."

"Bravo, Mother," Alicia replied, glad that the tide

had turned. Although revenge was not a motive to be encouraged, she trusted that her mother's desire for vengeance would last long enough to guide her smoothly through this current trial.

Chapter 14

Alicia was not feeling so positive half an hour later when she was forced to sit out the first dance of the evening because no one had claimed her hand. Her mother was still watching out, ever hopeful, for Mr Hampton's arrival. Surely he would not desert them in this crisis. If only he would arrive and dance with Alicia, perhaps their current disgrace would be forgotten.

Alicia felt increasingly uncomfortable. The ballroom was growing hotter and hotter from the warmth of the candles that lit the room and the heat being given off by those engaged in the dance. Every now and then, she caught a covert look in their direction and knew that word was passing around that the Countess of Harting had seen fit to snub them. There was no chance that those arriving late would escape the knowledge. The excitement of the evening was on the tip of everyone's tongues and Alicia soon perceived that her mother might have some justification for feeling so forlorn at the Countess' attitude.

After an hour of watching other people dance, Alicia began to think there was some merit in leaving. The strain of trying to appear cheerful whilst being obliged to observe rather than join in the dancing was beginning to take its toll.

Unfortunately, she had done such a good job of persuading her mother to stay, that Mrs Westlake was now determined to sit out the length of the ball in order to show that she was not intimidated by her enemy. Alicia was forced to remain at her mother's side, steadfastly trying not to meet the pitying gazes that were being cast in her direction.

"Would you do me the honour of the next dance?" a deep masculine voice enquired.

Alicia had been so engrossed in trying not to catch anyone's eye that she had not noticed Mr Merry approach. She jumped up from her seat, delighted at the sight of her friend.

"Of course, I will probably tread on your toes," he quipped as he led her into the set, "but as you have braved dancing with me once before and survived, no doubt you will do so again."

"I am indebted to you, Mr Merry. You cannot know what a painful thing it is to be obliged to watch a dance when what you really want is to be dancing yourself. I am aware that you do not share my enjoyment and am therefore all the more grateful for you putting yourself out like this."

"I am delighted to be of service," he replied politely, "and will endeavour to return you to your mother without any serious injury to your person or your dress. I confess I was surprised not to find you dancing already."

Alicia scowled. "I am afraid that the Earl of Harting, or rather his wife, saw fit to cut my mother. I believe that snub is responsible for scaring my partners away. Indeed, if you did not know, then you offered to dance with me under false pretences and I quite understand if you want to walk away from me too. I would hate for you to unwittingly come under the displeasure of society through lack of information!"

"I did not know," Mr Merry said in a small voice. "I

had not heard. But believe me, Miss Westlake, when I tell you that your words have in no way diminished my desire to dance with you." Mr Merry's eyes glinted with something that Alicia could not quite put her finger on. It was as if they had suddenly sharpened for battle. It was gratifying to think that she had given rise to such chivalry, but she had the nasty suspicion that it was not chivalry that had caused his eyes to glow like that.

Mr Merry might joke about his inability to dance, but Alicia could see no evidence of his supposed clumsiness. This was the second time they had danced together, and though he might not have the ease of movement that other partners, such as Mr Hampton, seemed to possess quite naturally, he was by no means as poor a dancer as he liked to make out. Alicia was by far the more nervous of the pair, fearing that all eyes were upon them because of the embarrassing episode earlier in the evening. However, after a little while, she managed to forget about the disagreeable incident in the pleasure of the moment and exchange a little conversation with her partner.

"I did not think to see you here, Mr Merry," Alicia commented, "knowing how little you care for balls. I thought you must be buried under manuscripts in the depths of the British Museum."

"It is true that I have spent many hours there, Miss Westlake, but even I have interest in other things."

Alicia thought he was paying her a compliment, but Mr Merry was rarely straightforward, and she could not be quite sure.

"Marbles, for instance?" she suggested. "Old pots, vases, statues?"

Mr Merry put on a look of mock affront. "Miss Westlake, are you convinced that I can only be interested in things that are old and dead? I assure you that I am most interested in some things that are very much alive and far from old."

Alicia felt her colour rising. There was no mistaking that comment. He was flirting with her! Despite her resolution not to be interested, she felt a satisfied glow spread through her. Unfortunately it did not last long. She could see the Countess of Harting standing to one side of the dance, barely concealing the anger that was brewing inside her. She feared that Mr Merry was in line for a set-down for daring to go against the Countess by dancing with her.

Alicia had to admit that Lady Harting was a striking woman. She was dressed magnificently with tall ostrich feathers in her hair in imitation of the style introduced by the Duchess of Devonshire and her person was adorned by a generous quantity of diamonds which were rivalled only by her mother's own. These jewels spoke of her wealth and position as much as her bearing and confidence did.

Mr Merry made no effort to avoid the confrontation. With a quick, reassuring look at Alicia, he took her firmly by the hand and boldly approached the Countess.

Lady Harting refused to look at Alicia. "Merry, please accompany me to the card room," she said, in a tone of voice that showed she was used to being obeyed. Alicia blushed at the older woman's rudeness. It was as if she were not there.

"Mother, may I present—"

For a moment, Alicia thought that she must have misheard. Mother? Was Mr Merry really calling the Countess 'Mother'? What must he have thought of her, complaining about his mother's dreadful behaviour? On the other hand, Mr Merry had told her that he did not see eye to eye with his parents. Alicia looked from one to the other but could perceive no likeness. The Countess' face was handsome, she supposed, but there was no softness around the eyes, none of the laughter lines that were so evident in her son's. She looked at Mr Merry's face. There was no softness in it now. She felt like a pawn in a game of chess being battled out by two master players. A weapon in Mr Merry's war against the parents whom he had told her, quite candidly, that he did not like.

"The card room, Christopher," the Countess interrupted, holding out her arm, waiting for him to take it.

"—Miss Westlake," Mr Merry continued, as though Lady Harting had not spoken. "Miss Westlake, the Countess of Harting, who has the misfortune to have me for a son. I am sorry to disoblige you, Madam, but I must return Miss Westlake to her mother."

Mr Merry took Alicia's arm, bowed briefly and walked away without a backward glance, leaving his mother seething, staring after her undutiful son.

"I am sorry," he said, as they walked across the room. "My mother is well used to having her own way and it can be most unpleasant when someone – usually me – provokes her."

When Alicia made no reply, his manner softened a little. "You look shocked. I should have told you who my parents were, but when you spoke of how badly my mother had treated you, I did not want you to think ill of me by association. I do not know why my beloved parent has taken against you, but—"

"I do."

Mr Merry was all eagerness. "Do tell." Instead of leading her back to her mother, he diverted their path to the refreshments, and, armed with glasses of orgeat, they sat down together on one of the benches provided for guests to sit and watch the dancing.

"There is not much to tell. Once upon a time, there were two ladies, both beautiful in their own way, who came to London in search of a husband. They were both much courted and the Earl of Harting, I believe, was something of a matrimonial prize. One – your mother – set her heart on the Earl; the Earl, alas, set his heart on my mother. The Earl needed to marry for money, so I am told, as the title did not have the fortune to support it—position and influence, but little money. The Earl should never have offered for her, but my mother's refusal was humiliating. Of course, she could have gloated. Instead, she married my father and withdrew from society. People said that the Earl had not come up to scratch – that he had cried off and not made her an offer – but she knew better. She chose money over position and married a mere Mr Westlake with a handsome face and very deep pockets which, if one looked too closely, smelt undeniably of shop. I am not sure what was the bigger crime—refusing the Earl or marrying a plain 'Mr' who was far more wealthy, but was somewhat tainted by the trade from which his fortune came. I expect you can finish the story for me."

Mr Merry nodded. "The Earl married my mother with undignified speed and gratefully accepted her huge dowry. But my mother was under no illusions; she knew that she was second choice and has waited thirty years for her revenge." Mr Merry sighed. "My mother was ever one to harbour a grudge. Brought face to face with her old adversary, I doubt she could resist the allure of delivering a rebuff. It would never have occurred to her to leave the past alone. I am sorry for it," he added. "It will make life in London uncomfortable for you."

Lady Melbourne's son, Mr Lamb, claimed Alicia's hand for the next dance, followed by the Marquess of Worcester. It appeared that her Whig friends were not going to desert her. She was not to know that as soon as the Duchess of Devonshire had discovered what had happened, she had begged them to dance with Miss Westlake as an act of rebellion against the Tories.

Mr Hampton arrived at last and Mrs Westlake, who had not ceased to keep half an eye on the door, spotted him as soon as he entered the room. With a gracious smile and bend of her head, she summoned him to her side. Mr Hampton needed no more encouragement. He had come expressly to dance with Alicia and eagerly responded to Mrs Westlake's invitation. Alicia's attention was fixed in quite another quarter. She was watching Mr Merry weave a path across the ballroom toward her and was disappointed when she saw him turn abruptly on his heel and walk away. As soon as she saw Mr Hampton, she realised why. Mr Merry's antipathy toward Mr Hampton had evidently not gone away.

The Countess of Harting took note of every partner Alicia danced with, as if putting them on an invisible blacklist. She did not give a second thought to her son's pursuit of Alicia. The boy would do anything to annoy her. No sooner had she to declare someone as unworthy of her notice, then what would the boy do but single her out? She did not feel quite so complaisant about Mr Hampton's attentions. She could not bear it if the Duke's nephew was ensnared by that insufferable woman's daughter. She determined to observe Mr Hampton closely and, if she felt that he was in any danger, she would take it upon herself to tell the Duke.

By the end of the evening, Mrs Westlake was feeling very melancholy. The Earl of Harting stared at her frequently, but did not dare incur his wife's wrath by approaching her again. However, she did not lack companionship. More than one enterprising matron thought there was more to the Countess of Harting's behaviour than met the eye and tried to wheedle information out of her that might explain her ladyship's actions.

But on the subject of her disgrace, Mrs Westlake maintained a dignified silence. She refused to stoop so low as to slander her enemies. Nevertheless, after an evening of sly comments and rude stares, her resilience was weakening and she wanted nothing more than to go home and retire to her bed. Her only comfort was that at least Mr Hampton's attentions showed no sign of abating. Perhaps he could be persuaded to offer for Alicia after all.

Chapter 15

In the days that followed the Duchess of Gordon's ball, the number of invitations that the Westlakes received decreased significantly. The Countess of Harting's behaviour caused those that had welcomed the Westlakes into the ton to think twice before including them in their entertainments. Though Lady Harting was not much liked, nobody doubted her ability to sniff out the slightest dent in anyone's reputation. If Lady Harting saw fit to cut the Westlakes, there was every reason to suspect that they were not as genteel as they appeared. The ton knew that to accept anybody branded as associated with trade was courting social disaster.

The Duchess of Devonshire and Lady Melbourne continued to stand by the Westlakes, but few others dared to follow their lead. The Duchess of Devonshire invited them to another ball, but there was no card for Lady Buckinghamshire's assembly. As the weeks went by, the influence of their few remaining friends visibly weakened.

By the end of February, it was evident that all the Whigs' plans would come to nothing. The King's recovery was assured; the Whigs were not going to be asked to form a government after all. Worse than that, their support for the Prince of Wales during what became known as the Regency crisis left them decidedly out of favour at court.

"Can you believe it?" Mrs Westlake whined to Alicia, bemoaning her ill luck. "The Duchess of Devonshire has been ruling the ton for years and now, when we most need her support, she has fallen out of favour. It is too aggravating for words."

"I am sure that she did not do so just to spite you, Mother," Alicia replied.

Mrs Westlake gave her daughter a withering look and continued. "The Duchess is determined to go ahead with the ball she has planned and Elizabeth says that all the Whigs have pledged to stand by her. I am afraid that it will not be the glittering success of her last ball, but we must certainly attend and show the Duchess our support."

Alicia had not supposed for a moment that their attendance was in question. It was not as though they were inundated with invitations after all. She was certainly not put off by her mother's fears that the evening might be rather flat. From her point of view, it was unlikely that it would be. The consequences of Lady Harting's behaviour were proving to be far more pleasant than she could have anticipated. Although their engagements were fewer, Mr Merry had started appearing regularly at the events which they attended. Whether to annoy his mother or protect her from Mr Hampton's continued attentions, Alicia was unable to divine, but she enjoyed his company and would have been quite content if only he had not determined on conducting a silent battle with Mr Hampton right in front of her.

The Duchess of Devonshire's ball was no exception. While she was dancing with Mr Merry, Mr Hampton hovered assiduously waiting for the dance to finish. When Mr Hampton came to claim her hand for the next dance, Mr Merry bowed, but would not speak to Mr

Hampton. He seemed to want to avoid having any conversation with him at all.

Miss Westlake was at a loss to explain Mr Merry's behaviour and could not resist asking Mr Hampton whether he could shed any light on it. "I cannot understand why Mr Merry should be so particular in his behaviour toward you," she said. "It seems unaccountable that he should be so angry with you on so little acquaintance."

"I, on the other hand, do not think it is surprising at all," Mr Hampton replied, uncharacteristically loquacious. "Forgive me for speaking bluntly, but with your wealth and beauty, Miss Westlake, you are a highly desirable matrimonial prize for any younger son. Mr Merry's mother has most effectively scared off the other rivals for your affections, but it will take more than Lady Harting's disapproval to drive me away. I only wish that Mr Merry had more justification for his jealousy."

Mr Hampton's words were most unsettling. Could Lady Harting really have gone to so much trouble to bring about a match between her younger son and the daughter of her oldest rival? It seemed unlikely, but the shadow of a doubt had been planted in Alicia's mind and she found it quite disturbing. Not as disturbing, however, as Mr Hampton's last words; they were the closest thing to a declaration that he had ever said.

Alicia was only too glad when the ball finally came to an end. Despite the Duchess of Devonshire's best efforts, the atmosphere was rather flat. The Duchess and her Whig friends were all trying just a bit too hard to be cheerful. The truth was that they could not forget that they were in disgrace for supporting the Prince of Wales during His Majesty's illness, and now that the King was better, they were facing a decided fall in popularity.

Alicia had found it a strain to keep her two admirers from drawing undue attention to themselves by their hostile behaviour toward each other. Mr Merry's stubborn conduct in refusing to talk to Mr Hampton was embarrassing and she was forced into being more attentive to Mr Hampton than she wished, simply to make up for Mr Merry's impoliteness.

As they waited for their carriage to be brought round, even Mrs Westlake admitted in a whisper to Lady Granger and Alicia that the evening had dragged. It was not to be compared to the success of the Duchess' previous ball. However, Mrs Westlake was not going to dwell on it; she had much more important things to think about. She was delighted to discover that Mr Hampton had not been put off by Lady Harting's outrageous behaviour and saw it as a good sign, a very good sign, of his genuine interest in Alicia. She did not despair of seeing her daughter married to the future Duke of Wessex.

She did not take Mr Merry's courtship very seriously. She assumed that he was just trying to annoy his mother—an objective with which she could completely sympathise. In fact, she was inclined to look upon Mr Merry's sudden pursuit of her daughter as rather fortuitous; a little rivalry was all that was needed to push Mr Hampton into making Alicia an offer of marriage.

Mr Hampton's words at the ball left Alicia in no doubt as to his intentions. She was sure that she could not marry him. Almost. She supposed he would make a good husband. He was a pleasant enough companion even though she deprecated his complete lack of a sense of humour. He invariably smiled when she exercised her wit, but she could not be quite sure that he had actually understood her meaning. From all that she had seen of him, he was a quiet gentleman of steady principles. From a worldly point of view, she knew it would be a good match. Her mother would be in raptures if she accepted him.

Alicia lay awake at night wondering what she would say if Mr Hampton asked. Her mother would expect her to say yes, but she was by no means convinced that she would. She dreaded the scene with her mother if she refused. But the more she thought about it, the more she felt that perhaps she would not have to make that decision. Surely the Duke of Wessex would have bigger matrimonial plans for his nephew and ultimate heir? Therein was her safeguard. The Duke would certainly oppose the match. She would not have to refuse Mr Hampton because he would never offer for her without his uncle's approval.

Alicia was not surprised that her mother welcomed Mr Hampton's suit. Her mother's enthusiasm for titles was unparalleled and marriage to a duke was about as high as she could go. Unless she were to marry into the royal family, that is, and not even her mother could expect that. What puzzled her more was her encouragement of Mr Merry. She failed to grasp that her mother was hoping to use his rivalry as a means of bringing Mr Hampton to the point.

The competition between the two gentlemen was intense as each tried to surpass the other in providing entertainment for Alicia and her mother. Mr Hampton escorted them to see the illuminations in celebration of the King's recovery; Mr Merry asked them to accompany him to Covent Garden to see *The Duenna*. Alicia loved the theatre and was vocal in her enthusiasm for Mr Sheridan's musical, loudly praising it as vastly superior to either Drury Lane's *Robinson Crusoe* or Covent Garden's *Aladdin*. She thought she may even have preferred it to *Macbeth*.

Mr Hampton immediately recommended trying another Shakespeare, to see if she liked it better, and invited her to the Drury Lane Theatre to see *Twelfth Night*. Not to be outdone, Mr Merry took them back to Covent Garden to see *The Comedy of Errors*. Seeing that *Macbeth* was on the playbill again, Mr Hampton accompanied Alicia and her mother to Drury Lane to see it. But he had reckoned without the absence of Mrs Siddons, and Alicia found it somewhat lacking.

Alicia thought it was as well that her mother was distracted by the constant attentions that Mr Hampton and Mr Merry were paying her as there was little else for her mother to smile about. The number of invitations from members of the ton had virtually dried up and there was no question of them attending the ball being held at the Pantheon in celebration of the King's recovery. Even had they not felt honour bound to join the Duchess of Devonshire and the other Whigs in boycotting the ball, they would have shied away from the risk of being cut or, worse still, refused entry, to an event over which the Duchess of Gordon was patroness.

Mrs Westlake sighed heavily and lamented, at least once a day, that things had worked out so ill for them. But then she looked at Alicia and smiled knowingly. A little push was all that Mr Hampton needed and with her daughter married to the future duke, no one would dare to continue to shun her.

Chapter 16

Whilst Mrs Westlake was working on a plan to persuade Mr Hampton to get to the point, her old adversary, Lady Harting, was, with equal determination, doing her best to prevent it. The Countess was concerned about Mr Hampton's continued attentions to Miss Westlake. In fact, they worried her excessively. The Duke's nephew seemed to be in earnest and she could not bear the thought that if Mr Hampton married the Westlake girl, her old rival's daughter would one day be Duchess of Wessex and outrank her. Lady Harting had often regretted that she had no daughter to marry the Duke's nephew. An alliance between the two houses would have been delightful. It was too late to do anything about that now, but at least she could prevent a misalliance between the Duke's nephew and that woman's daughter.

The Countess believed that a direct attack would be the best method of preventing such a disaster. She saw it as her duty to alert the Duke to the ruinous match that his nephew was pursuing as quickly as possible. None knew better than she that Mr Westlake's fortune come through trade. It was inconceivable that the Duke would countenance such an alliance.

She had briefly considered sending a letter to Mr Hampton's father, but she could place no reliance on Lord Richard taking her warning seriously. He was a singularly indolent gentleman and he would no doubt dismiss the whole affair, trusting his son not to act foolishly.

No, she would be far more likely to get a reaction from the Duke. She considered writing to him, but decided it would be better to see him face to face. A written note might not convey the seriousness of the situation with enough force to persuade the Duke to take action. No, inconvenient though it was, she must visit the Duke in person.

The Earl was surprised when his wife unexpectedly announced that she needed a few days in the country to recuperate, but he had long since given up questioning her decisions. It was far more comfortable to agree straight away; she always seemed to get her own way in the end. No doubt the Countess had her reasons.

"This would be an excellent opportunity to pay a visit to your old friend the Duke of Wessex, Harting. I am sure it is long overdue, but what with going abroad for your health and the King's illness, it has been impossible to find the time."

The Earl was not averse to visiting the Duke, but could not understand why his wife wanted to travel so far into Hampshire when their own estate was some twenty miles nearer. He guessed that the Countess had a different motive from the professed one of needing a few days of rest in the country. After all, they had only been in town a few weeks and her ladyship always seemed to have boundless energy when it suited her.

The Duke was genuinely pleased to welcome his old friend for such an unexpected visit. He secretly thought it was a shame that he had brought his wife with him, but he was by far too well-mannered to mention it. He was more than a little surprised that they should make the visit during the season, but assumed they had their reasons and thought no more about it. No doubt all would be made clear in time.

Lord Richard was less tolerant. He was inclined to see the arrival of uninvited guests as an intrusion. Not that he minded the Earl, but the presence of a lady would quite cut up their peaceful routine. He would be expected to make polite conversation instead of snoozing in front of the fire with a bottle of port for company. It was really most inconsiderate of the Earl to bring his wife into their midst.

Dinner was a formal affair. It could never be anything less at Swanmore. The continual presence of the servants kept the conversation at a very superficial level and Lady Harting waited restlessly for the meal to finish so that she could engage the Duke in a few minutes of private conversation.

She had no intention of losing the opportunity to talk to the Duke by allowing the gentlemen to sit for hours over their port. "I hope you will indulge my husband in a game of piquet, Lord Richard," the Countess said as she rose from the table. "I am afraid that I am a very indifferent card player and Harting would relish a worthy opponent such as you."

Lord Richard brightened considerably and immediately declared his willingness. An evening of cards would be far more entertaining than making stilted conversation with the Duke's unwanted guests and if he could succeed in winning a few guineas off the Earl as well, so much the better.

"Excellent," Lady Harting declared, as she left the room, confident that the gentlemen would soon follow.

The Duke was not taken in. It might seem that Lady Harting was arranging a pleasant evening for her husband, but he knew better. Clearly the Countess was eager to engage him in conversation of a particular nature. He had experienced the manoeuvres of match-making mothers and their daughters ever since he had turned eighteen and again after the death of his wife.

Even though it was many years since anyone had tried to ensnare him into marriage, he could still recognise that look, that eagerness that characterised a woman with a hidden agenda. He supposed that this was why his old friend had paid him an impromptu visit—his friend's wife clearly wanted a private word with him.

Reasoning that it was as well to let the Countess have her say as soon as possible, the Duke fortified himself with a generous quantity of port and suggested that they join Lady Harting in the drawing room. The Earl and Lord Richard were quick to follow his lead. They had their eyes fixed on the promised game and with barely a word to Lady Harting, they settled themselves down at the card table leaving the Countess to entertain the Duke.

"You must be missing your nephew, Duke," Lady Harting oozed. "Such a fine young man and so much like a son to you."

"Am I to understand that you have seen my nephew in town then, Madam?" the Duke enquired. "I encouraged him to take his place in society. After all, only two old men stand between him and the title. It is time he took a wife."

"Yes, I have seen him. Indeed, I was hoping for the opportunity of dropping a word in your ear, for I am a little concerned about him."

"In my ear?" the Duke asked with a haughtiness that suggested he was none too pleased at being spoken to with such familiarity. He did not take kindly to the thought of Lady Harting poking her nose into his affairs. "Surely you are addressing yourself to the wrong person, Madam? If there is anything to be said concerning Mr Hampton, I suggest you address your remarks to his father."

"I am sure that Lord Richard would agree that you, Duke, as the head of the family, would perhaps have more influence over Mr Hampton's behaviour. It is, as you will hear, a delicate matter."

"How so?" the Duke asked brusquely.

"Mr Hampton is most unfortunately paying court to a young lady of whom I am not at all sure you would approve."

"Go on, Madam," he urged, wondering whether there was any real cause for concern. "I am listening."

"The girl is a Miss Westlake. Her father was not at all the thing. His money came from trade."

The Countess paused dramatically, waiting for a reaction, but the Duke said nothing.

"Yes, I thought you would be shocked," she continued, assuming that her unwelcome news had left the Duke lost for words. "The girl and her mother had inveigled their way into the ton before I returned to London, but I soon put them in their places. I do pity Mr Hampton. The girl is extremely pretty and has cast out lures to draw the young gentlemen in. Alas, even my younger son – the foolish boy – has fallen victim to her charms."

"You interest me exceedingly. Her manifold attractions must be excessive to overcome the disadvantage of her birth. What of her mother? Is she tainted by trade too?"

"Well no, her birth is respectable, but it cannot make up for the other. I am sorry to be the one to break it to you, but a word from yourself and I am confident the affair will be at an end. Your nephew would do nothing to displease you."

The Duke nodded in agreement. No, he had every reason to believe that Joshua would obey him. "And what of young Merry? Will your son drop her equally obediently?"

The Countess looked firm. "Merry will do as he is bid or suffer the consequences."

The Duke's interest was aroused. A girl that could attract two noblemen's sons and continue to inspire young Mr Merry's devotion despite parental opposition must be something quite out of the ordinary.

The Duke had not seen Lady Harting's younger son since he was a boy, but he had a feeling he would like him. He had often lamented the lack of strength in his old friend's character. It would seem that Lady Harting had met her match in her younger son and the Duke thought wickedly that it was no bad thing.

"Are you sure that you have told me everything, Lady Harting? You have not mentioned the fortune. I am sure there is a fortune. Are you sure you are not trying to eliminate the competition so that your son can marry the heiress?"

Lady Harting coloured. "Wealth is nothing where there is a lack of breeding."

"Ah, so there is a fortune," the Duke concluded. "I see that I have stayed away from town too long. I will come and see the girl for myself. It is not often that beauty and wealth go hand in hand. Beauty, wealth and breeding—surely two out of three is good enough?"

The Duke laughed at the Countess' discomfort. He tolerated her for the sake of the Earl, but if ever there was a lack of breeding, surely it was in this cold-hearted, spiteful woman. He had heard rumours that the Countess of Jersey was following in her footsteps. But at least Lady Jersey had beauty to counterbalance her spite. The Earl of Harting's wife had little beauty or breeding. The Duke thought that the wealth she had brought to the marriage had been poor compensation for his old friend marrying a shrew.

Chapter 17

Within a week, the Duke was in London, dragging his reluctant brother with him. Lord Richard was quick to dismiss Lady Harting's concerns and was by no means persuaded that any intervention on their behalf was necessary. He grumbled incessantly about a wasted journey and how much his gout was bothering him.

"Are you not the least bit interested to discover what sort of girl your son has become entangled with?" the Duke asked his brother.

"Humph!" Lord Richard retorted. "If Lady Harting thinks the girl is unsuitable, I can hardly imagine that Joshua would be chasing after her. He knows what is due to the name."

"But perhaps he has fallen in love, Richard. That might make him forget."

"Humph!" Lord Richard reiterated. "If Joshua has fallen in love with the wrong sort of girl, Wessex, then there is no reason to suppose that he is contemplating marriage."

Mr Hampton was taken aback by the arrival of his father and uncle in town but quickly hid his surprise. It had been many months since the Duke had left his ancestral home. He wondered what rumours had reached Swanmore that were sufficient to provoke his relatives into making the journey to London.

Lord Richard did not travel well and immediately took to his bed to recover. The Duke, though two years older, was in far better health and keen to get to the heart of the matter as quickly as possible. He had come to London to find out what manner of girl his nephew was courting and to extricate him from the connection if it proved unsuitable. Lord Richard had shown such a disappointing lack of interest in his son's affairs that the Duke felt no obligation to wait for him to rejoin them before launching into his enquiries.

"I hear that your name is being linked with that of a lady, Joshua," the Duke said in a gruff voice, "a lady with some degree of scandal surrounding her."

Mr Hampton swallowed hard, but said nothing. He wondered exactly what tales had been told about him. He could not tell whether the Duke was pleased or not. He bided his time, waiting to see what the Duke would say next.

"Why did you not tell me?"

Mr Hampton hesitated, choosing his words carefully. "I did not think you would be interested."

"Of course I am interested, Joshua. Is she pretty?"

Mr Hampton nodded. "Very pretty."

"But not of noble birth."

Mr Hampton swore under his breath. He wondered who had been carrying tales back to his uncle. He hoped the Duke was not going to be awkward. "Well, no, Uncle."

"Are you in love with this lady who has been cast out from society?" the Duke asked. He paused, waiting for his nephew to respond, but for some reason Joshua seemed reluctant to talk about the object of his affections. "I understand she is very wealthy."

Mr Hampton smiled. "It is true she is an heiress, but

if she has been painted to you as a commoner, then you have been misled. You will see at a glance that her mother is quality."

The Duke nodded. "Very well, Joshua, but are you sure you know what you are about? It is no small thing to be excluded from the ton."

"The Countess of Harting has done her best to blacken their name, but the Westlakes are still received at Devonshire House."

"Then I will say no more about it until I have met the young lady for myself."

The Duke wasted no time in calling upon the Westlakes. Mrs Westlake was highly gratified when Mr Hampton introduced his uncle, but Alicia was more circumspect. She was afraid that Mr Hampton's attentions were even more serious than she had supposed and that he had called upon the Duke to approve his choice.

Mrs Westlake rapped Mr Hampton lightly on the hand with her fan with what Alicia considered quite inappropriate familiarity and gently reproached him for not giving them notice that his uncle was in town.

"Do not be too hard on my nephew, Mrs Westlake," the Duke said. "My brother and I arrived yesterday without warning and so you can hardly blame him for advising you of what he himself was not aware." So the Duke had not been summoned by his nephew, Alicia concluded, but had come of his own accord.

"But what has brought you to London in such a hurry, Your Grace?" Mrs Westlake enquired.

"The pleasure of making the acquaintance of you and your daughter, Madam," the Duke replied suavely.

Mrs Westlake responded suitably, but Alicia wondered what rumours about her had been told to bring the

Duke so precipitately to London. Perhaps it would be easiest if the Duke did not approve of his nephew's suit. Then she would not have to decide what she really thought about Mr Hampton. It certainly weighed in his favour that his uncle thought a great deal of him, but could she really contemplate marrying where she did not love? Would it not be misery to be married to a gentleman she could not laugh with, however reliable and upright he appeared?

"Lady Harting tells me that you have been ostracised from society, Miss Westlake. How did you come to offend such an influential personage?"

Alicia visibly stiffened at the mention of the Countess' name. She was not surprised to discover that it was Lady Harting who had been carrying tales to the Duke. She warmed to his direct approach and was equally direct in her reply. "I believe that my mother offended her years ago and that she has waited all this time to carry out her revenge."

"You interest me exceedingly, Miss Westlake. I wondered whether there was anything more to the Countess' enmity than an objection to the fact that your father's fortune came from trade."

"No doubt the Countess found my grandfather's aptitude for investing in industry objectionable, but without far-sighted people like him, the cotton industry would not have been able to progress, Your Grace," Alicia replied with spirit. "My grandfather invested well and reaped the benefits of thinking ahead of those that would not countenance change. But my father was brought up a gentleman, whatever you may have been told."

"Well said, Miss Westlake. Your loyalty to your family is admirable."

The Duke continued to talk with Alicia, asking her about her father, her home and how she liked London. He observed her carefully and was pleased with what he saw. He thought that she would make an excellent wife for his nephew.

For her part, Alicia had to admit that she liked the Duke. He was so easy to talk to that she soon forgot that he held such an elevated title. He was an entertaining conversationalist with a ready sense of humour and she was delighted to find that she did not have to explain what she meant when she made a joke. Alicia thought it was a pity that his nephew was not more like him.

The Duke was still deep in conversation with Alicia when Rowson announced the arrival of Mr Merry. Alicia was dismayed. She did not care to be found entertaining the Duke and his nephew—it gave such a look of intimacy. Alicia would have denied him if her mother had given her the chance, but Mrs Westlake was not going to pass up the opportunity of displaying her exalted connections. Mr Merry might carry the news back to his parents, and that might succeed in putting the Countess' nose out of joint.

Mr Merry entered the room expecting a warm reception from Alicia at least, but was brought up short by the sight that greeted him. His cheerfulness departed in a flash. Not only was Mr Hampton there before him, but he had the support of his uncle to further his suit.

He looked across the room and caught Alicia's eye. She blushed to the roots of her hair. From the look on Mr Merry's face, Alicia realised that the Duke's presence had all the appearance of intimacy that she had feared.

The Duke good-naturedly brushed away Mrs Westlake's proffered introduction, claiming an acquaintance with his old friend's son, though he had not seen him since he went up to Cambridge. The tight look on Mr Merry's face and the blushes on Alicia's did not escape his notice. It would seem that his nephew had a lot of work to do if he was going to be successful in his suit.

"I am attending the theatre at Covent Garden on Wednesday," the Duke said. "I have reason to believe that the Queen will be attending. Did you ever happen to see the Queen before, Miss Westlake?"

Alicia admitted that she had not.

"And would you like to see Her Majesty?" he asked her.

Alicia guessed that an invitation to join the Duke would follow. She wanted very much to see the Queen, but was loath to encourage Mr Hampton by accepting the Duke's offer. In the end, curiosity won.

"I would very much like to see the Queen, Your Grace."

The Duke smiled. "Excellent. Then you must join me in my box on Wednesday. The play is a comedy which I have not seen before—*He Would be a Soldier*. I cannot vouch for the play, but I believe you will find the evening entertaining. Merry, do join us. I am sure we can find room for one extra."

Mr Merry accepted the offer, but it was clear from the expressions on the two gentlemen's faces that neither was satisfied with the arrangement. Mr Hampton appeared to be decidedly put out by the whole affair whilst Mr Merry looked as if he had just agreed to a death sentence.

Chapter 18

Although slightly daunted at being abruptly brought into celebrity by association with the Duke, Alicia was looking forward to the theatre visit in his company. She had been introduced to the Prince of Wales at the Duchess of Devonshire's ball and heard herself spoken of as a pretty girl, but she was eager to see other members of the royal family. Until recently, the King and Queen had been shut away at Kew because of the King's illness and so she had not had the opportunity to see them or any of the princesses. She had heard that the Prince of Wales' good looks did not come from his mother and wanted very much to see if the Queen really was as ugly as she had heard rumoured.

The Duke's box was in a good position, close to the stage, and at his urging, Alicia seated herself on the front row with Mr Merry on one side and Mr Hampton on the other. The two gentlemen vied with each other to engage Alicia in conversation. Up until now, Alicia had managed to avoid having both gentlemen in attendance simultaneously, but on this occasion, she had been outmanoeuvred. If it had not been so awkward, Alicia would have laughed. The situation was most uncomfortable. Neither gentleman would talk to the other, only with her or occasionally with Mrs Westlake or the Duke.

Alicia greeted the Queen's arrival with some relief. It was wearing her out keeping the peace between her two suitors and she was unable to have a satisfactory conversation with either. The audience broke out into spontaneous applause as Queen Charlotte entered the theatre accompanied by two of her daughters. Her Majesty seemed quite overwhelmed by the rapturous welcome.

"Which princesses are they?" Alicia whispered under her breath.

"Augusta and Elizabeth," Mr Merry and Mr Hampton said simultaneously, making Alicia smile.

Alicia had quite a good view of the royal box and was surprised that the royal party looked so normal. The Queen was smiling graciously, but not even her smile could hide her plainness, though her bearing was certainly regal. The two princesses did not look much older than she was. She thought that Princess Augusta looked a model of elegance whilst Princess Elizabeth had a very sweet face.

Eventually the applause died down and the curtain went up. But to Alicia's surprise, this did not, as she had expected, herald the start of the play. Instead, a splendid back cloth displaying the King's arms was revealed with a scroll bearing the words 'Long live the King' above it and a second saying 'May the King live for ever' beneath.

No sooner had the audience taken in this carefully prepared tribute in recognition of the King's recovery then the theatre manager came forward with the theatre's singers and launched into *God Save the King*. Alicia joined in with the rest of the audience, enthusiastically singing the anthem three times. The Queen appeared to be most gratified with all the attention.

The play was, Alicia had to admit, nothing above the ordinary, but she was very glad they had come. Seeing the Queen for the first time was a memory she would always cherish. She was disappointed to discover that the second piece to be performed was *Aladdin*. She had already seen that once and had not found it very amusing the first time. Mrs Westlake had no particular wish to see *Aladdin* again either, but she was not going to drag herself away from the theatre a moment before she had to.

"How tired the Queen looks," Mrs Westlake observed. "It must have been dreadful with the poor King so ill. I believe he acted very strangely toward her. Ah well. I am sure she is at peace again now that the King is better and will soon appear more rested."

"I doubt very much whether the Queen is truly at peace, Mother," Alicia replied. "Whilst I am sure that she is delighted that the King has recovered, I suspect that, at the back of her mind, she must wonder whether the King will stay well."

Mrs Westlake murmured some inarticulate reply which suggested to Alicia that her mother was not truly interested in the Queen's state of mind and then promptly changed the subject.

"Princess Augusta is very pretty," Mrs Westlake said. "I am surprised she is not married yet. I thought that the King would have arranged a match for her by now. I mean, before he was ill, of course. I expect the Queen is glad to have her daughters with her. Daughters are such a comfort to their mothers."

Alicia grimaced, but forbore to make a reply.

Aladdin was as uninspiring as Alicia remembered. She found it hard to concentrate and her eyes drifted mindlessly across the stage until she was arrested by the behaviour of a rather striking actress playing a supporting role.

The actress in question kept looking up at their box

and when she spoke, she seemed to be saying her lines directly to them rather than to the main body of the audience. Alicia thought that perhaps acting before royalty was making the woman nervous and she had decided to fix her eyes on their box in an effort to stay calm.

The play was not engaging Mr Merry's attention either. He was staring vacantly at the stage, whilst his mind was wandering back over the manuscripts he had been looking at that morning.

"Who is that woman you are looking at?" Alicia whispered to Mr Merry. "She seems to be saying her lines right to us. Is she a particularly famous actress? I do not remember seeing her before."

Alicia's words brought Mr Merry back to the present with a jolt. He had not consciously been looking at anyone. He followed Alicia's gaze, and his spirits sank. He had inadvertently been staring at one of the most highly paid courtesans in London.

Mr Merry cleared his throat. "Um, that is, I believe, Mrs Martindale."

"And is she well known?" Alicia whispered.

Mr Merry hesitated. How could he explain the true state of affairs? Young ladies of quality were not supposed to know about such things. It would be a breach of etiquette even to mention it. How could he explain that Mrs Martindale's fame was not derived from her acting abilities? He had never felt so embarrassed in his life. "Um, yes. I suppose so."

Alicia stared at Mr Merry in surprise. What on earth had she said to disconcert him? All at once, an unwelcome possibility popped into her mind. She knew that actresses were not always respectable. Perhaps the woman was casting out lures to the gentlemen in her box. Or worse, perhaps she was already under the protection of one of them. Her mother had never hidden the fact that gentlemen sometimes had relationships with women who were not their wives, but Alicia had not for one moment considered that those gentlemen could be people she knew. The woman was certainly very attractive. She was built on majestic lines, with curves in all the right places, and was wearing a dress which was far more revealing than any that a lady of the ton would wear.

Alicia stole a covert look at Mr Hampton. As she watched, his eyes rested fleetingly on Mrs Martindale, but he immediately turned away, frowning in disapproval. His eyes became resolutely fixed on the action taking place in the centre of the stage and Mrs Martindale's unusual conduct failed to draw him back again. If she was trying to catch Mr Hampton's attention, Alicia thought, it looked like Mrs Martindale had failed.

Then an awful thought dawned on Alicia and her heart sank. Mr Merry had been staring straight at Mrs Martindale. No wonder he had sounded so embarrassed. What a fool she had been! The realisation left her feeling very subdued and she could not wait for the interminable *Aladdin* to end so that she could be alone. Why did she forget so easily that Mr Merry's life was not built on the same principles as her own?

Chapter 19

Alicia tried not to dwell on the incident at the theatre, but it was hard to put it completely from her mind. She wanted to challenge Mr Merry, to hear him deny that he had any association with Mrs Martindale, but she could hardly ask him outright whether the actress was his mistress. It really was not a subject for polite conversation. According to the dictates of genteel society, it was one about which she was supposed to know nothing at all.

So she remained silent, though all the while wondering, and found it difficult to resume their friendly banter. But her withdrawal from Mr Merry did not make her more sympathetic toward Mr Hampton. He was very worthy, but not very entertaining, and he did not have the merit of sharing her passion for antiquities. What is more, he had utterly failed to make the slightest impression on her heart.

The Duke thought it was a pity that Miss Westlake showed no inclination for his nephew's suit. She was not giving him any encouragement and there was certainly nothing lover-like in her behaviour toward him. To be fair, the Duke had failed to observe any such behaviour in Joshua either, but his nephew was certainly trying to fix his interest with her.

The Duke hoped Joshua was motivated by love and not by the size of Miss Westlake's fortune. But surely he was worryingly unduly; there could be no need for Joshua to marry for money.

The Duke had been so eager to show his support of the match that he was inclined to think he had over-whelmed Miss Westlake. He decided to try a different tack. The next time they called on the Westlakes, the Duke took a seat at the far end of the drawing room and devoted himself to Mrs Westlake, leaving the young people to themselves. He thought that maybe Joshua would fare better without his uncle keeping watch.

Mrs Westlake was delighted to have the Duke's full attention and set about captivating her audience. Her conversation exactly suited the Duke. It was bright and witty without being too clever and made a pleasant change from worrying over Joshua or listening to Lord Richard complaining about his gout.

During his lifetime, Mr Westlake had always paid for the early delivery of the London newspapers, and after his demise, Mrs Westlake had continued the practice. She devoured the latest fashion magazines and absorbed every morsel of gossip that happened to come her way. Even in rural Oxfordshire, she had known as much about what the ton was doing as the ton itself. She was familiar with what they were wearing, what they were reading and who was connected with whom, in both family relationships and romantic liaisons.

Reading the newspapers had become something of a habit. She had discovered that by doing so, even in London, she was sometimes aware of snippets of information that others did not know. There was nothing she liked better than being able to share what she had read in a conversational way and the Duke was very ready to listen. As a widow, she had more licence than a single woman, allowing her to share some of the juicier bits of gossip when she was sure that Alicia was not listening. She flirted delightfully, playing with her fan, making the Duke feel like a young man again.

"The whole country is delighted that the King has recovered. I believe that they would all come to the service at St Paul's to celebrate if they could. I hear that they are beginning to erect scaffolding along the route to enable as many as possible to see the King and Queen on their way to the cathedral. I daresay that you will be part of that procession, Your Grace."

The Duke nodded. "I confess that I do not much care for these formal occasions, but it is part of my heritage. From the time I was breeched, I knew that one day I would be Duke and would be required to play my part as a peer of the realm as my father had done before me. I had hoped that my own son would do likewise, but it was not to be. Since Denmead's death, I have had to accept that it will be my brother and not my son following in my footsteps. Unless my brother beats me to the grave, in which case the title will go directly to my nephew," he said, looking fondly at Mr Hampton, who was deep in conversation with Alicia.

"And does Mr Hampton accompany you in the procession?" Mrs Westlake asked.

"Alas, no, Mrs Westlake. I am required to take my place amongst the peers some way below the Duke of Norfolk, but young Joshua must sit with the rest of the nobility."

The Duke paused for a moment as an idea came to him. A moment later, he began again, having arrived at a quick decision. "Mrs Westlake, I would consider it a great honour if you and your daughter were to sit with my nephew during the service. I am able to offer you good seats in the cathedral with a fine view of the proceedings, even though I cannot offer you my company."

Mrs Westlake was extremely flattered by the Duke's suggestion. Her plans to accompany Lady Granger to the service were immediately thrown aside. Elizabeth would not have her turn down such an opportunity.

"Your Grace, I am overcome by such thoughtfulness," she replied, fluttering her fan in an agitated manner. "Alicia and I would be delighted to accept your kind offer."

After the Duke and his nephew had gone, Mrs Westlake was bursting to share her good news. She was in such high spirits that it did not occur to her that Alicia would not share her enthusiasm.

"Mother, I cannot believe that you have accepted the Duke's invitation without saying a word to me," Alicia complained. "I would much rather you had declined such a show of attention. It gives us such a very particular look, as if we were part of the Duke's family."

Mrs Westlake beamed at her daughter and patted her hand. "Which you may well become," she praised, "you clever thing."

Alicia angrily pulled her hand away. She had been so convinced that the Duke would be against the match that she had not tried very hard to dissuade Mr Hampton from courting her. Not that it would have been an easy feat as her mother had been busy encouraging him ever since he had first shown an interest in her. Evidently, she could no longer rely on the Duke's disapproval to dampen Mr Hampton's ardour.

Since the night at the ball when Mr Hampton had first revealed his intentions, she had been constantly examining her inmost feelings, trying to determine the right course. Only now, when she was being forced into a public display of intimacy with the Duke's family, did she know for sure that she could not marry Mr Hampton. She thought of a pair of cynical blue eyes that had a tendency to twinkle with unspoken understanding, and knew beyond a doubt that it would be wicked to accept Mr Hampton when she was always comparing him unfavourably to someone else. Even if that someone else was not a godly man and one whom she knew she could not marry.

"Please do not get any grand plans about my marrying Mr Hampton, Mother. I do not feel for him in that way. He is my friend. That is all."

Mrs Westlake looked at her daughter as if she were not in her right mind. "But he is the Duke's heir. You would be a Duchess one day. Think of it, Alicia— Duchess of Wessex! No, I will hear no more about it. We are going to the service with the Duke's family whether you like it or not."

Alicia objected profusely, but her mother was not listening. Mrs Westlake was aiming high and Alicia knew better than to get in the way of her mother's ambition.

The conversation with her mother left Alicia feeling very uncomfortable, but there was nothing she could do. Her mother had accepted the Duke's invitation to sit with Mr Hampton and so, unless she wanted to miss the service completely by taking to her bed, she would have to make the best of it. The dreadful weather did nothing to lighten her spirits. At least they would not have to stand out in the rain. The poor people who had been waiting all night for a sight of the King must have been drenched.

Mrs Westlake was lapping up the attention of being in company with the Duke's family in the cathedral;

Alicia's only pleasure was in being in such a good position to watch the service. As they waited for the procession to enter the cathedral, Mr Hampton did his best to entertain her, but he found her monosyllabic answers somewhat discouraging and soon lapsed into silence.

At last their Majesties arrived. The King was dressed in a smart blue coat with a red collar and cuffs and gold lacing that Alicia had no problem in recognising as the Windsor uniform. Alicia thought that the King looked very good-natured, beaming away, obviously happy to be among his people again. She did not think him very handsome though. His eyes were a bit too bulbous to be pleasant to look at, but maybe that had been caused by his illness.

The Queen was dressed in blue silk trimmed with white and wore a bandeau which Alicia had no doubt was inscribed with the words 'God Save the King'. She recognised the two princesses she had seen at the theatre and guessed that the two others must be the Princess Royal and Princess Mary.

The princesses were all dressed in blue, just like the Queen, complete with bandeaux. Alicia wondered whether they had had any choice about what they were wearing. No, she supposed not. She could not imagine any lady choosing to wear the same clothes as their mother, even if she happened to be the Queen. Alicia thought it was a blessing that she was not required to dress like her mother.

The Prince of Wales did not look happy at all. He looked like a grumpy boy who had just had his favourite toy confiscated. He was not behaving very well. Alicia thought that he really should have made the effort and at least given the appearance of being pleased that his father was better, even though it had spoilt all his plans. Such a sour attitude did not make him popular with anybody.

In the days that followed, Mrs Westlake continued to accept invitations from Mr Hampton and at every available opportunity she pointed out the advantages of a union with the Duke's nephew. Alicia was disappointed, but not surprised, that her mother continued to ignore all her protestations that she was not going to marry Mr Hampton. When her mother had an end in view, she was not one to give up easily. Mrs Westlake's sole aim in coming to London was to reestablish herself in the ton by marrying her daughter to a man of fortune and prospects. In Mr Hampton, she saw her best chance of achieving all that she desired. Alicia continued to object, but Mrs Westlake just would not listen.

"And do not think that your Mr Merry will offer for you, Alicia. He is a younger son. He needs connections to make his way in the world—connections that you cannot give him. You mark my words, he is just making up to you to spite his mother. If you do not accept Mr Hampton, you will be left on the shelf and we will be excluded from society for ever."

Alicia blushed. "He is not my Mr Merry, Mother. I do not plan to marry him any more than Mr Hampton."

"But, Alicia, Mr Hampton will be a duke one day. A duke! It is more than I hoped for you."

"Mother," Alicia said firmly. "Think how embarrassing it would be if you pushed Mr Hampton into making me an offer which I then refused."

Mrs Westlake stared at her daughter in disbelief. "You would not!" Alicia's face was unyielding. The truth of her words gradually sank in. Mrs Westlake's face dropped. She looked ridiculously crestfallen. All her plans were going to come to nothing. She could not understand why her daughter would not jump at the chance of becoming a duchess. The girl had no ambition—no ambition at all. Why, she would marry Mr Hampton herself if she were twenty years younger, though in truth, she preferred older men. Like the Duke.

It was one of those moments of blinding revelation. In a trice, Mrs Westlake's ambitions were transformed. The Duke was not a young man, but he was still very attractive. Such a man needed a pretty young woman to look after him. Not so young as to be giddy and always wanting to be at parties, but one who knew how to look after a gentleman. Someone with experience, who could attend to his comfort. Someone like herself. She did not know why she had not thought of it before. She rather liked the freedom that came with her widowed status, but it was nothing to the thought of being a duchess. She was sure that the Duke liked her company, but she would have to take some drastic action if she wanted to become his wife. The more she thought about it, the more the idea appealed to her, and not least because it would enable her to look down her nose at the Countess of Harting whom she would then outrank.

Chapter 20

Alicia expected a fight. Her mother wanted her to marry Mr Hampton and she had refused to consider his suit. Her mother was not one to accept defeat gracefully. Alicia waited with bated breath for the next onslaught. She fully anticipated that her mother would keep returning to the subject, trying to wear her down with her arguments as she had done on previous occasions when their opinions had clashed. She would appeal to her better nature, moan about her stupidity and urge her to take advice from her loving mother, who was so much wiser and more experienced in the ways of the world than she.

Though normally easy-going and adaptable, there were times when Alicia could be as stubborn as her mother. She was not going to be persuaded to change her mind about Mr Hampton. Perhaps if there had not been a Mr Merry she might have been tempted, but the comparison was too unfavourable. She did not love Mr Hampton, shared no interests with him and he did not make her laugh. No, she was not going to change her mind, but she did not like conflict and dreaded the confrontations that lay ahead before she won her point.

However, when Alicia next saw her mother, she found, much to her surprise, that she was in a sunny temper. No brooding, no recriminations, not even one reference to the subject of their disagreement.

"Mother, I am sorry that I cannot—" Alicia began, anxious to clear the air.

"Say no more," her mother interrupted with a big reassuring smile.

"But—"

"No buts. Let us forget all about that and talk about something much more exciting. Vauxhall Gardens open next week. How would you like to visit them?"

Alicia was becoming extremely nervous. She loved her mother dearly, but had lived with her too long to suppose that she was planning a visit to the gardens for her benefit alone. What mischief was her mother brewing? She hoped very much that she was not planning to throw her in the way of Mr Hampton in the hopes that she would change her mind.

"That would be delightful. You know how much I would love to see Vauxhall," she said. "But if you are planning to visit in the company of Mr Hampton and the Duke, I fear I will have to forgo the pleasure."

"What kind of mother do you think I am?" Mrs Westlake asked. Alicia thought it better not to respond.

"Mr Lamont has kindly offered to accompany us."

"Mr Lamont!" Alicia could not hide the dismay in her voice. On the only occasion that she had been obliged to dance with him, he had repeatedly squeezed her hand in a most familiar way and she had to admit that he made her flesh creep. "I thought you said he was a fortune hunter and not to be encouraged."

Mrs Westlake pouted. "He may not be of the highest ton but he pays me pretty compliments and if you are determined to refuse Mr Hampton's company, it is the best that I can do. It is not as if we are inundated with gentlemen offering us their company," she said crossly.

Alicia thought that this display of temper was much

more in character and she resolutely put aside her fears that her mother was not being entirely honest with her and set about soothing her back to her cheerful mood.

She would not have felt so confident if she had known that her mother was busy planning her visit to Vauxhall to coincide with that of the Duke, who had mentioned his plans to attend the opening night the last time they had met.

Alicia had heard her father talk about Vauxhall on many occasions. Since she was a child, she had been captivated by his descriptions of the magical gardens—a world of enchantment that had seemed more like fantasy than a real place. She could picture it now, standing in the gardens at dusk, waiting for the whistle blast that would announce the lighting of the lamps. Another blast and all the lamps would be lit simultaneously, bringing the fairytale world to life in a flood of lights, twinkling in the creeping darkness.

The only thing marring Alicia's anticipation of the visit was her mother's choice of companion. She supposed she had no right to complain, but she could not get over her mother's change of attitude toward Mr Lamont, whose company was certainly not going to increase their consequence.

It soon transpired that they were not the only people to be descending on Vauxhall for the opening night. They had to wait for more than half an hour for a boat to take them up river and by the time they arrived at the entrance to the pleasure grounds, it was already dark. Alicia was disappointed to have missed the lamp-lighting, but she was too excited to dwell on it for long. Mr Lamont paid their admission fees and they passed with a crowd of other visitors into the dim entrance hall. They emerged from the gloom of the passageway into a flood of light from the fairy-like illuminations for which Vauxhall was famous. The effect was all that Alicia could have asked for.

Mr Lamont felt his luck must be turning. Mrs Westlake was much more sympathetic than usual. The wealthy widow had not seen fit to smile on him before. He began to see prosperity around the corner and put himself out to please the lady and her daughter. He walked down the central walkway with Miss Westlake on one arm and Mrs Westlake on the other, well-pleased to be seen in the company of two beautiful and wealthy ladies.

At length, he conducted them to the supper table he had secured, and encouraged them to be seated. He was eager to display his valued guests for all the passers-by to see. Perhaps if word got out that he was making headway with the wealthy widow or her daughter, his creditors would stop breathing down his neck so assiduously. He magnanimously ordered some of the exorbitant fare that was on offer—the famous slices of wafer thin ham and other delicacies and a bottle of over-priced wine. He shuddered slightly at the cost, but saw it more in terms of an investment than an expense.

Alicia drank in the atmosphere of the busy gardens. She thought that she would never tire of it. It was fascinating to watch the constant stream of people going past their box. It seemed as if the whole world was in Vauxhall for the opening night. The moderate entrance fee allowed people from vastly different spheres of life to mingle and be entertained, side by side. At Vauxhall, everyone who had paid their entrance fee was equal. Gentlemen with their ladies walked the same paths as tradesmen and their wives, and working unseen all around them were the courtesans and pickpockets who

haunted the area, looking for their prey. Alicia was glad
that the faithful Rowson was keeping watch over them.
She had no confidence that Mr Lamont would be able to
protect them from the unwanted attentions of inebriated
aristocrats or encroaching tradesmen, but knew she
could rely on her mother's trusted manservant.

A few people she knew paused at the box to exchange a few words, but she recognised others who
walked on past, either oblivious to her presence or
choosing to ignore her. Among those she recognised was
the Prince of Wales. She was more than a little surprised
to see him strutting along with a host of his cronies and
Mrs Fitzherbert hanging on his arm. Clearly even royalty
was not above paying a visit to Vauxhall. She was
amused to find Mr Lamont quick to point out those
members of the ton that he spotted, nodding gracefully
toward them as they went by as if trying to prove that he
was on terms of intimacy with them. Alicia was relieved
that he did not catch the Prince of Wales' attention by
his manoeuvres; it would have been most embarrassing.

At the appointed time, a bell rang to announce the
nightly performance of the Cascade. Mrs Westlake
immediately expressed a desire to see the artificial
waterfall that had been so much improved since the days
of her youth. She had heard that the show now included
a storm. Mr Lamont readily rose to his feet and, with a
lady on each arm, led them to the area of woodland
where the famous spectacle was situated.

As soon as she reasonably could, Alicia withdrew her
arm from Mr Lamont's grasp and moved a little away
from her mother and her companion so that she could
watch the Cascade in peace.

"It is done by mechanics," a voice behind her said.

Alicia recognised it instantaneously. Despite her

recent doubts over his morals, she was heartily glad to see him. "Mr Merry, I quite thought you had gone out of town."

"And I thought you had become part of the Duke's party."

Alicia blushed. "I … my mother …"

"It is all achieved by a mechanical device that gives the illusion of a waterfall," Mr Merry said, changing the subject.

"Oh. But maybe I just want to enjoy the spectacle instead of analysing how it works."

Mr Merry considered this. "That does not seem very likely, but if the illusion gives you pleasure, then by all means, be amused. I could explain how it works, but if you are not interested, I will cease to bother you with my company."

Alicia was torn. She had seen so little of Mr Merry in the past few weeks and though she knew she should not encourage his attentions, she did not want him to go. Besides, she was inquisitive and wanted to know how it worked. Her mother was too absorbed to pay any heed.

"Very well. Tell me," she said.

Mr Merry grinned, making his face seem much younger. He proceeded to explain, very clearly and succinctly, the device behind the Cascade.

"You would make an excellent teacher, Mr Merry," she exclaimed.

"But my job is so easy when I have only one pupil and she is eager to learn."

"Alicia? Where are you?" Mrs Westlake's voice called out. The Cascade's performance was over and she had finally noticed that her daughter was not standing next to her as she had assumed.

"Mother, I …" How was she going to explain Mr

Merry's presence? It had all the appearance of a secret assignation. She turned to say goodbye, but Mr Merry had already gone. He had slipped away into the darkness. She felt a pang of regret. It was too bad that Mr Merry was so ineligible in every way.

They returned to the box for the supper that Mr Lamont had arranged. She was not very impressed with the food. The ham was as thin as it was reported to be, but this was anything but a virtue, as the amount of meat in each slice was minimal. Her mother and Mr Lamont laughed and flirted over the costly bottle of wine. Her mother's behaviour was incomprehensible. Alicia could not understand why she was making up to a man whom she had previously stigmatised as a fortune hunter. What was her mother up to? She soon found out.

Without warning, Mrs Westlake bounced out of her seat and announced her intention of going for a walk. Mr Lamont expressed himself happy to accompany her. He was thinking of the dark walks and of pressing his suit upon Mrs Westlake while she seemed so amenable.

"You look tired, Alicia," Mrs Westlake said to her daughter. "Stay here—Rowson will look after you." She laid a restraining hand on her shoulder when Alicia would have risen to announce that she was perfectly happy to join them for a walk. "No, no, dear. Stay here and rest. We will not be long."

Alicia was not very impressed at being left alone with just a footman, even such a superior footman as Rowson. Although she was sure that Rowson was more than able to protect her from the riff raff that mingled with the gentry at Vauxhall, she felt the lack of companions keenly. She was afraid that it gave the impression that she was inviting company, a view that only increased when two young gentlemen, decidedly the worse for drink, paused at her supper box and started flirting outrageously with her.

She recognised them immediately as the Duke of Bedford and the Marquess of Worcester, but soon realised that they were far too drunk to have any idea who she was. In fact, it soon became clear that they thought she was not entirely respectable.

"Well, 'ere's a pretty one, Worcester," the Duke of Bedford drawled, leaning over the table and squeezing Alicia's chin in a very familiar manner.

"Excuse me, Your Grace. This is not your table," Alicia said firmly, shrinking into the corner of the box.

"Now, now. Don't run away, my pretty," the Duke of Bedford continued, seating himself on the bench next to Alicia. "Let's 'ave something to drink."

The Marquess sat down on the opposite side and helped himself to a glass of wine, spilling a good deal on the table in the process.

Alicia felt trapped. "I think these gentlemen are leaving, Rowson," she said loudly. She looked meaningfully at the footman who needed no further encouragement.

"Very good, Miss," Rowson said, taking hold of the first of the befuddled lords and pulling him forcibly out of the box and dumping him unceremoniously on the path. He did not scruple to rid his young mistress of such unwelcome company, but was glad that the two young noblemen were far too drunk to remember his rough treatment of their persons.

"Where d'e go?" the Marquess of Worcester asked. He peered over the far end of the table and saw his companion spread across the ground. "We going?" he asked as Rowson grabbed him by the shoulders and threw him on top of his companion. "Glad you were there, old fellow. Might have hurt otherwise." He picked himself up and bowed eloquently to Alicia. "Very nice to have met you, Miss—" he muttered as he keeled over on top of his friend again.

Alicia sat back in the box and wondered how many more unsolicited visitors Rowson would have to get rid of before her mother and Mr Lamont returned. She wished that she could go after them, but she would hardly be better off out of the box than in it.

"Miss Westlake. Were these gentlemen troubling you? I could not help noticing their precipitate arrival on the footpath." Mr Merry looked around. "I do not see your mother? Have you lost her again?"

"Oh, Mr Merry. You cannot believe how glad I am to see you."

"I am flattered. How may I be of service?"

"Please could you accompany me to find my mother and Mr Lamont? I do not feel safe here. I should be most grateful."

"Your wish is my command," he said gallantly and helped her out of the supper box. "You looked like a damsel in distress. I am only sorry that you have suffered some unpleasantness. It is delightful to appear as a knight in shining armour coming to rescue a beautiful lady with so little effort."

Mr Merry guided her carefully round the two gentlemen sprawled on the path in front of the supper box. They seemed to be in no hurry to rise from where they had fallen. Alicia shuddered. Vauxhall was a lovely place, but the presence of a gentleman could be deemed a necessity to guard a lady from receiving unwanted attentions.

"You need not worry over them, Miss Westlake. They are unlikely to remember your face let alone the way in which they were despatched from your supper box! Just as well, as it is not usually the way one treats a peer of the realm."

Alicia grunted. "If one does not behave like a gentleman, one should not expect to be treated like one."

"Very good, Miss Westlake, but entirely too revolutionary for today's aristocracy. I see you are with the reformers."

Alicia shook her head, but the smile on her lips belied the words. "I know nothing of politics. It is a man's province."

"Just so, Miss Westlake."

Meanwhile, Mrs Westlake was hurrying the bewildered Mr Lamont down one of the darker paths, walking unfashionably fast.

"My dear Mrs Westlake," he panted. "You are putting me quite out of breath. Is there any hurry?"

Mrs Westlake was quick to dissemble. "Mr Lamont, if we linger, my daughter might decide to come after us and then we shall never be alone."

Mr Lamont took her hand and gave it a squeeze. "My dear Madam, my most ardent desire is to be alone with you."

Mrs Westlake tried not to shudder. Mr Lamont's hand was clammy and possessive and she wanted nothing more than to push him away, but that would not serve her purpose. With great resolution, she held onto his hand and by this means dragged her puffing beau behind her. They hurried along until, as they were turning a corner, she saw the two gentlemen she was looking for, strolling along the path toward them. She sighed with relief. She did not think she could stomach much more of Mr Lamont's repulsive person.

Hastily pulling her companion away from the corner,

she looked sweetly up into Mr Lamont's face, which was red and puffy from the exertions that she had just put him through.

"At last we are alone," she said, gazing up into his unprepossessing countenance and giving his hand an ardent squeeze.

"Mrs Westlake!" he oozed, and, taking her in his arms, he lent forward to plant a kiss on her lips. She managed to divert his intent by turning her face at the last moment, so that the kiss meant for her lips landed on her cheek. Undeterred, he followed it up with a second attempt. As he did so, she spotted the two gentlemen coming round the corner—the Duke of Wessex and his brother, Lord Richard.

Mrs Westlake gave a little squeal and pulled herself away from the astonished Mr Lamont's hold and ran toward the two gentlemen. "Please—help me!" she cried and fainted in the arms of the Duke of Wessex.

Lord Richard shouted after Mr Lamont, and took a few steps toward him. But Mr Lamont had too much respect for his own skin to hang around waiting to be accosted by some unknown gentleman. He did not understand Mrs Westlake's behaviour. One minute she had seemed receptive to his advances; the next, she was struggling to get out of his arms as if he were assaulting her. Women! However, he knew danger when he saw it. Self-preservation was his foremost priority at such a time and he hurried away as fast as his already tired legs could carry him, leaving Mrs Westlake to whatever fate she had run off to.

"Why it is Mrs Westlake!" Lord Richard declared, eyeing the apparently unconscious form in the Duke's arms. "How very odd."

The Duke thought that it was odd too. In fact, unless

he was very much mistaken, he would have said that it was a ruse. He looked down at the lady in his arms and smiled. She was certainly a pretty handful and he was not above feeling his pulses beginning to race at the thought of the feminine charms lying beneath his grasp.

Mrs Westlake decided it was time to stir. "Oh, thank you," she said in a feeble voice, opening her eyes and bestowing a grateful smile on the Duke. "Oh, Your Grace. How very fortunate that you should come along just at the right time."

"How very fortunate indeed," replied the Duke, with the hint of a smile. He gulped hard as she negligently pushed her body against him.

Alicia and Mr Merry were a few paths away when they heard Mrs Westlake's plaintiff cry.

"Mother!" Alicia exclaimed and started running along the walkway, followed closely by Mr Merry.

As she turned the corner, Alicia stopped short, so that Mr Merry almost ran into her. There was her mother, in the Duke of Wessex's arms, looking longingly up into the Duke's face as she slowly came out of her 'faint'. There was no sign of the hapless Mr Lamont. Her mother did not look like she was in distress. In fact, she looked remarkably contented for someone who just five minutes before had been heard screaming.

"Mother, I thought—" she began to murmur, more to herself than anyone else.

"Exactly what you were supposed to think," Mr Merry said cynically, looking over her shoulder at the charming tableau. "That your mother was in trouble and needed rescuing. It looks as if she has already been rescued. I do not think your presence is required. She will not thank you for extricating her too promptly from a situation which she has clearly taken such trouble to engineer."

Alicia was appalled. Surely her mother could not have planned the whole scene? The Duke was looking down into her mother's eyes with an expression of tenderness combined with amusement and, dare she admit it, desire. No doubt that was in response to her mother flickering her eyelids pathetically at the Duke and the rather compromising position in which the Duke was holding her.

Lord Richard stood by looking extremely uncomfortable. Mr Merry's expression was as cold as ice. She wished she could find an explanation to excuse her mother's conduct which appeared in such a bad light.

"I ... I ..."

"Words are quite unnecessary, Miss Westlake," Mr Merry said curtly.

Mrs Westlake was none too pleased to see Alicia's arrival, but hid her irritation admirably. "Alicia, my dear. How on earth did you find me?"

"I heard your cry, Mother."

"I had a fright, my dear, but, as you can see," she said, looking longingly up into the Duke's face, "I am quite safe. Mercifully the Duke came to my rescue."

Yes, Alicia saw. It was humiliating, but she had to make the best of it.

"Your Grace," she said, sweeping a curtsey. "What a happy chance that my mother came upon you in her distress."

"Yes," replied the Duke. "A lucky chance indeed. Mrs Westlake, do you think you can walk? Here, take my arm."

The Duke started walking back toward the main avenue with Mrs Westlake leaning rather more heavily on him for support than was warranted. Alicia looked round for Mr Merry, but he had gone. Reluctantly, she took Lord Richard's proffered arm and followed the Duke along the avenue in silence, dwelling miserably on her mother's atrocious behaviour.

Chapter 21

Throughout the journey home, mother and daughter maintained an unbroken silence. Mrs Westlake made no attempt to justify her behaviour at Vauxhall. She was well aware that she had violated her daughter's sensibilities by throwing herself at the Duke, but felt that she would be entirely vindicated if she managed to secure him.

Alicia was not just embarrassed; she was mortified. She was so angry and disappointed with her mother that she could not bring herself to discuss the subject. What must Mr Merry think of her mother? And what must he think of her, by association? How could she ever look him in the eye again?

But in addition to her personal humiliation, she feared the repercussions of the evening if it should ever become widely known that her mother had so pointedly set out to ensnare the Duke.

She decided that it would be as well if they kept a low profile for a while. No doubt, her mother was planning to pursue the object of her embarrassing farce, but Alicia intended to prevent her and had a very shrewd idea of how it could be achieved.

Mrs Westlake never rose early for breakfast, giving Alicia the perfect opportunity to put her plan into action. Without any preamble, she informed Lady Granger about the drama of the previous night.

"My mother has had quite a shock," Alicia announced in a confidential voice. "Someone tried to molest her in the gardens and if it were not for the fortuitous arrival of the Duke of Wessex, who knows what would have been the result."

Lady Granger's attitude was all that she could have hoped for. "How dreadful!" she exclaimed. "I will send for the doctor at once. Her poor nerves. I will talk to chef. He will know how best to tempt her appetite after such an ordeal. My poor cousin. I will go to her immediately."

When Mrs Westlake awoke, she found herself the centre of unwanted attention. Any attempt on her behalf to leave her bed was speedily quashed by her cousin. "No, no, my dear Susannah. On no account must you get up today. Such a shock. How dreadful for you. There is no need to be brave. The doctor will be here shortly. I am sure he will prescribe something to soothe your nerves."

"But I—"

"No, Susannah. You must rest." Lady Granger could be very firm when it came to matters of health. Mrs Westlake had no choice but to submit, or admit that it had been a ruse, which, of course, she was not prepared to do. She waited in vain for news that the Duke had called, but he did not. Marie did bring up a beautiful bouquet of hothouse flowers that he had sent, with his best wishes for her recovery, but he did not call. She was disappointed, but there was always tomorrow.

She agreed to see Dr Black with poorly concealed reluctance, but by the time he arrived, she had decided that it would do her no disservice for people to know that the doctor had waited on her for the delicacy of her nerves and gracefully submitted to the consultation. She had some trouble persuading the doctor that she had no need of being bled, and was grateful when Dr Black prescribed a bottle of restorative medicine instead. With the threat of bloodletting held over her head, she willingly agreed to stay in bed and rest.

The next morning, Mrs Westlake was obliged to keep to her room again. On no account would Lady Granger hear of her getting up until the doctor pronounced her fit to do so. Mrs Westlake hid her frustration and bore with her cousin's ministrations as best she could. But Lady Granger was in her element. She fussed and cosseted and talked incessantly of poor Susannah's nerves until she gave her cousin the headache. Eager to be released from Lady Granger's overpowering solicitude, Mrs Westlake seized upon her now genuine indisposition and begged to be left alone so that she could sleep.

Immediately Lady Granger's attitude changed. Mrs Westlake might as well have asked to be left alone to die in peace. Lady Granger crept around the room on tiptoe, pulling the curtains closed herself and whispering constantly that she was sure Susannah would feel more the thing when she had built up her strength again.

Alicia went to sit in her mother's room for an hour before dressing for dinner. She cheerfully informed her mother that the Duke had called to make enquiries after her health but that Lady Granger had given such an exaggerated account of her condition that she thought it unlikely that the Duke would repeat the visit for a week at least.

Mrs Westlake was frustrated that her cousin's concern had kept her in her room but was somewhat encouraged that the Duke had at least paid a visit to ask after her.

After ten days of enforced bed-rest, Mrs Westlake thought she could bear it no longer. Her natural inclination was always to be busy and her enforced confinement, coupled with her anxiety to see the Duke, was making her extremely irritable. Lady Granger scolded her, saying that it was always so when you began to feel better and that if she was not careful, she would fret herself into a fever.

Mrs Westlake made a supreme effort to be polite and gently asked her cousin to beg the doctor to call so that he could confirm that she was well enough to be up and about again. Lady Granger gladly sent a message to Dr Black, whom she was only too ready to consult on any and every matter of health.

She was still waiting for the doctor's visit when Alicia went to sit with her that afternoon. Mrs Westlake was eager to know whether the Duke had called again.

"Yes, Mother. He came with Mr Hampton a short while ago."

Mrs Westlake let out a contented sigh. "How very thoughtful," she cooed. "I am sorry to have missed them, but I shall be up to receive them next time they call."

Alicia said nothing, anxiously biting her lip.

Mrs Westlake saw the tell-tale sign of her daughter's nervousness and immediately demanded to know what she was not telling her.

"If you must know, Mother, His Grace called to take his leave of you."

Mrs Westlake looked aghast. "Take his leave? You must be mistaken. Surely he would not leave London now. Tell me you are teasing me, Alicia."

"I am sorry, Mother. They are leaving town at the end of the week."

At these words, Mrs Westlake became very agitated. It was so frustrating to be kept in bed. Aside from the anxiety caused by her continued incarceration, she felt perfectly well. What she wanted was to see the Duke. She felt sure that all that was needed was a little push in the right direction. She must get up and try to see him before he left town.

She would have rung for Marie and insisted that she dress her immediately, but at that moment, there was a knock on the door and Lady Granger crept into the room, followed by the doctor.

"Now here is Dr Black, Susannah, just as you requested." She turned to the doctor. "My cousin declares that she is quite well again, doctor, but I fear that she is far from it. She frets continually and complains of the headache. I am most anxious that she does not do too much too soon and suffer from a relapse."

The doctor nodded wisely. Lady Granger was a very valuable patient and although he saw little wrong with her relation, it was imperative that he did not fail to fulfil her expectations.

"I am sorry to see you still looking so pale, Mrs Westlake," he said.

Mrs Westlake grimaced. Pale. Of course she was pale. She had been cooped up inside for the best part of two weeks.

"I am convinced that all I need is a little fresh air, doctor," she replied.

"I am not so sure, Mrs Westlake. You have undergone a great trial and we must see you fully restored. A little sea air would undoubtedly prove beneficial, but I recommend sea bathing to complete your recovery. I am a great believer in seawater for restoring health."

"I am sure that is not necessary," she replied, but the

doctor continued as though she had not spoken.

"Doctor Russell was, of course, always in favour of Brighthelmstone, but a colleague of mine, a Doctor Crane, is a great advocate for Weymouth. Indeed, I have visited the town myself and cannot say enough to recommend it. The sands there have a very safe and gentle slope, making them ideal for sea bathing."

Mrs Westlake decided that her best course of action was to humour the doctor and hear him out and then find an excuse for not following his advice. She had no intention of paying a visit to the seaside. She nodded encouragingly as Dr Black warmed to his subject.

"The town is not lacking in polite entertainment. There are some excellent assembly rooms as well as several libraries and the scenery around the town is quite beautiful."

Mrs Westlake thought some enquiry was necessary to impress upon the doctor that she was seriously considering his recommendation. "What about antiquities? My daughter is very fond of castles," Mrs Westlake added facetiously.

"Then she will not be disappointed. Weymouth has its very own castle – a ruin called Sandsfoot – and there is a solid Tudor fortification over on the Isle of Portland which can be reached by a short ferry ride."

Mrs Westlake smiled. "It sounds like the ideal sea bathing resort, but I really do not feel—"

"Now you must not be worrying that Weymouth attracts no persons of quality," the doctor continued. "The Duke of Gloucester has a house on the seafront and," he whispered, "following the recommendations of my fellow doctors, the King himself will be staying there shortly to convalesce after his recent illness."

Despite herself, Mrs Westlake was interested. You

could not ignore the movements of royalty. "That is indeed a recommendation," she admitted.

Dr Black nodded. "You could do far worse than follow in the King's footsteps, and so I told Lord Richard Hampton."

Mrs Westlake's attention was now well and truly caught, but, irritatingly, the doctor seemed to feel that he had said enough and was not forthcoming with any further information. After waiting several moments for the doctor to resume, she casually asked: "And did Lord Richard listen to your advice?"

The doctor nodded, smiling broadly. "Indeed he did. Lord Richard has persuaded the Duke to quit town and take a sojourn in Weymouth at my personal suggestion. Lord Richard suffers terribly from the gout and I was quick to recommend sea bathing as a remedy. I was able to give him the name of an eminent Weymouth physician in whom I have every confidence. I could even recommend a suitable property in town whose owner I happened to know was wishful of leasing his house for a month or two whilst he went abroad."

Mrs Westlake could not believe her good luck. So that was why the Duke was leaving town. Quite by accident she had discovered both the cause of his departure and his destination and the doctor had, quite unwittingly, supplied her with the perfect excuse to follow him there.

Mrs Westlake appeared to consider the doctor's words. "So you believe that sea bathing would help restore me to full health?"

"Yes, yes, Mrs Westlake. Seawater cures many things," Dr Black assured her.

"And it is not too difficult to secure accommodation at this time of the season?"

"Weymouth is still relatively unknown, Mrs Westlake. I am sure you will find a number of suitable lodgings on offer. Indeed, the Duke was perfectly satisfied with the property I was able to recommend to him and waits only for the owner to depart for Italy in the second or third week of June before taking up residence."

"You cannot do better than follow the dear doctor's advice, Susannah," urged Lady Granger, who would have unhesitatingly obeyed whatever instructions the doctor cared to give her.

"Well, if you really think it will do me good, I suppose that I will have to go," Mrs Westlake conceded. But though her voice might suggest some reluctance, secretly she was overjoyed at how well things had worked out.

Chapter 22

Mrs Westlake did not raise any objection to staying in her bedroom the rest of the day, but the next morning, she insisted on being dressed and appeared at the breakfast table in the best of spirits.

"I shall be sorry to see you go, Susannah. It has been such a comfort to me to have your company," said Lady Granger.

Alicia looked at her mother enquiringly.

"Dr Black has recommended a visit to the seaside to complete my recovery," Mrs Westlake replied.

Alicia waited for her mother to continue.

"We leave for Weymouth just as soon as Rowson can secure us a house there."

Alicia could not conceal her amazement. She was immediately suspicious. She knew that her mother had not been ill, and yet here she was, meekly submitting to the doctor's advice for a recuperative visit to the seaside.

"Then we are to quit London?" she asked.

Mrs Westlake took her daughter's hand. "Forgive me for whisking you away before the season is quite over, but the doctor recommends the sea, and so to the sea we will go."

Alicia could not comprehend her mother's extreme haste to be removed from the capital, but was happy to comply with her wishes. She was not sure she had the courage to face Mr Merry again and could not complain at being precluded from the opportunity of doing so. On the other hand, she was prevented from offering an excuse for her mother's behaviour and the thought of being sunk in his esteem forever left her feeling much lower than her mother, for whose benefit they were supposedly making the trip. Perhaps the sea air would revive her spirits as well.

The whole household was plunged into chaos as the Westlakes made preparations to leave. In the meantime, Rowson quietly and efficiently made all the necessary arrangements to ensure their smooth removal to Weymouth. He returned to London the following day having secured a lease on a property on the seafront in York Buildings, just a few minutes' walk from where the Duke of Gloucester's house stood. He arranged for horses to be sent ahead along the route so that Mrs Westlake could travel the whole way served by her own stable and her own liveried postilions. He arranged for the staff to travel to Weymouth in advance to prepare the house and ensured that the chaise was adjusted for the long distance journey ahead by removing the coachman's box so that the Westlakes' view would not be obscured.

In less than a week, they were on the move. Alicia thought that her mother had been surprisingly good-tempered whilst they were getting ready for the trip south. She had not mentioned the absent Duke once. Then, after several days of unremitting rain, the sun finally broke through on the morning of their departure. Mrs Westlake declared that this was a good omen for their journey.

But her sunny temper did not last long. Marie was complaining vociferously about having to sit on the outside of the travelling chariot. For reasons best known to herself, Mrs Westlake had decided that Rowson and Marie should travel on the rumble seat behind her carriage rather than inside the coach bearing the luggage. Marie felt that it was beneath her dignity to sit outside, where she was subject to the elements, and did not scruple to protest to her mistress about such poor treatment. Mrs Westlake ignored all her complaints, but Alicia could tell that her mother's patience was wearing thin.

As she sat down in the carriage next to her daughter, she noticed for the first time what Alicia was wearing and scowled. "Why have you worn that old thing?" she asked, looking disapprovingly at the heavy brown travelling coat. "You should have worn your new blue one. It is so much more fashionable and it brings out the colour of your eyes."

Alicia looked at her suspiciously. "I do not see why it matters what I wear to travel in, Mother. I find the blue one does very well for going about town, but it is fashionably thin and this one will keep me much warmer on the journey. Besides, I do not want the blue to become travel-stained or I shall not be able to wear it around Weymouth."

Mrs Westlake mumbled that it was too late to do anything about it now anyway and let the matter pass.

The carriage was not running as smoothly as usual. The roads had suffered in the recent rains and it was a miracle that they were not completely waterlogged. Soon after entering Hampshire, they stopped for refreshments and a change of horses at the White Horse in Alton and Alicia took the opportunity to stretch her legs. When she returned to the carriage, her mother was deep in consultation with Rowson and the postilion. The postilion did not look very happy. He obviously did not like what he was being told and was shaking his head solemnly from side to side. Eventually he shrugged his shoulders and mounted, ready to leave.

"Is there a problem?" Alicia asked her mother.

"Not at all, but we need to alter our route, so do not be surprised when we leave the post road."

It seemed an unusual course to take, but when Alicia asked why, her mother mumbled something about the weather and she was too tired to pay much heed. All she cared about was reaching a nice warm bed for the night and it was some miles before they were due to stop. She closed her eyes and tried to sleep.

Half an hour later, she was awoken abruptly by the chaise lurching to one side and coming to a full stop. Alicia pulled down the window to try and see what the problem was. It soon became apparent that the wheels on one side had become stuck, firmly, in the mud. Once off the post road, the state of the lanes was indifferent. Even a slight deviation from the carriageway could be problematic and the area to the side of the road where the coach was lodged was a muddy swamp, deeply rutted by the constant passage of farm vehicles which used the road regularly.

Despite the postilion's attempts, the vehicle would not shift.

"There is nothing for it, my dear," declared Mrs Westlake. "We shall have to walk to find shelter whilst Rowson finds some help to extricate our carriage from the mud."

Alicia wondered if her mother was feeling quite well. "But Mother, it is so dirty. We will ruin our clothes."

"Nonsense. The exercise will bring the bloom back to our cheeks. This way."

"But surely we passed a village not that long ago?

Would it not be better if we stayed in the carriage while Rowson went back and got help?"

"Alicia—we are going to walk."

"Yes, Mother." Mrs Westlake could be very stubborn. Alicia knew that there was no point arguing if her mind was made up. She could refuse, of course, but she could hardly let her mother go off with just a grumpy maid for company and the servants had enough on their hands to manage the horses and arrange for the trapped vehicle to be freed from the mud without complicating matters further. Alicia reflected that it was just as well she had put on her old coat after all.

"Come along, Marie," Mrs Westlake commanded. Rowson handed the reluctant maid down from the chaise and she joined her mistress on the road. Mrs Westlake started walking purposefully along the carriageway.

Marie was grumbling. "'Dis is a fine way to treat your maid, huh? First, I 'ave to travel outside and now, I 'ave to walk in zis mud. In Paris, we have dignity. Zese roads are 'orrible."

"Never mind, Marie," Alicia consoled the disgruntled maid. "You can afford to put up with a few inconveniences for the immense salary that my mother pays you."

"But of course. If she did not, I would go."

They continued to walk along the road, but they did not seem to be any closer to finding refuge. There was no sign of a village or even a farmhouse where they could seek help. Alicia began to despair of discovering the assistance that her mother seemed sure they would find. She wished she had tried harder to persuade her mother to walk back the way they had driven. She was sure they would have reached the village they had passed in the carriage by now.

"I think we should have gone the other way," Alicia called after her mother.

"No, dear," Mrs Westlake replied brightly. "This is the right way, I am sure."

There was nothing for Alicia to do but follow.

In a short while, the road passed a farm track on the right-hand side and beyond the track, the road was banked by a wall, indicating that they had reached the edge of someone's estate.

"Oh look: an entrance!" Mrs Westlake exclaimed helpfully as they came upon an elaborate archway, complete with a splendid wrought iron gate. "Perhaps we could ask for help here." Alicia looked at her mother doubtfully. The surprise seemed feigned rather than genuine as if she had known all along where she was heading.

The lodge keeper was all concern when the ladies explained their predicament. He hailed a lad to bring round the pony cart and soon the two ladies and their maid were being driven up the driveway to a magnificent house. The avenue was lined on both sides with huge beech trees which joined above the road to form a near-perfect arch. All around them the parkland was scattered with deer and the prospect down the hill toward the house was breathtaking.

The lad stopped the cart at the front door and jumped down. He shouted to a stable boy to come and hold the reins and then handed the ladies down from their rather basic transport with great state. He then darted to the front door where he rang the bell with gusto. Clearly this was not a common proceeding, as the butler looked ready to send him packing round to the back entrance before he noticed the group of ladies behind him.

"Mr Robinson said as 'ow I was to bring 'em up to the 'ouse. Their carriage 'as 'ad a accident."

The butler nodded at the lad to dismiss him and Mrs Westlake stepped forward, handing him her visiting card. "We are so sorry to inconvenience you, but perhaps we may speak to your master? Our carriage has had a mishap and we are quite without transport home."

The butler glanced at the card, but the name meant nothing to him. However, he could recognise quality from a mile off and there was no doubt in his mind about the price of these ladies' gowns. And there was a maid. Bramber knew his duty. "Please step into the book room, Madam, and I will see if His Grace is at home."

The ladies were ushered into a small ante-room which had a fire blazing despite the time of year. Bramber closed the door on the uninvited guests and went in search of his master, but not before instructing one of the footmen to regale the lady's maid with refreshments in the servants' quarters. Marie brightened considerably. "Zis is very nice. It is a très belle maison," she confided to the footman, who gave her an encouraging smile once the butler was out of sight.

No sooner had the door shut then Alicia rounded on her mother. "Your Grace?" she asked incredulously.

"Mm. I believe it is the home of His Grace, the Duke of Wessex."

"What you mean is that you know very well it is his home and you have contrived an entry in the most despicable way. I only hope he will refuse to see us."

"How can you be so ungrateful, Alicia? This is all for you. If I were to become the next Duchess, your position in society would be secure."

"Mother, no!" Alicia snapped, her embarrassment exacerbating her normally placid temper. "I cannot control how you choose to behave, but do not, I beg of you, pretend that it is all for me. How could you do such a thing? First you throw yourself at the Duke in Vauxhall Gardens and now you thrust yourself upon him in his own home. How could you?"

Mrs Westlake had the grace to look guilty. "I am just helping things along, Alicia. A gentleman may have an inclination, but he may not act on that inclination without a little help. It is rather hard on our sex to be forever waiting for something to happen. It is a lady's right – perhaps even her duty – to help a gentleman see where his best interests lie. And if that gentleman is a duke, why, then the lady has to be a little more inventive or she will lose him completely."

Alicia shook her head in despair. "But how can I face the Duke, Mother? He must know that you have forced your way into his home. If word of this ever gets out, we will be labelled as title hunters, and it will be nothing more than the truth. Mother, please let us go before we have to endure the humiliation of being turned away."

"Go? Are you out of your mind, Alicia? No! I am not going to go after all the effort I have taken to get here. Just you wait and see. The Duke will be glad to receive us. I am convinced that something good will come of this. Now for goodness sake, stop scowling and tidy up your hair, or do you want the Duke to think you are a hoyden?"

Meanwhile, the Duke was dreading another tedious afternoon listening to his brother complaining about his gout, followed by another tedious evening playing cards. His visit to town had left him feeling restless and dissatisfied. He was struggling to readjust to having no one but his brother and nephew for company. After the excitement of London, life at Swanmore was sadly flat. The Duke thought with relief that at least they would be leaving for Weymouth at the end of the week.

Bramber's announcement that they had unexpected visitors could not have been more welcome. The Duke indulged in a silent chuckle as he read the name on the card the butler handed to him. He could not help admiring Mrs Westlake's audacity. He was well aware that she had contrived the Vauxhall rescue, but he chose to be entertained rather than offended and he was by no means immune to her charms.

It was with considerable reluctance that he had left London, but he had put his personal inclinations aside and taken pity on his brother who was in constant pain from his gout and agreed to accompany him to Weymouth. Besides, he was intrigued to see what Mrs Westlake would do next. Now he knew.

Lord Richard was contemptuous, damning Mrs Westlake and her daughter as social climbers and urging his brother to caution. "Wessex, how can you be so naïve?" he moaned. "Swanmore is not on the direct road to anywhere. How can you suppose that the ladies have need of your help by chance? Remember, this is the woman who threw herself at you at Vauxhall!"

The Duke smiled slowly. "Oh, yes, I remember. Are you jealous that she threw herself at me and not you?" he asked.

"Jealous? Of course not!" Lord Richard snapped. "But can you not see? The woman is hunting you!"

This time the Duke laughed out loud. "Ah well, you see, the Duke did not wait upon Mrs Westlake, and so Mrs Westlake has come to wait upon him."

Lord Richard snorted. "God knows I have tried to encourage you to get out a little, find some female companionship. After all, you cannot mourn Denmead forever."

The Duke gave his brother a long stare. Did his brother really think that he was still grieving for his good-for-nothing son? "Mourn Denmead? Why no. Nobody could mourn Denmead forever," he replied in a quiet, somewhat mocking voice.

"I believe that the ladies are awaiting our pleasure," said Mr Hampton, interrupting the awkward silence. "Perhaps we should invite them in to tell us their tale. I for one will be happy to see Mrs Westlake and her daughter again and it would do us good to have some company for the evening."

The Duke agreed. Ignoring his brother's disapproving grunts, he instructed the butler to invite Mrs Westlake and her daughter to step up to the drawing room. "And Bramber, bring some suitable refreshments—some Madeira and I think some lemonade for Miss Westlake."

"Very good, Your Grace."

Alicia was still seething when the butler returned. Her hopes of not being received were immediately dashed. "His Grace is ready to receive you. Please come this way."

The ladies followed the butler up the stairs and into the drawing room. "Mrs Westlake, Miss Westlake," he announced in a voice devoid of all emotion and then withdrew.

"Mrs Westlake, how lovely to see you again," the Duke said, taking Mrs Westlake's hand and kissing it in the grand manner. "You remember my brother, Lord Richard Hampton, and of course you know my nephew, Mr Hampton?"

Lord Richard bowed stiffly and Mr Hampton graciously. Alicia was heartily embarrassed and wished that they had been turned away at the door rather than be subject to such humiliation.

"But must you always be in distress, Mrs Westlake, for our paths to cross?" the Duke continued.

Alicia gasped incredulously. The Duke saw right through her mother, she was sure of it, and yet he was welcoming them into his home. Her mother's behaviour was despicable, but, incredibly, the Duke seemed to realise it and was not offended.

The Duke listened sympathetically to the story of the carriage getting trapped in the mud, merely expressing his surprise that they should have left the post road. Such directness made even the intrepid Mrs Westlake blush and she was grateful that the Duke did not pursue the matter. Instead, he dispatched his men to help extricate the carriage from its unfortunate predicament and bring it up to the house.

By the time that this operation was completed, the day was already far advanced. One of the carriage wheels had been damaged in the process and required mending. There could be no question of the ladies travelling further on their journey that day.

"Providence has brought you to my door," said the Duke, "and who am I to go in the face of providence? You and your daughter must be our guests tonight, Mrs Westlake, for we are in sore need of company. Poor Joshua has been condemned to listen to two old gentlemen's chatter for days and he will grow old before his time unless you take pity on him."

Mrs Westlake was effusive in her thanks and even Alicia was relieved that they would not have to continue their journey that evening. The Duke, still hopeful of making a match between Joshua and Miss Westlake, helpfully placed Alicia next to his nephew at dinner. It was a happy arrangement. Mr Hampton was exerting himself to please Alicia and engaged her in conversation on commonplace topics, distracting her from her mother's behaviour and helping to restore her composure.

Meanwhile, Mrs Westlake, seated with the Duke on her left hand and Lord Richard on her right, set out to entertain the gentlemen with the latest gossip from town.

"I do hope that neither of you gentlemen was much attached to the Opera House," she said, "for it has been burnt to the ground! There the dancers were, practising their steps like every other Wednesday evening, when their rehearsal was interrupted by the roof suddenly catching alight. Even as they fled the stage, a beam fell from the ceiling. Such was the ferocity of the fire that in no time at all, the whole place was ablaze."

"What a terrible calamity!" the Duke exclaimed.

"But that is not the worst of it," Mrs Westlake continued in a conspiratorial tone. "The manager is convinced that it was no accident." The two gentlemen were outraged and spent a considerable time berating the unknown felon who had wantonly destroyed the theatre.

Even Lord Richard had to admit that Mrs Westlake was a charming conversationalist. She shared a flow of inconsequential information in an amusing and interesting manner which kept both gentlemen very agreeably entertained over dinner.

The Duke refused to linger long over his port and hurried after the ladies almost immediately to avoid being confronted by his brother again. He had remained single for far too long. There was no subterfuge with Mrs Westlake. She had made a push to be brought to his notice and, he had to confess, she had succeeded. He thought that she was a remarkable woman. He supposed she must be at least forty as her daughter was a grown woman, but her face was still remarkably pretty with clear blue eyes that had twinkled mischievously as she had related the mishap to their carriage in a charming, musical voice.

He settled himself down at Mrs Westlake's side and listened while she chatted about her dear friend the Duchess of Devonshire, who was about to go abroad with her husband and that scheming Lady Elizabeth Foster, to visit Spa.

When Mrs Westlake revealed that she and her daughter were on their way to Weymouth, the Duke was unable to resist a smile.

"What a coincidence, Mrs Westlake," the Duke teased. "The doctor has recommended sea bathing for my brother's gout and we are planning a sojourn in Weymouth too. You must allow me to call upon you and your lovely daughter."

"We look forward to it, Your Grace."

Mrs Westlake lay in the four-poster bed to which she had been shown and thought how delightful it would be if this became her home. On that note, she fell asleep.

Alicia lay awake wondering what the future held. Alicia liked the Duke. But it was not the Duke's face that appeared in her dreams, but a handsome, young face filled with scorn. The Duke might forgive her mother's behaviour, but she doubted very much that Mr Merry would.

Chapter 23

Rowson was a genius. He was the youngest son of an impoverished Yorkshire clergyman who had come south in search of opportunity. Mr Westlake had hired him as a footman and he had risen almost imperceptibly to take charge of the whole household. He was tall and handsome and totally devoted to Mrs Westlake's interests. He ordered her household, hired her servants, ruled her stable and removed all the effort from running a large establishment.

Since her husband's death, Mrs Westlake had come to rely even more heavily on Rowson. He was, undoubtedly, her most faithful manservant and she trusted him implicitly. She often chose to have him accompany her in public to fulfil what was, strictly speaking, a mere footman's role. She was rather partial to having a good-looking man at her beck and call and felt that his presence added greatly to her consequence. And it was very fashionable; the Prince of Wales only employed tall servants.

By the time that the Westlakes arrived in Weymouth, a full complement of staff had been installed in the house that Rowson had hired for them in York Buildings and everything was running like clockwork.

Alicia sat on the window seat of her bedroom, sipping her hot chocolate and enjoying the view. The outlook was beautiful. The windows faced east, looking out across the bay, where the early morning sun was glistening on the surface of the water. Almost below the windows, just beyond the railings, the sands began sloping down toward the sea. She could see the rows of bathing machines lined up on the beach, ready for use by those who wanted to benefit from all the medicinal and healing properties of seawater.

Alicia watched with interest as a bathing machine attendant fitted a horse into the shaft and then, with the bather safely ensconced in the little hut on wheels, led the horse into the water. She was impressed at how docile the animal was, as though walking out through the waves was a perfectly natural thing for it to do. When the bathing machine had progressed far enough, the horse was unharnessed and led back to the beach, whilst the bather gingerly descended the steps into the water.

Alicia looked longingly at the lady tapping the water with her hands and, she imagined, squealing with delight, although she was too far away to hear. Alicia was somewhat sceptical about the healing properties of seawater claimed by Dr Crane, but this in no way lessened her determination to try sea bathing at the earliest possible opportunity.

Mrs Westlake was in high fettle. The Duke had sent them to Weymouth in his own carriage and promised to call when he arrived. Mrs Westlake could not stop talking about it. In point of fact, she could talk of nothing else.

Alicia could stand no more of her mother's self-congratulations. It was not as if the Duke had proposed. Although the Duke had been gracious and paid her mother a good deal of attention, she could not quite rid herself of the fear that he was just amusing himself.

To escape her mother's chatter, Alicia decided to go

for a walk. It was rather early in the morning to see many visitors on the promenade, but the sun was sparkling on the sea and the day beckoned to her. She determined to walk to the circulating library in St Thomas' Street and write their names in the subscription book. With the reluctant Martha in tow, she set out at a leisurely pace, resolving to make her expedition last as long as possible to keep her away from her mother's company.

Just as she was about to enter the library, Alicia was surprised to hear herself being hailed. "Miss Westlake."

She turned and found herself face to face with Mr Merry, who was slightly out of breath from the exertion of walking quickly to catch her up. Alicia blushed. She was all too aware of the circumstances of their last meeting, but Mr Merry seemed to have forgotten all about it.

"Good morning, Miss Westlake. What a beautiful day."

Alicia struggled to regain her composure. "Mr Merry! I thought you were in London. How did you come to be in Weymouth?"

"I could ask you the same question, Miss Westlake. We have both travelled a long way since our last meeting." Alicia held her breath and waited to see if he would say anything more about that awful evening at Vauxhall.

After a moment he continued. "As for me, I have come to keep my brother company. The King is coming to Weymouth and Droxford comes to play attendance on the royal party. And you?"

Alicia hesitated. "The doctor recommended that my mother should come to the seaside to convalesce."

Mr Merry raised his eyebrows. "I am sorry. Has your mother been unwell?"

"My mother—that is—her nerves were somewhat upset and the doctor felt she would benefit from the sea air."

"How strange," observed Mr Merry. "I could have sworn that your mother was made of sterner stuff than that." Alicia felt the colour rising in her cheeks once again, acutely aware that Mr Merry had not been taken in by her mother's act for one moment.

"You say that your brother is here. Are your parents here too?" Alicia asked nervously. "I hope that there will not be any unpleasantness between them and my mother."

"Have no fear of that. My honoured parents are not yet in Weymouth. They wait for the King to come."

"And your brother?" she asked tentatively, remembering how he had followed his mother's lead at the Duchess of Gordon's ball.

"Droxford will do anything for a quiet life." With which withering statement, he dismissed his brother entirely from his mind.

They entered the library together, chatting with the ease of old friends. Mr Merry then bid farewell and took himself off to the reading room, where the London newspapers awaited his perusal.

Alicia entered her own name and her mother's in the subscription book and consoled herself for the loss of Mr Merry's company by finding two very bad novels to take home to read.

Chapter 24

A few days of rain failed to dampen Mrs Westlake's spirits. Nothing would convince her that the Duke was not in earnest and she was constantly wondering aloud how long it would be before he would call. Alicia was less optimistic and waited with some trepidation for what she saw as the inevitable let-down of her mother's high ambitions.

In the event, it was Mrs Westlake and not her daughter who was proved right. Alicia was just suggesting to her mother that a walk on the promenade would be pleasant now the sun had come out, when Rowson announced the Duke and Mr Hampton.

Mrs Westlake dropped a deep curtsey and welcomed her visitors enthusiastically. Alicia could barely conceal her surprise when it transpired that the gentlemen had only just arrived in Weymouth. This was an honour indeed!

"Forgive me for waiting on you in all my dirt, Mrs Westlake," the Duke apologised with a smile, "but I wanted to offer to accompany you to the assembly rooms this evening and feared that if I took the time to change, the opportunity would be lost."

Mrs Westlake positively glowed. "How very kind, Your Grace."

Mr Hampton engaged Alicia in conversation. "Are you enjoying your visit to the seaside, Miss Westlake?"

"Yes, I am," she replied, "though it is much pleasanter when the weather is like today and the sun is shining and I can walk out along the promenade."

"You had better make the most of the peace and quiet while you can. The King is coming to Weymouth to convalesce and where the King goes, many others follow."

"It is strange to think that I might bump into His Majesty on my daily walk," Alicia laughed.

"Will you do me the honour of dancing with me at the assembly rooms tonight?" Mr Hampton asked.

Alicia hesitated. She did not want to encourage Mr Hampton to think that his suit might prosper, but she could not very well refuse the invitation without foregoing the pleasure of dancing completely. Reluctantly, she gave her assent with the appearance of cheerfulness. Mr Hampton did not seem to notice anything amiss and shortly took his leave with the Duke, confident that he had successfully furthered his own interests.

Mrs Westlake entered the assembly rooms on the Duke's arm and Alicia followed behind with Mr Hampton. Alicia might decry the lengths to which her mother was prepared to go to win the Duke, but she had to admit that the cachet of being in the Duke's party added greatly to their comfort.

The very first person they encountered was Lord Droxford. Alicia had not, of course, been formally introduced to him. She had only seen him once before, on that fateful day when his mother had so rudely snubbed her own. He was tall and fair like Mr Merry and, from a distance, she thought they looked alike. However, on closer inspection, she could see they were quite different. Some of Lord Droxford's height could be attributed to the elegant, red, high-heeled shoes he wore and his waistcoat was so elaborately embroidered that the handiwork outshone many of the dresses in the room. Alicia could not imagine Mr Merry tripping across the room in heels or wearing such a beautiful piece of apparel. She had never seen any evidence to suggest that he thought clothes had any purpose other than to keep him warm.

When she examined Lord Droxford's face more closely, she was surprised how dissimilar he looked from Mr Merry. She wondered whether she would have guessed the relationship if she had not known they were brothers. Mr Merry's features were strong and well-defined whereas his brother's features were much more rounded. Mr Merry had a firm chin, but Lord Droxford had his father's square jawline. It was not an ugly face. She supposed that many would call it handsome, but she looked in vain for the animation that characterised his brother's countenance, and realised that it was this that made Mr Merry's face attractive, far more than anything else.

Lord Droxford was a follower. He followed fashion, he followed the ton and he followed his parents. He was no match for his forceful mother and had long since forborne to argue with her. It was far easier and pleasanter to abide by her wishes. But his parents were not in Weymouth and here in front of him was no lesser person than the Duke of Wessex with the woman that his mother had chosen to ostracise on his arm. Lord Droxford did not have above ordinary intelligence, but in the world of fashion he was in his element. He knew what was required of him without any prompting. In a flash, his previous attitude toward Mrs Westlake and her daughter was transformed. His mother would never go against the Duke of Wessex.

"Duke, Hampton," he said, acknowledging the newcomers. "Pray introduce me to your so charming companions."

The Duke did nothing to conceal his amusement. The Viscount clearly thought that it was now expedient to recognise Mrs Westlake and her daughter even though his mother had refused an introduction just a few months previously. But rather than offer an apology for his former behaviour, Lord Droxford was acting as if he had never met them before. The Duke wondered whether the Viscount's mother would follow suit. He thought wickedly of the chagrin it would cause Lady Harting if she was obliged to recognise Mrs Westlake and her daughter after cutting them so openly. It really was most diverting.

"But of course, Droxford. How very backward of me. For some reason I thought that you had already met."

Totally oblivious to the barbed comment, Lord Droxford hastily assured the Duke that he was mistaken. Alicia bit her lip in an attempt to stop a chuckle escaping from her lips. She could not help liking the Duke; he really had a very droll sense of humour.

She bore the introduction with a good grace and was further amused when Lord Droxford proceeded to invite her to dance. How differently he was behaving now they were in the Duke of Wessex's party! She had the distinct feeling that he believed himself to be doing her a great favour by asking her and took no little satisfaction in being able to turn him down as she was already promised to Mr Hampton. She had not anticipated being grateful for the prior engagement, but she had to admit that she was. However, once he had made up his mind, Lord Droxford was not so easily put off. He immediately claimed her hand for the second dance and Alicia found it impossible to refuse.

In contrast to the pompous Viscount, Mr Hampton's unassuming company was pleasantly refreshing. Alicia gave him a dazzling smile as they took their places in the set that was forming. Mr Hampton was not sorry to see that she preferred his company to that of the Viscount. It was the most encouragement that he had received of late and he dared to hope that Miss Westlake was, at last, warming to his suit.

For the second dance, Alicia was obliged to keep her engagement with Lord Droxford. The Viscount came to claim her hand with great state and ponderously led her into the set. For a moment she thought that he would be a clumsy dancer, in danger of stepping on her train. But she need not have worried; the Viscount excelled in all polite attainments.

Lord Droxford complimented Alicia on her performance and asked her how she liked Weymouth.

"Very much so, thank you."

"I think it is a prodigious shame that the King chose Weymouth," he drawled. "Mother was all for Brighthelmstone. Her doctor even suggested it to His Majesty, but Dr Crane had got in there first and the King's advisors thought the quiet of Weymouth would suit him better." He sighed. "I would much rather have gone to Brighthelmstone."

"I think it is a pretty place," Alicia replied. "The view across the bay from our lodgings is quite picturesque."

The Viscount smiled condescendingly, as if pitying her poor taste. "The picturesque is all very well, Miss Westlake, but Brighthelmstone is so much more fashionable. Weymouth is dull. There is so little to do. The theatre is sadly provincial and the society, present company excepted, decidedly middle-aged."

"I believe there are some delightful drives to be had," Alicia continued. "I am eager to visit the Island of Portland where I have been told I will find some splendid scenery and the ruins of an old castle."

"Indeed." Droxford sank into a silence which Alicia made no attempt to interrupt. The Viscount thought very well of himself and was clearly unused to having his opinions challenged by those he considered his social inferiors. Alicia found it most amusing and wished that Mr Merry was there to share the joke.

But the Viscount's brother failed to put in an appearance and, loath though she was to admit it, by the end of the evening, Alicia was beginning to think that Lord Droxford had some justification for his superior attitude. After dancing with the Viscount, Alicia was besieged by requests for her hand and she was not obliged to sit out a single dance. It was the most exalted company she had been in. The King was coming to Weymouth and some of his retinue had come on ahead. The town was full of those not in the King's immediate party, but whose lives revolved around the court.

Alicia sipped a glass of orgeat that one of her partners had brought her. She looked across the room at her mother who had not left the Duke's side all evening. Perhaps her mother was right after all and the Duke really was going to propose.

Chapter 25

Mrs Westlake glided into the drawing room with a smug look on her face. She had just returned from taking tea at the rooms and was eager to share her news. "The Duke has invited us to go for a drive tomorrow," she announced. She was clearly waiting for Alicia to fall into raptures, but in this she was to be disappointed.

"Let us hope, then, that the weather is fine," Alicia replied unenthusiastically. She did not cherish the thought of another day in company with her mother employing all her arts to captivate the Duke. She was becoming more and more reconciled to the fact that her mother was succeeding. It was only a matter of time before the Duke asked her to marry him and she had no doubt at all as to what her mother's answer would be. On reflection, she did not think that it was a bad turn of events, though she had not expected her mother to marry again.

Mrs Westlake was disappointed to find that Alicia's response to the invitation was one of resignation rather than excitement. It irked her to think that her daughter disapproved of the advantageous match which she felt she was so near to securing.

"Well I think you could be a little more enthusiastic, Alicia," she moaned. "It is a great honour to be invited out by the Duke and it is not as if you have spent your whole life in the company of noblemen. It so happens

that His Grace has suggested we visit Corfe Castle and
when I heard the name of the place, I immediately asked
whether there was actually a castle there, and he told me
that there is a splendid ruin of a castle on a hill above the
village and so I knew at once that it was just the sort of
place you would like to visit and so I assured him that we
would be delighted to go with him and his nephew and I
thought that you would be more grateful for the
opportunity!" At the end of this outburst, Mrs Westlake
sat down rather abruptly on a chair. She pulled out her
vinaigrette from her pocket and started sniffing its
contents very loudly.

Automatically, Alicia applied herself to calming her
mother's unsettled sensibilities. It was a task she had
performed so many times before that it was not hard.
Her mother was quite a simple person. She wanted
everyone to love her and be happy with her. All Alicia
needed to do was reassure her mother that she approved
of the proposed visit and she would be all smiles again.
Alicia regretted the fact that the promised outing would
necessarily force her into pairing up with Mr Hampton
once more, but she had to confess that the destination
had her full approval. Corfe Castle was one of the places
she had read about in *The Weymouth Guide* that she had
purchased from the library in St Thomas' Street for the
grand price of one shilling and sixpence.

According to her guidebook, it was "one of the finest
ruins in Europe" and the King's Tower was allegedly the
scene of the horrific murder of Edward, King of the
West Saxons, by his mother-in-law Elfrida. It had also
borne a role in the Civil War, but the guidebook was
disappointingly brief on the subject. She wondered
whether the Duke knew about her love of ancient places
and was consciously trying to win her favour. Perhaps

Mr Hampton had told his uncle. If so, she was indebted to him. She hastened to convince her mother that the invitation was very welcome. Indeed, she had no need to pretend; she was most willing to visit Corfe Castle.

As Alicia had predicted, no sooner had she expressed her support for the trip than her mother discarded her vinaigrette and began discussing earnestly with Alicia what they should wear.

The next day dawned as brightly as any of the party visiting Corfe could have hoped for. The sun shone, but there was a light breeze coming in from the sea which prevented the temperature from becoming uncomfortably hot.

As they approached Corfe, Alicia could not resist the temptation to press her face to the window to see if she could catch a glimpse of the castle on its perch high above the village. The majestic ruin was silhouetted against the sky and Alicia wished for the hundredth time that she could paint like her father so that she could capture the image.

The carriages drove through the village, then over a bridge and through an archway which took them within the castle's outer walls. Inside was a relatively flat area of grass where the carriages stopped and the whole party alighted. Everyone wandered around, admiring the view of the countryside over the broken down walls, though Alicia could not help thinking that the Duke and her mother looked more engrossed in each other than in the ancient monument they had driven so far to see.

As Alicia wandered through the castle ruins, she felt transported to another world. Piles of rubble and collapsed walls were witness to the terrible destruction that had been vented on the stronghold. She imagined the castle filled with soldiers, struggling to hold it for the King in the Civil War. Sadly Mr Hampton's well-meaning comments brought her back to reality. He had attached himself to Alicia as her guide and had clearly come prepared to please. As they walked through archways and into the shells of ancient rooms, he spouted random facts about the castle and its history, all of which she knew already. It was rather annoying, but she had to give him credit for trying.

He pointed out the ruin of a tower in the corner of the main part of the castle which rose above them. "That tower is the very place where Edward, King of the Saxons, was murdered by his evil mother-in-law Elfrida," he declared dramatically. Alicia had read that bit in the guidebook too. I suppose he is going to tell me that it is called the King's Tower in honour of King Edward now, Alicia thought. Sure enough, in the very next sentence, Mr Hampton did.

"So how do you like the castle, Miss Westlake?" the Duke asked good-naturedly, coming up beside her as she stared up in awe at the walls towering above them. "Your mother tells me that you like a good ruin. Is it romantic enough for your tastes?" he teased.

"I believe Miss Westlake's expression tells all, Uncle. She is delighted with the prospect and lost for words," Mr Hampton said.

Alicia felt unreasonably annoyed that Mr Hampton had presumed to answer for her. It was only a little thing, but she did not care for it.

"Indeed, I am far from lost for words, Your Grace. It is a magnificent ruin and I could talk about its picturesque splendour and stories from its history all day."

"Well, well, you must not let an old man stop your

progress, Miss Westlake. You will not want to be slowed down by those of us who want to adopt a more sedate pace. I can see that you are eager to go and explore. My nephew will take care of you, Miss Westlake."

Alicia smiled and murmured an appropriate response but thought wryly that she was likely to take more time to look round the castle than the Duke and her mother, not less. She wanted to see in every room; look out of every arrow slit; admire every view. They left the outer bailey and climbed up a slight incline to the bridge that led further into the castle. The wall on one side was at a strange angle which meant that the archway above their heads did not meet in the middle. She would have liked to stop and stare up at it for a while, but was afraid that Mr Hampton might think her rather odd and proceeded through the broken doorway and into the west bailey. Wherever she walked, Mr Hampton patiently followed.

To her surprise, they came upon an area that had been cultivated. Inexplicably, someone had been using the area inside the castle to grow plants. "Who would have thought it? A garden!" she exclaimed. "I cannot think why anyone would plant a garden here. Only think of how far you would have to walk to weed it."

Alicia was disappointed to find that her sally was greeted by no more than a condescending smile and a nod of agreement. She refused to let her companion's lack of a sense of the ridiculous dull her enthusiasm. She walked all around the west bailey, peering out of the windows and examining the towers as far as the broken down walls would allow.

She stopped and stared longingly up the slope that led to the rest of the castle ruins. To reach them, you had to climb up a rather steep incline and she thought it would be impossible to ascend them in a ladylike manner, encumbered by her skirts and a partner whom she suspected would dissuade her from the attempt if she dared to suggest it.

"I wish I knew what had happened to make such a castle fall," she confessed to Mr Hampton as she gazed at the collapsed state of the walls. "There must have been a terrible battle fought here to cause such devastation."

"It is a lasting monument to the dreadful effects of anarchy and Civil War," replied Mr Hampton, quoting the guidebook almost word for word.

But Alicia was still puzzled. "Yes, but how did it happen? Did they blast it with cannon from below even though the castle had such a height advantage?"

Unfortunately, Mr Hampton did not know and could not even hazard a guess. Trying to have a discussion about the castle's role in the Civil War was impossible. The superficiality of his knowledge was all too obvious. As she had feared, all that he knew about the castle had been gleaned from the guidebook and he had no knowledge of the subject beyond that and no opinions of his own gained from personal study or otherwise. In fact, it soon became evident that he had no real interest in history at all; it was all a façade to amuse her.

"I wish that somebody could tell me about the castle during the Civil War," she confessed to Mr Hampton. "I would so like to know how so grand a castle fell."

Mr Hampton saw an opportunity to impress and immediately offered to go and see if there were any locals who might be more knowledgeable than he was. Alicia accepted the offer and sat down on a section of ruined wall to breathe in the atmosphere and wait for his return. But her curiosity soon got the better of her and she returned to the broken archway and, when she was sure that no one was looking, she craned her neck to look up. She could see the groove where the portcullis had once fitted, but the two sides of the arch were completely out of alignment.

"Hallo."

Alicia turned round, but no one was there. The hollow-sounding voice came again. It seemed to be emanating from somewhere nearby. Although she was not superstitious, the eeriness of the voice made her shiver. Her mind told her that someone was playing a trick on her, but the complete absence of any human form was puzzling.

"Hallo?" she replied.

"Beware! I am the ghost of Lady Bankes," the voice echoed.

"Most amusing," Alicia scoffed, "but surely the ghost of a lady should have a female voice?"

"Ah, a slight mistake," Mr Merry laughed as he emerged from a gap in the building next to her. He had to bend double to get out.

"Mr Merry!" Alicia exclaimed, blushing with pleasure. "What a surprise."

"Are you surprised to see me? I, on the other hand, am not at all surprised to see you."

"But what are you doing here, Mr Merry? Are you following me?" she teased.

Mr Merry was quite unabashed. "Well I thought that was quite obvious," he confessed. "I had not exactly planned to come to Corfe today, but the temptation was too great. Besides, just a short while ago you expressly wished for my company."

Alicia vehemently denied it. "Mr Merry, you are mistaken. I never said anything of the sort."

"Pardon me, Miss Westlake, but I distinctly heard

you wishing that somebody could tell you about the castle during the Civil War."

"Worse and worse!" she retorted. "Now you confess not only to following me, but to listening in on my private conversation as well."

"It was quite your own fault, Miss Westlake. Heed my warning and never have a private conversation in a public spot, especially not one with hiding places that you are not aware of."

"Hiding places? Are there really?" she asked, momentarily diverted.

Mr Merry smiled mischievously. "I could show you," he whispered.

Alicia bit her lip. Mr Hampton had not yet returned. The servants were busy setting out the food that they had procured from the local inn whilst the Duke and her mother were nowhere to be seen. Curiosity quickly outweighed any considerations of propriety. She nodded excitedly and took the hand that Mr Merry offered her. He showed her how to bend over in order to get through the collapsed doorway.

Once through the entrance, it was possible to stand up straight again. Alicia's face was flooded with colour, but though the rosy cheeks could be attributed to the nature of her exertions, the animated glow which accompanied them was more as a result of excitement and the rather improper closeness of the situation in which she found herself.

The inside of the tower was disappointingly ordinary. The whole of the upper floors had long since collapsed. There was little of any interest, but it was peaceful, with a layer of stone between them and anyone else. It felt altogether rather private. The intimacy of standing together away from all other eyes was borne upon her.

Had Mr Merry been inclined to take advantage of her, here was the perfect opportunity.

But nothing seemed further from Mr Merry's mind. "Not much to see, I am afraid," he said, "but at least you know that for yourself now. There is nothing quite like seeing these things with your own eyes."

They heard voices outside and Mr Merry quickly put a finger to his lips. He might act with a reckless disregard for convention, but he was all too aware that others did not and he had no wish for Miss Westlake to be found in what could easily be construed as a compromising situation.

"… my dear Mrs Westlake, need you ask? I will treat her as my own daughter—the daughter I never had. I am as giddy as a young man, Mrs Westlake. You have made me so happy …" The Duke's voice sounded loud and clear as he and Mrs Westlake passed the tower where Alicia and Mr Merry were concealed and then drifted away as they walked through the archway and back down to where the carriages were standing. Alicia blushed at the words. What a conversation to overhear. What had gone before was all too obvious, but Mr Merry made no comment.

As soon as the Duke and Mrs Westlake had gone by, he led the way out of the tower and they both emerged from their hiding place. Alicia brushed at her skirts which had picked up several patches of dirt. She looked after the retreating forms of her mother and the Duke.

Alicia's mind was full of the conversation she had heard. Was everything now arranged between them? It was one thing to suspect something is about to happen and another to face the reality of it. Part of her wanted to run after her mother and have the truth confirmed, but the rest of her want to forget what she had heard. Things would never be the same between her and her mother again.

"I suppose I should go," she said reluctantly, turning to follow them.

"She was betrayed, you know."

Alicia turned back, her interest piqued. "Betrayed?"

"Lady Bankes was defending the castle for the King and she was betrayed by one of her own officers. They let the Parliamentarians in."

"I knew it," she said triumphantly. "I knew that it was far too strong a castle to have been defeated in the ordinary way. But how did it become a ruin? Was it blown up from the inside?"

"Parliament decreed that it should be destroyed so that it could not been used by the Royalists against them again."

"What a waste."

"But think how ordinary it would be if it had not been destroyed. It would be just another old castle and my friend Bankes would be living here, on the hill, instead of in his much more comfortable home at Kingston Hall."

"Poor Lady Bankes. She must have lost everything," Alicia said sadly.

"Maybe not everything."

Alicia waited expectantly.

Mr Merry did not disappoint her. "It is rumoured that she threw her jewels down the well to save them from the Parliamentarians," he said.

"The well? What well? I have not seen any well, Mr Merry," Alicia declared.

Mr Merry looked expressively up the steep incline to the part of the castle that she had not been able to explore. Alicia caught sight of Mr Hampton on his way up the slope below them. She could not bear to exchange her current companion for Mr Hampton's uninspiring person.

While she was still hesitating, Mr Merry climbed nimbly up the slope and leaned back down to offer her a hand. The temptation was too great. She grabbed Mr Merry's hand and, with a very unladylike step, she was able to reach about half way up the slope. Mr Merry climbed to the top and turned back for her hand. This time he pulled with such an almighty force that she lost her footing when she arrived on the upper level and was promptly catapulted into Mr Merry's arms. She stood back, embarrassed, but Mr Merry seemed oblivious to her discomfiture and proceeded to lead the way along a little path carved out by the sheep which led to the far end of the ruin.

Every now and then he paused to point out something of interest—an arrow slit; holes in the stonework which used to hold the wooden beams that had supported the upper floor; a recess which had once been a fireplace. Every question she raised, he seemed to have an answer for.

Up three steps and they were inside the inner ward. Mr Merry showed her the well which had been the ostensible reason for the climb.

"An important feature if you want to survive a siege," he said.

"Do you really think that Lady Bankes' jewels are down there somewhere?" she asked, peering into the well.

"Well no. I think it is highly improbable. Who would throw their jewels down a well? I think it much more likely that she smuggled them out of the castle by secreting them on her person."

Alicia quizzed Mr Merry about the King's Tower. "What about King Edward? Was he murdered here like the guidebook says or not?" she asked.

"The *Anglo-Saxon Chronicle* states that he was murdered at Corfe Gate," Mr Merry informed her, "so it is likely that he was murdered somewhere nearby, but probably not just here. The castle may not even have been here until some one hundred years later when William I built on this area."

It was exhilarating to be up so high. Alicia felt as if they had the whole castle to themselves. From their vantage point, they had a bird's-eye view of the surrounding country and could see further than from anywhere else in the castle. Fields and trees stretched out as far as their eyes could see and Mr Merry directed her gaze so that she could even see the harbour at Poole in the distance.

But then Alicia's glance fell on the area below them and she realised that they were far from alone. She could see clearly what was happening inside the castle. Her mother and the Duke were making their way back to the outer bailey. They would soon come upon Mr Hampton who was wandering about, presumably looking for her. It would very soon be evident that she was with neither party and her disappearance would cause general consternation. Reluctantly, she knew she must return.

They walked back through the ruins until they came to the sharp descent that would take them back down to the west bailey. It had not looked quite so very steep from the bottom, and Alicia bit her lip, wondering how on earth she was going to get down.

"Take my hand, Miss Westlake. Find a foothold and we will get down, little by little. Trust me."

Surprisingly, she did trust him. She trusted him despite the fact that he seemed to forget her for days at a time; despite the fact that he did not get on with his family; despite the fact that he did not believe in God. She probably should not trust him, but instinctively she did. This insight did nothing for her peace of mind.

When they reached the bottom, Mr Merry applauded her. "Bravo. You are a mountaineer now." But then his face clouded over and he bid Alicia a hasty farewell before disappearing up the slope again.

It did not take Alicia long to realise why. Mr Merry had caught sight of Mr Hampton's approach before the archway had hidden him from view. As he came round the corner he exclaimed, "Miss Westlake. I began to fear that you had fallen over the edge somewhere. I found a man from the village who was most knowledgeable and was able to tell me all about the defeat of the castle in the Civil War."

Alicia murmured her thanks, but her mind was distracted. Mr Merry had gone again. He still refused even to pass the time of day with Mr Hampton. Was it all a matter of jealousy? If so, it was of the acutest kind. It was some moments before she appreciated that Mr Hampton was waiting for her to speak. "Do go on," she said, hoping that this was an appropriate response. Mr Hampton smiled and launched into a description of the castle's defence during the Civil War. Alicia suffered herself to listen to a repetition of the facts, which now lacked the novelty of their first telling, with every appearance of pleasure. Mr Hampton had gone to such efforts to please her that she took pity on him and was at her most charming for the rest of the day.

Chapter 26

Alicia had been embarrassed by her mother's behaviour before, but now that she was actually betrothed to the Duke, Alicia found her completely insufferable. Not only did she constantly refer to her forthcoming marriage and how that would make her a duchess, but her mother also found it necessary to repeatedly praise her own cleverness at bringing the matter about. Alicia thought this could not be forgotten too soon.

Poor Martha found herself being dragged out several times a day for walks along the seafront or to visit the circulating library so that Alicia could minimise the amount of time she had to spend in her mother's company.

"I gather that I missed the big announcement," Mr Merry remarked, when he met Alicia walking along the promenade the next day, "though after what we overheard, it was only to be expected. I do believe your mother is to be congratulated. How fortuitous that she should faint in the Duke's arms at Vauxhall. He might otherwise have failed to notice her existence."

All Alicia's pleasure at coming upon Mr Merry quickly dissipated. She felt all the justice of his words, but they stung nevertheless and were delivered in such a mocking tone of voice that she was left in no doubt of the contempt in which he held her mother.

"You are mistaken, Mr Merry," she retorted, rising to her mother's defence. "The Duke was well acquainted with my mother before that day."

"But then, of course, I believe your carriage met with an accident near the Duke's house. So maybe Vauxhall was unnecessary. To land on the Duke's doorstep was a much better plan. Every man likes to play the knight-errant, but surely once is enough?"

"The Duke is his own man," Alicia replied with some spirit. "He would not marry a lady simply because he kept coming to her rescue."

"Probably not. If your mother had been a hideous sight, no doubt the Duke's chivalrous instincts would have been curbed. But all is well that ends well: your mother has caught her duke and no doubt your own betrothal will follow swiftly behind."

"My own betrothal?" Alicia asked, puzzled.

"To the Duke's nephew. The two of you were as close as two peas in a pod at Corfe, despite my warning you against his company."

"For which you have given me no basis whatsoever," she snapped.

"I assume you intend to accept him. You can hardly avoid his company now as he will soon be part of your family."

"Mr Merry, let me assure you that—"

But she got no further. At that very moment they were overtaken by the subject of their discussion. With the merest nod of the head to acknowledge her companion, Mr Hampton pointedly addressed Alicia.

"Miss Westlake. I have some exciting news that I could not wait to share with you. Your mother said that you had walked out this way and I took the liberty of coming after you. Word has just reached us: the King is on his way to Weymouth. Their Majesties are due to arrive this very afternoon."

Though Alicia rued Mr Hampton's familiarity which seemed to confirm the betrothal that Mr Merry believed to be imminent, she was delighted to receive the news.

"This afternoon? I should like very much to be there when the King arrives."

"Of course you will be there, Miss Westlake. The Duke is part of the King's welcome party and you and your mother will naturally be included."

"And will you be there too, Mr Merry?" Alicia asked, attempting to draw him back into the conversation.

Mr Merry was annoyed that he had let his personal frustrations overcome his good manners. He had come after Alicia with the express intention of enlightening her about the King's imminent arrival, but he had lost the opportunity. Instead, he had wasted those precious minutes sarcastically congratulating her on her mother's betrothal and practically begging her to deny that she was about to become engaged to Mr Hampton.

"I will of course be there to welcome the King and my esteemed parents who accompany His Majesty. Pray excuse me."

A quick bow and he was gone, walking swiftly away from Alicia without a backward glance. There was nothing to be done but to take Mr Hampton's proffered arm and dawdle back to the house at the dignified speed suited to a lady whose mother was about to marry a duke. She found the pace intolerably slow and paid scant attention to what Mr Hampton was saying.

She wondered when she would have the opportunity of talking to Mr Merry again. The suggestion that she was about to be engaged to Mr Hampton was ridiculous, but she wanted to assure Mr Merry that it was so. Not that it was any of his business, of course, but she did not want him to couple their names together.

At around four o'clock, the King's entourage arrived in Weymouth. Alicia went down onto the esplanade with the Duke and her mother to watch the arrival. There was a magnificent procession with flags flying led by the mayor of Weymouth and accompanied by a band which played *God Save the King*. Guns fired, both from ships anchored in the bay and from the royal battery on the esplanade.

The King appeared to be well pleased with the prospect and was overhead to say: "I never enjoyed a sight so pleasing."

The town was delighted with the King's visit and the atmosphere of excitement was catching. In the evening, they wandered through the town, admiring the illuminations celebrating His Majesty's arrival.

The routine of their days was completely disrupted by His Majesty's arrival in Weymouth. Everything revolved around the King and whether the Duke's attendance was required. Alicia spent her time with her mother, consoling her for the loss of the Duke's company on those occasions that he was required to wait on the King. They went sea bathing, walked along the promenade, and were driven out into the Dorset countryside in the Duke's barouche. The Duke came when he could; Mr Hampton came oftener; Mr Merry came not at all.

On Sunday, Mrs Westlake and her daughter accompanied the Duke and his nephew to the parish church of Melcombe Regis which was situated in St Mary's Street. The church was so crowded with people wanting to see the King that there was not a free seat in the whole building. Alicia was glad that they were with the Duke. At least sitting in the Duke's pew allowed them a little more space than if they had come on their own.

She tried desperately to concentrate on the sermon, but found her attention slipping and her eyes wandering as she scanned the congregation. Her gaze fixed on the rear view of a gentleman seated two pews in front of her. Her heart beat a little faster; she recognised that fair head of hair. It had been several days since she had seen Mr Merry. There had been no opportunity of continuing the conversation that had finished so abruptly. She was aware that appearances would seem to be supporting rather than refuting Mr Merry's suspicions. Since her mother's engagement, she had rarely been out in company without Mr Hampton being present.

She glanced at the lady seated beside him. She had no difficulty in recognising the profile of the Countess of Harting. She knew that Mr Merry did not get on with his mother and was, perhaps, a little surprised that he should be with her in church. She hoped that the Countess was not going to be difficult. As if he could feel her eyes upon him, the gentleman turned, and she realised in a flash that she had been mistaken. It was not Mr Merry, but his brother, and she blushed at having been caught staring.

Too late she remembered how improbable it was that she would meet Mr Merry in church. This was one place that she would not bump into him by chance. She allowed her gaze to wander around the church. She supposed that there were others there who believed quite as little as Mr Merry did, but had chosen to conform to the expectations of society and attend church services. At least Mr Merry was not guilty of double standards, but that was not much comfort. It was a melancholy thought that the most engaging gentleman of her acquaintance made not the least pretence of sharing her beliefs. Resolutely she put all other thoughts aside and dwelt on the Reverend Groves' words.

As they left the church, the Duke drew Alicia and her mother forward and presented them to the King and Queen. Mrs Westlake glowed with pride as the Duke presented her as his affianced wife. The King was a true romantic and smiled kindly on them. Everyone should be as happy as himself in marriage. The Queen smiled too, but Alicia was sorry to see that she still looked tired. The King's illness had taken its toll on her. Perhaps the sea air was as much for her benefit as for the King's.

Two days later, Alicia was taking her early morning walk along the esplanade, when she heard a band playing. Since the King's arrival, there had been no end to the celebrations of the local people who feted their King at every opportunity. Consequently she thought nothing of it until Mr Merry came hurrying toward her, beaming from ear to ear.

"Well met, Miss Westlake," Mr Merry said brightly. "The very person I was hoping to meet. I am sure that you will enjoy the joke."

"Good morning, Mr Merry," Alicia replied in a reserved tone of voice, determined that he should not be allowed to ignore her for days and receive no reproof.

"Now do not disappoint me, Miss Westlake," he laughed. "The King has been sea bathing this morning."

"We are in Weymouth, Mr Merry," Alicia replied without emotion. "People come to Weymouth to go sea bathing. I fail to see why the King going sea bathing should cause you such amusement."

"Let me continue, Miss Westlake. The King was

pulled out to sea in a bathing machine, just like anyone else. But then, what do you think happened?"

"Pray enlighten me," she said.

"As the attendant opened the door to let the King out and down the steps into the sea, the door of the next bathing machine burst open and revealed a band inside who started to play *God Save the King* whilst His Majesty was being dipped! Can you imagine how surprised the King must have been to have received such a noisy reception among the waves? And yet he did not seem to be perturbed a jot. Just smiled and nodded and carried on with his bathe. Now tell me you are amused."

Alicia shrugged. She was amused, but she was loath admit it.

"I saw your brother in church," Alicia said.

Mr Merry made some nondescript noise that sounded rather like "Humph".

"You were not there."

"You should have known better than to look for me."

"Who said that I looked for you?"

"You must have looked to have known I was not there, but you could have saved yourself the bother— you knew that I would not be."

"Not even for the King?"

"I am no hypocrite, Miss Westlake. I would only go to church if I wanted to worship."

There seemed nothing that she could say to that and she was not sorry to see Mr Hampton approaching. The conversation had become awkward and she was not surprised that Mr Merry made a hasty bow and walked off in the opposite direction. She began to wonder if all her encounters with Mr Merry would leave her feeling as if she had been hit by a whirlwind.

Chapter 27

Having received the King's blessing, the Duke was anxious to claim his bride and departed at once for Hampshire to make preparations to receive Mrs Westlake and her daughter. He was conscious of having wasted too many years on his own and knew he was not getting any younger.

Though Mrs Westlake had hoped for a big London wedding, she was happy to submit to the Duke's impatience. To return to London in the autumn not as the outcast Mrs Westlake but as the Duchess of Wessex would be a triumph.

The ceremony was to be a small affair at the chapel at Swanmore, just close family and a few chosen friends. Mrs Westlake took great delight in extending an invitation to the Earl of Harting and his family. She was keen that the Countess should be there to witness her greatest hour.

As Mrs Westlake had long ago realised, Lady Harting was an ambitious woman. She was naturally resentful and had taken a great deal of malicious enjoyment from disrupting her old adversary's path back into society, having nurtured her hatred of Mrs Westlake over many years. It had hurt her pride to know that she was the Earl's second choice and that she had only succeeded because she had a large dowry and the Earl had been too weak to stand up to his own mother.

On the other hand, the Countess was not above shifting her behaviour if it was in her interests to do so. With studied politeness, she accepted the barbed olive branch. The exasperating Mrs Westlake could be treated with disdain, but the future Duchess of Wessex was a person to be reckoned with. Lady Harting could not pretend to like the woman, but she admired the persistence that had won her the prize. She expressed her delight in icy rhapsodies and set about planning how she could manipulate the current turn of events to her advantage.

It did not take her long. Mrs Westlake's approaching marriage to the Duke changed things. A union between her old adversary's daughter and one of her own sons was now highly desirable. The Countess watched Miss Westlake with growing interest. Up until now she had dismissed her younger son's assiduous courtship of Miss Westlake as irritating but inconsequential. She had not hesitated to attribute his pursuit of the girl to a deep-rooted desire to vex his mother. It was quite impossible for her to believe there was any other motivation; he was simply trying to annoy her. Lady Harting observed Miss Westlake and was inclined to believe that the girl favoured her younger son.

Mrs Westlake had reached the same conclusion. Matters had not gone according to her plans. She had encouraged Mr Merry's courtship in order to prompt Mr Hampton into making an offer for Alicia's hand, but her daughter had obstinately refused to consider marrying the Duke's nephew. Mrs Westlake had seen the way her daughter looked at Mr Merry and thought, with a sinking heart, that Alicia was doomed for disappointment. Like Lady Harting, Mrs Westlake believed that Mr Merry was courting her daughter simply to aggravate his mother. In an effort to protect her daughter, she was now doing everything she could to discourage Mr Merry.

Lady Harting was quick to notice Mrs Westlake's change in behaviour. She had not seen any signs in the past to suggest that Mrs Westlake objected to her son's courtship of her daughter. Maybe Mrs Westlake had promoted the match for much the same reason that Christopher had pursued it—to annoy her. Clearly Mrs Westlake's approaching nuptials had changed her perspective. Petty rivalries were thrown aside for the sake of advantage. The future Duchess of Wessex no longer found the match acceptable. No doubt, the new Duchess would want to see her daughter married well, preferably to a titled gentleman.

Droxford could be that man. In a flash, her younger son's courtship was dismissed. Christopher no longer met the criteria, if he ever had. Christopher rarely met any criteria. He delighted in going against her very wishes. He was disrespectful and difficult, unlike Droxford in every possible way. If she wanted to bring about an alliance with the Duke's family, it would have to be through her elder son.

The future Duchess could probably look higher than a viscount for her daughter. After all, the girl was as pretty as a picture and had a fortune that would delight any prospective husband. Despite this, she believed that the Duchess would not be averse to a match between her daughter and Droxford. Mrs Westlake's satisfaction in being accepted by those that had rejected her would make the match highly desirable. Lady Harting under-stood such feelings only too well.

Lady Harting was a ruthless woman and when she decided on a course of action, she swept any objections out of her way without mercy. Christopher had become one of those objections. She did not believe that he was genuinely attached to Miss Westlake, but it made no difference to her if he was. He had become an obstacle in the path of her ambition. He needed to be removed as Miss Westlake's growing affection for him could jeopardise Droxford's chances.

The Earl of Harting and his family left Weymouth for Holybourne House at the same time as the Westlakes travelled to Swanmore. They were to join the ducal party the day before the ceremony.

The Countess waited until her husband had gone out riding before summoning Christopher to an interview. She was pleasantly surprised when he came.

"Christopher, we need to talk."

Mr Merry waited in silence. He had no idea why his mother had sent for him, but was just interested enough to make the effort to come.

"It is about Miss Westlake."

Now his mother had his full attention.

"You must give her up."

Mr Merry stood absolutely still as if he could not believe what he was hearing.

"I beg your pardon?"

"For once, I believe I understand you, Christopher. You have pursued Miss Westlake in order to aggravate me, but now you must give her up."

"And may I know your reasoning, Madam?"

"Because her mother wishes it."

"I am sure that Mrs Westlake wants nothing more than her daughter's happiness. I do not believe that Miss Westlake is indifferent to me."

"You are missing the point, Christopher," Lady Harting continued impatiently. "You are not good enough for her. Miss Westlake's mother will soon be a duchess and looks for a titled match for her daughter. Unless I am much mistaken, you have neither title nor wealth to offer. Droxford has both."

Mr Merry coloured. There was nothing he hated more than being compared to his brother.

"It is true that Miss Westlake may believe she has feelings for you, which is all the more reason why you must give her up. Her mother wants her to make a good match and you will just get in the way."

"Miss Westlake is not like her mother. She is not interested in such worldly things."

Lady Harting saw her opportunity and pounced. "I believe you are right, Christopher. Miss Westlake takes her religion very seriously. Perhaps if you had followed my advice and made the church your profession, you would have been the right sort of husband for her. She would be admirably suited to being the wife of a bishop. But I think you are forgetting the choices you have made. Your refusal to attend church causes comment and would cause Miss Westlake great pain."

The discord of their last conversation came promptly to Mr Merry's mind. In a single moment, all the fight went out of him. He could not, would not, believe that Miss Westlake was mercenary, but the truth of his mother's words cut deeply. He would not disrupt Miss Westlake's peace by causing her to choose between him and her beliefs.

Lady Harting sensed her triumph was near.

"Droxford will make her a good husband. She might never get a title if she married the Duke's nephew. Who is to say that the Duchess will not give the Duke a son?"

The mention of Mr Hampton put Mr Merry on edge. If only he could be sure that Miss Westlake would not choose Mr Hampton over his pompous brother. His brother was a fool, but Mr Hampton made him nervous. He could not rid himself of the conviction that Mr Hampton was not to be trusted.

"Christopher, I am waiting. Your father and I must return to the King in Weymouth as soon as the Duke and Duchess leave on their wedding trip. Promise me that you will not pursue Miss Westlake."

Mr Merry let out a long sigh. "You may go back to Weymouth in peace, Mother. I give you my word that I will not seek out Miss Westlake's company while the Duchess is away. After that, I cannot promise, but you have made your point only too well. I would never forgive myself if I forced Miss Westlake to compromise her religion."

Lady Harting smiled warmly at her son. It was a rare moment when she felt in harmony with him. "You are making the right choice, Christopher," she said softly, putting her arm around his shoulders.

Mr Merry pulled away from her embrace in disgust. "I might be doing what you want, but it is for Miss Westlake's sake, not yours or Droxford's," he snapped. "And I do not have to like it."

He stormed out of the room, barely containing his emotions. His mother made no attempt to follow him. She had very little sympathy to spare for anyone and none whatsoever for her younger son. She had succeeded in her object and was very well pleased with herself.

Alicia found it hard to hide her disappointment when the Earl and Countess of Harting arrived for the wedding without their younger son.

When she made a tentative enquiry, the Countess apologised lightly for his absence. "There is not the least use placing any dependence on my son, Miss Westlake. When he buries himself in the library with his books, there is no doing anything with him at all," Lady Harting said gleefully. "I am afraid that not even your manifold attractions could entice him away from his studies today."

Alicia blushed and wished she had not asked.

Twenty miles away, Mr Merry was indeed ensconced in the library of Holybourne House. He was burying himself, quite ineffectually, in his studies and trying to forget.

The ceremony was followed by a wedding breakfast in the splendid dining room where the new duchess glowed with pride as people offered their felicitations.

Lady Harting was regretting making her previous enmity so public. The Duchess received her congratulations with malicious pleasure. She could see how much it cost the Countess to put her true feelings aside and accept her as the Duke's new bride.

The Duchess commiserated with the Countess on not having been blessed with a daughter. "Alicia has been such a comfort to me. Now my only desire in life is to see her well-settled."

The Countess of Harting forced herself to smile. "With such beauty and connections, I am sure that the foremost families in the land will seek her hand for their sons," she replied with studied politeness. "I myself have been blessed with sons."

She paused and looked the Duchess in the eye. "The advantage of sons is that they can inherit their father's titles."

The Duchess raised her eyebrows. "Indeed!"

"I feel sure that your daughter could one day be a countess," Lady Harting continued.

"Do you really think so?" the Duchess asked, hardly daring to believe what her old enemy was implying.

"But of course. I am a strong believer that connections should always take precedence over personal inclination."

The Duchess positively beamed at the Countess. Despite cordially disliking her, Lady Harting was actually promoting a match between her daughter and Lord Droxford. But it would not do to get too carried away. At this moment in time, it was no more than an idea.

"I thank you for your kind thoughts, Madam, but I have observed that children do not always behave as their parents would like."

Lady Harting dismissed the Duchess' concerns out of hand. "Droxford is a most dutiful son. He never gives me a moment's unrest."

The Duchess glowed with satisfaction. She knew that Lord Droxford was considered one of the biggest matrimonial prizes on the market. What an incredible achievement it would be if she could see her daughter married into the family that had so rudely cut her just a few months before. All thoughts of trying to persuade her daughter to reconsider Mr Hampton were forgotten. This was the match she had longed for.

Oblivious to the plans her mother was making for her, Alicia was feeling miserable. Since her father's death, she had been her mother's sole companion and she was not at all sure what it would be like now that her mother had a husband to care for. Mr Merry would have laughed her out of her fit of dejection, but Mr Merry had not come. Alicia was angry with him for failing to support her on what he must have known would be a difficult day. Sadly she acknowledged the melancholy truth that he found his studies more engaging than her company.

At his mother's prompting, Lord Droxford sought Alicia out and conducted a condescending conversation with her.

"You must be very proud of your mother becoming a duchess," Lord Droxford said.

"I am pleased that my mother is so happy," Alicia replied.

"The Duke is very rich. No doubt he will be a generous father to you."

"The Duke is very kind to me and my mother."

"It will be your turn next."

"I beg your pardon?"

"It will be your wedding next. Now that your mother is a duchess, there will be many gentlemen eager to seek your hand in marriage. How should you like to become, shall we say, a viscountess?"

Alicia's mouth went very dry. Was Lord Droxford actually saying what she thought he was saying? "I have no plans to marry just yet, Lord Droxford."

"Ah, but you ladies cannot plan, Miss Westlake. You have to be asked." And with these smug words, he smiled broadly and yielded his place to Mr Hampton, satisfied that he had done what his mother had asked. He had given Alicia a hint as to her future expectations without committing himself in the slightest. Should he choose to pay his addresses, he had no doubt that they would be welcomed without reservation.

Mr Hampton had watched Lord Droxford in conversation with Alicia, but judging by the look on her face, he was not a threat to his own plans. It was obvious that Alicia found the Viscount's company irksome. Alicia was still flustered by whatever Lord Droxford had been saying to her. Mr Hampton immediately adopted a brotherly attitude and talked about commonplace matters until her equanimity was restored, putting Alicia quite in charity with him.

Chapter 28

After the bustle of all the preparations and the excitement of the wedding, Swanmore was eerily silent. The Duke and Duchess had left for Ireland immediately after the wedding breakfast. The Duke had intended to take his bride to Paris, but the recent disturbances had caused him to change his plans. He would not risk being caught up amongst the revolutionaries in France. He would take his new Duchess to visit his Irish estates instead.

Lord Richard had taken to his room with gout and rarely showed his face, even at mealtimes. The Hartings had finally left. The Earl and Countess had returned to Weymouth to wait on the King, whilst Lord Droxford had departed for Holybourne House, with promises to call regularly to see how Alicia was doing. Alicia hoped that he would not feel the need to ride over too often.

Left with only Mr Hampton for company, Alicia was in danger of falling into a state of melancholy. She felt strangely bereft now her mother was married. Since her father's death, it had been just the two of them and although they did not always see eye to eye, they had been each other's companions, through good times and bad. Now she was on her own.

Lord Droxford's words still rang in her ears: "It will be your wedding next." But she was not ready for that. Not ready at all.

Alicia wished she could have gone away with her mother and the Duke. The kindly Duke had even suggested it, but she had quickly declined. She had no wish to play an awkward third.

Alicia was glad of Mr Hampton's undemanding company. There was nothing lover-like in his behaviour toward her. His kind attention to her comfort was more in the nature of a brother than a suitor. Little by little, she began to relax when she was with him.

Often he would accompany her on her daily ride, out onto the estate and beyond, into the hills of the Meon Valley. He did not say much, but they enjoyed a companionable silence. On the few occasions when Mr Hampton was occupied with estate business, she rode with just a groom for company.

If the weather was inclement, she would reluctantly forego her ride and retreat to the Duke's library. It was a wonderful place—a large rectangular room with a raised walkway and bookcases on every wall, both on the ground floor and the raised area. Every now and again, there was a window embrasure in which might be set a chair or a desk.

Alicia liked to curl up in one of these chairs and read, oblivious to the raindrops battering against the window-panes. Even on fine days, she liked to spend some time there reading, bathing in the warmth of the late summer sunshine which streamed brightly into the room.

In the afternoons, the local gentry would call and she would sip tea out of the Duke's beautiful Wedgwood teacups. She would talk about parish business with the rector's wife or listen to the squire's wife and her garrulous daughters gossiping about their neighbours.

All too often, Lord Droxford rode over from Holybourne House, to see how she was doing. Alicia took no pleasure in these visits. If she had not been so annoyed by his presumption, it would have been amusing. It was as if the Viscount thought that his presence alone was all that was required.

He sat and talked at Alicia rather than with her, making little effort to engage her in the conversation. He laughed at his own witticisms and seemed to require no encouragement at all to keep talking. Mostly he spoke of London, giving her a detailed account of the ton's activities which he had gleaned from his newspaper or heard about in a letter. If she interrupted his flow with questions, he smiled at her condescendingly and answered her as if she was a poor, ignorant girl who needed educating in the ways of fashion. And he kept coming back.

Once, she spied his horse from afar and sought to avoid his company by fleeing from the house for a ride. But her escape was foiled. Sensing a romance, a misguided footman urged the Viscount to head for the stables to catch up with the young mistress, and Alicia was forced to allow Lord Droxford to accompany her. The experience was as painful as drinking tea with him. He rode alongside her, dictating a pace which he thought suitable for a young lady and refused to be goaded into a gallop or even a canter.

Frustrated by his overbearing attitude, she was provoked into an ungracious moment and refused to invite him in for refreshment before his ride back to Holybourne House.

But if she thought this would put him off, she was mistaken. Two days later he was on her doorstep again. The man was impervious to snubs! They sat drinking tea while Lord Droxford babbled on in his usual way, talking about nothing of any real importance.

"How are your parents, Lord Droxford?" Alicia asked, taking advantage of a slight pause in his monologue to enter the conversation. "Are they still in Weymouth?"

"My parents are quite well, thank you. They have gone to Plymouth with the King. They are all staying at Saltram House—"

Lord Droxford would have been happy to expand on the movements of the royal party, but Alicia gave him no chance. "And your brother?" she interrupted, trying to sound casual. "Has he gone to Plymouth too?"

Lord Droxford looked confused. "Merry? Why would Merry go to Plymouth? No. He is with me at Holybourne House."

The reply surprised her. She had seen nothing of Mr Merry since arriving in Hampshire and had supposed that he had gone to London or returned to Weymouth with his parents. "Is he much occupied?" she asked innocently.

"He writes." The normally loquacious Viscount seemed to have nothing else to say on the subject.

"And what does he write?" Alicia asked, ignoring Lord Droxford's lack of inclination to talk about his brother.

Lord Droxford wriggled uncomfortably in his chair. He did not want to talk about Merry's studies. Although he was secretly proud of his brother's intellectual abilities, he always felt inadequate when they were being discussed. His tone of voice made it quite clear that he found the subject distasteful.

"I believe he writes about Rome."

Despite the disapproval, Alicia could not resist continuing the discussion. "I would love to go to Rome. I believe your brother has been there. Have you?"

The Viscount raised his eyebrows at her imperti-
nence in continuing a conversation he clearly did not
want to have. But manners were his byword. The
question had been asked and in politeness, he must
answer it.

"Merry is not the only one to have made the Grand
Tour."

"Oh yes, I remember. You went on the Grand Tour
together." She knew she was being wicked, but she could
not resist the temptation. "And did you visit the
excavations at Pompeii and Herculaneum too? There is
so much we can learn about the people who once lived
there from what they have uncovered. I believe that Mr
Merry was fortunate enough to bring back some
interesting pieces with him."

The Viscount felt that he had let Miss Westlake run
on for long enough. The conversation was making him
feel uncomfortable and he knew that it was time for him
to take control again. "No doubt my brother finds them
fascinating, Miss Westlake," he said in a disdainful tone
of voice, "but there is no accounting for taste. Merry is
welcome to his bits of antiquity. What he can find to
interest him in broken pieces of stone and marble is
beyond me. I am more interested in things of real
beauty."

"Such as?"

The Viscount smiled condescendingly. He was in his
element once more. In all matters of fashion he knew he
was vastly superior to his brother. He looked down his
nose at Alicia and proceeded to explain his reasoning to
her as if she were a child or an imbecile.

"Fashion, Miss Westlake, fashion. The elegance of a
well-performed dance; the exquisite embroidery on a
waistcoat; a perfectly manicured hand; the whitened face

of a beautiful woman—these are things of real beauty."

Alicia disagreed. The beauty of the things that the Viscount admired was only skin deep. At least there were stories behind Mr Merry's antiquities. But she was unwilling to argue with Lord Droxford and so kept her thoughts to herself.

When Lord Droxford rose to take his leave, he took her hand and lifted it to his lips. He lingered over it a moment, kissing it delicately. She felt the heat flooding into her face with embarrassment. She did not like the look on his face. It bore all the signs of possessiveness. It was clear that he believed that all he had to do was to ask and she would be his.

At that very moment, Mr Hampton walked in. Alicia immediately withdrew her hand, but it was too late. Mr Hampton was quick to assimilate the situation. Perhaps the Viscount presented a bigger threat than he had hitherto given him credit for. He noted the smug look on his rival's face and Miss Westlake's cheeks suffused with colour. "Has Lord Droxford outstayed his welcome?" Mr Hampton demanded brusquely, looking Alicia directly in the face.

Alicia was quick to deny it. The last thing she wanted was a scene. "No, no, Mr Hampton. Lord Droxford was just leaving."

Instead of being cheered by these words, Mr Hampton feared that Alicia was trying to protect her suitor. Perhaps the Viscount was making headway with Miss Westlake after all.

Chapter 29

The next morning, Alicia sat with her needlework on her lap, wondering how she would ever get through another wet day.

The sound of a carriage sent her scurrying to the window. She peered out in an unladylike fashion and saw that a travelling carriage had drawn up outside the house.

"Mother!" she exclaimed joyfully and hurried out to greet the Duke and Duchess.

"Well, my dear. How nice it is to be home again. Not that Dublin was not beautiful and the temperature more amenable than here. We will have to light the fire in the drawing room tonight or I will positively freeze to death."

She held out her hands to Alicia and greeted her affectionately. The Duke followed suit, kissing her soundly on both cheeks before stepping back to admire her.

"It does me good to look at you, Alicia. I have never had a daughter of my own and now I have been blessed with such a pretty one, fully grown up, in the blink of an eye."

The Duchess noticed that Alicia seemed rather pale. It would not do for her bloom to go off now that she could claim exalted connections in addition to her beauty and wealth. She wanted at least an earl for her daughter and she had fixed on the very one. During her weeks away, the idea had grown in her mind. It would be so amusing if Alicia married Viscount Droxford who would one day inherit his father's earldom. Lord Harting would be Alicia's father-in-law when, had her mother chosen differently, he might have been her father.

There was necessarily a good deal of bustle with the arrival of the Duke and Duchess. Six weeks in Ireland had flown by for the newly married pair; time had moved slowly for Alicia.

The Duchess glided into her daughter's bedroom as she was dressing for dinner. "Have you missed me, darling?" she asked, putting her hands on Alicia's shoulders as she glanced at her reflection in the mirror.

Alicia looked up and gave her hand a quick squeeze. "More than I can say."

The Duchess was far from displeased with the answer. It was comforting to know that her importance in her daughter's life had not diminished.

"How have you gone on?" she asked casually. "Have the neighbours been attentive?"

"I have walked and ridden every day that was dry. I have read countless books and improved my pianoforte playing—a little at least. I would not care to count how many cups of tea I have drunk with Lady Henry and her very talkative daughters. But I have not had a dance the whole time you have been away and fear you will label me a bluestocking for all the reading that I have done. I have written and received letters from all my London friends and long to see them again."

"And have you had no other visitors?" she asked pointedly.

"The Earl and Countess stayed on for a few days after the wedding before travelling back to Weymouth. They regretted that they would not be in the locality whilst I was most in need of company, but I assure you that I have been able to bear the deprivation. I only wish that they had taken their son with them!"

The Duchess frowned. "Is that Merry boy making a nuisance of himself? I will get the Duke to warn him off."

"No!" Alicia replied with a little too much enthusiasm for her mother's peace of mind. How ironic that her mother should accuse Mr Merry of pestering her when she had seen nothing of him the whole time her mother had been away. "No, it is rather Lord Droxford who has been troubling me."

The Duchess frowned. What had the Viscount been doing to make himself unpopular with her daughter? Bother the man—surely he had not made improper advances toward her?

"How so, my love? Lord Droxford is a very suitable young gentleman. He is heir to the Earl. Do you not like him?"

Alicia could not believe it. After the Countess had cut her mother, she had not been able to say a good word about her or her pompous elder son. How could she now countenance a match with him? "No mother. I do not like Lord Droxford. He talks incessantly of nothing of any importance and makes no effort to hide the fact that he believes himself to be a superior being— no effort at all."

The Duchess was disappointed that Alicia seemed to have taken a dislike to Lord Droxford. She was not going to drop her cherished scheme so lightly, but was astute enough to see that this was not the time to persuade her daughter of the advantages of the match. "I suppose he is somewhat proud, but maybe he will improve with time. Let us say no more about it."

In the weeks that followed, Lord Droxford was a frequent visitor to the house. The Duchess did all she could to encourage him but Alicia's reception of him remained cool. Mr Hampton continued to act like a brother to her and, in this manner, they continued on very friendly terms. Mr Merry still did not come.

Alicia kept telling herself that it did not matter whether Mr Merry came or not. She was only causing herself heartache by yearning after his company. Unfortunately, her other suitors fell far short in comparison. Clearly she would have to remain a spinster all her life and set up home as an eccentric bluestocking with a huge library and some impoverished relation as her companion. Perhaps she could write a book as Miss Burney had done. Better that than marry where her heart was not engaged.

Chapter 30

In the middle of September, the royal family returned to Windsor and the Earl and Countess of Harting came back to Holybourne House. The Countess was frustrated that her son had made so little headway with Miss Westlake. She was as eager as the Duchess to promote an alliance between the two houses and was determined to move things along.

She decided to hold a ball, ostensibly in honour of Lord Droxford's birthday. Droxford always shone in the ballroom. She made sure to consult the Duchess before setting the date and then, to minimise the inconvenience to the Duke and Duchess, she invited them all to stay at Holybourne House for a few days. The Duchess was gratified at the attention and was delighted to accept.

Alicia had mixed feelings about the ball. On the one hand, it was obviously being staged to bring her and Lord Droxford together. On the other, it was being held at Holybourne House where Mr Merry had hidden himself away. Even if he refused to come to the ball, surely she could not be under the same roof as him for two days without them meeting.

It was Alicia's first visit to Holybourne House. She had to admit that the approach was impressive. All along the road was a stone wall, seven feet high, marking the edge of the estate, and even from the carriage, she could spy nothing inside except the abundance of trees. After a considerable distance, the coach passed what she assumed was the back entrance to the park. The impressive stone archway was topped with the figure of a stag standing proudly looking out over the surrounding countryside. A short while after, they came to the principal entrance—another magnificent stone archway, this time with a rampant lion on top. They entered the park and followed the drive, adorned with statues on either side which Alicia had an excellent opportunity to examine as the coach made its unhurried way up to the front door of the house.

The house had been built for the current earl and was a magnificent building in the Palladian style with a perfectly symmetrical frontage. Although she was no expert in architecture, Alicia was quick to recognise the Portland stone with which the entire house was faced. What was good enough for St Paul's was clearly good enough for Holybourne House!

The Duke's party arrived at Holybourne House early in the afternoon. The Duchess wanted to allow plenty of time to get ready for the ball. The whole family was assembled to welcome their arrival. The Countess greeted them as old friends which Alicia found difficult to cope with. It seemed so hypocritical that Lady Harting should be welcoming them into her home as honoured guests when six months before she had shunned their society and urged the rest of the ton to do likewise. It may have been her imagination, but she thought that the Countess' smile looked very superficial. Perhaps she was so aware of it because she was conscious of the empti-ness of her own.

The Earl seemed more genuine. She had the feeling that he would have welcomed the relationship all along. Lord Droxford echoed his mother's insincerity. Where

Lady Harting led, Lord Droxford would surely follow. Had Alicia been inclined to his suit in other respects, this weakness in his character would certainly have put her off.

Mr Merry did not know how to face Alicia. "Good day, Miss Westlake. How nice to see you again."

His words of welcome sounded hollow even in his own ears. Alicia thought he looked ill and wondered if it was sickness that had kept him away.

"Good day, Mr Merry. I hope you are making good progress with your studies. They must be quite extraordinarily absorbing to keep you from visiting your friends."

Mr Merry could see the hurt in her eyes but felt helpless to do anything about it.

"Did you never think to come and visit me at Swanmore? Lord Droxford found plenty of opportunities. You must know that your company would have been as welcome as his," she added confidentially.

Mr Merry could feel his resolution wavering. After all, he had only promised his mother that he would stay away while the Duke and Duchess were in Ireland. "I am sorry," he mumbled, "but it was not in my power."

Alicia wanted to demand why it was not in the power of a grown man to act according to his inclination, but at that moment Lady Harting interrupted their conversation with offers of refreshment. When she turned back, Mr Merry had disappeared.

The Duchess was too focused on preparing for the forthcoming entertainment to pay much notice to the bleak look on Alicia's face. She whisked her disconsolate daughter away to her room and immediately set Martha to work on her hair. It was of the utmost importance that they were looking their best.

Their new sack dresses were fashionably striped, the Duchess in grey and silver and Alicia in ivory and peach. The Duke had given Alicia a pearl necklace and earrings to wear with her ball dress. They were simple, but just the right adornment to go with her gown and eminently suitable for a girl of her age. The Duchess was looking forward to dazzling the other guests with the ruby and diamond necklace that the Duke had given her as a wedding present. It truly was the most stunning piece of jewellery she had ever owned.

The ball was splendid. The decorations were splendid. The band was splendid. But Alicia was disappointed. She opened the ball with Lord Droxford, danced twice with Mr Hampton and never lacked for partners the rest of the evening. But of Mr Merry there was no sign.

Had she but known it, Mr Merry was observing the progress of the evening from a discreet viewpoint on the first floor balcony, but he did not come down to the ballroom floor and so Alicia was not to know of his interest in the proceedings. He could not resist standing there, watching her, jealously noting all her partners and hoping, somehow, that she could still be his.

Chapter 31

By the end of the ball, Alicia was feeling distinctly aggrieved. How dare Mr Merry pursue her so avidly in London and in Weymouth and then ignore her completely when she was living only twenty miles away? And now, when she had attended a ball right here in his own home, he had not deigned to be present. He had not danced nor come to supper nor even put in an appearance at the breakfast served at the end of the ball. Alicia was adamant that she was not going to leave the house until she had received an explanation of Mr Merry's behaviour.

She wished she could face him right then, but she could hardly go to his bedchamber and demand an audience. It was almost eight o'clock in the morning. The guests not staying over had left after breakfast and the few like themselves who were privileged to remain had retired to their bedchambers. But the house was far from still. Whilst the family and their guests slept, the servants were busy cleaning and tidying and putting the rooms to rights. By the time she awoke, there would be no evidence that there had ever been a ball. She would just have to wait. They were to stay one more day before returning home. Surely Mr Merry could not avoid her completely.

Although she might have been tempted to dwell on her disappointment, the exertions of the evening were sufficient to send Alicia to sleep as soon as her head touched the pillow. She awoke, refreshed, barely four hours later, eager to track down Mr Merry and very ready for the second breakfast which Martha informed her was being served.

Alicia's enthusiasm did not last long. Mr Merry was at breakfast, but it seemed as if her arrival was a signal for his departure, and he stayed but a few moments after she sat down to eat. The situation did not improve. Lord Droxford attached himself to her quite particularly and stayed at her side, giving his opinion on every aspect of the ball, for the entire afternoon. Mr Merry reappeared at dinner, but he was seated about as far away from her as possible. She had no opportunity for private conversation with him, or indeed, any conversation at all. After dinner, Lord Droxford was once more seated beside her, and she was obliged to endure yet more of his small talk. Before she could find an opportunity to escape, Mr Merry had left the drawing room.

It was the end of a very disappointing day. Alicia was angry at Mr Merry's desertion. Was he really so absorbed in his studies that he could not give up a single hour to talk with her? Now that there was no possibility of speaking with him, she could not wait for the evening to end. She began to count the minutes until she could retire and was not sorry when the Duke noticed her stifled yawns and recommended that the party break up early.

Back in her bedchamber, Alicia dwelt miserably on the defection of her friend. She had felt so sure she would have had the chance to talk to Mr Merry at some point during the day. But she was going home in the morning and apart from their unnatural conversation when she had arrived, she had not exchanged two words with him. It was a lowering conclusion, but one she had to face up to: he was avoiding her. But why? She could not understand his change in attitude.

She paced up and down her bedroom until Martha became quite concerned. She had never seen her young mistress so worked up.

"Come along, Miss Alicia. Let me undress you and then I will go down to the kitchen and get a nice cup of hot milk for you."

"Thank you, Martha, but I think I will need something more than milk to calm my mind tonight."

Martha slipped the snowy white nightgown over Alicia's head and persuaded her to sit down while she brushed her hair out. But Alicia did not seem to be able to sit still tonight.

"Do stop fidgeting, Miss," Martha pleaded.

"I wish I had brought a book with me. Maybe if I had something to read it would help me to settle. It never occurred to me that I would want one while I was here."

"The Earl has a fine library, Miss. Perhaps I could fetch you one when I go to get your milk."

"No thank you, Martha. No doubt you would come back with a book of sermons and I am not in the mood for that tonight."

Martha tucked Alicia into bed and scurried off to the kitchen. She soon returned with a cup of warm milk and at Alicia's request, she bade her goodnight and withdrew, leaving her mistress to sip her drink and blow out her own candle.

Alicia finished her milk but it did not calm her spirits. She tossed and turned but was so restless that she could not get comfortable. The confinement of her bedroom was irksome and she wanted to be doing something. If she had been at home, she might have stolen outside into the gardens for some fresh air, but she had no wish to cause a scandal by walking through the Earl's grounds in the moonlight.

Perhaps she could creep downstairs and find herself a book in the library. She would have to be quick. She knew that her mother would give her a tremendous scold if she was discovered jaunting about the house in her nightclothes.

She jumped out of bed and grabbed her dressing gown, pulling the cord tight across her front. Picking up her candle, she opened the door and listened. Not a sound. Everyone had gone to bed. All the candles in the sconces had been snuffed, leaving the hallway in darkness. Even the last of the servants must have retired for the night.

Fortunately, she remembered how to get to the library. She made her way along the corridor and down the stairs without incident and crossed the huge vestibule, with hardly a noise. The library was the second door on the right. Her own candle burned brightly in the darkness of the hallway. She turned the handle and pushed the door open. On the far side of the room, the last embers of the fire were still glowing in the grate. So he had been in here, studying, as she had supposed.

She carried her candle to the first column of shelves and started to read the titles, hoping that something would grab her fancy before she had scanned every book in the place.

"Do you normally wander around other people's houses at night?"

Alicia jumped violently, nearly dropping her candle. It was him of course. He had a habit of coming up behind her and making her jump.

"Come to the fire," he said, taking her hand. "It is not much of a fire, but it is still giving off a bit of warmth."

She allowed him to lead her across the room to where the fire was slowly dying in the grate. She felt she owed him some kind of explanation and turned toward him as she started to speak.

"I expect—ugh!"

The smell on his breath was overwhelming. Alicia wrinkled her nose in displeasure.

"Brandy."

"Oh."

"I am drunk."

How was she supposed to respond to that?

"I thought it only fair to warn you. You can go if you like."

"You have my hand."

"Oh. Sorry." He dropped her hand immediately, but perversely, she did not leave.

"Why do you get drunk, Mr Merry?" Alicia asked.

"I beg your pardon?"

"I said, why do you get drunk?"

"You have lived in society all these months and you ask why I get drunk?"

"Mr Merry, you are not like other men. In the whole time that I have known you I have never once seen you act in the way that society dictates. So I repeat, Mr Merry, why do you get drunk?"

Mr Merry struggled to think. He really was most awfully drunk and he was not sure that he was up to dealing with Miss Westlake in this condition. Somewhere in the dark recesses of his brain he remembered that he must not kiss her. He must not tell her that he was as drunk as a wheelbarrow because he was so depressed at the thought of her marrying his brother. He had drunk to forget for so long that it had seemed the natural thing to do. But he must not tell her. Otherwise all his sacrifice would be for nothing.

He resorted to anger and sarcasm to keep his softer feelings in check.

"Does your mother know you are here, Miss Westlake?" he asked, abruptly changing the subject.

Alicia shook her head.

"Ah, I thought not. She would never forgive you if you let yourself be compromised by a mere younger son, the black sheep of the family. Have you a soft spot for a black sheep, Miss Westlake? I assure you that it is not advisable. Have you not considered that I might want to snare an heiress?"

He took a step toward her, so that she could smell the brandy on his breath, but she refused to budge. "You do not scare me, Mr Merry. Why are you so determined to try?"

"Perhaps I am trying to scare you away for your own good. Remember, I am drunk and can hardly be held accountable for my actions. You really should go, Miss Westlake. Your reputation would be in tatters were you to be found alone with me in a state of, shall we say, dishabille."

Alicia's cheeks glowed as she recollected the fact that she was ready for bed. She had not expected to meet anyone. She pulled her dressing gown more tightly around her.

"You have carelessly happened upon the wrong brother, Miss Westlake. I am an embarrassment to my family; Droxford is perfection itself. Surely you have noticed? He is everything that my parents want in a son. He does all things well. He has no opinions of his own but agrees heartily with every word my mother utters. He gambles a little, drinks rather more, but never behaves in an indecorous manner. He has just enough religion to convince everyone that he is a good man without ever having to do anything to prove it. He moves in the best circles, dresses in the height of fashion and never causes my revered parents a moment's anguish. At my mother's bidding he pursues a lady who is unsuited to him in every possible way and no doubt he will offer marriage to that lady at the exact moment that my mother suggests it. It will be a very proper arrangement without passion or emotion and my parents will be immensely pleased at the exalted connections they have made."

"It must be hard to live in the shadow of such a paragon," Alicia replied.

"Quite. In fact, I choose not to live in his shadow at all. Droxford never sends out ripples wherever he goes; I tend to make a splash and people get wet. I am an embarrassment to my family—no, not an embarrassment, a disappointment. I have made the fatal error of being unconventional. If I was truly depraved, I think I would be more acceptable. Droxford passed through Cambridge as a matter of course. I, on the other hand, discovered an aptitude for learning. But was I praised for my achievements? No! I was criticised for consorting with the wrong set of people. As if Pitt and Wilber were somehow inferior because they were untitled! I wanted to go into Parliament like my friends, but that was not allowed. Droxford must go into Parliament. That was the role of the elder son. I was too passionate. There was no telling what I might say. Without my family's support, I had no hope of obtaining a seat. As a younger son, I did not have sufficient income at my disposal to buy a seat like Wilber. I daresay my father could have used his influence to get me one, but he declined to intervene. He would never go against my mother. My mother wanted me to enter the church. She thought it would suit my academic inclinations. The church! When she knows that I do not believe. I refused. I am not such a hypocrite. And so I am labelled the black sheep of the family: the son who refuses to go to church and disobeys his parents."

"That is pitiable indeed," replied Alicia, "but hardly sufficient to give you the reputation of a black sheep."

Mr Merry raised his eyebrows in surprise. "What? Is that not sufficient for you? What do you really know of black sheep, Miss Westlake?" he asked, advancing toward her. "Do they seduce young ladies of quality who carelessly put themselves in their power?"

Alicia bit her bottom lip. Mr Merry was standing so close, towering over her, that he had almost completely blocked out the light. She gulped. She was not afraid. Whatever Mr Merry said, he did not seem to be able to scare her. He was much easier to trust than his brother. She did not think that she would care to be alone like this with the Viscount.

They stood for a while in silence, gazing into each other's eyes, almost daring the other to make the first move. At last Mr Merry looked away. He walked back to his table and picked up his glass of brandy and took a large sip as if nothing particular had happened.

He had to act naturally. Being so close to Miss Westlake in a state of undress was having a powerful effect on him. He had to forget that she was here, with him, alone in the library, in the middle of the night, dressed in—

"Can I ask you a question, Mr Merry?"

"But of course," Mr Merry replied, welcoming the

interruption. It would not be helpful to pursue his current train of thought.

"Do you think I should marry your brother?"

Mr Merry spluttered, almost choking on his brandy. "Marry my brother? What kind of question is that to ask me?"

"You are my friend, Mr Merry. If I said I was going to marry your brother, would you see fit to tell me – to warn me – if he had a mistress?"

This time Mr Merry did choke. Alicia had to stop and pat him on the back.

"Miss Westlake, I—"

"Yes?"

"It is not considered fit to talk of a man's mistress in front of a young lady like yourself."

"So it is something I am supposed to discover after I am married?"

"Are you going to be married?" he asked.

"Have you got a mistress, Mr Merry?"

This time he choked so badly that it took him several minutes to get his breath back.

"After all, you have just told me that you are the black sheep of your family. Does that make you without morals too?"

"Miss Westlake, I think you had better leave."

"Have you got a mistress?" she repeated urgently.

Mr Merry put down his glass and advanced toward her. Despite her previous assurances that he could not scare her, she retreated from the intense look on his face. She backed away from him, never once taking her eyes off his face, until she bumped into the bookcase. Mr Merry leaned over her, placing one hand on the book-case either side of her head, so that she felt quite trapped. Alicia bit her bottom lip anxiously.

"No, Miss Westlake, I have not got a mistress," Mr Merry said with slow deliberation.

"Then Mrs Martindale—?"

"No, Mrs Martindale is not my mistress."

"Oh."

"And no, Miss Westlake, I most definitely do not think that you should marry my brother."

For a moment Alicia thought that Mr Merry was going to kiss her, but no sooner had the thought popped into her head, then he turned abruptly and walked out of the room, leaving her quite alone.

Chapter 32

The Holybourne House ball left Alicia feeling completely dejected. Despite their night-time encounter, Mr Merry had made no effort to see her before she returned home and had not visited since. Perhaps her boldness had given him a disgust of her. Lord Droxford continued to call, but Mr Merry did not.

It might have cheered her somewhat if she had known that Mr Merry was feeling quite as dejected as she was. When he went over their conversation in his mind, he realised that she had not denied that she was going to marry his brother. The inevitable conclusion was that she was going to marry him, but did not have the heart to admit it.

Alicia would have liked to put all thoughts of love and marriage aside, but it was impossible. The Duke gently suggested that his nephew would make a good husband whilst her mother persisted in promoting Lord Droxford's suit. Alicia wondered what it would take to make them both realise that she did not want to marry either man.

The Duchess was overjoyed at Lord Droxford's continued attentions and thought he must be about to pay his addresses. She could not, or would not, believe that Alicia was indifferent. "The Viscount is the biggest prize on the matrimonial market. I know that you find him a tad arrogant, but his superiority in all matters of the ton gives him some right. He is the catch of the season."

"Mother, how can I say this plainly to you so you will understand? I do not want to marry Lord Droxford."

"But Alicia, I so want you to have the position in society that your father could not give you."

"Mother, you threw yourself in the Duke's way and succeeded in winning his affection. You have raised my position in society by these dubious means, but I do not want to marry for wealth and position. I want more than that. If I marry, I want to marry a man of integrity whom I can both love and respect."

"But I do love the Duke," the Duchess whimpered. Alicia put her arm round her mother. She did not doubt that her mother loved the Duke, though she questioned the depth of her affection. Her own feelings ran far deeper, and not in the direction of the Viscount.

But when, a few minutes later, her mother started to put forward the benefits of the match again, Alicia was so exasperated that her ordinarily calm disposition deserted her and she lost her temper. "Mother, please stop!" she shouted. "I do not love Lord Droxford. I do not even like him. Please give up the notion that I can be persuaded to accept him. I am not interested. I can neither love nor respect him. Do you hear me, Mother? I will not marry Lord Droxford."

To Alicia's amazement, her mother burst into tears. Her mother never cried. Not really. She often had hysterics – what Alicia thought of as mock tears – but rarely, very rarely, did she truly cry.

"I am sorry," she sobbed. "I just want you to be happy, secure, in case—"

"Please do not cry. I did not mean to shout."

The Duchess sniffed loudly. "It is just that I am not young and—"

"Mother, you are hardly in your dotage."

"Yes, but at my age, there is a greater risk."

Alicia stopped. She went absolutely still. Surely not. This just could not be happening. The Duchess sniffed again.

"I just want to be sure that, if anything happens to me, you will be safe, secure. I want you to have your own home, so that if—"

"Tell me you are not going to have a baby."

The Duchess found that she could not meet her daughter's eye. "Well, it is not what I was expecting. After all, I was married to your father for years and no brother or sister ever came after you so I thought—"

"Oh, Mother! Are you sure?"

"Yes, yes, of course I am sure. A woman knows these things. And the nausea is a rather convincing little clue. I cannot get up in the morning without eating a dry biscuit in bed. The Duke is so caring, so considerate. If I admit to feeling not quite well, he insists that I take to my bed and rest."

Her mother sniffed again. "I am afraid, Alicia. It should be you having a baby—not me. The Duke's first wife died in childbirth. She did not live to see her baby. The Duke was left alone with his son and then Denmead was killed in those horrid riots. The Duke has been on his own for so long that I think he is afraid of being left alone again. He is petrified that something will happen to me. And I think, perhaps, that it is his overwhelming need to cosset me that is making me feel so anxious."

The Duchess would have preferred not to tell anyone else during the early months of her pregnancy, but the Duke was so protective of his wife in her delicate condition that it was impossible. Having confessed to a slight dizziness during the afternoon, the Duchess was obliged to lie down until the dinner hour at the Duke's bidding. Although the rest had completely restored the Duchess to her normal state of health, the Duke was more than usually solicitous for her welfare and could not refrain from repeatedly asking her if she was feeling quite well all through dinner.

Such behaviour could not pass unnoticed and Mr Hampton remarked that he was unaware that the Duchess had been indisposed.

"No, no. She is quite well, Joshua. Just a slight dizzy spell this afternoon. Nothing to worry about. The doctor assures us it is quite normal."

Lord Richard and Mr Hampton stared at the Duke expectantly. The Duke was so pleased with the prospect of fathering a child at his time of life that he welcomed the excuse to share his secret.

"Oh well, I can see that you have guessed. It is hard to keep such good news to myself. Congratulate me, Joshua," he said to his nephew, patting him on the back. "I am going to be a father again!"

Alicia watched to see how the Duke's family would receive the news. A flicker of something went through Mr Hampton's eyes and was gone. It might have been shock; it might have been anger. She could not be sure. Whatever his true feelings, he was quick to offer his congratulations. A little too quick, Alicia thought. After all, his hopes of inheriting the dukedom one day were slipping away. If the baby was a boy, he would never be duke, and even if the baby was a girl, no doubt the Duke would lavish all the property not tied to the dukedom on his own daughter rather than his nephew.

"At your age, Uncle!" Mr Hampton teased.

"Aye, aye. It is a good joke, is it not?"

Lord Richard was undeniably shocked. Alicia watched as he sat there, not speaking, for fully ten minutes.

It was not until the gentlemen had been left alone with their port that Lord Richard finally gave vent to his feelings. His tone was far from congratulatory.

"Why must you be setting up your nursery again at your age?" grumbled his brother.

"Now, now, Richard. You must not think I will forget you. You have been my heir for these past nine years and I will, of course, make adequate provision for you. But I am sorry that young Joshua here might not inherit the title after all. You have been like a son to me, Joshua." He sighed. "More of a son to me than ever my own boy was."

Mr Hampton gave a superficial smile, but the Duke noticed nothing amiss. "I am glad that you are happy, Uncle."

The gentlemen sat over their port a long time. The Duke was euphoric; Lord Richard was resentful; and Mr Hampton—Mr Hampton was thoughtful.

At the Duchess' request, the Duke agreed to keep the news within the family. She did not think she could bear everyone knowing if she were to lose the baby. Just a few months, she begged.

The Duchess refused to give up on her hope of changing Alicia's mind about Lord Droxford. She continued to invite the Earl and Countess and their son regularly to dinner, but said nothing, trusting in time to win her daughter over.

Unwilling to upset her mother again, Alicia played along. Outwardly she smiled, while inwardly she gritted her teeth and looked forward to going to London where there would be some relief from the self-important Viscount's company. In contrast, Mr Hampton's friendly conversation was a distinct relief.

After a particularly long afternoon of paying visits in the neighbourhood, the Duchess was exhausted. The Duke bid her rest and she was only too glad to obey him. Marie put her to bed with strict instructions not to wake her. Accordingly, when Marie went to dress her for dinner and found her still fast asleep, she sent down a message to the Duke that the Duchess would not be joining them.

As the Hartings had been invited to dinner, some excuse was necessary. "Well, I see that I cannot keep our secret from you," the Duke confided. "My wife is in an interesting condition, but I must swear you to silence or the Duchess will rake me down! It is only known within the family."

The Countess' bosom swelled with pride. She had thought that the Duke wanted Miss Westlake to marry his own nephew, but nothing could have shown his approbation of the match with Lord Droxford more clearly. By including them in the secret, he was practically welcoming them into the family.

When the Duchess joined the ladies in the drawing room, she apologised for the slight indisposition that had prevented her from sitting down with them at dinner.

"There is no need to dissemble," the Countess said. "I confess that the Duke has let us into your little secret."

The Duchess was far from pleased, but there was nothing she could do but accept the situation graciously.

Lady Harting was unable to resist making pointed

comments about how careful the Duchess would have to be "at her age". The Duchess replied in kind. Outwardly they might appear to be the best of friends, but inwardly, their rivalry still burned.

"How brave of you to face the trials of motherhood given your advanced years," the Countess jibed.

"Indeed, but it is most gratifying to find that I am able to present the Duke with an heir at my age."

"What a disappointment if it turns out to be a girl."

"Not at all—the Duke always wanted a daughter."

"What a sacrifice you are making. Such a late foray into motherhood could seriously damage your health."

"I quite understand that you would not wish to take such a risk," the Duchess said with satisfaction, "but fortunately, the doctor says I am as healthy as most women are at half my age."

Meanwhile, Lord Droxford sat staring at his wine, trying desperately to avoid listening to the conversation. His father was heartily congratulating the Duke and reminiscing about the time when his own boys were born. It sounded as if he was envious. The Viscount felt heartily embarrassed. He was ready to get married at his mother's bidding, but the thought of being a father made him feel quite ill.

When the gentlemen adjourned to the drawing room, the Duke and Lord Harting were still deep in conversation about fatherhood. It seemed as if no other topic could draw their attention. Lord Droxford was quick to move as far away as possible from the discussion.

Alicia noticed his discomfort and could not resist taking the opportunity of depressing his suit once and for all. "I confess I never anticipated having a new brother or sister, Lord Droxford," she said.

The Viscount wriggled about nervously in his seat. Some answer was evidently required. "Indeed, no. It must have come as quite a shock to you."

Alicia beamed. "But such a pleasant one, do you not think?"

Lord Droxford was lost for words.

"I am sure it will not be long before I am setting up my own nursery," she said innocently, "and my mother's child will be a playmate for my own."

The Viscount looked aghast, but Alicia continued relentlessly. "I have always regretted being an only child. I do hope that I am blessed with a large family. I think that bringing up a large family would be most rewarding. Would you not agree?"

"I ... I ... have never given the matter much thought," the Viscount replied feebly.

"Just imagine all the noise. A large sitting room filled with children, laughing, crying, and squabbling, with urgent requests for a game or a story or—"

"I believe that is what a nursery is for," the Viscount countered weakly.

"Oh no? Do you think so?" Alicia enquired. "I would not always want to be sending my children off to the nursery. That is the joy of a large family."

"Pray excuse me, Miss Westlake," Lord Droxford intervened, before Alicia could say another word. "I believe my mother is beckoning me."

"But of course," she said meekly, trying not to smile. Her tactics had worked beautifully.

Lord Droxford rose hastily and walked quickly away from the lady he had been ardently pursuing for the past three months. He shuddered. What a lucky escape! He had been on the verge of proposing, but the scene that Alicia had just painted filled him with dread. He knew that it was his duty to provide an heir, but he had never envisaged a whole household of children and certainly not ones who made a noise or made demands on his attention.

The Countess frowned when she noticed the expression on her son's face. She knew that mulish look. Droxford was going to back down from the match. He was allowing his personal inclinations to affect his judgement. If that was the case, she needed to force the issue, or at the very least, help it along. Droxford was too much the gentleman to back down if the match was thrown at him.

The Duke was talking about his concern for his wife. He did not want to take any chances. The Duchess was to have the best care that money could buy. He thought perhaps it would be as well to consult a London physician. The Earl agreed that this was most assuredly the best course of action.

The Duke needed little encouragement and announced his intention of taking the Duchess to town as soon as possible. "I do not mean to make a fuss, my dear," he said, fondly patting his wife's hand, "but there is no harm in getting a second opinion on these dizzy spells you keep having."

The Duchess knew it would be useless to object. Maybe if the physician reassured the Duke, her husband would not feel the need to cosset her to death.

"I am perfectly ready to go to London, but I confess to being somewhat daunted by the journey," said the Duchess. "It is a long way to travel when you are feeling nauseous before you begin."

Lady Harting saw her opportunity. "I am not surprised that the thought of the distance puts you off. It would be most inadvisable to travel the whole way in one day in your condition. If you broke the journey up, you would find it much easier to endure. Let Holybourne House be your first stop and you may proceed in gentle stages from there."

The Duke agreed and gratefully accepted the offer. "If we set out for London on Tuesday and rest at Holybourne House, then we could easily reach Guildford on Wednesday. I will send word to my old friend Lord Onslow. I am sure he would be only too glad to provide accommodation for us at Clandon Park and then we could complete our journey on Thursday. What do you say to that, my dear?"

The Duchess was satisfied. If she could travel to London without being made to feel too unwell, she was not sorry to go. Although it was too early for the season, there would be entertainment enough to keep her occupied in town.

It was not until after the Hartings had left that the Duchess broke the news to Alicia who had missed the entire conversation. The Duchess did not think her daughter would be averse to going to London, but she was afraid that she might not quite like stopping off at Holybourne House en route. She was right.

"Holybourne House is hardly any distance at all from here. Stopping there is quite unnecessary. We could just as easily reach Guildford in a single day. Why do you want to spend three days on the road instead of two?"

"The Duke thinks it is a good idea to travel in easy stages, Alicia. A little break would be most welcome."

"What you mean is that it will give you yet another opportunity to throw me in Lord Droxford's way. Did you fail to notice the look on the poor man's face this evening? Believe me when I say that he is no more inclined for the match than I."

"What have you been saying to him?" the Duchess demanded.

"Merely hinting at the large family I am looking forward to having," Alicia replied.

"Alicia! You did not say anything so improper?"

Alicia bit her lip. She did feel somewhat guilty at the tactics she had employed, but although she was ready to apologise for her lack of propriety, she did not regret what she had said.

"Forgive me, Mother, but the temptation was too great. Besides, any man who cannot stand the thought of children is really not the right one for me. It would be unkind of me to continue to plague him. You go ahead and break your journey with the Countess. I am sure that you will find her conversation invigorating. Perhaps I will linger a few days longer here and travel up to London when Mr Hampton is free to accompany me."

"What an excellent idea," barked the Duke, who had just joined them. He had not quite given up the hope that Alicia would choose his nephew over Lord Droxford. "What say you, Joshua? Can you undertake to bring your cousin safely to London?"

Mr Hampton looked at Alicia's animated face and smiled warmly. "It would be a pleasure, Uncle. I have a little business to attend to which will take me away from home for a few days, but I will be free to accompany my new cousin to London by the middle of next week."

The Duchess was annoyed, but there was little she could do. If Alicia had really talked so improperly to Lord Droxford, perhaps she was fighting a lost cause anyway.

First thing on Monday morning, Mr Hampton rode off on estate business, anxious to be ready to fulfil his more pleasant commitment the following week. Meanwhile, the house was in an uproar, packing the cases that were to be conveyed to London and making the travelling chariot ready for the long journey.

Alicia wandered around the gardens disconsolately. She had acted on impulse when she had refused to accompany her mother and stop over at Holybourne House and now she was destined to stay in the country even longer when she really wanted to be in town.

It was not that she disliked the country; it was rather the company that she hoped to stumble across in town. She assumed that Mr Merry would soon be going to London, if he was not there already. Perhaps if she visited Mrs Montagu again she would see him and they could talk some more. Even if all they could do was talk, it was more satisfying than trying to make conversation with his brother. She wished that she had not acted so precipitately. Maybe Vauxhall Gardens would still be open as the weather was so fine and she could wander along the walks and remember her visit there in the summer. But perhaps that was not the best night to remember. It had brought her mother a step closer to being a duchess, but it had also brought Mr Merry's disapproval down on her.

Her thoughts were interrupted by a summons from her mother. She wondered what scarf or trinket her mother was now unable to find and slowly made her way to her mother's dressing room where the Duchess sat, surrounded by neatly filled packing cases.

"Oh, Alicia. What do you think? The King held a levée at St James' and hardly anyone attended. The first one since his splendid recovery and it was held at such short notice that nobody went. The Duke is mortified. He means to travel to London post-haste, for there is to be another on Wednesday and he is determined to be there. I wish I could go with him, but I cannot travel so fast. Even a slow coach makes me feel nauseous these days. I intend to follow him at the slower pace we had planned. Please say that you will come with me tomorrow, for I do not care to be apart from the Duke for long and I really cannot travel alone."

"And do you still intend to stop over at Holybourne House?" Alicia asked cautiously.

"It is not to be thought of. We have just received word from the Earl that they too are going to London for the levée. They said that Droxford would stay behind to receive us, but even I can see how particular that would look. After all, it is not as if you are engaged! No, no—I have abandoned the plan to stop over in Holybourne. Provided we set out early, I am sure we can make it to Guildford where the Duke has arranged for us to receive a warm welcome at Clandon Park. Another day's travel should see us safely in London. I only hope that it does not make me feel too unwell. Please say you will come with me, Alicia?"

"Of course, Mother," Alicia assured her. "Martha has already packed most of my things. We can leave first thing in the morning."

In little more than an hour, the Duke was on his way to London. The Duchess looked truly crestfallen and Alicia was smitten with remorse; perhaps her mother's feelings for the Duke were deeper than she had realised.

The rest of the day dragged and it was with relief that the two ladies retired soon after dinner. Alicia thought it was as well they had agreed to leave early the following morning. She feared that if they had not, her mother would have fallen into a fit of melancholy and, no doubt, it would have been her lot to talk her out of it.

Chapter 33

A licia did not care much for the six o'clock start, but
her mother was so anxious to set out, that she had
readily agreed to the early departure time. They were
travelling in her mother's chaise, the same one in which
they had journeyed to London almost a year before, but
with the Duke's arms newly emblazoned on the doors.
The Duchess had always said that the only thing missing
from her travelling chariot was a coat of arms and she
was quite content with the effect.

Rowson had made all the arrangements. The Duke's
head coachman, Wilby, was to drive them to London,
riding postilion so as not to obscure their view. Rowson
had agreed with Wilby where they would change horses
and had arranged for the Duke's own teams to be ready
for them. A guard armed with a blunderbuss was to
accompany them for protection from highwaymen; the
maids were to follow behind in one of the Duke's
coaches, with Rowson himself and most of the luggage.
There was nothing for them to do but sit back and enjoy
the journey as best they could.

Their route skirted the Earl of Harting's estate. Alicia
gazed through the window as they went by, staring at the
imposing stone wall and wondering what was happening
in the house beyond. Was Lord Droxford sitting, waiting
to see if they would come? Or was he nervously biting
his fingernails, hoping that he would be spared the effort

of entertaining the Duchess and the daughter that she so clearly wanted him to take off her hands?

As they passed the main entrance, she looked down the driveway as far as her eyes could see. She wondered idly who had made all the statues that lined the avenue leading up to the house. Perhaps Mr Merry had bought them for his father in Rome. She had not thought of that before. Perhaps they were centuries old and not newly carved marbles as she had assumed. Maybe her father had painted them in situ, before they were transported to England.

Maybe … She was still absorbed in her thoughts when the stonework suddenly came sharply into focus as the carriage swerved terribly. The horses were in complete chaos. She could hear Wilby shouting furiously.

Alicia looked out of the window. A coach and four was heading along the road toward them at breakneck speed. On one side of their carriage was the wall and on the other, the ground fell sharply away from the road and ended in a ditch. Wilby was trying to pull over to let the oncoming carriage pass, but the rapidly approaching vehicle seemed to be out of control. It swerved this way and that, from one side of the road to the other, so that the coachman did not know which side to pull to in order to get out of its way.

Alicia could hear Wilby yelling: "Pull over, man. Pull over!"

But the other vehicle could not or would not. The Duke's horses were wild with panic and despite the highly experienced coachman's best efforts, the erratic driving of the approaching carriage was forcing them off the road. Desperate to avoid a collision, the horses plunged this way and that, stumbling as they tried to keep their footing.

The carriage swung wildly behind them until a final swerve was too much. With a loud cracking noise, the pole broke as the carriage overturned, falling heavily into the ditch. As the body of the chaise made contact with the ground, Alicia and her mother were thrown from their seats.

It took Alicia a moment to realise what had happened. Her head was throbbing. She must have hit it when the carriage tipped over. She could hear the noise of the frightened horses mingled with the shouts of those struggling to bring them under control. Her ears soon blocked out the cacophony of noise outside and became focused on the sounds inside the carriage. Everything was strangely quiet. No, not completely quiet. Somewhere in the distance she could hear something. A small whine. Heavy breathing. As her thoughts became clearer, she remembered that she was not alone.

"Mother?" Her urgent shout was unanswered.

She reached across the capsized coach to where her mother was lying, crushed against the window frame on the opposite side. Her face was covered with cuts from where it had made contact with the broken glass.

"Mother, wake up!" No response. Panic began to consume her. She took a deep breath, trying to calm herself. She could not afford to lose control now; her mother needed her. Dear God, please let my mother live, she prayed, as she shook her vigorously, trying to get a reaction.

To her relief, the Duchess began to whimper.

"Mother? Are you hurt?"

"I cannot move, Alicia," she sobbed. "My ankle is caught."

Alicia gently raised her mother's skirts and saw that her foot had become trapped in the wreckage when the side of the carriage had smashed into the ground.

"Try to stay calm, Mother. I will get help. Wilby must be somewhere nearby. He will be able to free your foot and pull you out. Just hold on."

The body of the carriage was lying at a strange angle. It was on its side, crushed in the ditch, whilst the wheels were still more or less level with the road. As a result, the floor was pitched at an angle that made it more like a steep slope than a flat surface. Alicia was grateful that the current fashion was for looser fitting dresses than in the days of her mother's youth. She could not even begin to imagine trying to climb out the window wearing a hoop! She would have been obliged to strip down to her petticoats and that was not a prospect she fancied, even when in dire straits.

She hitched her dress up as best she could and tried to pull herself up using the carriage seats. If only she could reach the window, she would have more leverage. But alas, this was one time when her inches let her down. She was not tall enough to secure a firm hold and slithered back down to the bottom of the coach in her attempt.

Urged on by her mother's whimpers, she resolved to try again. This time she discarded her shoes and stockings and her bare feet gave her added grip which enabled her to scale the slope more effectively. "Be brave, Mother. I will be back soon," she cried as, with one final effort, she threw open the carriage door and clambered outside. Unfortunately her dress caught on the doorway and she heard a loud ripping noise as she pulled herself out of the carriage and gingerly climbed over the body. With a sigh of relief, she slid down over the side and found that her feet were on solid ground again.

She looked down at her appearance and laughed. Her dress was torn, her feet were bare and her hair was hanging down in several places having come loose from her exertions in climbing out of the carriage. Then she recollected that her mother lay trapped in the broken carriage and chided herself for thinking about such insignificant things as how she looked.

How on earth had such an accident happened? Where the carriage had left the road, she found the groom struggling with the horses, frantically trying to calm the animals. He must have jumped clear before the carriage had gone over. She did not dare to interrupt him; he clearly had his hands full. But where was Wilby?

She soon found the Duke's coachman, lying on the road some little way away from where the groom was trying to bring the horses under control. Alicia was relieved to find that he was still conscious.

"Thank God," she cried with feeling. "What happened? Are you hurt?"

"Some blundering idiot who couldn't control his animals drove us off the road, Miss. Didn't even stop when he saw that we were going over. Can't blame poor Comet for rearing. I didn't stand a chance. Poor beasts. I've never seen 'em so frightened."

"Wilby, my mother is trapped in the carriage. You must help her."

"Happen I can't do that right now, Miss. I'm afraid I landed some'at awkward like and I think this leg of mine is broken. Maybe my shoulder too, for it hurts like the devil, Miss, if you'll pardon my speaking so freely."

There was no sign of the guard. She called out, but there was no response. Alicia did not like to think of him lying crushed beneath the carriage.

Wilby was more optimistic. "Happen young Tom has

gone for help, Miss. James jumped free so happen he did too. Those poor horses! They were proper worked up by that fool of a driver. Happen the idiot's lying in a ditch somewhere yonder with his own broken coach. Shouldn't be allowed on the road. And mighty early in the day to be at his liquor. Happen he had been drinking all night. That would explain it."

"Yes, that must be the explanation," Alicia agreed. "But I cannot just stay here assuming that Tom has gone for help. My mother's ankle is trapped in the wreckage. She cannot get out. And you need a doctor if your leg is to mend properly. I will go for help myself. Fortunately, I know who lives here, Wilby."

"Happen you do, Miss."

"Lord Droxford will send help." Even in the midst of her troubles, mentioning her erstwhile suitor's name still caused her to blush.

"Happen he will, Miss."

Alicia started to make her way along the road, back to the entrance that they had passed a short while before the accident had occurred. Every time her naked foot trod on a pebble, she cringed, but she did not stop. Her mother was depending on her. She looked at the unyielding stone wall and shuddered. The ditch was bad, but the wall would have been worse. At that speed, the solid stonework would have smashed the carriage to pieces. But it was not helpful to dwell on such things, unless it was to be grateful. With a quick prayer of thanks that the carriage was pushed left and not right, she determined to put such negative thoughts behind her and set her mind on rescuing her mother.

Chapter 34

Alicia was disappointed to find no one at the lodge at the entrance to Holybourne House. It meant that she would have to make the long walk up the driveway by herself. In bare feet. It would be mortifying to arrive on the Earl's doorstep in such a dishevelled state, but Alicia was too concerned about her mother to give more than a fleeting thought to her appearance. That said, it was a relief to know that Lady Harting was from home. Despite everything, she would have shrunk from appearing before that lady in her current state. But the Countess had gone to London and it would be Lord Droxford who saw her like this. She had no wish to make a good impression on him. If her current appearance gave him a disgust of her, so much the better.

She rang the bell vigorously and waited impatiently for the door to open. The butler did not betray by so much as a flicker of an eyelid that her appearance was anything out of the ordinary. In the back of her mind, Alicia stored away the information that if ever she set up her own establishment, she must obtain such an invaluable member of staff.

"Good morning. Is your master at home? There has been an accident."

"Be so good as to step this way, Madam, and I will inform him directly," said the butler, showing her into the Red Room.

Alicia paced up and down the room. Every moment of delay was a moment leaving her mother trapped inside that horrid carriage. She had walked as rapidly as she could, but her bare feet had hampered her progress and it had taken her well over half an hour to reach the front door.

She paused at the mirror and grimaced at her reflection. Her hair had come out of all its restraint and was poking out wildly from under her hat which was sitting at a very odd angle. She quickly unpinned her battered bonnet and made an attempt to straighten her hair as best she could before restoring the crumpled headgear. She was still wiping a smut of dirt from her face when she heard the door opening.

"Lord Droxford," she said eagerly as she turned to the doorway, but the words died on her lips. "Oh!" she cried. "Oh, but I thought—"

"A miscalculation on your behalf, Miss Westlake, and one that I hope will not inconvenience you," Mr Merry said in an icy tone that froze her blood, as he paced up and down the room in much the same way that Alicia had been doing a moment before. Without even looking at her, he continued in the same caustic tone.

"He said that you would come. He said that your mother was set on having him for a son-in-law. I thought I knew better. But no matter—clearly he was right. But there really was no need to go to all the trouble of contriving an accident on my father's doorstep. You see, Droxford took fright and ran to London and so you find only his reprobate brother in residence. You can trap me, but I am afraid that I am no great catch. I am, alas, only a younger son and so do not meet your mother's very obvious criteria. I will never be a viscount let alone an earl. A sad situation for you, I am afraid, but—"

"Mr Merry!" she interrupted, too distracted to let his cutting words affect her, though she was mortified at his interpretation of her actions. Surely he knew her better than that? "If you do not stop talking I will have the worst fit of hysterics you have ever been privileged to witness. I know what this might look like, but believe me when I say that appearances can be deceiving. Our carriage has had an accident. This is no contrivance. My mother is lying hurt inside, trapped in the wreckage. God knows how badly she is injured. The coachman has broken his leg. I left the groom struggling to control the frantic horses and the poor guard, as he clearly has not come here for help, may be lying crushed beneath the vehicle. Please will you give us some assistance before it is too late?"

At Alicia's words, Mr Merry stopped pacing and looked at her properly for the first time. In a single glance, he took in her torn dress, her bare feet and her hair, still falling, tangled, around her face, despite her best endeavours. He saw the strain on her dirt-smeared face and cursed himself for not believing in her, despite the incriminating circumstances. He had so steadfastly declared to his brother that she would not come that her arrival had thrown him into complete disarray. He so wanted to believe that he had been right, that she was different from her mother, that he readily accepted what she was saying, however unlikely the explanation appeared. He heard the note of desperation in her voice and with difficulty restrained himself from taking her in his arms and offering her the physical reassurance that she stood desperately in need of. He immediately took charge of the situation.

"Miss Westlake. I have been a fool not to realise that you are in genuine distress. I can only apologise for my unfeeling behaviour. Let us not waste any more time in ruing my lack of sensibility. Can you tell me where the accident happened?"

The change in Mr Merry's tone of voice almost undid her. Her heart had been beating hard and fast whilst she had resolutely made her way to the Earl's house for help. Anxiety had helped her to remain composed even when Mr Merry was ranting at her.

But now that he was talking to her with gentleness, she became momentarily overwhelmed and found that she was shaking from head to foot. Mr Merry anxiously watched her. How could he have been so blind to her obvious anguish? "Can I get you a glass of wine to calm your nerves? You have had a very distressing experience."

"No, no," Alicia replied, rallying her spirits with a supreme effort. "My mother lies trapped. We must go and help her at once. The carriage came off the road but a short distance past the lion gate."

Mr Merry strode out of the room and barked instructions to the staff. Within a very few minutes, the Earl's second travelling carriage was pulled up behind Mr Merry's own phaeton, into which he invited Alicia to climb. Motioning to the coachman to follow, he spurred his horses into action and drove them down the driveway and out of the park as fast as safety would allow.

"Tell me what happened."

"We were going along the turnpike road just south of Alton. As you know, the road passes alongside your family's estate. I knew we were next to your land as soon as I caught sight of the wall. I was just wondering where the statues came from when a madman came driving his carriage toward us as fast as his horses would go. Our coachman tried to pull to one side to let him pass, but his horses were out of control. Wilby thinks the driver must have been drunk to let his vehicle career from side to side like that. Fortunately, he was able to steer us into the ditch, as the lesser of two evils. But the ditch was not very forgiving. The horse Wilby was riding reared in its distress and he landed badly. He thinks his leg is broken and maybe more besides. The groom jumped clear when the carriage tipped over, but my mother and I were trapped inside. When I discovered that my mother could not move, I managed to climb out of the overturned carriage and came to you for help. I am just so thankful that Wilby managed to steer the carriage into the ditch and not the wall. At that speed, the carriage would have been smashed to pieces and us with it."

Mr Merry nodded curtly and concentrated on his driving in silence. The thought of Miss Westlake's carriage being smashed against the wall that ran around his father's estate made his blood run cold. Half an hour before, he had been prepared to damn Miss Westlake as a title hunter, but now he wanted to wipe away the anxious frown on her face. He wanted to cherish and protect her. It was something he had never felt before and he was entirely unprepared to deal with it.

His contemplations were interrupted by an exclamation from Miss Westlake. "Here, Mr Merry, here. Stop the carriage."

Mr Merry brought the phaeton to a halt and jumped down, handing the reigns to his groom who ran quickly to the horses' heads. When he saw the tattered wreck that had been the Duchess' very smart chaise, Mr Merry became seriously alarmed. Without waiting for his servants to arrive, he started to climb down into the ditch, next to the wreckage.

"Your Grace, can you hear me?" he called. When he failed to elicit a response, Alicia joined in, shrieking in a most unladylike manner.

"Mother!" she yelled. "Mother, I have brought help. Can you hear me?"

The reply was weak but audible: "Alicia."

By this time, several men who worked on the estate had arrived and Mr Merry discussed with them the best way forward. They could try to right the carriage, but the Duchess could end up more injured than she was already. They would have to get the Duchess out before any attempt could be made to lift the battered carriage.

"I will go," volunteered Mr Merry. He stripped off his coat and cast it aside before approaching the tilted carriage. He hoped to goodness that it was wedged in its ungainly position and not balanced precariously on some tree or shrub that might collapse under the addition of his weight and shift the carriage's position. Several men held onto the exposed parts of the carriage while he lowered himself through the doorway that Alicia had climbed out of an hour before.

He immediately saw the problem. The carriage had fallen on a boulder which had smashed the side of the carriage and the Duchess' foot had become trapped in the broken wood when she had been thrown from her seat in the impact. It took some time to free the Duchess. Little by little he worked at the wood around her foot with his knife, all the time talking to the Duchess as if they were having afternoon tea. At last he was able to pull the Duchess free, but when she tried to put pressure on her foot, she squealed with pain.

"Her Grace's foot is free but she's unable to use it. I am going to need a rope to get her out," he called up through the open door.

A rope was swiftly found and tied firmly round the waist of a stocky farm worker who stood on the road above the wreckage. Mr Merry secured the other end underneath the Duchess' arms and, at his signal, the rope gently hauled the Duchess up to safety.

By the time Mr Merry had dragged himself up and out of the carriage, the Duchess was safely ensconced in the Earl's coach with her daughter beside her.

Almost as soon as the door was shut, the Duchess' courage deserted her and she burst into tears. "My baby. Oh, my baby."

Guiltily, Alicia realised that she had not given her mother's condition a moment's thought. She looked at the tears streaming down her face and wondered how resilient unborn babies were to sudden impact. And as she sat in silence, with her arm around her mother's bruised and sobbing body, she had to acknowledge just how much this unborn child meant to her. To her surprise, it hurt. She would no longer be the centre of her mother's attentions—this new baby, if it survived, would be. It was a very melancholy thought.

Mr Merry hurried over to the Earl's travelling coach. He was eager to ensure that the Duchess had been made as comfortable as possible. But as his hand went to the door handle, he heard the noise of wailing coming from within and hastily withdrew it. He was not accustomed to such excessive shows of emotion.

No one cried at Holybourne House. He doubted whether his mother had ever cried in her life. As children, he and his brother had been chided if they wept over a cut knee or a broken toy. "Stand up to your problems like a man," their mother had always said. And if they could not control their passions, they had been sent straight back to the nursery. Such a show of emotion had never been acceptable at Holybourne House.

He stood back from the coach and gave instructions for it to be driven back up to the house as smoothly as possible. He had sent a man for the doctor before they had set out to rescue the Duchess. With any luck, the man would be waiting for them by the time they reached the house. The coachman had been lifted onto a farm cart and transported up there already. The doctor would need to set his leg, but the man did not seem to be suffering from any concussion, which was a mercy considering how far he had fallen.

The guard had been discovered at some little distance from the wreckage where he had been thrown when the carriage went over. He had been knocked unconscious, and it seemed as if his wrist was broken, but he could have suffered much worse. Mr Merry thought he was lucky to be alive. There would not have been much hope for him if he had been trapped under the falling vehicle. It was a nasty business.

The doctor was just leaving the Duchess' room when Mr Merry arrived back at the house.

"The Duchess is doing as well as can be expected, Mr Merry. It has been a terrible shock, but her injuries are superficial. She has a swollen ankle and a few cuts and bruises, but she is more worried about the baby than herself."

"The baby?" he asked incredulously.

"Oh yes, the Duchess is with child. She is most anxious for it. There was little I could say to reassure her. It is too early to say. I have prescribed two weeks of bed rest. All we can do is to wait and see. And now I must see my other patients. I believe there are some broken bones to be set. Be so good as to show me the way."

Mr Merry summoned a servant who conducted the doctor to where the Duke's men had been laid. He was left alone, hovering outside the Duchess' room, wondering what to do.

Chapter 35

The Duke's travelling coach arrived shortly after the doctor had left, bringing the ladies' maids and the ubiquitous Rowson. As soon as Marie heard that her mistress had been injured, she demanded to be taken to her side at once. The Duchess had her complete devotion. It was the summit of Marie's ambitions to be lady's maid to a duchess and she revelled in her mistress' elevated status. Now she had the position she craved as well as a huge salary and she was not going to lose it by any negligence on her part. Mr Merry showed her up to the Duchess' room, adjuring her to send Miss Westlake along to the drawing room for a cup of tea as soon as her mistress was settled.

Marie immediately took control of the sick room, plumping up the Duchess' pillows and adjusting the fire screen, and managing to make her mistress feel a good deal more comfortable by her zealous attentions. In less than half an hour, the Duchess was asleep and there was nothing for Alicia to do but obey Marie's urging to join Mr Merry for a cup of tea.

Mr Merry was anxious to make amends for the unpardonable callousness of his words to Alicia when she had arrived that afternoon. Admittedly, as soon as he had realised the true situation he had sprung into action and worked unceasingly, but that still did not excuse the fact that he had been excessively rude. He could try to justify himself on the basis that the circumstances were too similar to what his brother had predicted, but he was angry with himself for failing to depend on his own judgement. For the first time in his life he had trusted his brother's opinion over his own.

He did not really want to consider why his reaction had been so violent. Perhaps it was plain, stark jealousy that, yet again, his brother was going to get something that he wanted. And he did want Alicia, even though it was beneath his dignity to admit his feelings for someone whom he still feared was on the catch for bigger fish than he.

He was quick to notice the fatigue on Alicia's face. She looked worn down by the distresses of the day and her anxieties were far from over. "How is your mother?" he enquired tenderly.

"She is resting now. Her ankle pains her somewhat, but her real anxiety is for the baby."

Some response seemed required. "The doctor mentioned it—I was not aware that the Duchess was with child."

"No. Not many people are. It is too early. Mother wanted it to be a secret. Only the family knew," Alicia replied. "And your parents and brother," she added awkwardly.

Mr Merry sighed. His brother really was being welcomed as part of the family. No doubt his brother would eventually submit to his mother's wishes. Droxford could never stand up to her for long. "Holybourne House is at your disposal for as long as you need it."

"Thank you."

"And you?" he asked gently. "How are you?"

The tenderness of Mr Merry's tone took her by surprise. Was this really the same man who had ranted and raved at her when she had arrived on his doorstep? She had not really stopped to think how she felt. It was over. Her mother would recover. But the baby? Maybe the baby would not survive and her mother would be devastated. And poor Wilby's leg was broken and he would be laid up for weeks. And the Duke would be so distressed. And it had really been a most dreadful day. Such an awful, horrible accident.

Alicia burst into tears. It was something that she rarely did. Perhaps it was the sense of relief that they were still alive. Perhaps it was just the reaction to all that had occurred. Perhaps, now that she had stopped, now that she no longer had to be brave and in control, the shock of what had happened was setting in. Her whole body was racked with sobs.

Nothing in Mr Merry's life had prepared him for comforting a lady in distress. But Miss Westlake was in trouble and his heart went out to her. He acted on instinct. He walked across the room and put his arms around her and held her while she sobbed. Then he led her to the sofa and sat down beside her, his arm still firmly draped around her shoulders.

Alicia was too upset to think about her undignified pose and allowed herself to rest her head against Mr Merry's broad shoulder as she sought to control herself. The distraught figure sitting next to him tugged hard at Mr Merry's heart. It seemed natural to offer her what comfort he could. And so he gently lifted her chin and kissed her in what he tried to convince himself was a brotherly way.

Alicia stopped crying immediately. It was impossible to keep on crying while you were being kissed. Her body was responding to the kiss in anything but a sisterly way. If she had been standing, she would surely have fallen.

That kiss told her more about the state of her heart than her head had ever done. She had thought herself above temptation. She had rebuffed any suitor that had come close to embracing her. And now the unbelieving antiquarian had done it—and she did not want him to stop. Somewhere in the back of her mind she knew that she must not be drawn in. It would not – could not – work. She thought of her parents' unhappy marriage. She had seen the pain caused by having too many differences to overcome in a relationship. Mr Merry's attitude toward everything she believed in was too big an obstacle. Even if she did love him. Why did people fall in love with such unsuitable individuals?

With a great effort of will, Alicia pulled away from the comfort of Mr Merry's arm and stood up.

"Pray forgive me," she blurted out. "I do not know what overcame me. I do not usually indulge in such a show of weakness. Thank you for being such a comfort to me in my distress. It is what I always thought a brother would be like."

Mr Merry was speechless. Whatever his original intention had been, that was no 'brotherly' kiss. It had been magical and he felt sure that, just for a moment, it had been magical for Miss Westlake too.

"The kiss—I was just trying—I am sorry—"

"Mr Merry, there is no need to apologise. You were offering me comfort when I was in distress and you have my gratitude. I am perfectly in control now. I think that I will go and see how my mother is doing. Pray excuse me."

Gratitude! She was offering him her gratitude? He was no flirt. No doubt his brother would have known what to say to get Miss Westlake back in his arms. If he had been his brother, no doubt she would still be curled up in his arms. She would not have drawn away in the first place. Yes, it had been magical—magical for both of them, but while he was marvelling in the tenderness of the embrace, Miss Westlake was making sure she did not compromise herself any further with an untitled younger son.

Chapter 36

Mr Merry sat for a long time unable to move. How was he going to face Miss Westlake now? What had he been thinking of? She was upset and he had taken advantage of her. Putting his arm around her was intimate enough, but what on earth had possessed him to kiss her? He savoured the memory of that kiss. It was probably the only one he would ever have. And he had been sure, just for a moment, that she had returned his embrace. But then she had come to her senses. She was kissing the wrong man. Had it been his brother, no doubt she would have carried on. She did not choose to throw herself away on a mere younger son. Never had he felt so angry about his lack of birthright. If only he had been the elder son, he would have been eligible.

As the dinner hour approached, Mr Merry became acutely aware of the awkwardness of entertaining Miss Westlake alone after what had passed between them. It was something of a relief when her maid brought a message to say that she would take her meal in her mother's room. He was sorry not to have the pleasure of her company, but could not help thinking that it was for the best. Alicia had withdrawn from him. For a moment she had forgotten, but then the realisation that he was the impoverished younger son must have hit her. He found it hard to forgive her for putting rank and wealth above love.

Alicia could not avoid Mr Merry's company at breakfast the next morning, but his manner toward her was so uncharacteristically formal that she felt as if they were strangers. Perhaps she had imagined the connection during that kiss. But if that was so, then she should be thankful for his withdrawal. Following her heart would only lead to a lifetime of unhappiness and regret.

A letter arrived post-haste from London. Alicia thought absent-mindedly of the poor man who must have ridden through the night to bring it. The letter was from the Duke. Mr Merry had sent news of the Duchess' misfortune the previous afternoon and the Duke had immediately dashed off a reply. He was extremely distressed to hear of the accident and shuddered at the thought of what might have happened. He was grateful to Mr Merry that he had been able to rescue his wife and relieved to hear that the Duchess was not seriously injured. Only the King's levée prevented him from riding down to Holybourne House on the spot. He regretted the circumstances that had caused him to change his plans. With a complete lack of logic, he reasoned that somehow his presence would have prevented the mishap. He requested frequent updates on the Duchess' condition and promised that he would set out as soon as the King's levée was over.

After Mr Merry had read the letter, he passed it to Alicia to peruse. She read it and handed it back and then an awkward silence fell between them. Neither knew how to carry on as they had done before.

Just as Alicia was thinking of excusing herself, the door burst open and Mr Hampton strode, unannounced, into the room. His eyes fell on Alicia and he hurried round to where she was sitting and took her hands in his own.

"Thank God you are safe!" he exclaimed loudly. He threw his head back as if sending up a silent prayer before sitting down heavily in a chair at the table. "I came as soon as I could," he continued. "I was so distressed when I heard what had happened. Your mother?"

"The Duchess is recovering well."

"And the baby?"

"It is too early to say."

Mr Hampton nodded. He turned to regard Mr Merry and sneered. "How fortunate that the carriage should be overturned so close to friends. If it had been planned, the location could not have been more convenient."

"If it had—" Alicia repeated in a tone of disbelief mingled with outrage. She stood up abruptly. She did not like Mr Hampton's insinuations. "My mother is hurt, Mr Hampton. We might have been killed. I think that you could spare us from hinting that the accident was premeditated."

Mr Hampton hastened to assure her that he had meant no such thing. "It was an unfortunate choice of words," he apologised. "Of course I did not mean that you had planned it. The only person to benefit from your misfortune is your host who has had the pleasure of your undivided attention."

Alicia thought that Mr Hampton's apology sounded more like a thinly veiled accusation. She was immediately on the defensive. To suggest that Mr Merry had planned the accident was ridiculous. No one could have predicted the outcome of the carriage being driven off the road. Both she and her mother could have been killed. Hardly a good way to pursue a courtship!

"And a great privilege it was that Miss Westlake could call upon me for aid. I am only thankful that I was at home and had not gone to London with my brother."

"Yes, indeed," Mr Hampton replied with mock sincerity. "How very fortunate."

Alicia sighed. The silent battle that had been raging between the two men had escalated into open war. It seemed that it was now impossible for them to meet without sparring and she did not much like being caught in the middle. "Pray excuse me, gentlemen. I am going to sit with my mother."

Both gentlemen rose and watched Miss Westlake until the door closed behind her. They both sat down, painfully aware of the antagonism between them, but neither knowing how to execute a graceful exit.

"Dare I ask what became of my uncle's horses?" Mr Hampton asked.

"The horses are in the stables, Mr Hampton, in the care of my own groom. Fortunately the traces broke before the animals were dragged down into the ditch with the carriage body and escaped with little hurt."

"And the wreckage?"

"I have made no attempt to lift it yet, though I am afraid that it is far beyond repair."

"I should like to see it."

"Very well. There is no time like the present." Mr Merry led the way, glad to be doing something. Anything was better than sitting, thinking about that kiss.

While they walked to the stables, Mr Merry seethed in silence, a silence that Mr Hampton made no attempt to break. Mr Hampton's words had been insulting. To suggest that he had put Miss Westlake and her mother at risk in order to gain the pleasure of her company was outrageous. Mr Hampton was doing nothing to improve the opinion he had formed of him the very first time he had seen him, all those years ago. It would seem that Mr

Hampton would go to any lengths to turn Miss Westlake against him. The competition should have depressed him, but strangely enough, it did the opposite. If Mr Hampton thought him a threat, then maybe, just maybe, he did have a chance with Miss Westlake after all.

As he went over the conversation in his mind, one thing began to trouble him. Perhaps the accident was not the result of an evil mischance. Heavily laden coaches were notorious for toppling over. No one else had seemed to think it odd that the coach had been capsized into a ditch by a drunken driver pushing them off the road. But now that he had been accused of contriving the mishap, he could not rid himself of the impression that perhaps it was not so accidental after all.

Having gone over the wreck with Mr Hampton, he left him to his groom and rode off to make some enquiries. He could have sent his man, but he decided he had endured quite enough of Mr Hampton for one day. He made a tour of all the local coaching inns to see if an unknown carriage had arrived some time the previous afternoon, but everywhere he enquired, he drew a blank. The more negative responses he received, the more convinced he became that there was something more here than had at first appeared. Surely a drunken driver would have, sooner or later, driven his own coach off the road or at least stopped for refreshment? But everywhere he went, he got the same response. There had been no news of an accident and no unknown coaches stopping yesterday afternoon. It was all very strange.

At the same time, Alicia sat with her mother and mulled over Mr Hampton's words. She did not believe for a moment that Mr Merry was guilty of what Mr Hampton had covertly accused him of, but his words had made her wonder. She longed to ask Mr Merry whether he thought there was any possibility that the accident had been planned. It was an unsettling thought that someone had purposefully tried to push their carriage off the road.

She determined to take Mr Merry aside and ask him, but no opportunity for private conversation presented itself.

Out of courtesy, Mr Merry reluctantly offered Mr Hampton a bed for the night, an offer which Mr Hampton eagerly accepted. "I feel in some measure that I am standing proxy for my uncle," he said. "I know that the Duke would want me to be here, in case the Duchess took a turn for the worse."

Mr Merry managed a forced smile, and muttered something polite, but he foresaw a long evening ahead of him. Having Mr Hampton's face continually in front of him reminded him too forcibly of what he wished he could forget.

Alicia left the gentlemen to their port and went to sit with her mother. The Duchess had slept intermittently throughout the day and was happy for her daughter to read to her. Alicia had managed to find all four volumes of Samuel Richardson's *Pamela* in the Earl's library and had borrowed them for her mother's entertainment. It was not her favourite, but she decided she would rather read that than Henry Fielding.

"Dear Father and Mother, I have great trouble, and some comfort, to acquaint you with. The trouble is that my good lady died of the illness I mentioned to you, and left us all much grieved for the loss of her: she was a dear good lady, and kind to all us her servants …"

Oh my, thought Alicia. She would not have chosen to read *Pamela* to her mother if she had remembered how it began. What a depressing way to open a novel! She read on, but stopped when she noticed that her mother's eyelids were closing, just as she was reaching the bottom of the first page.

"Do go on, my dear. I am awake, truly."

Alicia continued, but very soon stopped again. This time her mother did not speak. She closed the book and put it on the bedside table and crept out of the room. She let Marie know that her mother was asleep and deliberated about whether to go downstairs or retire to her room. She decided on the latter course. No doubt Mr Hampton would wait up until Mr Merry retired and she would be forced to endure an hour of uncomfortable conversation without securing a moment's private talk with Mr Merry. No, she had a far better plan for achieving her object.

Chapter 37

Alicia retired to her room but she had no intention of going to bed. She desperately wanted to talk to Mr Merry. She needed to voice her fears, and be told that she was being foolish. But more than that, she wanted to be assured that Mr Merry was still her friend. She could not abide him acting as if they were little more than strangers.

The clock struck midnight before she heard noises in the hall. The gentlemen were retiring for the night. At least, Mr Hampton was. She would wait until she heard him passing along the corridor before creeping out of her room. She was determined to talk to Mr Merry tonight and she was confident she knew where to find him.

She dismissed Martha and stood silently just inside the doorway to her bedroom, listening hard for the sound of footsteps. It seemed likes hours before she heard Mr Hampton passing her door, but it could not have been more than a few minutes. She waited a little longer and then opened the door as quietly as she could and slowly made her way downstairs.

The house was in darkness. The only light was that coming from her candle. She felt like a robber, creeping around someone else's house late at night. Every creaking floorboard made her jump. She made her way across the hall to the library. As she had expected, she could see a warm glow coming up from under the closed door. She hesitated a moment and then confidently turned the handle and entered the room.

"Hallo?" she called out tentatively.

Mr Merry sprung out of his chair by the fireside and stared at Alicia in surprise.

"Miss Westlake!" he exclaimed.

"I am sorry to disturb you, but we need to talk."

Mr Merry gulped hard. He was not sure that this was a good idea. The intimacy of being alone together in the semi-darkness, especially with him in his current state, was working powerfully on his senses. His breath quickened as she came toward him. This was definitely not a good idea. He was not sure he could trust himself to behave.

"You have been avoiding me," Alicia accused him.

"I thought it was best."

"Why?"

"Because I kissed you."

"Oh."

"I was trying to comfort you. You were upset."

"So you did not really want to kiss me?"

"I did not say that."

Alicia nervously bit her bottom lip. He had all but admitted that he wanted to kiss her. It was most improper, but very gratifying.

"Do you want to kiss me now?"

"Miss Westlake. That is a very dangerous question to ask a man who has drunk half a bottle of brandy. I want very much to kiss you right now. And no, I do not think you stand in need of any comfort."

Alicia assimilated his response and smiled. She had not meant to say that at all. She really could not afford to flirt with Mr Merry. It was too dangerous.

"As I said before, Mr Merry, we need to talk."

"At this hour, Miss Westlake? Believe me, I am at your service, but did your mother never tell you that you really should not visit a gentleman in his study, particularly not at this time of night?"

She ignored him and carried on. "I cannot stop thinking about what Mr Hampton said."

Mr Merry waited. "Yes?" he prompted.

"What if the accident was not an accident?" Alicia blurted out, unable to keep the suspicion to herself any longer.

"I see," he replied quietly. "So you have come to accuse me in private?"

"Do not play with me, Mr Merry. You know very well that I am not accusing you. But tell me, if you please, do you think that it is possible that someone deliberately forced our carriage off the road?"

Mr Merry hesitated. Should he share his own suspicions and risk worrying her unnecessarily? On the other hand, if the accident had been planned, Miss Westlake should be on her guard.

"Yes."

Alicia did not know whether to laugh or cry. She had not expected such a direct answer. "What makes you think so?"

"I can find no trace of the supposedly drunken driver who forced your vehicle off the road."

"And you think that is significant?" Alicia asked.

Mr Merry nodded.

"But why?"

"If the driver were drunk, he would surely have crashed his own carriage or at least stopped to rest. I can find no evidence that he did either, which implies, perhaps, that he was not drunk after all." Now came the difficult part. "Your mother is with child. If someone was afraid that she would give birth to an heir—"

"Are you suggesting—?"

"I am not suggesting anything. I am merely looking at the facts. Who stands to lose from the birth of an heir?"

"Are you asking me to believe that Lord Richard attempted to kill me and my mother?" Alicia asked incredulously.

"Either Lord Richard or his son. For my part, I think Mr Hampton is the most likely contender."

"I might have guessed," Alicia retorted. "You seem to be incapable of rational thought where Mr Hampton is concerned. I cannot believe that you are accusing him in the same way he accused you this morning. Are you sure that you are not letting your own antipathy for Mr Hampton cloud your judgement?"

"Miss Westlake, I have told you before not to trust Mr Hampton. Now I have even more reason for telling you so again."

"But you will not tell me why, Mr Merry. Mr Hampton has shown me nothing but kindness and you want me to repay this with thinking him capable of such a heinous crime?"

"I have my reasons."

"Then tell me, that I may judge for myself."

Mr Merry hesitated. He was afraid that if he once opened the door on those awful memories, he might never be able to shut it again.

"Please?" Alicia begged.

Again Mr Merry hesitated. He was afraid that the alcohol was affecting his judgement—that in the morning he would regret having said so much. But Miss Westlake's safety was at risk. That was motive enough.

"You asked me once why I got drunk. I will tell you. I drink to forget. Have you ever known fear, Miss Westlake? Fear that completely overwhelms you and renders you incapable? That returns, time and time again, disturbing your peace?"

Alicia shook her head.

"I felt that fear once, Miss Westlake, and I have been running away from it ever since."

She reached out and laid her hand on his in sympathy. "Tell me."

Mr Merry's eyes glazed over—the effect of the alcohol in his bloodstream. With a supreme effort of will, he transported his mind back to the night he wanted to forget and began to unlock the memories. Miss Westlake gave his hand a reassuring squeeze and somehow he found the courage to begin.

"Do you remember the day we visited Mr Townley's house in Park Street, and he told you how I had rescued his favourite marble—the one he jokingly called his wife?"

Alicia nodded.

"That was the night it all happened—the night of the rescue. I was in London for the express purpose of visiting Townley's collections. I had visited several times that week already, but he kept encouraging me to go back. I think it was a rare experience for him to come across someone who shared his passion and we formed a firm, if unlikely, friendship as a result. You know what I am like. The town was exploding with anti-Catholic unrest, but I was so consumed with all the incredible objects I was seeing that I had not really noticed."

Alicia understood. Mr Townley's collections had evoked a similar reaction in her.

"It was on my fourth visit that the trouble reached

us. When I arrived at Townley's house, I found him in a pitiful state. He had heard that the mob had burned Lord Mansfield's house and was scared for his collections. I had not even realised he was a Catholic. The riots seemed to be moving toward his house. I helped him rescue Clytie, but refused a place in his carriage, foolishly assuming that I could make my own way back to my lodgings. By this time, there were people everywhere. In the distance, I could hear the sound of guns firing. They had sent soldiers in to restore the peace. The mob went wild, desperate to get away from the gunfire. I was carried along by the crowd moving in the opposite direction and lost my way. I ended up in an alley with nowhere to go. Before I could retrace my steps, a man came running down the street toward me. He was well-dressed, a gentleman, and I assumed he was escaping from the mob like me."

Mr Merry looked deeply into Alicia's eyes, hoping that she would not condemn his cowardice. "I was scared. The man looked like he was running for his life. The natural conclusion was that we were both in danger—that the mob was close behind. I panicked. I ran for cover and shouted to the man to join me, but he tripped and fell. I wanted to help him, but I could not move. I was frozen to the spot with fear. It seemed like an eternity, but it must have been only a few minutes later that a soldier on horseback came thundering down the street toward us. The soldier rode right up to the man cowering on the floor. The next moment, his horse suddenly reared and its hooves crashed down on the man's head, crushing his skull."

Alicia gasped.

"I am sorry. I did not mean to shock you. I have never had a strong head for things like that myself. It makes me feel sick just to remember. The images of that evening are forever imprinted on my mind and I have tried so hard, so very hard, to block them out."

Alicia squeezed Mr Merry's hand again in sympathy. "I am so sorry."

He pulled away from her grasp abruptly and started to pace the room.

"Do not feel sorry for me, Miss Westlake," he spat out. "It is not the memory of the horror that upsets my peace, but the shame. I saw a man killed in front of my eyes and I did nothing. I was so afraid I could not move."

"I doubt there was anything you could have done. It was just an accident."

"Was it?" he demanded angrily. "As the full horror of what I had seen began to sink in, I kept thinking what a terrible waste of life. What an awful mishap. But then I looked up and caught the expression on the soldier's face. It was a look of sheer hatred. He looked glad that the man was dead. And it made me wonder whether it was not an accident after all."

Mr Merry stopped in front of the fire and stared vacantly into the flames. "When my feelings overcome me, I drink. I drink to forget."

"But I do not understand. What has this got to do with Mr Hampton?" Alicia asked.

"It is his face that is imprinted on my memory. He was the soldier."

"No!" Alicia cried. Every feeling revolted. "Nine years is a long time, Mr Merry. Surely you must be mistaken?"

"I do not think so. The likeness is too strong."

"But if you are convinced, why do you not bring him to justice?"

"How could I ever prove that it was not an accident? He was a soldier doing his duty, Miss Westlake. Maybe he could have controlled his horse, maybe he could not. Either way, I am utterly convinced that he meant that man to die. I cannot forget the look on his face. Such a man is not to be trusted. That is why I urge you to be on your guard. I have no proof, just a strong antipathy that will not go away."

"I do not know what to think," Alicia said. "I find it hard to accept that Mr Hampton could have acted like that and yet I do not doubt that you believe what you say. What a dreadful thing the riots were to have stirred up such savagery in people."

"And do not forget, it was all over an argument about religious freedom. I decided that night that if that was what religion did to people, I wanted none of it. So I determined to eat and drink and laugh at life, for it could be me tomorrow."

"And what if it was?" Alicia retorted.

"I beg your pardon?"

"What if it was your time to die tomorrow? Would you stand before your Maker and explain that you drank to forget? And tell him that you do not believe in him and so cannot accept his judgement?"

"Miss Westlake, you cannot understand."

"That is the worst excuse ever—'I cannot under-stand'! I will not claim to know what it was like to see someone die like that, but I watched my father die, in peace, ready to go to his Maker. It was sad for me, because I miss him so much, but I know he has gone to a far better place."

"Your sincerity almost convinces me, Miss Westlake. But what if you are wrong?"

"What if I am right, Mr Merry? Would you throw

away the chance of eternal peace because faith is a risky business?"

"Now that I have never considered. I have always seen religion as a crutch. To comfort the poor and motivate the few, like my friend Wilber, to do good. He has tried time and time again to convince me and Pitt of the truth of what he believes, but, as you see, he has failed. Perhaps I am too much the cynic to live by faith."

"Perhaps you are too little a risk-taker."

Her words hung in the air.

Alicia shivered. She dreaded to think what time it was. She really should return to her room before Martha missed her. "I must go," she announced.

Mr Merry grabbed her by the hand as if he would prevent her from leaving. "Be on your guard, Miss Westlake." The earnestness in his voice chilled her more than the words. It was not an easy thing to see Mr Hampton as a potential threat; he had always been a friend to her.

Alicia nodded. "I will. Thank you, Mr Merry. Goodnight." She pulled her hand free and Mr Merry made no move to regain it. At the door, she paused and turned back toward him. "God bless you."

The door closed and Mr Merry was left alone with his thoughts and a dying fire. Even as the last vestige of warmth disappeared, he sat heavily, not moving. He drank no more, but sat and listened to the sound of her voice singing in his head, over and over again: "Too little a risk-taker. Too little a risk-taker."

Chapter 38

Mr Merry spent the rest of the night sitting in his chair in the library. He slept little. He was afraid that now he had stirred up those awful memories, they would once more overshadow his dreams. He had never told anyone what had happened that night. Not even John knew the whole story—only what he had blurted out when he had arrived back at his lodgings, nauseous with the shock of witnessing the most harrowing event of his life. John had never asked. That was the beauty of a loyal manservant. But at last it had come out and he had to admit that it was a relief. Perhaps the whole thing had been blown out of all proportion in his mind from having kept it to himself for so long. Maybe his hatred of Mr Hampton was prompted by more than a memory. Maybe he was underestimating the power of jealousy.

Before dawn, he rose and went to his room to change his clothes. He always ensured that he retired before the maid came to clean out the grate. He had once made the mistake of staying till morning and he had almost scared the poor girl out of her wits. Besides, he was anxious not to miss a chance of seeing Miss Westlake over breakfast. Her nocturnal visit had encouraged him to believe that she was not as indifferent to his kiss as she had claimed at the time.

Miss Westlake was at breakfast. Unfortunately, so was Mr Hampton. Mr Merry was quick to note that the conversation was all on Mr Hampton's side, with Miss Westlake returning little more than monosyllabic answers. He smiled to himself. She may not share his antipathy, but he had certainly succeeded in making her wary.

"Did you sleep well, Miss Westlake?"

"Yes, thank you."

"And have you seen Her Grace yet this morning?"

"Yes."

"And how is she?"

"She is doing well, thank you."

"Do you ride this morning, Miss Westlake?"

Alicia raised her eyebrows in disbelief. "No, Mr Hampton. I am going to sit with my mother. Pray excuse me."

Mr Merry bid a hasty retreat. He had been unable to avoid asking Mr Hampton to stay in his parents' house, but that did not mean he had to be sociable with a man he disliked and had good reason to mistrust.

Alicia spent the whole morning with her mother without respite. She felt weighed down by all the thoughts that were bombarding her peace and it was with difficulty that she kept up a cheery dialogue with her mother, interspersed with sections from *Pamela*.

But neither the conversation nor *Pamela* failed to keep her attention. Her thoughts kept drifting back to the conversation in the library. She blushed at the remembrance of her own forwardness that had led to Mr Merry admitting that he wanted to kiss her. She brushed the thought aside quickly. She must not dwell on that kiss. It was too dangerous for her peace of mind.

She thought with horror about Mr Merry's dreadful disclosures and wondered what she should believe. It was hard to keep her thoughts to herself and not share her fears with her mother. After all, it was no small matter to suggest that the Duke's nephew might be trying to kill them. Of course, in the broad light of day, the idea seemed preposterous.

If Mr Merry had hoped for a tête-à-tête with Miss Westlake, he was out of luck. She had still not emerged from her mother's room when the sound of carriages heralded the arrival not only of the Duke, but of his own beloved family as well. He might have guessed that his mother would have deemed it opportune to return home to act hostess to the Duke.

The Countess had not given up her darling plan of marrying her dutiful elder son to the Duchess' daughter. As soon as she heard about the accident, she criticised Lord Droxford for persisting in following them to London. It should have been her elder son on the scene, not her younger. She feared that Christopher would take advantage of the situation to pursue his own interests. The foolish boy probably thought that he could snare a fortune for himself, but she knew better. He would ruin his brother's chances and then the Duchess would look elsewhere for a match for her daughter.

"Good afternoon, Mother," Mr Merry said.

The Countess had no time for the preliminaries. "How is the Duchess, Christopher?"

Before he had a chance to answer, the Duke and his father walked in. "Good afternoon, Your Grace," Mr Merry said, pointedly addressing the Duke. "I am happy to say that the Duchess has passed a good night."

He turned to his father who acknowledged his greeting and then fell silent. For the hundredth time, Mr Merry wondered why his father had married a lady who ruled his house for him. He supposed that his father must like to play second fiddle, but he knew it would not suit him. It might suit Droxford, he thought, as he nodded to his brother who brought up the rear of the party. Droxford would be lost without someone telling him what to do. Mr Merry despaired of his brother. Despite what Droxford had told him about not wanting to marry Miss Westlake, here he was again, in their mother's train, presumably being constrained to make another push for the heiress.

Mr Merry saw the look in his mother's eye and guessed that she was not pleased that it had been he and not Droxford who had been able to aid the Duchess in her hour of need. He suspected that he would get the blame for Droxford having left for London; his mother would never believe that her elder son had dared to upset her plans. He dreaded the forthcoming tirade. He always stood up to his mother, but that did not mean it was pleasant. And as he had no intention of repeating his promise to stay away from Miss Westlake, his mother would not be pleased with him. Of course, that was something he had learnt to live with at a very young age, and would not vex him unduly, but it would make things unpleasant.

The Duke's arrival released Miss Westlake from the sickroom, but Lady Harting made sure that her younger son had no opportunity to be alone with Miss Westlake. Alicia expressed a wish for fresh air and Mr Merry promptly offered to accompany her for a walk around the gardens. But his mother claimed a prior demand on his time in a very public manner which he could only refute with extreme rudeness—something he was not prepared to do, for Miss Westlake's sake. Lady Harting suggested that Miss Westlake take a walk with Lord

Droxford instead. It would have been churlish to have forgone her walk for the lack of good company, though she was sorely tempted to do so. Lord Droxford looked so miserable that Alicia could almost feel sorry for him.

Dinnertime afforded Alicia as little of Mr Merry's company as the afternoon had done. She was seated as far away from him as possible, and when the gentlemen joined the ladies in the drawing room, Lady Harting hovered near her like a shadow, never leaving her side, thus precluding any private conversation.

After a day of his mother's company, Mr Merry could stand it no longer. He did not want to leave Miss Westlake to his mother's mercy, but he had to get away. He could not stand by and watch his mother continually pushing Droxford to make up to Miss Westlake. It was unbearable. He hated to see his brother being manipulated by their mother but there was nothing he could do to prevent it.

He also needed space to think and he could not do that with his mother breathing down his neck. He was constantly in Miss Westlake's company and yet thwarted at every turn from having any meaningful conversation with her. So far, he had managed to keep his temper, but sooner or later his mother was going to push him over the edge. He did not want to subject Miss Westlake to such a scene.

He was still fretting over his last conversation with Miss Westlake. He was sure that she was not indifferent to him, but he was by no means convinced that she would agree to marry him. Although increasingly confident that she would not marry his brother or Mr Hampton, he was also increasingly unsure whether he could make her truly happy unless he was able to embrace her faith. Perhaps his mother was right and he was no good for her.

These doubts only served to make him more protective of the object of his affections. His deep-rooted mistrust of Mr Hampton made him nervous. If his worst fears were confirmed and Mr Hampton was responsible for the carriage accident, then Miss Westlake and her mother could both be in danger. If only he had something more concrete against Mr Hampton than an ingrained belief in his ruthlessness and a possible motive, he could try to warn the Duke. But how could he voice his suspicions as they stood? It was unthinkable. He would be laughed out of the house by Mr Hampton's doting uncle and would be in utter disgrace with his mother.

Even if he was right, Mr Hampton could hardly be a threat in such a busy household. Miss Westlake and her mother would be safe enough while surrounded by so many people.

Mr Merry determined to leave the following morning, but not without speaking to Miss Westlake. This might be his last opportunity to see her. If he decided that there was no future for them together, he would not be coming back. He persuaded John to deliver a note to Miss Westlake at an opportune moment, asking her to join him in the garden before breakfast the next morning. He hoped that she would not condemn his forwardness and be too prudish to accept.

Alicia was worn out with Lady Harting's chatter, which was laced with subtle and not so subtle references to the excellent prospects of her elder son and the happiness that would accrue to his future wife. It was clear that Lady Harting was going to give her no opportunity of speaking with Mr Merry and rather than face another hour of Lady Harting's company, Alicia pleaded the headache and retired early. She was on her way to her room when she was arrested by a voice.

"Madam?"

It was Mr Merry's manservant. What on earth could he want with her? Her mother. Perhaps her mother was worse.

The servant hastily assured Alicia that his mission was only to deliver a note from his master. He put the letter into her hand, bowed and disappeared. Alicia hurriedly secreted it away, afraid to be seen receiving a note from a servant. It would only excite comment, and provoke questions that she had no intention of answering. Not until she was undressed and tucked up in bed did she draw out the letter to read. It was not, as she half-feared, half-hoped, a love letter, but it was a request for what she could only deem an assignation. She knew she ought to refuse; she also knew that she was going to accept.

Alicia did not sleep well. Martha begged her to take her breakfast in bed, but she declared, quite truthfully, that she needed some fresh air before breakfast and hurried down to the garden for her secret tryst. She walked briskly toward the stream, hoping that she would not be seen. Mr Merry was waiting for her. They walked in silence, neither knowing how to begin what they wanted to say.

Inevitably, they both began to talk at the same moment. Mr Merry immediately backed down and begged that Alicia would continue.

"Mr Merry, I have thought at length about what you said to me. I understand how concerned you are for my safety and that of my mother, but I find it impossible to believe that Mr Hampton tried to kill us."

"Miss Westlake—"

"No, please let me finish. I understand the way you are thinking. You have seen him at his worst, appearing to revel in another man's death. And he is the ultimate heir to the dukedom and stands to lose it all if my mother has a son. But what I cannot understand, if what you suspect is true, is this: why would he try to kill me? It makes no sense. He has more or less told me that he wants to marry me. Would he really try to kill me if such was his intention?"

Mr Merry shrugged his shoulders. "I do not know. I have nothing further to say to persuade you, Miss Westlake. All I can do is to beg that you will not trust him." He paused. "I am leaving today."

"Leaving?" Alicia was completely taken by surprise. "How can you be leaving?" she asked in disbelief. "If you think that Mr Hampton is dangerous, why do you not stay to protect us?"

Mr Merry heard the disappointment in Alicia's voice and felt his resolution waver. "I do not believe that you are at risk whilst my parents and brother are at hand. Their assiduous attentions must make it impossible for any harm to come to you while you are here. I need space to think, Miss Westlake. You have stirred up memories that I have been trying to bury for years and I am not quite sure what to do with them. I wish …"

He stopped short. To make a declaration now would be madness. He lifted his hand to her cheek in an intimate gesture. "Goodbye, Miss Westlake."

Alicia watched his retreating figure with a sinking spirit. She could not believe that he was leaving her to the mercy of her fears and the relentless manoeuvres of his mother trying to force her into a marriage with Lord Droxford. Did he really care so little for her after all?

Mr Merry sought an interview with his mother whilst she was still in her dressing room.

"I am going to London to see Mr Wilberforce," he declared to his astonished parent.

"Indeed." Lady Harting could not believe her luck. She suspected a deeper purpose, but could only delight in his seeming capitulation. She was pleasantly surprised that her rebellious younger son had decided to make such a hasty exit. She had seen the way that he looked at the Duchess' daughter and had felt sure that he would try to prevent Droxford from marrying her.

"Your presence here means that my own is no longer necessary. I am sure that I can leave our guests in your capable hands, Mother."

Within the hour, Mr Merry was gone.

Chapter 39

Alicia missed Mr Merry's company acutely. It was no use pretending any more. She was in love and it was a hopeless case. In his absence, she dwelt heavily on all the disadvantages of the match. As to wealth, she was indifferent. What she would inherit would be more than enough for them to live on. But the difference in their beliefs weighed upon her mind. For so many years she had watched her father and mother pulling in different directions—her father to an evangelical mindset and her mother to the world of wealth and fashion. She could not face the thought of her own love withering because of the conflict that their different life views would cause. How could she bring up her children to be good Christians when the example of their father was always pulling them in the opposite direction? She could no sooner marry the man she loved than his pompous brother. Both would be doomed to fail. Love was not enough.

It was several weeks before the Duchess was well enough to be moved. Alicia had endured as much of the Countess and her biddable son as she could bear. She had avoided their company as much as she could by taking long walks. The grounds were beautiful. An infinite variety of autumnal shades was displayed in the leaves that were beginning to drop from the trees and carpet the ground beneath.

The Duchess was very shaken by her ordeal but was not oblivious to the sadness she saw in her daughter's face. She thought it was a pity that Mr Merry had taken such a hold of Alicia's affections and then disappeared. She had always believed that he was just trying to annoy his mother and his abrupt departure seemed to bear out the truth of her supposition.

The doctor declared that the Duchess and her baby were out of danger, but he strongly recommended a spell by the seaside to complete the Duchess' recovery.

"In November?" the Duchess exclaimed. "Surely the weather will be all sea mist and rain?"

"I understand your concern, Your Grace, but you will find that Weymouth has an exceptional climate," said the doctor. "The bay is so sheltered that it is quite safe to bathe all year round."

The Duchess was not convinced, but her husband was. "A few weeks by the sea would be the very thing, my dear. There will be so much more to occupy you in Weymouth than hidden away at Swanmore where you might fall into a melancholy."

"But why can we not go to London as we had planned?" she moaned. "I am sure that there will be plenty to entertain me there."

The doctor shook his head. "I really would not recommend the London air to Your Grace this winter," he apologised. "Not for you or the baby."

The Duchess pouted. She had not anticipated this level of cossetting and it was beginning to irk her. "Very well," she snapped. "I will go to Weymouth if you really think it best. For the baby's sake."

The Duke seemed relieved and immediately sent Rowson to secure lodgings in Weymouth before his wife changed her mind. It would be pleasant to go back to the

town when it was not so busy. The King had delayed the
opening of Parliament until December, so there was no
need for him to be in London. A few weeks by the
seaside would give them both a chance to regain their
peace of mind after the exigencies of recent events.

The Duke wanted to ensure that there was sufficient
company in Weymouth to satisfy his wife and eagerly
invited the Earl and Countess of Harting and their sons
as well as his brother and nephew to swell the numbers.

The Countess was delighted. How kind it was of the
Duke to invite them. Unfortunately, they would have to
decline the invitation on behalf of their younger son who
had gone to stay with friends in London.

Lord Richard grumbled. "Why must you be off to
the seaside again? You will get nothing but sea fog and
squalls at this time of the year. The seawater did nothing
for my gout in the summer and I will be damned if I am
going back there again."

"The doctor has recommended the sea air for the
Duchess. He maintains that it is fresher than London air.
And besides, you will not get away from the fog in town.
Come with us and at least we will have enough people to
play cards even if the weather lets us down. The Duchess
is very fond of cards, Richard, but perhaps you are afraid
she will cheat you out of your wealth?"

Lord Richard looked hard at his brother, but the
Duke did not seem to realise that his words could be
deemed in bad taste.

"I am sure you will manage very well without me,"
Lord Richard snapped and nothing that his brother
could say succeeded in changing his mind. The Duke
transferred his attention to his nephew whom he
encouraged to make one of the party, despite his father's
refusal.

"You cannot leave Miss Westlake to the mercy of Lord Droxford," he teased. "He might prove to be the only gentleman in town under the age of forty!"

"Rest assured, Uncle. If Miss Westlake is going to Weymouth, there is nowhere else on earth I would rather be."

The Duke thought, belatedly, that perhaps it had been rather unkind of him to encourage his nephew to go with them. He hoped that Joshua was not deluding himself. He had never noticed Alicia being more than sisterly toward him. There was certainly nothing to suggest that she would prefer Joshua as a husband rather than Lord Droxford. On the other hand, the Duke had not noticed Alicia being particularly receptive to the Viscount's advances. He was more inclined to believe that her preference was for the Viscount's brother. But Mr Merry had gone and as Lord Droxford seemed to have resumed his courtship with renewed enthusiasm, the Duke supposed that Alicia must have given him some encouragement.

The Duke hoped that Alicia would not mind going to Weymouth. He took her aside and explained that the doctor had recommended a period of convalescence by the sea.

"Oh—so we will not be going to London until later in the season," Alicia said, disappointed.

"Actually, my dear," the Duke said gently, "the doctor has advised us against going to London at all this year."

His words gradually sank in. Mr Merry was in London. If they were not going to London there would be no chance meetings. He would bury himself in his books and forget all about her. Tears began to fill her eyes. It would only prolong the agony, but somehow she could not accustom herself to thinking of a world without Mr Merry's friendship.

The Duke saw her tears and was horrified. "My dear girl, please do not be distressed. I could ask the Countess of Harting to take you to London with her when she goes, if you would like. I am sure she would be happy to do so—she is always so willing to oblige me."

Alicia could not think of a more unwelcome offer. "No, please do not. I am perfectly happy to come with you. I am just sorry to think that my mother is not well enough to go to London."

The Duke breathed a sigh of relief. "Yes, yes, my dear. It is natural for you to feel upset after what has happened. Maybe a few weeks of Weymouth air will lift your spirits."

Alicia did not believe that any amount of sea air would mend her broken heart, but she did not choose to enlighten the Duke. Once she had overcome her resentment at having their family party once more extended to include the Hartings, Alicia became resigned to the change in plans. She decided that it was probably just as well that they were not going to London. She did not feel equal to facing the world until she had regained control of her emotions.

The journey down to Weymouth was uneventful. Alicia was looking forward to the prospect of long walks by the sea. Maybe the sea air would help dispel her melancholy state of mind or at least shake off the lethargy that had descended on her with Mr Merry's departure.

But if she had hoped for solitude, she was to be disappointed. Lady Harting cooed continually about the Duke's generosity in treating them like family in a way that set Alicia's teeth on edge. The Countess was relentless in urging her elder son to pay his addresses and Alicia found it virtually impossible to avoid Lord Droxford's company. Every time she thought she was going for a peaceful walk, she found that Martha's presence had been exchanged for that of Lord Droxford or his domineering mother. The Viscount talked incessantly of what was happening in London whilst his mother repeatedly pointed out to her all the advantages of marrying an elder son with a title and an unassailable position in society. But if the Countess thought these tactics were going to persuade her to accept Lord Droxford's hand, she was very much mistaken.

Chapter 40

Mr Merry had far too much time on his journey up to London to think about all that happened in the previous few days: the unexpected arrival of Miss Westlake and his ghastly treatment of her; the horror of the accident; the apology; the kiss; and the awful suspicion of foul play that had grown on him. His mind kept going back to Miss Westlake's fantastical visit to his den, late at night, when he was far from sober. It was a wonder that he could recall the conversation at all and yet he could not forget it. And then there was that last pathetic meeting when he had told her he was leaving and her eyes had pierced his heart as they accused him of not caring.

He wondered whether Miss Westlake would have accepted him if he had asked her to marry him. Part of him thought that she might have. Why would she have looked so hurt when he left if she did not love him? But what if they were married and lived to regret it? He could not bear to think of it. If only he had that quiet assurance that characterised her. If only he were at peace. His fears had been locked away for so long that he had rarely been forced to look at them. Now he was faced with the dismal truth that he was just not worthy of the woman that he loved.

By the time he arrived at Mr Wilberforce's home in London, Mr Merry's spirits had plummeted and he began to think that he should have gone to visit Mr Pitt instead and drunk his sorrows away. He knew that drinking did not really make things better, but it dulled the pain of his own feelings of inadequacy. He hoped that Wilber would be able to lighten his mood. His friend could usually be relied on to talk him out of a fit of melancholy.

Mr Merry was relieved to find Wilber at home.

"How are you, my friend?"

"Sick as ever, I am afraid," Wilber replied in a cheery voice which seemed oddly at variance with the words. "My gut seems to be constantly arguing with the food I feed it and the only way I can keep it in check is with this wretched laudanum, but I have high hopes that I will be fit enough to attend once the House is in session."

"Poor fellow. Then it is as well I have come to cheer you up!"

"Seriously? You look awful, Merry. Are you ill?"

"I am quite well I assure you."

"Ah, it is a sickness of the heart then," he said in a sympathetic tone, nodding his head wisely.

"You are very astute this evening. And what, pray, do you know of matters of the heart?"

Wilber ignored his friend's jibe and continued in the same vein. "Who is she?"

Mr Merry kept a dignified silence.

"O come on, Merry. You know that I will wheedle it out of you sooner or later. You might as well confess and tell me now. It will save a lot of effort and I am, after all, a sick man."

Mr Merry gave a reluctant laugh.

"Her name is Miss Westlake."

"Miss Westlake? The daughter of the new Duchess of Wessex? My, my, Merry. You are setting your sights high. Well go on, man. What is she like?"

"Where do I start? She is small and fair with the bluest eyes you have ever seen. She can look quite severe when she is concentrating, but when she smiles, it is like the sun coming out and her whole face lights up."

"An angel, I perceive."

Mr Merry frowned at his friend. Wilber held up his hand to apologise for the interruption and Mr Merry continued.

"She is as passionate about antiquities as I am but as passionate about God as you are."

"I am willing to overlook the passion for antiquities. When can you introduce me to this paragon? I am half in love with her myself."

Mr Merry pulled a face. Wilber was not being very sympathetic. However, his friend begged forgiveness and by dint of careful questioning, Wilber extracted the whole story. Nearly. There were certain parts that Mr Merry kept to himself. He was not going to acknowledge that precious kiss or the intimate meetings in the library to the Saint or anyone else. He also kept his distrust of Mr Hampton out of the narrative. He had never told Wilber about what had happened in the riots of '80 and he did not feel equal to doing so now. Without that, his hostility toward Mr Hampton would simply be put down to jealousy.

"So what is the problem?" Wilber asked when Mr Merry finally stopped talking. "I take it there is a problem, otherwise you would not look so forlorn. Does the lady not return your affection?"

"Yes—no—I do not know."

"You do not know?" Wilber asked incredulously.

"I have, I think, some chance with her, but I am afraid to put it to the test."

"Afraid, Merry?"

"I am afraid that she will not have me and even more afraid that she might accept me and that we would both live to regret it."

Mr Wilberforce was puzzled. "But from all you have said, Merry, and perhaps even more from what you have not said, I would have concluded that she had a decided preference for you. Do you suspect her of being on the hunt for a title like her mother? The tattle has died down now, but the gossip surrounding the Duke's marriage was not very flattering to the Duchess."

"No, I do not think that Miss Westlake is like her mother. If she were after a title, she would accept Droxford."

"Why would she not have you then? You are an honest man, Merry. You will not beat her and have no inclination for gambling, so she is unlikely to find herself in the Fleet. You become a trifle preoccupied when you are working, but if, as you say, she likes antiquities too, I assume she would make some allowance for that."

"I am not at peace, Wilber. Not with myself and certainly not with God. I am not sure that I could cope with being continually reminded of that."

"Ah, I see. She makes you aware of your own lack of peace? You are right. She is definitely not the woman for you. You must introduce me at once."

"Wilber, be serious."

"No, no. There is no doubt about it, Merry. She will make you unhappy. You will only find peace with God through faith in Jesus Christ and that is a path you have determined not to take."

"She said I was too little a risk-taker."

"I beg your pardon?"

"She said I was too little a risk-taker," he repeated slowly, "because I would not take a step of faith."

"Ha! And that irks you, my friend?"

"She was calling me a coward, Wilber! She said that I needed to take a risk—to dare to believe."

"I like this Miss Westlake of yours more and more."

"What if she is right? What if I am too afraid to discover what I have so resolutely ignored?"

Wilber laughed. "Merry, I am hardly the person to ask for an objective opinion."

"I have prided myself on my logic," Mr Merry continued as though his friend had not spoken. "Throughout history, religion has been the cause of hatred and bloodshed and so I turned my back on it. I decided that I wanted nothing to do with it."

"I have no argument to put forward against that except that the best things when corrupted become the worst," Wilber replied. "Do not dismiss religion because some have twisted it to meet their own ends."

"There may be some truth in what you say," Mr Merry conceded. "I have always abhorred the duplicity of those who go to church on Sunday and yet are still unfaithful to their wives on Monday, but maybe they too are guilty of perverting religion to satisfy their own needs. Religion sops their consciences, but makes no difference to their way of life."

"I am at one with you there, Merry. Hypocrisy is indeed detestable. I wish that I could shake people out of that superficial kind of religion."

Mr Merry sighed. "I suppose that if I am to have any peace of mind, I must give this faith thing a try. I must take a risk or be damned!"

"That is not quite how I would have put it, Merry, but nevertheless true. It will be an experiment of faith. I like it!"

"How do I do it, Wilber? I have steadfastly ignored

every jibe you have poked at me urging me to trust God. Yet here I am, wondering whether I dare to believe in a God who I would much rather ignore."

"One step at a time, Merry. Come with me tomorrow and meet my good friend Newton. He can tell you how God turned his life upside down. He is a staunch supporter of the abolitionist movement, but he was once a slave trader. Take a chance that God might speak into your heart. Take a risk."

"Very well. I will come."

It seemed such a small step, but Mr Merry's heart immediately felt lighter. His willingness to go and listen seemed to release the block that he had put in place all those years ago. After the first step, the second seemed to follow more easily. Mr Merry listened to the Bible being preached as if he had never heard it before. In truth, he had not heard it since his days at Cambridge in the chapel of St John's.

Mr Merry listened and questioned; Wilber reasoned and persuaded. The more he read the Bible, the more he realised that it was not about what he had done, but about faith in what God had done for him. He was a hard man to convince, but once convinced, there was no going back. Within a fortnight, Mr Merry had taken that step of faith and had made his peace with God.

Mr Merry was eager to go back home and tell Miss Westlake about his new-found faith. His mother would disapprove. Maybe the Duke would disapprove. Regardless, he meant to ask Miss Westlake to marry him. But whether she would have him or not, he was a changed man.

Chapter 41

The day before Mr Merry was due to leave, a letter arrived from Lord Droxford to say that he was in Weymouth again. Mr Merry snorted loudly as he read and Wilber begged to know what was so funny.

"Why less than a year ago, my mother cut Miss Westlake's mother and now it seems they cannot be separated. My parents have gone to Weymouth with the Duke and Duchess of Wessex and poor Droxford has gone too. No doubt my mother is still trying to further her cherished plan of uniting our family with the Duke's."

"But is that not your plan too?" Wilber teased.

"Why yes, but my mother would not think me worthy of that honour for a moment. Droxford writes that my mother is acting as if the knot is already tied, but he assures me it is not. I think Miss Westlake terrifies him; she is too clever for him by half. Poor Droxford. He sounds so miserable. He would be so uncomfortable with a bluestocking for a wife. But I expect my mother will bully him into proposing. He never could stand up to her. Droxford would do anything for a quiet life!"

"You do not seem to be unduly perturbed."

"I do not believe that Miss Westlake will accept my brother," Mr Merry said confidently. "You were absolutely right in your estimation of her character and I am sure that worldly advancement will not influence her decision. Besides," he added smugly, "I am so very nearly sure that she is in love with me."

"You conceited nincompoop!" Wilber replied. "Had you not better go and claim your lady before she gives up on you and marries someone else. She is an heiress, is she not? Perhaps I will come to Weymouth myself and try my luck with her."

Mr Merry grinned. "I tell you, she only has eyes for me."

Wilber could not forbear to tease his friend. "But surely you said that the Duke's nephew was another contender for her hand. Are you so sure that the virtuous Mr Hampton will not get there before you?"

"Virtuous!" Mr Merry spat out. "Do not make me sick. Mr Hampton is a mean, vicious, loathsome beast of a man!"

"Steady," Wilber urged. "Those are hefty accusations against a man of supposedly good character. I will admit that I have heard rumours that he has the highflying Mrs Martindale in keeping, but that hardly merits such a reaction."

"Mrs Martindale," Mr Merry repeated, distracted for a moment by the memory of that dreadful evening at Covent Garden Theatre. So Mr Hampton was responsible for the actress' strange behaviour that evening. Perhaps he had been ignoring her whilst he pursued Miss Westlake.

"Well that makes sense," Mr Merry said. "On one occasion she attracted so much attention by acting her part to our box that Miss Westlake asked some very awkward questions. It did not even cross my mind that she could be Hampton's mistress. She must cost a king's ransom to keep."

"But if that was news to you, why did you react so

fiercely to my suggestion that Hampton was virtuous?"
Wilber asked.

"I have my reasons."

"And would you care to share those reasons?"

Mr Merry hesitated. Apart from Miss Westlake, he
had never shared his ghastly experiences at the riots with
anyone. But telling Miss Westlake had started to lessen
the hold that those dreadful memories had over him.
Perhaps he had kept quiet for too long. Mr Merry took a
deep breath and began. It was not so bad the second
time. When he reached the end of his narrative, his
friend was full of sympathy.

"I was so ashamed. I saw a man's life extinguished
before my eyes and was helpless to do anything. I
decided in that moment that if there was a God, he
would certainly reject a coward like me. It was less
painful to believe that there was not a God than that he
would reject me. So I blocked out the blackest day of my
life and when it reared its ugly head in my memory, I
drank to take the painful memories away. And I was
doing it quite successfully until I discovered that the
soldier I had seen on that dreadful night was courting the
woman I had fallen in love with."

"What!" Wilber had been listening in silence to Mr
Merry's narrative, but at this he exclaimed.

"I am absolutely convinced that Hampton was that
soldier."

"Are you telling me that it was Hampton's horse that
crushed that poor man's skull?"

Mr Merry nodded.

"And that it was the look on Hampton's face that
made you doubt whether it was an accident?"

Mr Merry nodded again.

"Just one man, lying helpless in the street, with no

mob, no gunfire, nothing that could have scared the horse."

"I know Hampton used to be in the Horse Guards. He told Miss Westlake that he had sold out after his cousin's death."

"Merry, did you ever find out anything about the man who died that night?"

"No. I closed my mind to that awful scene, so that I did not have to face my own failure. I was horrified by my own inability to do anything to save the poor fellow because I was frozen with fear."

Mr Wilberforce got up and paced up and down the room. "Merry, I have just had the most terrible thought. You do know that the Duke's son was killed in those riots, do you not?"

"During the riots? Are you sure?"

"If my memory serves me correctly, he was caught up in the fleeing mob and trampled to death."

The two men looked at each other with growing horror as they simultaneously reached the same conclusion.

"If Hampton's horse killed a man—" Mr Merry began.

"—then that man could well have been his cousin who we know died in the riots," finished Wilber.

"Hampton had nothing to lose. He must have grabbed at the opportunity that presented itself. No one was going to question Lord Denmead's death in the riots. It was only by chance that I saw what happened and even I could not be sure that he had been killed deliberately."

"On the other hand, he had everything to gain," Wilber added. "By eliminating his cousin, he became heir to the dukedom after his uncle and father. I have no doubt that he could live on those expectations for years."

"He must have been responsible for the accident to the Westlakes' carriage then," Mr Merry declared. "It is not widely known that the Duchess is expecting, but we can be sure that Hampton knew. If he had been borrowing on his expectations, maybe he could not afford to risk being ousted from the succession."

Now it was Mr Merry's turn to pace up and down, forcing his brain to make sense of it all. "Miss Westlake refused to believe that Hampton would try to hurt her and so held that he could not be responsible for the carriage being driven off the road. It is true that he has by no means given up his pursuit of her hand and seemed genuinely distressed after the accident. I must be missing something."

"Slow down, Merry. However ominous the circumstances, you have no proof. Now, if you discover that the Duke's son did, indeed, die of a crushed skull, that would be closing the net, but it would still only be your word against his."

"But you must see that there is no time to slow down. I cannot hold back because I have no proof. I must see the Duke," Mr Merry said. "I must try and convince him of the truth. If Hampton has murdered once, he could murder again. Just pray that I will not be too late."

Chapter 42

Despite all Lady Harting's manoeuvres, Lord Droxford seemed to be exceedingly reluctant to come to the point. The Countess was becoming exasperated. She could not understand why Droxford was hesitating to claim such a suitable wife whom she believed was his for the asking. Whatever Miss Westlake's natural inclinations, the Countess was sure that she would not turn down such an advantageous offer.

"Droxford, I am at a loss to understand why you still have not fixed your interest with Miss Westlake. Surely I have made my feelings clear? The match is all that your father and I desire. The connection to the House of Wessex is highly desirable. The Duke's influence is significant and Miss Westlake's fortune considerable. And on top of this, the girl is extremely pretty and, in contrast to her mother, her behaviour is unlikely to ever put you to the blush. I ask you, Droxford, what more do you want in a wife?"

Lord Droxford could have told her, but he did not think that his mother would appreciate plain speaking when his opinions jarred with her ambitions. The truth was that he was by no means convinced that Miss Westlake would make him a comfortable wife and he did so like to be comfortable. She was a very attractive young lady, but lately she had started to make him feel somewhat inadequate. She had developed the habit of asking his opinion on subjects about which he knew nothing. Worse still, sometimes when she talked, he thought that she was not being serious, but he was never quite sure. He was always wondering whether he had understood her right. He did not think he could cope with that for the rest of his life. It would be exhausting.

She was much better suited to his brother. Merry might be unfashionable and too much inclined to make trouble, but Droxford had always stood somewhat in awe of his intelligence. He doubted whether Merry ever felt out of depth in Miss Westlake's company. He liked to feel in control without having to exert himself unduly. No, he did not think that Miss Westlake would be a comfortable wife.

Furthermore, ever since she had hinted at the large and noisy family she hoped to have, he had wondered whether it might be worth the effort of going against his mother's wishes.

"I am afraid, Mother, that we should not suit," Lord Droxford said tentatively.

"Not suit?" Lady Harting scoffed. "I daresay you might not suit, but why should that prove an obstacle? You need not live in each other's pockets. Do not tell me that you have fallen prey to some romantic notion that you need to be in love in order to get married?"

"No, no, of course not," he hastened to reassure his irate parent. "Perhaps it is just that I am not ready to take such a monumental step. Maybe if I knew Miss Westlake a little better ..."

"I cannot credit what you are saying, Droxford," Lady Harting sneered. "How can you not be ready? You have been acquainted with the girl for months. What more do you need to know? You need not be afraid that she will turn you down. It is not necessary for you to spend any longer wooing her when your rank and position in society are recommendation enough."

"Indeed, no, Madam, but I cannot rid myself of the impression that Miss Westlake requires more than I can offer her."

"Do not be ridiculous. You are a viscount, Drox-ford."

In the end it was self-preservation that forced him to the point. He would have no peace from his mother unless he made the offer. Not even marriage to Miss Westlake could be as bad as his mother's continual nagging. If Miss Westlake said yes, as his mother assured him she would, he would make the best of it. She was very pretty and he was not averse to the idea of having a pretty wife, but he did wish that he felt more at ease in her company. Lord Droxford resigned himself to the inevitable. With grim determination, he set out to pay a call on Miss Westlake.

Alicia sat down in the window seat looking out over the sea and took out her embroidery. Her lack of ability with watercolours might have made her father turn in his grave, but no one could find fault with her tiny stitches. She determined to meditate on the scripture verse which she was meticulously bringing to life with a myriad of brightly coloured silks. She thought perhaps she would get it framed and put it up on the wall of her bedroom. It was a verse from the book of Psalms: "Delight thyself also in the Lord, and he shall give thee the desires of thine heart."

Alicia sighed. It was hard to take delight in anything at the moment. Her mother was becoming increasingly fretful, possibly because she was concerned about the baby, but more probably because the Duke was fussing around her like a mother hen.

Mr Hampton gave every appearance of being trustworthy and dependable. Any suspicion she might have harboured that he had played a part in causing the accident had melted away over time. It no longer seemed possible that he could have done anything to cause her harm. He did not make her feel uncomfortable by paying her too much attention, but he was always considerate to her needs and she felt that he only needed a little encouragement in order to declare himself. This encouragement she made sure she did not give.

Mr Merry remained in London. She heard nothing of him. On the other hand, Lord Droxford was constant in his attendance and Alicia was obliged to listen to him rattling on about all the latest gossip. She supposed that many a young lady of fashion would be only too glad to receive his attentions. He was obviously not used to such an unenthusiastic reception of his company, but he must have set it down to her lack of experience, if he noticed it at all, as it had not prevented him from continuing his visits. He was quite capable of holding a conversation almost entirely on his own. There was really not much for Alicia to do except smile and endure. She found his conversation insipid. He never talked of anything but the most superficial subjects. Was that all that he expected of a lady—an interest in fashion and what was going on in the ton?

Now if it had been his brother, they could have talked about history or politics or something with a bit more depth. She could even have asked his opinion on the verse she was embroidering. He might not share her beliefs, but he would be bound to have an opinion.

"Lord Droxford," the butler announced.

Alicia jumped. She had not heard the door open and barely had time to stow away her embroidery before the Viscount marched into the room.

"Lord Droxford. What an unexpected pleasure," she said with a touch of sarcasm. "What brings you to visit me today?"

Alicia's sarcasm was lost on Lord Droxford who greeted her with his usual well-polished grace and launched into a monologue about what he had read in the newspaper that morning. Alicia could not resist making a comparison with his graceless brother. Really, they were so completely unalike in all but a faint resemblance in looks.

"Do you not find Weymouth rather dull?" he asked. "There is even less entertainment here now than there was in the summer."

"The weather is unseasonably fine, Lord Droxford. I like to walk and watch the sea. It is always changing. I think I like it best when the wind gets up and the waves come crashing down with some force. Do you not agree?"

Lord Droxford had never giving more than a passing thought to the sea. "I prefer London," he replied, perfectly seriously, "especially at this time of the year. Weymouth is more than a little thin of company. Excepting our own party, there is not another person of my acquaintance in residence."

"I am surprised, then, that you do not go to London, since there is so little here to engage your interest."

"I would like very much to return to London, Miss Westlake, but at the moment, it is not possible." He paused, looking miserable.

"Do you know what I miss the most?" the Viscount confided. "My club. There is nothing quite like the ease of male company, away from the demands of family."

Alicia bit her lip to prevent herself from smiling too broadly. Lord Droxford had all but admitted the need to get away from his mother. Poor man! She had some sympathy. Lady Harting was a bully!

"Many married men escape to their clubs," Lord Droxford continued. "The domestic scene is a woman's province. There is not much for a gentleman to do. If he becomes too familiar with his children, then he cannot make them mind him. As my wife, I would be happy to relinquish the children entirely to your care."

Alicia thought she could not have heard aright. "I beg your pardon?" she asked in astonishment.

"You must not think too poorly of me, Miss Westlake. I cannot help it. I am not cut out to deal with children. But you are a very capable lady. You will know just how to manage them and there will be no shortage of nursery staff to help you." He stopped when he realised that Alicia was staring at him and shaking her head in amazement.

"You do not think you could do it? Well, I cannot say that I blame you. Indeed, I am sure that there is no need for you to be involved if you do not wish it. I am sure it can be arranged."

"I have every intention of being involved in the lives of my own children, Lord Droxford," Alicia replied. "But there is one thing I need to make clear: you will not be their father."

Lord Droxford looked shocked. "Well, I think you will find me a liberal husband, but I would expect you to provide me with an heir before you took a lover. As long as you are discreet—"

Alicia's face turned red with embarrassment. "Lord Droxford, I fear that you mistake my meaning. I believe wholeheartedly in the sanctity of marriage vows. When I marry, I will be faithful to my husband, but I have absolutely no intention of marrying you."

It took a moment or two for Lord Droxford to fully digest her words. His mother had instilled in him such a belief in his own worth that he had not stopped to question it. His face reflected his confusion.

"You are refusing me?"

"I cannot refuse what I have not been offered."

"Miss Westlake, will you marry me?"

"No. I will not."

"You have no desire to be a viscountess?"

"No. I do not."

"Amazing! My mother values her title highly. She was convinced that you would not be able to resist the lure of being a countess one day."

Alicia laughed. "I believe that my mother and yours do have something in common after all!"

"But not you? You do not value a title?"

"No. I do not."

Lord Droxford gave a satisfied smile. "So Mother was wrong. I thought she was always right, but not this time. She said you would have me if I asked, but she was wrong. Ha! I knew better. I always thought it was Merry you preferred."

Alicia blushed again. She did not dare to look Lord Droxford in the eye.

"I like your brother's company, Lord Droxford, but I do not think we would suit."

"No?"

She thought of the verse she was embroidering. Mr Merry did not 'delight' himself in the Lord. He did not even believe God existed.

"No," she replied sadly.

"Pity," Lord Droxford said. "I think I should have liked to have you as a sister. I do hope you will still stand up with me next time we are at a ball together in London. You are the lightest little dancer I know and it will always be a pleasure to partner you."

Lord Droxford took his leave as gracefully as ever and Alicia was once more left alone. She did not know whether to laugh or cry. In the end, she cried tears of relief—relief that she would not have to endure Lord Droxford's attentions any more. Perhaps she would laugh later, when she told Mr Merry of his brother's proposal. But then she remembered that Mr Merry had gone. There would be no more shared laughter. Then she cried in earnest.

It was not every day that you had the opportunity to reject a viscount's offer of marriage. Alicia dreaded the embarrassment of having to face the Countess or her son again after causing the ruin of all her plans. Lord Droxford was quick to relay the news that he had done his duty, but been rejected. Lady Harting could not believe it. In the quiet of her room, she ranted at the girl's wilfulness and quickly decided that her younger son was to blame. He had put his elder brother in a poor light and turned Miss Westlake's head.

Heartily relieved that obeying his mother had not led to a betrothal, Lord Droxford hastily departed for London. He was not going to wait around for his mother to force him into a second attempt. That would be too humiliating for words.

When Mr Hampton came in almost an hour later, Alicia was still recovering from the episode. "You look upset," he observed, taking his seat beside her.

"No, not really. Just a little unsettled."

"Tell me," he urged. Alicia obliged. After all, the rejection could not remain a secret for long.

"Lord Droxford asked for my hand in marriage."

"Ah," replied Mr Hampton.

"Now I look back, I suppose that the whole experience was laughable," she continued. "The poor man was doubtless only obeying instructions and his mother had clearly persuaded him that all he had to do was to drop the handkerchief and I would rush to pick it up. He looked as if he was on his way to the scaffold, not making a proposal of marriage. The look on his face when I declined his offer was nothing short of relief!"

Mr Hampton sighed. "Titled men of wealth and good prospects cannot be blamed for expecting women to fall at their feet—they frequently do."

"Well I do not," Alicia huffed.

Mr Hampton smiled. He had been right all along. He had been sure that Miss Westlake would refuse the tiresome viscount and now he had been proved correct. Things were beginning to go his way at last. Mr Merry had withdrawn from the competition for Miss Westlake's hand and now Lord Droxford had failed to win her too. Surely now was the right moment to declare himself.

"Nobody who knew you would suppose that you would marry for the sake of wealth and connections, Miss Westlake. And you need not fear—the Duke will never make you marry against your inclinations."

"I do not fear it, Mr Hampton. The Duke is all kindness."

"Your mother has made him happy again."

"Yes, I do believe she has."

"I wish I could make you happy," Mr Hampton said tentatively.

Alicia felt all the awkwardness of being unable to offer him any assurance that his wish would be fulfilled. The very last thing she wanted was to be subject to a second declaration. Instinctively she wanted to run, but she decided to laugh it off.

"And so you have, Mr Hampton," she replied lightly. "You have reminded me that the Duke will support me in the face of my mother's chagrin. I only hope that it will not be of long duration as my mind is quite made up against Lord Droxford."

Mr Hampton smiled. Clearly Miss Westlake was not ready to face another proposal. He could wait. He was good at waiting. He had been waiting for years. "I am always glad to be of service, Miss Westlake."

She acknowledged his bow and tripped out of the room, glad to have made her escape without enduring another proposal. It was as well she did not look back. The glance that followed her departing figure was very possessive.

Chapter 43

On his journey to London, Mr Merry had been consumed with melancholy. Now that he was on his way back, he was no longer depressed, but he was overwhelmed with anxiety for the woman he loved and her mother.

As the post-chaise sped along, Mr Merry turned over the facts again in his mind. The evidence was strong enough for him to believe that Mr Hampton had murdered his cousin and covered his tracks in the chaos of the riots. Whether the Duke would see it that way or not was another matter, but he had to confront him with what he knew. It would take all his ingenuity to persuade the Duke to listen to him. Why should he believe evil of a nephew who had been more of a son to him than his own boy had been?

Mr Merry knew he had to try. If, as he believed, Mr Hampton had murdered his cousin without compunction, surely he was capable of removing anyone else that he thought was in his way. If the Duchess gave birth to a son, that child would inherit the dukedom. It would be unlikely that either Lord Richard or his son would ever inherit. It was the perfect motivation for the accident.

Much as he would have liked to blame Mr Hampton for what had happened, there was no getting away from the fact that Alicia had been with the Duchess in the carriage when it was mercilessly driven off the road. He could not accuse Mr Hampton of having wilfully tried to harm Alicia. Mr Merry had been there after the accident and he remembered the sincere look of distress on Mr Hampton's face. No, of that he must acquit him, though no other explanation presented itself.

Unless, of course, it was Lord Richard who was responsible, acting without his son's knowledge or consent. Lord Richard had made no secret of the fact that his brother's second marriage had come as a complete shock to him and that he resented the possibility of being pushed out of the succession.

But the carriage accident had failed to eliminate the Duchess or the possible future heir. Mr Merry was worried that its failure might force the perpetrator into doing something desperate. Although he thought that Alicia was safe, he had no such assurance that the Duchess would not be attacked again.

As the journey progressed, Mr Merry found that he was growing increasingly anxious on another score. What if he was wrong and Mr Hampton had been successful in pressing his suit? His own absence was unlikely to have helped his cause. His eagerness to see Miss Westlake again was tinged with the fear that he had miscalculated and somehow Mr Hampton had successfully ingratiated himself with her.

"I assume we'll be resting at Holybourne House tonight, Sir," his valet said, when they stopped to change horses.

Mr Merry was not fooled by John's deferential tone. It was little more than a veiled command. He was anxious to get to Weymouth as quickly as possible and had planned no such halt.

"It is fortunate that you understand how important it is to arrive at your destination in a state fit to be seen,

Sir," John continued. "Some gentlemen would not recognise the need to refresh themselves or replenish their wardrobes, but even though you are not one to make a fuss of your clothes, so to say, it is amazing how much more attentive to such things you have become since there's been a lady on the scene. It is just as well you know when to stop, Sir, for even if there were a full moon, I don't doubt you wouldn't want to arrive exhausted at your destination. I am so glad I don't have to point out the cloudiness of the night which makes it highly unlikely that we will have even a glimpse of the moon, and the likelihood of turning the carriage over in the darkness. Right glad I am that I have such a sensible master."

Mr Merry huffed. He supposed it would be wiser not to drive all night as he had intended. He chaffed at the delay of even a few hours, but while his family were surrounding Miss Westlake and her mother, they must surely be free from harm. "Very well, John. We will stop over at Holybourne House, but I intend to leave for Weymouth before sunrise, so do not linger over your liquor tonight."

John knew that such a comment was meant to provoke him, but he did not give his master the satisfaction of rising to the bait. He had achieved his intent and was satisfied.

It was already well past two o'clock when the chaise rounded the sweep of the road from Dorchester and started the descent down into Weymouth. It was a fine day and the bay presented a magnificent prospect, but Mr Merry was too absorbed in his thoughts to pay it much attention. He knew from Droxford's letter where his parents were lodging and the carriage set him down outside the house just before three o'clock. He was not perturbed to find that his parents were not at home. In fact, it saved him time as he did not have to go and pay his respects. A few words with the butler should be all that was required.

"Dawson, I need to see the Duke of Wessex. Can you tell me where he is lodging?"

"Good afternoon, Sir," Dawson replied in his characteristically inexpressive voice. "I believe the Duke can be found in York Buildings, in the same house where the Duchess lodged in the summer."

"Excellent! You are a gem, Dawson."

"Very good, Sir," Dawson replied, with just a glimmer of a smile. He had always had a soft spot for young Mr Merry.

It took only a few minutes to walk along the seafront to York Buildings. Mr Merry wondered how on earth he was going to begin his story. "Did you know that your nephew killed your son?" hardly seemed a propitious way to start. Perhaps he should just tell his story and leave the Duke to draw his own conclusions. Or maybe he should talk about the carriage accident first. If the Duke could be persuaded to believe that the vehicle had been driven off the road intentionally, perhaps he would more readily accept the rest of his story.

The door was opened by Rowson. "Is His Grace at home?" Mr Merry asked.

Rowson showed him into the library. "His Grace has been closeted with his agent all day, Sir. I will ascertain whether he is at liberty to see you."

"Thank you, Rowson. And Miss Westlake?" Mr Merry asked.

Rowson smiled sympathetically. "I am sorry, Sir.

Miss Westlake has gone out with her mother." Mr Merry was disappointed that he would have to wait to see Miss Westlake, but perhaps it was as well. He would not be able to rest until he had convinced the Duke that his nephew was a threat to the Duchess' safety.

A few minutes later, Rowson returned. "His Grace was about to go out, but he can see you now if you would care to step upstairs."

"Has he got company?"

"No, Sir."

Mr Merry followed Rowson up the stairs. He was glad to find the Duke alone. He would not have had the temerity to share his fears with the Duke in front of Mr Hampton or Lord Richard and it would only create awkwardness if he had to seek a private audience.

The Duke welcomed Mr Merry in and invited him to sit down.

"What brings you back to Weymouth, Merry, or need I ask? Have you come to try and succeed where your brother has failed?"

"Ah, so Droxford was refused?"

"Indeed he was. Did you not know?"

"No, but I am not surprised, either at the proposal or the refusal. They would not suit." Mr Merry paused for a moment and then started again, quite tentatively.

"I also came to see you. Your Grace, I do not know how to begin. There is no easy way to say what I have come to tell you, but I beg that you will hear me out. Nine years ago, I became embroiled in the riots in London—the same riots that claimed the life of your son. I lost my way in the crowds and inadvertently witnessed a scene that has disturbed my peace ever since. A mounted soldier pursued a lone man down the empty street where I had ended up. He stopped right over the man who had tripped and was lying, trembling on the ground. Suddenly the horse reared and its hooves came down on the man's head, killing him in one foul strike."

The Duke was listening intently. "Go on."

"I have come to believe that the man I saw being killed was your son."

"I do not know how you have come to that conclusion, Merry," the Duke said, shaking his head. "My son did die of a crushed skull, but he was not found in any back alley. I was told that he was trampled by the mob and saw no reason to doubt it. But does it really make any difference? Denmead has been dead for nine years and finding out that he did not die exactly how I thought is not going to change anything."

"There is more. I saw the look on that soldier's face as he stood over the man that his horse had killed. What I saw was a look of unadulterated hatred. It made me wonder whether it was an accident or whether the soldier had, in fact, urged his horse to behave like that."

"Murder?" the Duke asked sceptically. "That is a huge accusation to make against a member of the King's Horse Guards."

"It certainly looked like that to me. But I had no proof. It would only have been a boy's word against a soldier's. So I said nothing."

"Until now," the Duke said.

Mr Merry nodded and took a deep breath. This was going to be the hardest part. "A few months ago, I came face to face with that soldier. That soldier was Mr Hampton."

The Duke looked at Mr Merry in amazement. "Let me get this straight. Nine years ago, you saw a man being killed, whom you think was my son. Because of the look on the soldier's face you think it was murder. And now you are telling me that you think the soldier in question was my nephew. I think you have said enough, Mr Merry. Your jealousy of my nephew has blinded your powers of reasoning. Do you really expect me to believe that my nephew murdered my son?"

"I know it is hard to credit, Your Grace, but think of the motivation. Since Denmead's death, Mr Hampton has been in line to inherit the dukedom and all that goes with it."

"But why are you telling me this now, Merry? Even if you were right, do you expect me to bring Joshua to justice for something that happened so long ago, with so little proof, for I tell you now, I will not do it," the Duke said defensively.

"I am telling you this now, Your Grace, because I fear that the Duchess is in danger."

Mr Merry's words made the Duke sit up. He leaned toward Mr Merry. "Just what are you saying?"

"I believe that the Duchess' carriage was deliberately forced off the road. That it was no accident. Mr Hampton has been living off his expectations and I do not believe that he could afford to risk your wife giving birth to a son."

"Preposterous! Have you forgotten that Miss Westlake was also in that carriage? Trying to kill the woman you want to marry is hardly a good way of forwarding your suit. I give you every allowance for being a man in love, Merry, but this is too much. Let us say no more about it. I am sure you are anxious to see Miss Westlake again. Come with me and see her and forget all these disturbing thoughts."

Mr Merry took the Duke's outstretched hand and willingly accompanied him to join the others, but he was frustrated that his words had made so little impact.

But his words had been more influential than he realised. The Duke had drunk in every word that Mr Merry had said and was weighing them in his mind. He did not want to believe that there was any truth in what he had heard, but he knew he would never forgive himself if he did nothing and something else happened to his wife.

Chapter 44

The Duchess was disappointed, but not surprised, when Alicia told her that Lord Droxford had paid his addresses and she had turned him down. She would very much have liked Alicia to marry the Viscount. It would have been so satisfying to refer to her daughter as Lady Droxford. But she had finally realised that Alicia was not going to succumb to worldly ambition and marry for the sake of wealth and position. She was too much her father's daughter.

She thought it was a pity that Alicia had developed so decided a preference for Mr Merry, a preference that showed no sign of abating. Of course, her daughter denied it, but nothing else could explain her want of spirits. Mr Merry had lost interest, but she feared that her daughter had not. He would not have been her first choice for Alicia, but the younger son of an earl was not entirely contemptible. And it would still have been an amusing twist for her daughter to marry her old admirer's son. Not such a splendid match as marrying the Viscount, of course, but that was quite out of the question now that Alicia had refused him.

In the course of time, the Duchess hoped that Alicia would recover from her disappointment. Her daughter was still young. Next season would be different. Alicia would be presented at court as the Duke's new daughter and those who had previously been scared off by their precarious position in society would flock to ally themselves with one of the most illustrious families in the land. Alicia would have her pick of the eligible bachelors. Surely there would be someone who could supplant Mr Merry in her daughter's affections?

In the meantime, what Alicia needed was distraction. The Duchess mentioned her concerns to her husband who promised to support any endeavour that his wife thought would cheer her daughter up. Remembering how Alicia had enjoyed their visit to Corfe Castle in the summer, he proposed a return trip. The Duchess groaned.

"Oh, no! It is much too far to travel at this time of the year," she complained, "especially in my condition." Although the Duchess confessed to having a soft spot for the place where the Duke had proposed to her, she was adamant that she was not going to sit around in the cold whilst her daughter spent hours trudging about the ruins in the mud.

"Perhaps we could go and visit that pretty little castle overlooking Portland Roads that we have sometimes passed in the carriage. Alicia has often asked whether we might go and explore it, but somehow we have never quite managed to do so. If you want to cheer Alicia up, that would be just the thing. Then, if I feel poorly," or bored, she said to herself, "I can return home without inconveniencing anyone."

The Duke was quick to change his plans. If the Duchess thought a trip to Corfe would be too fatiguing, then Sandsfoot Castle would be a much better option. Alicia was thankful for her mother's intervention. Though she knew that her mother was thinking purely of herself, she had inadvertently served her daughter's interests too. Alicia could not think of a more depressing thought than going back to Corfe, though she had not had the heart to say so. Much as she loved Corfe Castle, all her memories of the place were tied up with Mr Merry. And this time there would be no Mr Merry.

On the day of the planned expedition, the Duke found himself unexpectedly detained by his agent with some business that needed his urgent attention. As the weather was the best that it had been all week, the Duke was unwilling to postpone the outing, and suggested that the others went on ahead and he would join them as soon as he could. The party travelled the short distance to Sandsfoot Castle in two carriages. Mr Hampton rode alongside the first carriage carrying Alicia and the Duchess, whilst the second vehicle contained the Earl and Countess of Harting.

Alicia had driven past Sandsfoot Castle in the summer but had never yet had a chance to explore. It was not a large castle. She reckoned that it would have fitted inside Corfe Castle several times over. She thought it was curious that it was built the same time as the equivalent castle over on the Island of Portland and yet, whilst the other had remained more or less intact, Sandsfoot seemed to be busy falling to pieces. The outside walls were still standing, but the roof had long since gone, and the whole of the east side was in danger of falling into the sea.

A light wind was blowing, but as it came from the south, it was mild and did not make the temperature unpleasantly cold and when the sun came out, it was easy to forget that it was November and the year was rapidly drawing to a close.

Alicia was not surprised when Mr Hampton attached himself to her, but she was reluctant to be alone in his company. She had dissuaded him once from making a declaration, but she was by no means convinced that he would not try again if a suitable occasion arose. Ever since she had become aware of the seriousness of his intentions, she had tried to keep him at a distance. She did not think she could face the awkwardness of turning down another proposal.

For once, she was grateful for the presence of the Countess of Harting, whom she invited to walk with them, leaving the Earl to attend her mother. But if Alicia was hoping for some protection from the Countess' company, she was doomed to disappointment.

Lady Harting was bemoaning the fact that she had ever agreed to visit the castle. She had joined the party more from a wish to be seen with the Duke than from any desire to see the ruins and made no effort to hide her displeasure that the Duke had been unable to join them. She resented every moment that she was obliged to spend in Alicia's company rather than the Duke's.

The Countess could not forgive Alicia for upsetting her plans by refusing her son's hand in marriage. It showed a regretful lack of ambition and she despised those who made no attempt to improve their position in life. She was also far from contented leaving her husband to squire the Duchess. Alicia thought wickedly that she was probably afraid that her mother would rekindle the Earl's passion for her.

Barely fifteen minutes after arriving at the ruin, the Countess professed that she was tired. She sent her maid scurrying off to fetch the Earl immediately. He smiled apologetically at Alicia before conducting his wife back to the carriage. Five minutes later, a footman brought a message from the Countess saying that she was unwell and that the Earl was going to accompany her home.

The Duchess had some sympathy with Lady Harting, but was unwilling to deprive her daughter of her afternoon's entertainment. "I am feeling a little tired as well, Alicia. Perhaps I will just go back to the carriage for a while and close my eyes."

Alicia immediately offered to abandon her exploration of the ruin, but her mother would not hear of it. "You two go and explore. Marie will keep me company. I will be all the better for a short rest."

There seemed to be no way to escape being left alone with Mr Hampton without being extremely rude. Reluctantly, she walked with him toward the ruin. She would be obliged to listen to his proposal and feared his chagrin at being refused. It was just the situation she had been trying to avoid.

It was not that Alicia still suspected Mr Hampton of foul play. Mr Merry's accusations seemed incredible now. Perhaps he no longer believed them himself. Surely if he really thought that Mr Hampton was dangerous, he would have come back to protect them?

Or perhaps he did not care about her after all. It was a lowering thought, but did it really make any difference whether he loved her? Her heart might be breaking, but even if he came back, she knew she could not marry him. How could she ever be happy with a man who did not believe in God and refused to go to church? She told herself that he was doing the kindest thing, taking himself away, but it did not stop her hankering after his company.

When they reached the castle, Mr Hampton offered her his hand to climb over a low section of wall. Alicia was so lost in her thoughts about Mr Merry that she took it without thinking. Mr Hampton did not let go. He pulled her close toward him and she was helpless to resist. She could feel the warmth of his breath on her face as he talked.

"You would not let me speak before, but you must listen to me now, Miss Westlake. I adore you."

"Mr Hampton—" Alicia tried to pull away, but he turned her back to him.

"Miss Westlake, I need you. I cannot offer you much, but what I have is yours."

"Mr Hampton. I really do not know what to say."

"At least give me some hope."

Alicia did not attempt to hide the truth. "I cannot."

Mr Hampton dropped her hand as if it were a burning coal. He started to pace up and down the length of the ruin, his voice growing desperate with his frustration.

"I do not understand, Miss Westlake. You refused Lord Droxford. Surely you cannot intend to refuse me too?" Then an unwelcome thought crossed his mind. He stopped pacing and stared at Alicia in disbelief. "Please do not tell me that you have set your heart on his brother?"

Alicia made no reply.

"Your mother will never let you throw yourself away on a younger son," he said scornfully. "Merry is a complete heathen with no prospects—no prospects at all. Marry me and be a duchess one day."

"You forget, Mr Hampton, that if my mother gives birth to a son, it is unlikely that you will ever be duke," Alicia said frostily.

"Yes, yes of course. I was forgetting."

Alicia could not believe what she was hearing. "Forgetting? How could you forget that my mother is expecting a baby after all that has happened?" Perhaps Mr Merry was right after all and Mr Hampton was in some way responsible for the accident. "Or maybe you hoped that there would be nothing to forget? Perhaps you hoped that her baby would not survive the carriage being overturned into a ditch."

"Just what are you trying to say, Miss Westlake?"

"That maybe you wanted that baby out of the way so badly that you forced our carriage off the road."

"I suppose Mr Merry planted that thought in your mind," Mr Hampton snapped. "How dare he suggest that I would deliberately set out to hurt you," he ranted. "I want to marry you. I was devastated to learn that you had gone with your mother and been involved in the accident. I could not rest until I had been assured that you were unharmed."

Alicia stood perfectly still, hardly daring to breathe. Had she heard Mr Hampton right or was it a mere slip of the tongue? "I was devastated to learn that you had gone with your mother," he had said. Not devastated to learn of the accident. In a single moment, everything fell into place. How could she have been so stupid? Their plans had changed after Mr Hampton had left. It should have been the Duke with her mother in the carriage, not her. That explained how shocked Mr Hampton had been when he arrived at Holybourne House. The accident had been meant for them, not her.

Mr Hampton grabbed Alicia's hand again and pulled her into an alcove where he pushed her up against the wall and held her there by the weight of his own body. With one hand he held hers tight and with the other, he tilted her face toward him and lent forward to kiss her.

She moved her head one way and then the other in order to avoid his embrace. "Mr Hampton, this is no way to further your suit," she spat out. "If you do not unhand me, I will scream."

"I need you, Miss Westlake," he whispered huskily. "I just need to convince you that you need me too."

Alicia closed her eyes, unable to free herself from his hold. She braced herself for the assault on her mouth, and prayed fervently that by some miracle she would escape from Mr Hampton's most unwelcome advances.

Chapter 45

"Unhand Miss Westlake. Now."

Mr Hampton spun round to see who was interrupting him.

"You!" he exclaimed, casting Mr Merry a look of loathing. Cursing loudly, he disappeared through the archway behind them.

Mr Merry was furious. He had arrived at the castle with the Duke a few moments earlier to find the Duchess sitting in her carriage with her maid, and her daughter and Mr Hampton nowhere in sight. He could not believe that, after all his warnings, Miss Westlake had still gone off alone with Mr Hampton.

"Of all the foolish things to do, Miss Westlake," he chided. "How many times have I told you that Mr Hampton is not a man to be trusted? And now, I come back to find you struggling in his arms."

Alicia just stood there, staring at Mr Merry. "You came," she said in a hollow voice. "I prayed and you came."

"Yes, and lucky for you that I came back when I did," he snapped.

Alicia sniffed loudly. It had been an unnerving experience. Her body began to shake with the shock of what had happened. Mr Merry's anger was gone in a moment.

"My poor girl," he said, putting his arms around her. Alicia did not object. It made her feel safe and for the moment, that was all that mattered. It was some time before her composure returned, but Mr Merry was not sorry for the excuse to hold her.

At length, she pulled away, but she immediately became agitated again. She was remembering the awful truth of what she had learned. "It was him. Mr Hampton was responsible for the accident. He did not know that I was in the carriage. We changed our plans after he had left. He never meant to hurt me. But he meant to hurt them—the Duke and mother and mother's baby. Especially mother's baby. Mr Merry, we must tell them."

Mr Merry laid his hand on her arm to prevent her from running off directly. "Wait. There is something I must tell you. I have just been talking with the Duke. When I was staying with Wilber, he persuaded me to repeat the story that I told you of what happened nine years ago."

"Yes?"

"As we talked, the pieces fell into place. We realised that it was not some random person that Mr Hampton killed, but his own cousin."

"No! Surely not."

"The circumstances are too damning."

"The poor Duke. He must be heartbroken."

"He did not believe me."

"But if he knows that Mr Hampton was responsible for the accident, surely he will change his mind?"

"Maybe. Maybe not. Mr Hampton has a lot of influence over his uncle. He may yet be able to convince the Duke of his innocence."

"But my mother is in danger. I know it. Mr Hampton must have been feeling quite desperate to have mauled me about like that. The Duke must be made to see before it is too late."

Mr Merry nodded. He took her by the hand and together they went in search of the Duke.

The Duke watched Mr Merry striding off through the doorway to the castle and then gave his full attention to his wife. Now that she had rested, the Duchess declared that she was ready to look round the castle, provided that the Duke gave her his arm. As the Duchess looked up into her adoring husband's eyes, the Duke felt a primitive stirring of protectiveness over his wife. It was his duty to look after her and if that meant confronting his nephew with Mr Merry's terrible accusations, then so be it.

Arm in arm, the Duke and Duchess started to walk down the grass slope toward the castle. A few moments later, they saw Joshua hastily leave the ruins and start to make his way up the bank toward them. The Duke decided that he should take this opportunity to talk to his nephew. This matter was too weighty to put off.

The Duke was unwilling to bring up such an unpleasant subject in front of his wife. He turned to the Duchess, saying: "Forgive me, my dear, but I need to talk to Joshua in private." He adjured Marie to look after her mistress and motioned to his nephew. "Walk with me, Joshua."

The Duchess complained loudly at being deserted so readily. "Please do not be too long," she grumbled. "I have no wish to still be looking around the ruins at sunset. It will be quite cold once the sun has gone in."

The Duke walked in silence with his nephew until they were out of earshot and then he began. "Joshua, how did my son die?"

Mr Hampton went pale. He had anticipated being accused of causing the carriage accident, but this was totally unexpected. "I have told you before, Uncle. Denmead was caught up with the rioters. I found his mangled body in the street along with other unfortunates, some caught in the soldiers' gunfire, some crushed."

"Would you say that his injuries were caused by a horse's hooves?"

Mr Hampton felt his mouth go dry. "Yes, they could very well have been caused by a horse. Excuse me, but I do not understand. We have been through this before. Why are you asking me this now, Uncle?"

"Then he was not crushed by the hooves of your horse?"

Mr Hampton stopped walking and turned to stare at the Duke, apparently outraged at what he was hearing. "Crushed by the hooves of my horse?" he repeated. "What a dreadful thing to say, Uncle. Who could have put such an idea into your head? Next you will be saying that I did it on purpose."

"Did you?"

"Did I what?"

"Did you kill your cousin on purpose, Joshua, or was it an accident?"

Mr Hampton stood in silence, not knowing how to respond.

"You were seen, Joshua. There is no use pretending. Tell me what happened," the Duke urged.

"I suppose that as that fellow Merry has just turned up again, it is not hard to guess who has being pouring this poison into your ears!" Mr Hampton exclaimed. "How could you believe a godless man like that over your own flesh and blood?"

He laid his hand on the Duke's shoulder and continued to speak, this time in a quiet, reassuring way. "I told you what happened. I brought your son's body home. Denmead was like a brother to me."

It was at this moment that Mr Merry and Alicia stepped out through the castle doorway. Mr Hampton thought the conversation was going his way. He was inclined to think that the Duke believed him when he said that Mr Merry was either mistaken or wilfully telling lies about him. Time was on his side. After all, it was a long time ago.

Mr Merry did not doubt that the Duke was confronting Mr Hampton with his suspicions, but he could not tell from looking at him whether the Duke was convinced that his nephew was responsible for his cousin's death or not. His conversation with Alicia had provided him with fresh evidence that Mr Hampton was also responsible for the carriage accident. He knew he had to tell the Duke as soon as possible, but he feared that Mr Hampton would react badly to his intervention.

Unwilling that Alicia should have to face any more unpleasantness, Mr Merry encouraged her to join her mother who was just about to enter the castle. Alicia had been through enough this afternoon already. He waited until the two ladies were out of sight before walking up to the Duke and Mr Hampton. They had their backs toward him, so it was not until he was almost upon them that they were aware of his approach. Mr Hampton shot him a look of such venomous hatred that Mr Merry visibly recoiled. He had seen that look before.

Confident that he had persuaded the Duke of his innocence, Mr Hampton did not feel the need to stay any longer to defend himself. "Forgive me, Uncle, but you will understand if I do not want to be in this man's company. He has done me a great disservice and that is not something I can readily forgive." He took leave of his uncle and walked away without a backward glance.

Mr Merry thought that the Duke looked tired. He did not like to force him to listen to him again, but he feared the consequences of delay. "Your Grace, I have just been talking to Miss Westlake. It would seem that she has had a conversation with Mr Hampton which provides an answer to the question of the carriage accident."

"I am listening," said the Duke.

"You would not consider for a moment that Mr Hampton could be responsible because Miss Westlake, whom he professes to love, was also inside the carriage. The obvious answer, which we failed to grasp, was that he did not know. According to Miss Westlake, you changed your plans at the last minute, after Mr Hampton had left on estate business. If that is true, the accident was not meant for Miss Westlake—it was meant for you and the Duchess."

The Duke was horrified. It all fitted together. He wanted to deny it, but he knew, deep down, that it was true. He just stood there, staring into nothingness, not saying a word. Mr Merry had expected the Duke to exclaim, to try to defend his nephew's actions, but he did nothing. He just stood and stared. He seemed to have aged ten years in a single moment.

Meanwhile, Alicia quickly caught up with her mother. She was concerned that it was getting cold and sent Marie back to the carriage for another shawl. She took her mother by the arm and gently led her into the ruin. She understood and applauded Mr Merry's motivation in sending her away. She had no wish to remain within earshot of what she did not doubt would be a distasteful conversation.

"Come and look at the sea, Mother. There are some splendid views."

"I have seen enough splendid views to last me a lifetime," the Duchess grumbled, but allowed herself to be led through the ruined entrance and along the side of the castle to the edge facing the sea. "Hmm, I suppose it is pretty enough," she conceded.

Alicia left her mother standing looking out to sea whilst she wandered through the rest of the ruin. There was not really much to see. Most of the walls above the first floor level had collapsed long ago leaving piles of rubble around the base. She noticed the foot of a spiral staircase in the far corner and clambered over one of these piles in order to reach it. The base of the stairway seemed to be intact and she cautiously climbed the first few steps. But she was destined for disappointment; after a dozen steps, the staircase ended in mid-air where the stone had crumbled away.

Reluctantly Alicia climbed back down again. The sun was setting and she knew that her mother would be wanting to go home and rest before dinner. She glanced over to where she had left her and received a shock. Mr Hampton was standing next to her mother in front of the largest opening on the east side of the castle.

Alicia was fully alert to the danger her mother was in. On the other side of that hole was a steep drop down onto the rocks below. She realised that she had been so bent on shielding her mother from unpleasantness that she had never given her the slightest hint that the carriage accident was anything more than an unfortunate mischance. Her mother certainly had no idea that Mr Hampton was responsible. She had no way of knowing that Mr Hampton was dangerous at all.

Mr Hampton's voice drifted across to where Alicia

was standing with amazing clarity. "This is the best view of all, Your Grace. From here you can see all the way down to the beach. Look, there is a dog running about on the sand."

The Duchess peered down through the opening, but was unable to see the beach. The long drop down made her feel giddy.

"If you lean out just a little more you will be able to see," he urged.

Alicia could hear her mother beginning to panic. "I cannot. I do not like heights." Mr Hampton's hand moved to the base of her mother's back. Was he really going to push her over the edge? Alicia wanted to call out and warn her, but she did not want to drive Mr Hampton into acting precipitately. On the other hand, surely he would not harm her mother if he knew that she was there to witness his treachery. She decided that it was imperative that Mr Hampton should be aware of her presence at once. She did not dare to wait until she could reach where her mother was standing.

"Mr Hampton, I quite thought that you had left," Alicia remarked in a loud voice as she clambered back over the pile of rubble and made her way toward them.

Mr Hampton turned and scowled. He had never been less pleased to see her. "No, as you can see, I am still here," he retorted, unable to keep the annoyance out of his voice.

"And have you no apology to make for your behaviour?" she asked as she reached where they were standing.

"Forgive me, Miss Westlake. I was overcome by my feelings."

The Duchess looked puzzled. "Alicia? What are you talking about?" she asked.

Alicia ignored her mother and carried on talking. If she could make Mr Hampton realise that his secret was out and his plans had no chance of success, then surely he would run to save his skin rather than try to hurt her mother.

"Feelings? Is that what it was? How can I have been so stupid? I thought it was revenge on me for refusing your hand. I will never marry you, Mr Hampton. I was right, was I not? You were hoping that my mother's baby would not survive the carriage accident."

"Alicia, what a dreadful thing to say!" the Duchess exclaimed.

"Yes, dreadful, but not as dreadful as the truth. Mr Hampton wanted it so badly that he caused the accident."

"Impossible!"

"Dreadful, yes, but not impossible, Mother. I did not believe it for a long time. I could not see how he could have planned the accident when he wanted to marry me. But something he said this afternoon made me realise what a fool I had been. I had forgotten that we changed our plans after Mr Hampton had left. He thought that it was you and the Duke in the carriage. His shock at finding that I had gone in the Duke's place was genuine enough. I truly believe he never intended to hurt me. If I had been killed, he would never have been able to acquire my fortune. Because it was money you wanted, was it not, Mr Hampton? I do not know whether you would have been glad if the Duke or my mother had been killed, but you did not want my mother's baby to survive, did you?"

As Mr Hampton listened to Alicia, his rage grew. So this was what Mr Merry was telling his uncle right now. Would it be enough to convince the Duke of his guilt?

He did not know. But somehow he knew that if the Duke believed he was guilty of causing the carriage accident, he would believe that he was responsible for his cousin's death as well. Even if he succeeded in keeping the Duke's favour, Mr Hampton knew that his situation was becoming critical. Already his creditors were closing in. Somehow, word had got out about the Duchess' condition. Speculation was rife as to what the child's sex would be. Without his prospects of one day becoming duke, he needed a rich wife. If Miss Westlake would not marry him, he would be ruined.

His plans had gone awry and it was all Mr Merry's fault. If he had not appeared out of nowhere after all those years and turned Miss Westlake against him, everything would have worked out the way he had intended. "Of course I did not want your mother's baby to survive!" he screeched. "How could you expect me to rejoice in the birth of a child that might deprive me of my inheritance?"

The Duchess looked up at Mr Hampton, her face full of horror. "Then what Alicia says is true?"

"Oh yes, quite true. Of course, she omitted to tell you that I killed my cousin as well."

"No!" The combination of fear and shock was too much for the Duchess and she crumpled in a heap at Mr Hampton's feet.

"You had better come and see to your mother," Mr Hampton said. "She appears to have fainted."

Alicia hurried over to where her mother had fallen. Now, surely, Mr Hampton would run. She bent over her mother's figure and was so intent on what she was doing that she did not see it coming. Mr Hampton rammed into her with the full force of his body weight and pushed her through the gaping hole in the wall.

As she screamed out in fear, Mr Hampton drowned out her cries with those of his own. "Miss Westlake. No! Hold on, I will save you."

Chapter 46

The screams shattered the silence that hung between Mr Merry and the Duke. In a trice, Mr Merry was running toward the ruin. Beneath Mr Hampton's cries he had heard another cry, one that pierced his heart. That was Miss Westlake's voice. He should never have let Mr Hampton walk off while he talked to the Duke here, out in the open. He should have made sure that Miss Westlake and her mother were safe.

His heart beat quickly as he sped across the ground, dreading what he might find. The Duke was running too, but he was not a young man and could not hope to keep up with his companion. As he entered the ruin, Mr Merry could see Mr Hampton with the Duchess in his arms, but of Miss Westlake, there was no sign.

Mr Hampton was concentrating all his efforts on moving the insensate Duchess whilst keeping up a dialogue that suggested he was trying to save her rather than deposit her body over the edge of the cliff. "Do not panic, Your Grace. I will save you," he cried as he moved toward the opening in the side of the castle, but the unconscious Duchess made no response.

He did not see Mr Merry diving at him until it was too late. Mr Hampton went flying backwards into the wall, dropping the Duchess to the ground in his efforts to maintain his balance. He quickly got to his feet again and started to move toward the doorway.

Mr Merry was a peaceable man, but Mr Hampton's treacherous behaviour had made him furious. He had not survived Eton without learning how to fight and before Mr Hampton could make it to the exit, he was floored again by a mean right hook which landed full in his face.

At last the Duke reached the scene and went immediately to his wife's crumpled body. He was relieved to find that she was still breathing. He took off his jacket, folded it and gently inserted it as a pillow underneath his wife's head. Then he stood up and turned to face his bloody-nosed nephew who was being held by the scruff of the neck by Mr Merry.

"You have sealed your own fate, Joshua. I can no longer have any doubt of your guilt. You have tried to kill my wife as you killed my son. But why, Joshua? Why did you do it? How could you profess to love me when you had murdered my son?"

"I was doing you a favour," Mr Hampton spat out. There was no use pretending. It was all over. Years of waiting had come to nothing. He had taken a risk and lost everything. "Denmead was a scoundrel. This way he died with some honour. Had he lived, he would have caused you nothing but shame and misery."

"But why, Joshua. Why? You said you loved him as a brother."

"Oh no," Mr Hampton said bitterly. "I said he was like a brother to me. Very different. I was jealous of Denmead: money, position, everything that he had and I did not."

The Duke sighed heavily. "And now, Joshua? What is your excuse now? Why are you trying to destroy my happiness? I have treated you like a son."

"A son who is about to be disinherited in favour of

the mewling infant of your upstart Duchess. I have been living on my expectations for years. Your marriage has ruined me."

"If only you had told me," the Duke lamented. "I could have given you more money."

Mr Hampton laughed bitterly. "I do not think I could settle for a competence now. It would seem such a let-down after living as heir to a dukedom. I am truly sorry about Miss Westlake. I would have married her but she would not have me. A pity—"

Mr Merry moved his hold to Mr Hampton's throat. "Where is she, you worthless scoundrel?" he growled.

Mr Hampton gagged at the tightness of the hand around his windpipe. He saw his life being extinguished before his eyes and pointed weakly to the opening in the wall. Mr Merry loosened his hold on Mr Hampton with such suddenness that his erstwhile prisoner collapsed and hit his head on the ground. Mr Merry's heart fell. Surely he had not come so far to lose her now?

The Duke stood beside him and together they peered over the edge. All they could see was the rocky descent from the castle to the beach, fifty feet or so below. There was no sign of a body, dead or alive.

"I am going down after her," Mr Merry declared. "Send for help. A doctor. There is a track down to the beach a little further along. Send a cart down, in case …"

The Duke assured him of his compliance. Mr Merry stripped off his jacket to give himself more manoeuvrability and the Duke supported him as he lowered his body through the gap in the castle wall and down onto the cliffside below. He found his footing, let go of the Duke's hand and searched for something to hold onto so that he could lower himself further down the cliff. In this manner, he descended half way down the rocky face.

At last he caught sight of her. She was lying very still on top of one of the blackberry bushes that freely covered the side of the cliff. Her skirt had mercifully caught in its brambles and prevented her from crashing onto the rocks below. He called out and thought he saw a faint movement in response. Mr Merry began to hope that all was not lost.

Alicia was not prepared for the sudden shove. Mr Hampton's presence should have put her on her guard, but she had believed his professions of regard and did not think that he would try to hurt her. How wrong she had been! As she went over the edge, she wondered whether she would die. She had been miserable, but while there was life, there was hope. She prayed urgently. She did not want to die. The cliff was not a sheer drop, but the force sent her reeling backwards giving her little time to stop herself from falling down and being crushed on the jagged rocks at the foot of the cliff.

Desperately she reached out with her hands, trying to grab onto anything that would break her fall. But her hands were too far away from the cliffside to yield her any assistance. Her skirts billowed out with the unexpected angle of her descent and caught on some bushes. She grabbed wildly, trying to right herself, but before she could find her feet, the undergrowth gave way under her weight and she fell another few feet until her progress was interrupted by the bush on which Mr Merry found her. She tried to move, but her skirts were caught and she was afraid that if she pulled too hard, the bush might give way and she would fall onto the rocks below.

Mr Merry moved swiftly toward her position, calling her name all the time. Alicia raised her head. He had come.

She would be safe now. When Mr Merry saw the movement and heard her answering cry, his heart leapt for joy. Quickly he made his way across to her and freed her skirts from the brambles that held her captive. Gently he helped her to find her footing and together, slowly, little by little, they made their way down to the beach below. The sand felt so good beneath her feet. Alicia shut her eyes and sent up a silent prayer of thanks. She was bruised and scratched, but miraculously, she was otherwise unhurt.

She wanted to stay there with Mr Merry, just savouring the joy of being alive. But the Duke had been good to his word and it was not long before a cart came trundling over the sands toward them. Mr Merry tucked her up with a blanket and sat down next to her. "Thank you," she whispered, resting her head on his shoulder. "I knew that you would come."

In less than half an hour, they were back at the Duke's lodgings. Mr Merry handed Alicia out of the cart, but he was soon ousted from her side by her mother who had recovered from her faintness and greeted her with unrestrained delight. She smothered her with an embrace that set poor Alicia squealing with pain as new, as yet unrecognised, bruises came to light.

Alicia was whisked off to bed and the doctor waited on her. Doctor Warren pronounced her lucky to have got away so lightly with her fall and cautioned her to take more care when she was near steep drops in future. So they had told the doctor it was an accident, had they? Well, perhaps it was for the best.

Chapter 47

While the Duke and Mr Merry were distracted by Miss Westlake's plight, Mr Hampton made his escape. He did not fear that he would be brought to justice. Even if the Duke were prepared to brave the scandal, there was little enough evidence to convict him. The fact that Mr Merry had witnessed him murdering his cousin was awkward, but not overwhelmingly against him. No one could prove that it was not an accident and it would be easy enough to claim that he had changed the facts about Denmead's death in order to protect his uncle from the truth.

His behaviour toward Miss Westlake and her mother would be harder to excuse. No one could prove that he had caused the carriage accident and no one had seen him pushing Miss Westlake over the cliff edge, but Mr Merry had seen him trying to throw the unconscious Duchess over the precipice in the same way, and he did not think that he would be able to talk himself out of that one.

Once Miss Westlake had begun to suspect him, he knew that his hopes of persuading her to marry him were over. In his desperation, he had tried to get rid of Miss Westlake and her mother, but Mr Merry had arrived before he could complete his plan. Another accident would have looked suspicious, but if it had not been for Mr Merry, he might have got away with it.

Even before the news of Miss Westlake's accident had reached the servants, Mr Hampton had mounted his horse and ridden back to town. He was not sure where he should go. He knew he could not remain in Weymouth. It was too much to expect that the Duke would forgive him and let him carry on as if nothing had happened.

However, that would not have solved his problems anyway. He needed money. He supposed that he could stay and see whether the Duke would pay him to leave, but he thought that was a risky strategy. Even if his uncle could be persuaded to pay up, Mr Merry was on the rampage. He had already been knocked down twice by the aggrieved lover and if Miss Westlake's injuries proved to be fatal, he did not think that even the Duke would be able to save his skin.

His natural inclination was to go to London where at least he could find comfort in the arms of his mistress. But if he stayed in London, sooner or later his creditors were bound to catch up with him. If only he had money, he could flee the country. If his mistress would agree to flee with him, he did not think it would be so bad. It was rumoured that you could live in some style on the continent for considerably less money than in London.

He wondered whether he would be able to persuade Mrs Martindale to run away with him. The timing was working in his favour. At their last tryst, she had told him she was carrying his child. Perhaps her husband would kick her out of his house once he discovered. It was doubtful whether she would find it quite so easy to find a new protector just at the moment. Yes, the timing of his exile was certainly working in his favour.

Mr Hampton rode back to his lodgings on the seafront and collected his belongings together as quickly as possible. He rapidly came to the conclusion that his best hope for money was his father. He was not sure what tale he would tell him. Maybe he would confess the whole and throw himself on his father's mercy. Perhaps he would play the persecuted man who was innocent of all that he was being accused of. Or perhaps he would just ask for money.

He told Rowson that he had received a message to say his father was ill and he needed to return to Swanmore immediately. He could not wait for the Duke to return, but required the second travelling carriage to be made ready for the journey without delay. Rowson thought it was odd that a message had found him at the castle without coming first to York Buildings, but it was not his position to question what he was told. He ordered the chaise to be brought round immediately and whilst Alicia was still being rescued, Mr Hampton left town.

Fortunately the Duke had his horses stabled along the route in readiness for whenever he decided to return home, and so Mr Hampton's journey back to Swanmore was as smooth and swift as possible. His father's supposed illness was justification enough for travelling all night. The sunny day had been followed by a cloudless night and the carriage made its way along the post road by the light of a full moon.

When Mr Hampton arrived at Swanmore, he went immediately to find his father. Lord Richard had fallen asleep in the drawing room, a half empty bottle of port at his side. His gouty leg lay raised on a footstool and a newspaper rested on his chest where it had fallen from his hand.

Mr Hampton thought what a pathetic creature his father looked.

"Wake up, Father. We need to talk."

Lord Richard awoke with a jump. "Joshua!" he exclaimed with delight. "Back from Weymouth already? Has she accepted you after all?"

"No."

"Then you have given up and come home?"

"Not exactly. I cannot stay. I need to go abroad."

Lord Richard thought he could not have heard right. "Go abroad? But why? If it is money you need, I can help. Surely there cannot be any need to leave here?"

"I am sorry to disappoint you, but there is every need for me to leave. Let us just say that I am out of favour with the Duke and will never be in favour again."

"Nonsense, Joshua. Your uncle is not one to harbour a grudge. Whatever it is you have done, he will get over it."

"Ha!" Mr Hampton scoffed. "No, he will not."

Lord Richard looked unconvinced.

Mr Hampton looked his father in the eye and pitied him for the air of trust he saw there. It was not often that he felt regret for what he had done, but just now, gazing at his father, he felt a pang of remorse at letting his father down.

However, if he wanted to stay in control of his own destiny, he needed to leave, and leave soon. It was not easy to find the words to confess his guilt to the one person whom he thought might understand his motivation, if not his actions.

"When Denmead died, how did you feel?"

"Joshua, what are you talking about?"

"Humour me, Father. His death—how did it make you feel, knowing you had become your brother's heir?"

Lord Richard looked uncomfortable. "I suppose I was glad. Glad that my son would one day be duke.

Denmead was ever a wild one. I was not surprised that he died young. If it had not been the riots, he would likely have been killed in a duel, for he was ever meddling with other men's wives."

"And when the Duke married again, were you not angry?"

"Yes, I was angry. I begrudged your uncle finding happiness when my life seemed to have been consumed by old age and bitterness."

"But what about me? Were you not angry that I might never be duke?" demanded Mr Hampton, his voice rising in volume with emotion.

"Not, I fear, as angry as you are, judging by the sound of your voice. Just what did you say to your uncle that you think he will never forgive?"

"Say? I did not say anything."

Lord Richard went pale. "Joshua, what have you done?" he asked weakly.

"Where shall I start? Nine years ago, I was stuck in the army while Denmead was idling around causing trouble. It was not fair. He had everything and I had what was left over. Quite by chance, I came upon him during the riots. He had been drinking and did not hesitate to hurl abuse at me. I was angry, angrier than I had ever been before. I chased him down and urged my horse to trample him."

Lord Richard was shaken, but it did not prevent him from sympathising with his son. "You were angry, Joshua. It was just an accident. Do not be too hard on yourself," he said, rising from his chair and putting a comforting arm round his son's shoulder.

Mr Hampton shook it off. "You are missing the point, Father. I meant my horse to kill Denmead. He did not deserve to live. I knew I would make a better duke than he ever would. Most unfortunately, it turns out that there was a witness. I was seen that day by Mr Merry of all people. And I thought all his animosity was due to jealousy over Miss Westlake! Do not look so shocked, Father. You said you were glad when Denmead died."

Lord Richard just stood and stared at his son.

Mr Hampton went on. "I had no money of my own apart from the allowance that the Duke gave me and the occasional gift from you. It was not enough for the life I wanted to lead. I developed a passion for a certain actress. I knew she would be a very expensive mistress. I started to borrow on my expectations. Then Miss Westlake came to London and I thought that marriage to her would rescue me from the moneylenders. But my plans went sadly awry. Miss Westlake fell in love with the man who has turned out to be my worst enemy and her mother married my uncle. When I discovered that the Duchess was with child, I could see my life falling apart. I could not afford to be cut out of the succession. I was driving the carriage that drove them off the road."

"What?" Lord Richard screeched.

"You heard me, Father. Mr Merry suspected foul play from the first, but apparently my genuine horror at the thought of possibly killing the woman whom I hoped would remake my fortune saved me from immediate discovery. Regrettably, the Duchess survived. So, alas, did her child. Rumours about the Duchess' condition had got out. My creditors were breathing down my neck. I made one final attempt to gain Miss Westlake's hand, but when she started accusing me, I knew I was lost. I pushed her over the side of the cliff and her mother would have followed, but I was interrupted. Do you still think the Duke will forgive me?"

The look of horror on Lord Richard's face said what

words could not. Like a man walking in his sleep, he led the way to the library and sat down at the desk. Taking pen and paper, he wrote a letter to his bank giving his son authority to draw on it up to an unspecified amount. Mr Hampton took the letter with a word of thanks.

Lord Richard thought of the property that his father had left him and how he had refused to sell it in case his son wanted to set up an establishment of his own before he became duke. He had not wanted Joshua to be obliged to always live at Swanmore. There was no point keeping it now.

"I will sell the estate," he said quietly, as he wrote another letter, this time to his solicitor. "You might as well have the capital as you will never be setting up house in this country now. Goodbye, Joshua. I do not think we will ever meet again."

"Goodbye, Father." He paused for a minute. "I am sorry to disappoint you."

Another minute and Mr Hampton was gone. Lord Richard continued to sit and stare sightlessly at the desk. A maid found him still sitting in the same position the next morning. He had suffered a stroke and, although he was still breathing, his body was completely paralysed down one side. The dreadful disclosure of his son's ruthless ambition had been too much for an already frail constitution.

Chapter 48

The bells rang out, calling the people of Weymouth to morning service. It had been three days since her fall and Alicia was tired of being in bed. It was not as if she had any broken bones. It had been a terrifying experience and not one she was going to get over lightly. Just that night, she had awoken in a cold sweat in the early hours of the morning having dreamt that she was still falling. Then she had remembered that Mr Merry had come to save her. Whenever she thought of the fall, she always remembered that Mr Merry had come to save her.

But the memory of it was bittersweet. She recollected with a heavy heart that nothing had changed. She reminded herself over and over again of her parents' unhappy marriage, trying to convince herself that it would still be foolish to marry Mr Merry. The thought depressed her so much that she knew she had to get up or she would go mad. She needed to go out instead of staying in bed feeling sorry for herself.

She had seen no one apart from Doctor Warren and Martha. Mr Hampton, she was told, had gone abroad. He would not be coming back. A message had come from Swanmore to say that Lord Richard had suffered a seizure. He had taken his son's crimes to heart and was not expected to recover. The Duke was saddened by the news and planned to return to Swanmore just as soon as his wife was fit to travel. The Duchess was still in bed resting after her ordeal and the Duke refused to leave her side.

Lady Harting was annoyed to discover all the drama she had missed by leaving Sandsfoot Castle early. She was astonished to discover that Christopher had proved to be the hero of the hour, managing to save Miss Westlake after her fall. As she could not imagine a situation where she would put herself in danger for another human being, she found her son's behaviour impossible to comprehend.

The Duke, however, was profoundly grateful for her absence. The less people who knew about Joshua's treachery, the better. He had not been sorry to find that his nephew had chosen to disappear while they were busy rescuing Alicia. He was horrified at what Joshua had done, but enough of his love for his nephew remained that he did not want to bring him to justice.

What distressed him the most was how little he had really known him. It made him feel guilty. If he had loved his son more, perhaps Joshua would not have thought he was doing him a favour by killing him. If he had not been so wrapped up in his own happiness with his new wife, perhaps he would have realised how devastating it was for Joshua to face the possibility of never becoming duke. He had spent nine years grooming Joshua to succeed him and yet he had not invested a single hour in reconciling him to his change in circumstances.

Martha fussed over her darling and made no demur about her decision to get up. She could see the gloom in Alicia's demeanour and thought that some new diversion might relieve it. Perhaps a little bit of fresh air and a good sermon would put her into a more favourable frame of mind.

It was not far to the parish church of St Mary's and not even the Duke raised any objection. If Alicia felt strong enough, he saw no harm in her going out. With the faithful Martha at her side, dressed in her Sunday bonnet, Alicia made the short walk to the church in silence.

It was a crisp, cold winter's morning and the sun was shining brightly. Normally she would smile at the very sight of the sea and the familiar sound of seagulls screeching. But not today. Today her heart was heavy and the cheerfulness of the morning was glaringly at odds with the way she felt.

Alicia took her place in the Duke's pew and thanked God for preserving her life. Presumably she had been saved for a purpose, but just at the moment she could not see beyond the aching chasm in her heart. The sermon was based on the beginning of Colossians chapter three—set your heart on things above not on earthly things. How ironic, she thought!

The last notes of the final hymn sounded. The vicar gave the blessing and the congregation began to pour out of the little church. Alicia was in no hurry to leave. Judging by the covert glances in her direction, news of her accident had spread quickly. If she tarried long enough, she might be able to avoid the well-meaning enquiries which she felt unequal to dealing with. If anyone asked her how she was, she had the most dreadful feeling that she might burst into tears. A cough, a sneeze and then all Alicia could hear was the sound of shuffling feet. And then silence. Alicia stood up and turned to leave her pew.

She was not alone after all. In the pew behind her was a familiar face. A very familiar face. And the last one that she had expected to see at church. She stared. She knew it was unladylike, but she could not help it. What was Mr Merry doing here? What could it mean?

"Good morning, Miss Westlake. I hope you are feeling recovered?"

After what seemed like an eternity she found her tongue. "Yes, thank you," she mumbled. She wanted to ask why he was there, but somehow the words would not form.

"May I walk you back to your lodgings, Miss Westlake?"

"Yes, of course. Thank you."

Martha was hovering outside the door, but dropped back instantly when she saw that her mistress was not alone.

Together, they started to walk away from the church. Mr Merry kept glancing at his companion's face. He was shocked to see how pale and drawn she looked. He had not seen her since that awful day when he had thought he had lost her. He had not come out this morning with the intention of declaring his love, but he longed to wipe away that desolate look on her face.

It was a struggle to find the right words. "Miss Westlake, I must speak to you."

Alicia's heart sank. The urgency of his words left her in no doubt about what he was going to say. It was all a front. He had come to church to besiege her with his proposals. She did not think she could bear it. "No!"

Mr Merry was taken aback. She had seen him in church. Surely she realised what that meant? Why should he not speak? He had been so sure that she loved him. They walked in silence along St Mary's Street and turned down Petticoat Lane toward the sea.

At length, Alicia realised that the silence was worse than facing her problems head on. When they reached the seafront, she paused. Asking Martha to wait for her on the promenade, she suggested that they take a walk on the sands. Mr Merry was very willing and together they walked down to the water's edge.

As soon as they were out of Martha's earshot, Alicia determined to get it over and done with. She could not look him in the face; it was too painful. So she stood, looking out to sea, as she sought to find the right words. "I am sorry, Mr Merry," she said in a strained voice that cost her some effort. "That was rude of me. If you wish to speak, I will listen. Pray continue."

"Miss Westlake, it is not my intention to distress you," he said gently. "I was fool enough to believe that the only objection you had to my suit was that I did not share your faith. That you harboured some feelings for me too."

Alicia coloured and stumbled over her words. "I believe that it is not wise to confess to feelings that it is not possible to satisfy."

Mr Merry began to smile. At first it was just a slight turning up of the ends of his mouth, but soon the emotion welled up inside him and a great big grin spread across his face.

"I do not see what there is to smile about," she snapped, "or are you so conceited that it gratifies you to know you have broken down my defences?"

"Miss Westlake. My dear Miss Westlake," he said, shaking his head as he looked down on her face which was still resolutely turned toward the sea. For a second, Alicia glanced up at him, but she quickly averted her eyes. His face was so full of love that she was in danger of being overwhelmed.

"I went to stay with Wilber and he told me that you would never make me happy."

"Oh!" Perversely, Alicia had suddenly gone off Mr Wilberforce.

"That you would remind me continually that I was not at peace with God."

"Oh!" Maybe Mr Wilberforce had a point.

"I came here to tell you that I had taken the risk. I took your words seriously, you see. I went to London, despondent that I would never be accepted by you and found to my surprise that, after all, I was accepted by God. I dared to believe and found that I could be at peace with God and myself."

"Oh." Was that all she could say? She could have screamed with vexation.

"And to warn you about Mr Hampton."

"And so you came to Weymouth. At just the right time."

"The timing was, you have to admit, miraculous."

"I was never more glad of seeing anyone in my life."

"They say that God works in mysterious ways."

"But who would have thought it? Mr Hampton, a murderer?"

"Miss Westlake, I would like very much if you could forget about Mr Hampton for a moment and think about me." He gently put a finger under her chin and tilted it upwards so that she had to look him in the eyes. Alicia blushed at the intimacy of the gesture. "Miss Westlake. I have decided to take orders and go into the church after all. Preaching this gospel gives purpose to my life. I have wasted years and I do not intend to waste the future."

"But what will your mother say about that?"

"Why, nothing at all. Miss Westlake. It was, after all, her wish that I should go into the church. I cannot give you great wealth and I am afraid I have no title, nor am I likely to ever inherit one, but I offer you a heart that loves you so much that even if you refuse me, I shall never look at another woman."

"But I rather fancied being a viscountess—perhaps I should marry your brother after all," Miss Westlake responded with a wicked smile.

"Well then. I shall have to elope with you. Or abduct you if you will not come willingly."

Her smile widened. "Not a good example to your parishioners."

Mr Merry grinned. "Miss Westlake. Will you marry me?"

"For the sake of your parishioners."

"They are not, at this moment, my primary concern."

"Yes, yes. Of course, yes. I loved you when my head forbade it. And now you have convinced my head, my heart is only too happy to acquiesce. It is, after all, a perfect match."

With a contented sigh, Mr Merry took Alicia in his arms at last and kissed her.

Chapter 49: Epilogue

Although the Duchess had hoped for something grander for her daughter, the Duke was delighted with the match and soon persuaded his wife to come over to his way of thinking. He had every confidence in the man who had rescued his wife and her daughter and exposed his nephew's treachery. Mr Merry might only be a younger son, but he was an honourable man, and that, declared the Duke, was more important than the size of his fortune. Besides, as the Duke insisted on settling a generous amount on Alicia in addition to the £30,000 dowry prescribed in the late Mr Westlake's will, there was no fear that lack of wealth would cause them any inconvenience.

The Countess of Harting did not know whether to rejoice at her younger son's catch or berate him for stealing Miss Westlake from her favoured elder son. In the end, self-interest prevailed. She had achieved her wish of being allied to one of the most influential families in Hampshire and magnanimously forgave Alicia for her lack of taste in choosing Mr Merry over Lord Droxford.

She was gratified that her son was finally taking her advice and going into the church, but her enthusiasm waned over the years that followed, as it soon transpired that her son had no ambition to distinguish himself and become a bishop. The Earl said little, but he was pleased to have acquired a daughter and on days when his wife was being particularly domineering, he thought wistfully of what might have been had he married Alicia's mother.

Lord Droxford was relieved. For the first time in his life, he had hesitated to yield to his mother's wishes and it had been most uncomfortable. Perhaps it hurt his pride a little that Miss Westlake preferred his younger brother, but he was always very courteous to his new sister.

But he was the heir to the earldom and it was unthinkable that he should remain unmarried for long. His mother found him a lady who was very much formed in her own mould. Lady Beaumont was a rather forceful, ambitious young widow who had already proved her child-bearing abilities by producing a son by her short first marriage to a viscount twenty years older than herself.

Lord Droxford proposed and was accepted and the new viscountess proceeded to present him with a whole nursery full of children – all, without exception, girls – with whom he had very little to do.

With the money his father had provided, Mr Hampton successfully persuaded his mistress to flee the country with him. They travelled to Vienna where Mrs Martindale lived as his wife and gave birth to his son with all the appearance of legitimacy.

However, when the money ran out, so did Mrs Martindale. She abandoned Mr Hampton and their eight-year-old son without a second thought and ran off with a wealthy Italian Count. Mr Hampton was obliged to work as an ostler and his fiercely loyal son worked alongside him, never once doubting the truth of his father's claims that he would have been Duke of Wessex if it was not for the interference of a scoundrel named Mr Merry.

Mr Merry and Alicia were married in the first week of January, just a few days after Mr Merry's ordination as a clergyman. The Duke had a living at his disposal that providentially became free at just the right time and Mr and Mrs Merry moved into a large house next to the church, ready to be filled with children.

The parish was delighted to have a minister who was prepared to live amongst them and very soon, Mr Merry and his wife were beloved by their parishioners. No one could doubt that the vicar believed the message that he preached. Everyone noticed the peace and joy that emanated from him and Mrs Merry and more people were convinced of the truth by what they saw in them than by what they heard from the pulpit.

One morning, Alicia ran into her husband's study with a mischievous grin on her face and an open letter in her hand. She stood there impatiently tapping her foot until he looked up.

"I have news from the Duke," she declared.

"I gather from the look on your face that all is well."

"Are you not interested to discover whether the Duke has his heir or not?"

"I am sure you are going to tell me whether I am interested or not."

Alicia pouted and determined to elicit a more active response. "I thought you loved me and here you are, married to me for just a few months, and already you are telling me that I talk too much."

Mr Merry laid down his pen and pushed his chair back. He had learned very quickly to recognise a demand for attention in his wife's playful words. He got up and walked across the room to his wife.

"Of course I love you," he said, wrapping his arms around her. "And the only time I think you are talking too much is when you should be kissing me instead," he continued, promptly following his words with an embrace that left her breathless.

As this was an entirely satisfactory response, and needed to be repeated to make sure the message had sunk in, it was some time later that Alicia recollected the contents of the letter.

"You will never believe it, but my mother has given the Duke his heir—"

"Wonderful!"

"—and a daughter!"

"Twins! I wager no one was expecting that."

"No, it was a complete surprise. Not even my mother knew. What a shock it must have been—wonderful, but still a shock." Alicia bit her bottom lip in a way that was now perfectly familiar to her husband. It usually meant she was thinking deeply about something. He waited for her to speak.

"I do hope that I do not have twins, this time at least. It will be hard enough to get used to being the mother of one baby—" But she got no further. It was one of those times that Mr Merry objected to his wife's chatter and he silenced it in the most effective way he knew. It was not a time for words. It was a time to embrace and marvel at the prospect of new life and the new adventure that lay ahead of them.

Glossary

Bailey: An enclosed courtyard within the external walls of a castle. Also called a **ward**.

Barouche: A four-wheeled carriage which was popular for summer excursions. It could accommodate four people on two seats facing each other and had a single, foldable hood which could be raised to protect those travelling in the forward-facing seat. It could be driven by **postilions** or by a coachman.

Beau: A gentleman admirer or suitor.

Blood-letting: A rather gruesome medical procedure often used in Georgian times where the patient was made to bleed, either by cutting the skin or applying leeches. Unsurprisingly, it was not very effective and could cause considerable harm to those already weak from illness.

Bluestocking: A nickname for a lady who took learning more seriously than was fashionable which was often used in a derogatory sense. The term originally applied to a group of people who met together to converse rather than play cards or take part in other frivolous entertainments. Although the original bluestockings were not all female, the bluestocking circle was led by ladies.

Breeched: Dressed in breeches or trousers. In the Georgian period, boys were dressed in petticoats until they were breeched, usually between the ages of four and seven, after which they wore men's clothes.

Brighthelmstone: An old name for Brighton that derived from the fishing village that grew into the fashionable seaside resort.

Chaise: A carriage, typically with a single seat for two people. A **post-chaise** was a chaise designed for travelling **post**. A private post-chaise could also be called a **travelling chariot**.

Chaperon: A female companion for an unmarried lady.

Competence: An income that was considered sufficient to live on, but not enough to support many of the luxuries of life.

Dishabille: From the French, meaning undressed.

Drawing room: Short for withdrawing room. Ladies retired to the drawing room after dinner leaving the gentlemen at the table to imbibe stronger drinks, such as port. The Queen held receptions which were called drawing rooms.

The Fleet: A London prison used mainly for debtors and bankrupts during the late Georgian period.

Levée: A morning reception held by the King for gentlemen only.

Olympian Dew: A Georgian lotion for washing the skin, also known as Grecian Bloomwater. According to advertisements, it could remove freckles and redness and make wrinkles disappear!

Orgeat: A refreshing drink made from barley or almonds and orange flower water.

Phaeton: A light, four-wheeled carriage that was driven by its owner rather than by a coachman.

Portland Roads: The name for Portland Harbour before the breakwater was built in 1849-1872.

Post: Literally, with post horses, hence rapidly. From this we get **post-chaise** (see chaise), **post-haste**—as quickly as possible—and **post road** (see below).

Postilion: A person who rode one of the horses pulling a carriage. A postilion-driven carriage had no coachman, but was guided by one or more postilions riding the nearside horses. A postilion could also work alongside a coachman, particularly if the coach was being pulled by three pairs of horses. A postilion was also known as a post-boy.

Post road: A road used by those delivering the post. There was a system of inns or post houses at stages along a post road where horses and postilions or post-boys could be hired and replaced. This enabled travel to take place at the highest possible speed by continually refreshing the horses. Post roads were typically among the first roads to be maintained by **Turnpike** Trusts.

Rumble seat: A seat on the outside of a carriage which could be used for transporting servants. It was located over the boot behind the main body of a **chaise**.

Sconce: A wall bracket for holding a candlestick.

Season: The season was the time of year when the upper classes went to London to socialise with each other. It was the best opportunity to meet a suitable marriage partner. During the late Georgian period, it typically ran from October or November through to May or June, roughly coinciding with the sitting of Parliament.

Set-down: A snub, often by a person of some importance to someone of inferior social standing.

Tête-à-tête: A private conversation between two people.

Ton: The fashionable set of Georgian London (pronounced to rhyme with the French word 'bon', with a short, nasal 'o' sound and a silent 'n'). It can also refer to the social standing required to belong to that set. Hence people of good ton belong to the ton.

Tory: One of the two main political parties during the Georgian period. The Tories supported the monarchy and the existing system and opposed religious toleration and reform. William Pitt the Younger was the Tory Prime Minister from 1783 to 1801 and again from 1804 to 1806.

Travelling chariot: A four-wheeled, **postilion**-driven carriage with a single seat for two people.

Turnpike: A toll gate or a road with a toll gate. Turnpike Trusts were set up by Acts of Parliaments during the 18th and 19th centuries in order to improve the state of the roads. Trusts were responsible for maintaining individual stretches of road and had the right to levy tolls on road users to finance this.

Vinaigrette: A small container holding an aromatic substance generally soaked in vinegar. It was used for reviving faintness and to mask unpleasant smells.

Ward: Another word for a **bailey**. The most important buildings in a castle would be located within the inner ward.

Whig: One of the two main political parties during the Georgian period. The Whigs believed in the power of the people and favoured economic and political reform. Key Whig politicians included Charles James Fox, Richard Brinsley Sheridan and Charles Grey, later 2nd Earl Grey.

A historical note from the author

A Perfect Match is a not a true story. Mr Merry and Miss Westlake and their families are fictional characters—products of my imagination. However, I have chosen to place my story against the backdrop of late 18th century England and I have tried to paint their world as accurately as possible. Many of the people that they interact with were real people and I have endeavoured to represent them as my research has suggested.

The historical events referred to at various times in the course of the story really happened. I have kept to the actual dates when I have known them and drawn on contemporary reports in an attempt to bring the events to life.

The rescue of Mr Townley's marble, Clytie, during the Gordon Riots of 1780 is based on a story that was told, but that may not have been true. Part of the reason why its truth is doubted is that Mr Townley would not have been able to carry the marble down the stairs and out of the house by himself. I have built on this by providing him with a strong, young helper—Mr Merry.

I have spent many hours editing my manuscript with an etymological dictionary to hand, trying my best to eliminate words and phrases that were not in use in late 18th century England, particularly in speech. It is a formidable task and I hope that you will forgive me if I have missed anything.

You will find more information on many of the historical characters and events on my blog: www.regencyhistory.net

Lightning Source UK Ltd.
Milton Keynes UK
UKOW04f1533150615

253529UK00001B/7/P